THE NORMAN PRETENDER

BY VALERIE ANAND

Gildenford
The Norman Pretender

THE NORMAN PRETENDER

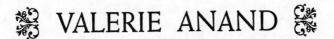 VALERIE ANAND

CHARLES SCRIBNER'S SONS ❈ New York

Library of Congress Cataloging in Publication Data

Anand, Valerie.
    The Norman pretender.

    1. Great Britain – History – Edward, the
Confessor, 1042-1066 – Fiction. 2. Harold, King
of England, 1022?-1066 – Fiction. 3. William I,
the Conqueror, King of England, 1027?-1087 –
Fiction. I. Title. PZ4.A5328No [PR6051.N34]
823'.9'14 79-26365 ISBN 0-684-16099-4

1 3 5 7 9 11 13 15 17 19 F/C 20 18 16 14 12 10 8 6 4 2

Printed in the United States of America

In equal parts, and with much gratitude,
to my mother and my husband, for their
unfailing encouragement and heroic endurance
of my relentlessly rattling typewriter

❧ CONTENTS ❧

✺ ACKNOWLEDGMENTS ✺

The excerpts from the two anonymous Welsh poems *The Elegy on Cynddylan* (see Part III, Chapter 8) and *Dinogad's Petticoat* (see Part III, Chapters 5 and 8) appeared in *The Oxford Book of Welsh Verse in English*, chosen by Gwyn Jones, copyright © Oxford University Press 1977. They are reproduced by kind permission of the Oxford University Press.

I should also like to thank Mr. A. D. Carr, M.A., Ph.D., Lecturer in Welsh History, University College of North Wales, for his help and advice when I was carrying out research on Gruffyd'ap Llewellyn, and Mr. David Howarth for his kind and prompt reply to enquiries.

The books which have assisted me are too numerous to list in full, but ranking high among them are Professor Frank Barlow's *Edward the Confessor*, George Slocombe's *William the Conqueror*, Denis Butler's *1066, The Story of a Year*, David Howarth's *1066, The Year of the Conquest*, J. E. Lloyd's *A History of Wales from the Earliest Times to the Edwardian Conquest*, Volume 2, and T. H. White's *The Goshawk*.

V.A.

❧ ENGLISH AND NORMAN ❧ RULING HOUSES
996-1087 A.D.

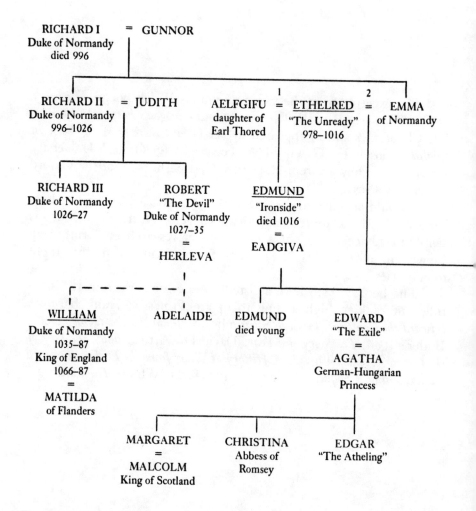

The names of kings of England are underscored for clarity. Dates given are, of course, only those of rule.

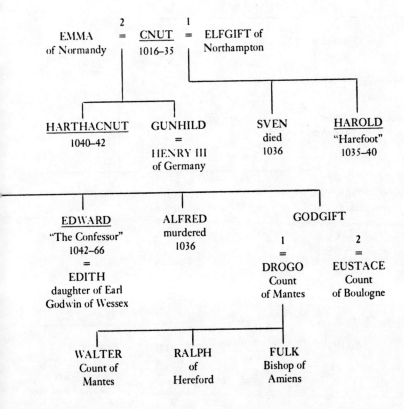

EMMA
of Normandy

2

=

CNUT
1016–35

1

=

ELFGIFT of
Northampton

HARTHACNUT
1040–42

GUNHILD
=
HENRY III
of Germany

SVEN
died
1036

HAROLD
"Harefoot"
1035–40

EDWARD
"The Confessor"
1042–66
=
EDITH
daughter of Earl
Godwin of Wessex

ALFRED
murdered
1036

GODGIFT

1
=
DROGO
Count
of Mantes

2
=
EUSTACE
Count
of Boulogne

WALTER
Count of
Mantes

RALPH
of
Hereford

FULK
Bishop of
Amiens

✣ HOUSE OF WESSEX ✣

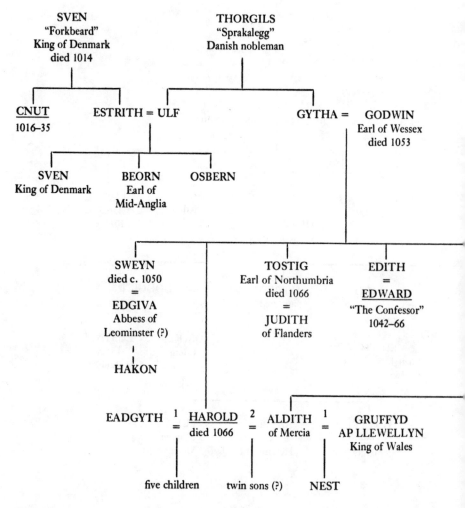

The names of kings of England are underscored for clarity. Dates given are, of course, only those of rule.

GYRTH	LEOFWIN	GUNHILD	ELFGIVA	WULFNOTH
died 1066	died 1066	entered convent	died young	entered church

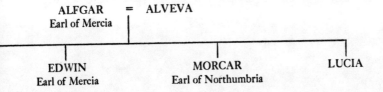

ALFGAR = **ALVEVA**
Earl of Mercia

EDWIN	**MORCAR**	**LUCIA**
Earl of Mercia	Earl of Northumbria	

THE NORMAN PRETENDER

Before . . . 1017 A.D.

"If I meant to do as Cnut asks," said the King of Sweden testily, "would I talk to you about it? I should do it, that's all. But as it happens, whatever customs they may have in that foggy island of yours, here in the north lands we don't murder our guests. You have eaten my salt and slept under my roof and your safety is my care. Your safety is what we must discuss. And his."

They both looked down at the baby lying in his basket cradle on the floor between them. The nurse sat cross-legged beside it, crooning now and then to the child. He was small and not very healthy; just now he was snuffling miserably. But from the point of view of King Cnut of England, he was healthier than was at all desirable. His mother, facing King Olaf across the cradle, shivered.

It might have been a shiver of cold. Winter was passing, but it was still very cold here in Sweden, even in the south. The Swedish king's hall and guesthouses were draped, curtained, upholstered, and coverleted in the comfort of fur. So were the people. The nurse, it was true, had to make do with a woollen mantle, but she was a thrall. The seven-month-old baby was swathed in sealskin outside his linen swaddling bands, King Olaf was vast and furry in a bearskin mantle, and the child's mother, Eadgiva, clutched a marten cloak tightly round her. But it was not the chill air that she sought to exclude, not the winter that made her shudder. It was fear.

"I trust you," she said to Olaf. "It isn't that. But Cnut's men have come here and asked you to murder my son. If you refuse, what will they do? Go meekly home? Can you protect us day and night, in every coming and going of our lives, for years to come?"

"No," said Olaf shortly. "I can't. Exactly."

At least he hadn't had to explain that to her. She wasn't a fool. Nor had she lost her dignity, even in her white-faced dread. She was a great lady still, in spite of destitution and defencelessness, in spite of her plump, homely appearance. Her husband had been a man of high position, Edmund Ironside, the last living son of King Ethelred of England's first marriage, and for a short time king over part of England himself. During that time, King Cnut had held the rest, by right of conquest. Now Edmund was dead and Cnut had seized the whole country and, with a son of his own and a new marriage that promised more, did not like it that his rival's child survived.

Olaf said in his gruff voice: "Cnut did not ask me to kill *you*, only your son. But he didn't know that you were pregnant. And now that his men have seen you . . ."

"It will be interesting to see," said Eadgiva bitterly, "whether they wait to find out if the child is male or female . . . or not."

"It would be better not to wait." Olaf ignored the bitterness. "When will the child be born?"

"In four months' time."

"Can you travel?"

"If I must," said Eadgiva wearily. Her voice sharpened. "There are only two of Cnut's men. Couldn't you . . . ?"

"Take them hunting in the mountains and arrange an avalanche or a crevasse?" Olaf's large frame rumbled with laughter. "I could. But they also are my guests. Nor do I want to make Cnut too much an enemy. Listen. You understand that you have no chance of going back to England? Cnut has his own heir and there are other descendants of Ethelred in the world too, ones Cnut may have reason not to touch. By the time your children are of an age to rule, power in England will be firm in someone else's hands."

"I know. And I don't care. If only I could make Cnut and everyone else understand that! Then we shouldn't be hunted any more. Fighting over the throne didn't do my husband any good, did it? He was killed, fighting Cnut. I don't want to fight Cnut. I want to *get away* from him!" Her voice rose, uncontrollably.

She did not feel safe even here in this room, in Olaf's palace, under his protection. The danger which had followed her like her shadow, ever since her friends had warned her of Cnut's intentions, was closing in on her. She was too tired to hide her terror; it had gone on too long. The warning had come within a week of her husband's death, early in the winter. *Cnut is claiming all England. Flee or take sanctuary with your son if you want him to live.*

She had taken the handful of guards and servants who were loyal and fled by ship, down the Thames, out into the questionable safety of the December seas. God was kind. The winter held the north in a light grip still. It didn't shut the seas until after Christmas and by then she was in Sweden. But when the winter passed, Cnut's men came, hinting, not too delicately, that the King of England would take it as a friendly gesture on the part of her host if he would dispose of the English lady's son. She clasped her hands tightly, holding down hysteria. In her womb, the second baby stirred.

"If you know that you can't go home to England," Olaf said calmly, "if you understand that, then our way is clear. If you go far enough away, that will be a way of saying that you and yours are not interested in England. Convince Cnut of that, and you are safe. I have an embassy leaving soon for Norway, by ship."

"Norway? But that's not very far. It's only . . ."

"They will touch at the Polish shore on the way. They are landing some merchants there, bound for the court of Poland. You will go with them. I will give you letters of introduction to the Polish court and to others. You can have your child in Poland. Then, if you take my advice, you'll travel on to King Stephen's court in Hungary. That is as far away from England as you can well get and still stay in Christendom. Cnut won't pursue you there. It will be a long time before he even knows where you are. I shall put it about that you went to Norway. By the time the truth gets to Cnut, you'll be learning the Magyar tongue. Stephen's court is Christian, cultured, and hospitable. Your children will have a future there. Make a life in Hungary for yourself and for them and learn to call that country home. Then you will all be safe."

Eadgiva, while the wind whined in the pines outside, gave the matter thought. Another long journey, to another strange country, and then to yet another. Further and further away all the time from everything familiar. She would never see England again. Childhood, girlhood, the days of her marriage, all beloved skylines and contours must be abandoned. A new life to make and a new language to learn. Not to hear English spoken again.

Not quite that, perhaps. She could teach the children. But, of England, that was all that she could keep.

It would be a lonely, empty life, in exile. But it would be a life. The alternative was death for her son, and perhaps for herself and the unborn one too. "When does the embassy sail?" she asked.

"Tomorrow," said King Olaf.

Part

I

THE EXILING OF ALFGAR

1053–1056 A.D.

1 ❈ Feast, with Spectre

King Edward's Easter Feast, 1053, was gravid with catastrophe before it even began, and the Godwin family knew it. But only Earl Godwin himself guessed at the likely nature of the calamity and he had no power to prevent it. There was a time when he might have done so. But his exile had aged him too much.

His return from that exile, seven months before, was magnificent enough. He had sailed up the Thames with his sons and his followers, on a tidal wave of warships edged with bright spears like foam. He had secured his earldom of Wessex again and first pressured and then wooed the reluctant king into a semblance of friendship. At Christmas 1052 there was an imitation of a Yuletide Feast, with a truncated guest list, no ladies, and by sheer good luck some trouble on the Welsh borders, which gave all those present something to occupy their minds and into which to channel their aggressions. Now, at the Easter Feast, it was to be a full-scale banquet, a sealing of the peace between King Edward of England and his chief earl. Round the porch of the king's great gabled hall at Winchester, lanterns twinkled in the fading afternoon, in honour of the Resurrection of Christ and the rebirth of friendship after quarrelling. And in a guarded strongroom beside it, guests had been asked to deposit their weaponry.

It was not, of course, customary to go armed into the king's hall. But usually it was assumed that guests would leave their blades behind in their guesthouses, of their own accord. That they should be officially disarmed in this manner was without precedent. Tassels of silk in various colour combinations were provided to identify the more anonymous blades for when their owners reclaimed them. Earl Godwin's sword with its great amethyst-studded pommel would not need labelling, however, and nor would the sword of thirty-one-year-old Harold Godwinson, the earl's eldest living son. Harold's had a row of notches on its silver hilt. They had not achieved their return without bloodshed, and there were those at this feast who wouldn't forgive them for it. And if they hadn't actually killed the Archbishop of Canterbury, Robert Champart, King Edward's old friend from Normandy, they'd obliged him to make an unforgiveably undignified exit from England. Just how undignified, they had only just learned. And, thought Harold Godwinson grimly, if his three high-spirited young brothers didn't stop indecently rejoicing in the details and clowning all over the guesthouse where they awaited the summons to the hall, if they took this mood of crude merriment into the feast with them, the situation could erupt into violence like dry straw when bonfire sparks blow into it. If only their father would raise his voice to control them . . . But Godwin sat quiet, unnaturally quiet, without the vitality to comment, and Harold, glancing at his lined face, felt anxiety. Before their exile, Godwin had never looked like that.

Meanwhile, as the eldest son of the house, the onus of restraining the wild younger men was his. He said, as his brother Tostig dragged a bench into the middle of the room and climbing on it began a realistic, even an inspired, impression of a deposed archbishop in a leaky boat: "Tostig, and you two others as well, *will* you stop that fooling? Save it for our hall at home!"

"Let them enjoy themselves," Countess Gytha of Wessex murmured. She sat with hands folded in her lap, watching her lively offspring with pride. Her head, with the high cheekbones and the crown of silvered plaits, was held erect. It was her triumph too that Champart was gone. For years she had had to watch her husband being elbowed aside for him. It was Champart she blamed for the grey which had ousted the copper from Godwin's hair and so drained his vigour that now he looked shrunken inside his rich clothes, as if they draped his body more than they adorned it. "Today we have reason to rejoice," she said.

"Rejoicing is one thing," Harold retorted. "Lunacy is another. *Tostig!*"

Tostig, energetically tossing the contents of invisible pails over the side of the bench, grinned and lobbed several gallons of imaginary sea water into his elder brother's face. "Oh, my embroidered mantle!" he wailed histrionically. "Oh, my beautiful boots! Oh, why was the only ship willing to take me from England this ruinous tub with gaps in her planking? What a fate for an archbishop, to drown like an unwanted kitten . . . !"

"Tostig, did you hear me?"

"Land!" cried Tostig, shading his eyes. "I see land! What shore is it? Where are we?"

The two younger boys, Gyrth and Leofwin, waiting their cue propped against the tapestried walls, zestfully entered the game. "We," said Gyrth inaccurately, "are poor Norman fisherfolk, rude and unlearned, come from our huts to see what the gale has blown to us. Hoping for pickings. But unluckily no one seems to be drowned, like a kitten or otherwise . . ."

"I wish all three of you were drowned!"

"Tell me, fellow!" cried Tostig shrilly, "where are we and who are you?"

"Strangers," said Gyrth in a dreadful parody of a rustic accent, thumbs hooked in a gold-buckled belt, "should name their own names first."

Despite the handicap of a snub nose and freckles, Tostig managed to express an extreme degree of offended dignity. "I, my man, am the Archbishop of Canterbury!"

"Are you now?" said Gyrth, hazel eyes sparkling. "Then maybe we *had* best introduce ourselves. *I'm* King of the Magyars, and *he's* Emperor of Cathay!"

The trio fell, whooping with laughter, into each other's arms.

". . . Archbishop of Canterbury!" yelped Tostig, "dripping wet and . . ."

"Seasick!" hooted Gyrth.

". . . Clutching a bailing bucket!" Leofwin held his ribs. "Oh, glorious, glorious . . . !"

Harold, the freshly barbered ends of his thick blond hair glittering under the torchlight, pounced upon his brothers, thrusting Gyrth aside and yanking Leofwin back. Reaching past them he grabbed a handful of Tostig's hair. "Behave yourself or by the Elbow of Odin I'll roll you in the rushes and spoil your fine clothes

too! Have you no sense? You damned fool, Tostig! I should think
they can hear you all the way to the king's apartments!"

Tostig, pink with rage, tore himself free. "What's the matter
with you? Aren't you glad to see the back of Champart? Wasn't he
our enemy? Aren't you glad to be home in spite of him?"

From where he sat, Godwin at last spoke, and his voice was
weary. "We are all glad, Tostig. But now we are home, we want to
stay. And our real enemy—mine, at least—was and is King Edward
and not Champart. Today I hope to bury that feud. Your brother is
right. We must go softly in the hall. Quieten yourselves, all of you.
There go the trumpets for the feast."

"That green mantle is very becoming," said King Edward to his wife
Edith, in careful, social accents.

The royal apartments were not especially luxurious but they
had become more comfortable, he noticed, since Edith's return from
the convent where she had spent the year of her father, Godwin's,
exile. Edith had always taken thought for her husband's comfort.
Despite his fury with her family, he had missed her during that
year. He wished to resume their relationship in a friendly manner.

Which might not be easy. He knew already that Countess
Gytha had taken three days to persuade Edith out of the convent and
back to her royal throne. Edith loved her father, and Edward knew
it. Edward detested him, and Edith knew it. Also, there were other
difficulties. Edith had found that one could live celibate and at peace
in the cloister, whereas to live celibate and at peace within a marriage took a level of saintliness to which she could not aspire. She
said so to her mother.

"I know," said Gytha, with genuine pity in her face. "I know.
But your family needs someone who has Edward's confidence. He
will never really forgive your father, I think. But you can do a great
deal to make things . . . smooth. Remember, your brothers have
their futures to make."

So for their sake she had agreed, and returned to this marriage
which for years had been no marriage. She had begun to think of her
brothers as her children—the children that Edward had never given
her and now never would. As she sat quietly on her stool beside the
chair where Edward rested, his long white hands clasped lightly on
his knees, awaiting the summons to the hall, she raised her eyes to

his. She, like Gyrth, had hazel eyes. They were Godwin's eyes and
Edward never looked into them without knowing it. But he had
learned to smile at Edith all the same and did it now. She returned
the smile. They had to make this partnership work by means of
keeping the rules.

He had just paid her a polite compliment. She must make a
suitable reply. "This is a great occasion. We must look well. I . . . I
am glad you let my father come home. He looks so ill these days."

"He's getting older," said Edward. "It might be wise if he retired soon from public life and let your brothers do more." His eyes,
light grey and sometimes cold, were remote. She did not know what
he was thinking. He said, half to himself: "His offence was very
great. You must forgive me, Edith, if I find it hard to forgive him.
My brother Alfred was very dear to me."

The hall, like the guesthouses, was already torchlit because the day
was passing into a dull and early dusk. The space between the sooty
crossbeams and the rooftree above them was full of shadow and the
faint rustlings of the sparrows that nested in the thatch. But below,
where the red-gold light was, the walls were hung with tapestries in
rich and lively colours, and garlanded with spring flowers and ever-
greens. A great fire burned in the central stone hearth and tables
were spread with white cloths and set with flagons and bowls: silver
above the salt and turned wood below it. The place was full of the
strong, composite smell of feasting: the sweetness of herbs in the
bulrushes underfoot, the bitterness of hearth and torch smoke, the tit-
illation of cooking from the adjacent kitchens, the pungency of the
hounds that roamed about hoping for titbits.

There was another odour, too, harder to define. But recognis-
able to men who were used to violence. The odour of tense, excited
humanity in whom violence lay near, very near, the surface.

The hall was packed. Taking his seat beside his father at the top
table, Harold observed that the only places still empty were those
that awaited King Edward and his queen. How many of those
present had come expecting trouble, and hoping for it? A tribe of
redheaded Northumbrian thanes who had ridden in that morning
with Earl Siward of Northumbria were already laughing noisily
together, though the drinking hadn't yet begun, and were glancing at
the Godwins sidelong, as if this were an entertainment and the fam-

ily of the Earl of Wessex were the prospective performers. Even that uninhibited old Viking, Siward, was bristling his bushy eyebrows at them in disapproval.

God send that they would be disappointed. In King Edward's dignified, aesthetic presence, no one, surely, would start a disturbance. Simmer and seethe, the company might, but surely nothing more than that.

Harold studied his fellow guests at the top table. The archbishops and other chief prelates were here. The See of Canterbury had had to be filled again after Champart's departure, whether Edward liked it or not. Harold's own father and brothers all but filled this end of the table; Siward was beyond the king's waiting chair, and beyond him again was old Earl Leofric of Mercia and his son, Alfgar.

Alfgar. There was one who wouldn't like this new peace. For entirely understandable reasons, furthermore. Before going with his father into exile, Harold had been Earl of East Anglia. Now that he was home, he was Earl of East Anglia again. In the interim, Alfgar had held the earldom. Harold's return had thrust him back into the state of earl-in-waiting, and report said that Alfgar and his wife were both furious. That was the wife, Alveva, at the ladies' table, three seats away from the queen's chair. Alveva was petite and olive-skinned, half-Norman; she would have been pretty had her dark eyes not been so sharp. That must be her young daughter with her, rather overdressed—no doubt they were bringing the girl out in hopes of getting her a good marriage. The daughter had an unusually youthful attendant, a child of no more than eight, who was at this moment arranging her mistress's cloak with a care older than her years. Harold, glancing at her idly, caught her eye. She immediately gave him a smile of such delighted recognition that for a moment he forgot Alfgar and Alveva and the nagging unease of this splendid, ominous gathering in wondering who she was and where he had seen her before. He had, undoubtedly, seen her before. That mature little face and its remarkable bright blue eyes were already lodged in his memory from some past encounter. And she clearly knew him. But when and where . . .

The trumpeters stepped into the doorway, taking up positions on each side of it. They raised their instruments to their lips. The fanfare sounded. He set wondering aside and watched the door instead, as King Edward and his queen, Edith Godwinsdaughter, walked through it.

"I have a tale to tell the company," announced King Edward.

The feast had begun. Relays of servers were carrying meats and pastries, white bread, mead and ale among the tables. The service was not as flawlessly smooth as it should have been; the servers were conscious of the tense atmosphere and here and there things were being dropped and spilt. The entertainers, sitting at the side of the hall and waiting to be called on for songs or foolery or acrobatics, had not been called on yet, which at first had seemed surprising: they were a good means of soothing an irritable atmosphere. But it seemed that the king proposed to undertake this task in person. Edward was at the centre of the high table, on the dais that stretched along one side of the hall. He wore blue, and a crown of gold fleurs-de-lys was on his silky, smoothly combed white hair. Skilfully, he touched the lyre he held and sounded a gentle opening chord. The servers became cat-footed.

The company, its noisy talk subsiding, turned towards its host. One of the ushers struck a mallet on the table to silence those who were slow to respond. Quiet fell.

"It's the tale of a bygone hero who fought for the Christian faith," King Edward declared. "I tell it each year to my Royal Housecarles"—he inclined his head towards the Royal Bodyguard of thanes at the second table—"but this year I have been asked by my wife to recite it for the whole company. Hear me!"

Edward was a good raconteur and this story of Olaf Trygvason, the pagan of the North who had been converted and had dedicated his sword to the conversion of other heathen, was one he was, as he said, well used to telling. He could hold an audience with it. Harold relaxed thankful muscles against the bench-back and exchanged a smile with his father. With the king's embarkation on this famous and unexceptionable tale, the atmosphere had grown calmer. Perhaps this would prove to be just an ordinary Easter Feast after all. Perhaps.

Just what King Edward had felt when he took up the sceptre a decade ago and became aware that his chief earl, without whom he could not keep that sceptre safe, was Godwin, of all people, *Godwin*, no one could well imagine. A few tried. Siward of Northumbria, though he personally liked Godwin, had also sympathised with Edward over having to accept "yon crafty southron." From Edward's point of view, this was a legitimate attitude to Godwin and the old Northumbrian understood it. Prince Gruffyd ap Llewellyn, of North Wales, who considered all the English to be his natural foes and took no sides, commented dispassionately: "I would not be in Godwin's doeskin boots for all the treasure in Christendom, man. Edward has a long, long memory."

And in mead-hall and ale-house, controversy raged over whether, before Edward came to power, Godwin had or had not deliberately handed over Edward's younger brother and his six hundred men to mutilation and death at the hands of a previous ruler. It was certain that, in 1036, the young exiled Prince Alfred and his followers had visited England, and certain that Godwin had met them at Dover, undertaking to escort them to Winchester, where the prince's mother lived. It was equally certain that one night on the road, in Godwin's Surrey town of Gildenford, the king's men swooped and seized the visitors from Godwin's hands. What was uncertain was whether or not Godwin knew of the plan beforehand.

For a long time, nothing happened. Edward seemed to lay aside his suspicions, and Godwin, swearing his innocence, insisting that the victims had been taken forcibly from his protection, even succeeded in marrying his daughter to the king ("There's resourceful for you," said Gruffyd admiringly). But no children came to seal the bond, and one day a man called Brand Woodcutter, who knew the truth of that night in the town of Gildenford, blurted it out and Godwin and his family departed into exile. They had dreamed of providing the heir to the throne, said Archbishop Robert Champart moralistically, and now they were as nothing.

But they had forced their way back and it was Champart who was as nothing today, and what was King Edward thinking now?

The recital neared its end: Olaf, surprised by foes while voyaging, sprang from his ship *Long Serpent* to die in the wild seas. On the lyre the waves rolled and the black-backed gulls cried for the dead hero. The Royal Guard and the rest of the housecarles banged their drinking horns in applause. Edward laid his lyre aside and said to the Earl of Wessex: "Olaf Trygvason wouldn't be your choice of hero, perhaps, Earl Godwin. You have never been devout. But he was a great man, who dedicated his blade only to honourable causes."

From the start of the feast, Harold had clung to the belief that although many who were present had reason to dislike the return of the Godwins—such as Alfgar, who had lost his earldom, and others who had lost kin in the raids the exiles had made on English shores—no one would actually start trouble in the presence of the king. What he hadn't foreseen was that Edward might start it himself. But the accent on the last four words he had spoken could not be mistaken.

In the guesthouse, before they came to the hall, Godwin had foreseen it.

He looked tired now, and badgered, and he emptied his mead-horn before he spoke. Then he said, courteously and cautiously: "I have always admired him. I admire the art with which you tell his story, too." The once-resonant voice had a crackle in it now.

At the ladies' table, Lady Alveva put her head on one side and then called boldly, in her light, French-accented voice: "I have not heard the tale told all through before. I thank the king for reciting it. But there was something in it I didn't understand."

Edward smiled across the hall to her. "And what was that?" he enquired kindly.

"Well, my lord, would a man converted to Christianity at swordpoint be likely to stay faithful once the sword was sheathed?"

Edward gestured to his prelates, offering them this religious point to settle. Stigand, the new Archbishop of Canterbury, cleared his throat. "Men are creatures of habit. The sword may encourage them to form good habits."

"And," added Bishop Aldred of Worcester, "once a man has grown used to the happy news of the heaven the faithful hope for, he rarely wants to return to heathen hopelessness."

"I've doubts of such conversions myself," Earl Siward broke in in his heavy northern speech. He grinned. "Wouldn't work on me, that's certain. I'd give Trygvason some of his own physic."

Everyone laughed, including the king. He and Siward, though so unalike, were friends. Graciously, Edward turned again to Godwin. "What is your opinion?" he enquired.

Godwin visibly thought it over, choosing words as he would

choose swordstrokes in a fight. To uphold Trygvason's attitude too
heartily: sycophantic. To quarrel with it openly: inflammatory. He
took a middle course.

"I'd watch such a convert," he said, and took another draught of
mead. "Men will pretend to much to save their lives."

"Perhaps." Edward nodded. "But while they pretend, at least
they don't spread heathenism. The infection is contained if not destroyed. One need not always kill outright to contain a foe. Would
you not agree, Godwin?"

"Boy!" said Archbishop Stigand loudly to the nearest server, as
the eyes of king and earl met, hard with the recognition of the double meaning, and under the table Harold Godwinson clenched a
furious fist. "Bring that mead here! Can you not see that the Earl of
Wessex has an empty horn?"

The server approached the bristling row of Godwins with a
nervousness which he could not hide. The anger in them was as tan-
gible as the heat from the fire. Harold shot warning glances at his
brothers and they held their tongues. But the flush on Godwin's
cheekbones spoke of a fury which might at any moment get beyond
his control. He had counselled quiet behaviour in the hall and he
was trying to take his own advice, but here was a degree of provocation which no man could be expected to endure. He held out his
horn automatically to be filled, but his eyes remained steadily fixed
on Edward's face, in a contest not the less savage because it was
without speech or movement.

The horn, to which he was not attending, was at an awkward
angle. The server bit his lip and tried to pour. Mead splashed and
dripped. Godwin's head jerked round.

"I'm s . . . sorry, my lord!"

"Be careful, can't you? This is a royal hall, not a cheap tavern!
Here!" He thrust the horn closer to the stammering server, mercifully adjusting its angle at the same time. He turned back to the
king and the unhappy mead-bearer resumed his task, this time completing it safely. With obvious relief, the man turned to leave the
dais and its terrifying occupants.

With too much relief. In his haste he did not look carefully at
the dais steps as he trod on them and missed his footing. For a
moment, diverted from their quarrel, king and Godwins alike waited
for him to choose between dropping his heavy amphora and pitching

headfirst on to the floor. Adroitly enough, he did neither, but shot out a foot instead and thrust himself upright against a table leg.

Godwin leaned back and folded his arms. "Very clever," he observed. His voice was a fraction, a single note, higher than normal. "One leg gives way so the other comes to the rescue, like brother supporting brother. Of course, it's natural for brothers to support each other. One must admire it."

He had counselled quiet behaviour. "We must go softly in the hall," he had said. But Edward had gone too far and Godwin could not keep his own resolution. Harold and his brothers sat still, eyes on the tablecloth, waiting.

"A brother," said Edward coolly, rejecting the challenge, "is a precious possession. So are sons. You have a fine brood, Godwin. You should let them begin to take your responsibilities over. You're not young any more." He raised a hand and a group of tumblers rose to their feet. "Shall we have some light entertainment?" said the king. The Godwins, speechless with outrage, saw that he intended to wound their father and walk on.

The tumblers ran on to the floor and began their routine. Siward of Northumbria, addressing Godwin across the backs of the king and both archbishops, said in a booming voice which attempted by sheer lung power to soften the atmosphere, like someone forcefully kneading a cramped muscle: "I heard your eldest boy died on pilgrimage. I'm mighty sorry to hear it. If I lost my eldest, I'd be like a tree with no leaves. My condolences, Godwin."

"Thank you," Godwin murmured, civilly, but with eyes remote and the hand that was not gripping his mead-horn now nervously crumbling bread. "These things happen. He was travelling in wild places."

"Unexpected death is always with us," Edward remarked. "Just as much in England as on wild roads in the East."

"God's Teeth!" Godwin's hand came down flat on the table. Godwin himself, the red flush now staining his whole face and forehead, rose abruptly to his feet. Harold stared at him aghast, having seen nothing especially objectionable—for a change—in the king's last remark. Outlaws and accidents were always subjects for talk. Edward's comment had been practically a cliché. But Godwin had been driven past endurance and now even an accidental touch set his scars throbbing. "My lord, do you seriously expect me to sit here and tolerate these—these—pin—pinpricks?" He stumbled over his own words and made an impatient gesture.

At the ladies' table, Gytha of Wessex said to her daughter the queen: "What is the matter with Edward today? Every word he speaks is a stab at your father."

"I think he wants Father to retire," said Edith helplessly. "I don't think he feels he can work with Father in the future. He's trying to make it obvious. But I didn't know he meant to . . ." She gave up trying to explain, shaking her head.

Edward was considering his chief earl with what appeared to be genuine astonishment. "Godwin, if you feel pinpricks where no pins were used, one must put it down to conscience. It is true, is it not, that danger attends us everywhere and that men may die by violence or pestilence, in any land, on any road? Believe me, I meant nothing more. Did I offend you?"

"Do you not know?" asked Godwin in a shaking voice.

Edward half turned in his chair, his smile narrow and triumphant. "So. My brother Alfred and that night at Gildenford do trouble your dreams, after all?"

Godwin was gripping the table edge. "Gildenford! Will it never be forgotten . . . ? Very well, since everyone is thinking of it now, shall we speak of it as well? Let's have it out, once and for all. I had no part"—he faltered, as if his anger, or the mead, had again disturbed his coherence—"no part in the slay . . . slaying of Alfred Atheling or his men, and no part in his mutil . . . ilation or any of their deaths. I arrested him and his men, no more. They were in this land unlaw . . . lawfully, foes of the realm. If I did wrong, even so, then the score was settled long ago. It's time it was for . . . forgotten!"

"What was the score settled with, Godwin?" asked the king with deceptive gentleness. "Your life? How many lives have you? Six hundred men were slaughtered like cattle on that hillside. You still walk in the sun. Or did you pay with your eyes? I see nothing wrong with your eyes. My brother died of blinding, to make him harmless without killing him, though he died in the end, anyway. A slow, wretched death, given by a gutless nithing of a king, because he feared my brother as a rival. He was a poor king, that Harold Harefoot. His father Cnut would have been ashamed of him. Too weak, too cruel to kill outright. And you served him, Godwin. And now you hope to make peace with me."

On the last phrase, the king also stood up. They faced each other like duellists. They were duellists. They had never been anything else, since that night at Gildenford. They never would be anything else, till the Last Trump sounded.

"I had *nothing to do* with the slayings or the blinding!" Godwin shouted. "I've sworn ten thousand oaths . . ."

"Men," said Edward implacably, "will pretend to much to save their lives . . . or their positions."

Godwin swore. A pulse thudded in his temple like a small heart beating. He raised his right hand slowly into the posture of oath-taking. But irritation got the better of him and he banged his palm down a second time, harder. Cups leapt. Ale spilled and bread bounced across the cloth. A piece rolled against his fingers. He snatched it up.

"Before God," said the Earl of Wessex furiously, "if those deaths are on my conscience, may this crust stick in my throat and choke me when I eat!"

"And may God's blessing be on the crust and the judgement that it makes," said Edward suavely. Godwin paused for a single vibrating moment and then, still holding Edward's eyes, bonded to him in mutual anger, he rammed the crust entire into his mouth.

The hall was quiet, staring. Lady Alveva saw that her daughter, Aldith, and her daughter's maid, Wulfhild, had their mouths open, and ordered them sharply not to gape, but then the drama seized on her too and she forgot them. Edith and Gytha were half on their feet, Gytha already moving to leave the table and go to her husband. For the Earl of Wessex was trying to chew, and above his working jaws, his face was purple-red and his eyes were bulging. They saw him try to swallow. They saw his hand rise to clutch his throat, saw the purple tone deepen, saw amazement and terror in the starting eyes. He must have swallowed successfully at last, for he opened his mouth to gulp air. But when he tried to speak, only hoarse incoherence came out and then his eyeballs rolled upwards and his knees gave way. He fell, clutching at the cloth and dragging it after him, cups and platters tumbling to the floor.

The hall was filled with outcry, with the scrape and crash of benches hurled backwards, and the scurry of feet. Countess Gytha was crying Godwin's name as she ran towards him. Edith came with her, tears on her face. Edward stood still, looking down at Godwin, his own face bone-white. Across the fallen man, Godwin's family confronted him.

"I accused him," he said steadily. His eyes met all of theirs in turn: Godwin's hazel eyes in the faces of Gyrth and Edith, Gytha's Scandinavian blue-grey in those of Tostig and Leofwin, Harold's brilliant blue like July seas, a throwback to some other Nordic ancestor. "I accused him," he said again, "but I did not judge him. God did that. And I swear that when I spoke of danger awaiting men on any road, I meant nothing by it. I had put provocation aside by then. It was his conscience that made him read a second meaning into that."

Tostig's face was aflame with fury but the others were only stunned. Harold pressed a hand to Tostig's shoulder, either in comfort or in warning, or both. "We too should call a man enemy, who harmed any brother of ours," said Harold. "It is true. *Yes, Tostig!*" His tone said, as if he had uttered the words: *Help me to save the peace and our tomorrows.* "But the score is settled now, I think," he said evenly to Edward. "Settled for ever, even if he recovers, my lord. May we take him to his chamber?"

"Yes. Take him," said Edward.

Tostig and Leofwin went to their father's shoulders, and Harold to his feet. As Harold straightened, lifting the weight which was so horribly, suggestively heavy, he once more caught the eye of the little girl who was attending Alveva's daughter at the lady's table. She was looking at him, and her unchildlike eyes were full of sadness for him.

They carried Godwin through the hall, past the upset benches and the disordered tables and the ribs of dismembered swans standing up like the remnants of old shipwrecks. Godwin was breathing, but noisily, and his face was dragged down on one side as if he too found his flesh heavy. Spittle ran from the corner of his mouth. Gytha wiped it with the edge of her mantle as she walked in stricken silence beside him.

In the hall, Alfgar Leofricson made his way to where his wife stood with the two girls. "This will interest Normandy," he said. "You'll write to your brother, of course?"

Alveva's brother was a close friend of the Norman duke. And Duke William, a cousin of King Edward, had during the days of Godwin's exile been nominated Edward's official heir. And despite the demotion of Champart and the surge of English opinion against all things Norman, he still was.

2 ❧ Cargo, without Profit

The truth of that night in Gildenford had emerged like an erupting boil in the midst of a quarrel between King Edward and Earl Godwin about something else. Specifically, about the appalling—said King Edward—behaviour of Godwin's folk in Godwin's town of Dover in attacking a party of French noblemen travelling home from a visit to Edward. The Dover man who began the riot, under the impression that he was defending home and privacy from invasion by impertinent strangers who were demanding lodgings rather than asking for them, had given history a nudge without knowing it. He died in the riot, still unaware of it, and disappointed because he was dying too soon, with a long-held ambition unfulfilled. His son, Rolf, very shortly hoped to fulfil it for him . . .

Rolf's contentment was with him like a following wind as he stood in the bows of his merchant ship *Bridegift*, coming upriver towards London's only bridge. He sniffed, with pleasure, the tang of the cargoes at the wharves. Here was an exotic olfactory confusion of spices and sweating livestock, leather and cheese and bitumen, with river water as a background. A good smell always, but doubly good when mixed with wood smoke and bread baking and meat on the spit in nearby houses: the welcoming aromas of home. He was glad to be back, and above all glad to be back under such promising conditions, carrying a cargo which was to be his passport to the future. Rolf Ericson was a small man with dust-coloured hair and a nondescript face and neither was any clue to the power of his ambition. But it was his father's legacy, and Rolf was his father's son.

The *Bridegift*'s rowers changed stroke to avoid a string of warships manoeuvring in the river. They were slim, high-prowed vessels, the lead ship flying the Golden Dragon of Wessex. Rolf signalled his men on as the convoy passed, and immediately found his progress impeded again by a great wallowing Mediterranean trireme, attempting to turn and doing it awkwardly. Forgetting his daydreams, Rolf swore heartily. He did not want to be delayed in berthing. It would mean being last in the queue at the Port Reeve's office. Which in turn meant waiting for his dinner, and he was hungry.

He had moved to London from his old home in Dover because London was the growing mercantile centre now. But there were drawbacks. The regulations were more rigid here. In any port, it was required that a merchant, on landing, must go to the Port Reeve's office to state his name and that of his ship, declare the nature of his goods, and, if a foreigner, take an oath on behalf of himself and his companions to keep English laws. But only in London were the authorities so strict that one could not go and have a bite to eat on shore first. Rolf cursed again, expressively.

The Port Reeve's office was a shabby shed in which two clerks in dun-hued clothes sat marking tallies and noting names. As Rolf had feared, the place was crowded. But it seemed at first that his wait would not be too long. A big, broad, fair man was ahead of him and displaying a pushful disposition. In his wake, Rolf moved steadily across the trodden-earth floor towards the clerks. Only when the fair man himself reached their table did a hitch occur. The fair man objected to the Strangers' Oath. He was going to make an issue of it. Rolf's dinner receded once more into the distant future.

". . . This is most utterly ridiculous! I am a Bristol man!" The accent was as thick as oil and redolent of Norway. "My ship she is the *Bristol Maiden* and . . ."

"You don't sound like a Bristol man to me," said the clerk, unimpressed. "If you will place your hand on this rood . . ." He held out a small ivory cross towards the indignant Norwegian-Bristolian. ". . . and repeat after me . . ."

"I was born in Norway, yes, yes, that is so. But my father he bring me to Bristol when I am twelve and since then I trade from that port, and never have I been asked to take such an oath as if I were a foreigner, never in my life!"

"The regulations," said the clerk patiently, "have been tightened lately."

"That I know! Restrictions about this, bans on that. Some old statute against exporting horses over fourteen hands is revived— livestock is my trade—and now there is this! It is an outrage, I tell you!" A massive fist threatened to splinter the clerk's table. The clerk began to look worried.

He didn't want, obviously, to lower the dignity of his office or break the regulations by giving in, but the objector was burly and angry. There was no sympathy forthcoming from the rest of the crowd, whose impatient annoyance was taking the form of muttering against the clerk rather than against the stranger. "What did you say your ship was called?" he asked, stalling.

"If it's the *Bristol Maiden*," said Rolf, pressing forward, suddenly and thankfully dredging a recollection up from a visit to Bristol five years before, "then—how long have you been her master, sir?"

"Eleven years, my friend." The big man turned round. "And Lyfing Thorkellson I was then, of Bristol, and I am now and . . ."

"I can vouch for him," said Rolf to the clerk, to the equal relief of both of them. "He does come from Bristol, whatever he sounds like. I have met him there."

"My friend!" said Lyfing, dropping a heavy palm on Rolf's shoulder.

"If you identify him, I'll be happy to leave it like that," said the clerk gratefully. "I know you, of course, Master Ericson. I have a message for you, by the way. There's a guild meeting this evening, at the house of Edmund Edmundson the hide merchant, if you wish to attend. He saw your ship coming upriver."

"Are guests allowed?" Lyfing Thorkellson enquired. His elbow prodded Rolf encouragingly in the ribs. "Much business one can find in the company of other merchants."

"I'll invite you as my guest," said Rolf, amiable now that he was almost through the formalities, with his meal in sight again. He added: "I remember in Bristol you had a reputation for never missing a chance of business."

Lyfing's bushy blond beard shook to his bass laughter. "And you, do you miss much, my friend?"

"If we could just finish listing your goods . . . ?" suggested the clerk, with one eye on the restless queue.

"By all means," said Lyfing affably. "Barbary horses, that's my main cargo. With a little makeweight in olive oil, pepper, ginger, and purple Tyrian dye. As to quantities . . ."

"And yours, Rolf Ericson?" said the clerk when his furiously scratching quill had caught up.

"Chiefly Burgundian wine . . ." said Rolf.

"Wine?" said Edmund, the purveyor of hides. A round, pink person, copiously trimmed with fur, he spoke across the guild meeting table to Rolf, in a voice full of commiseration. "My dear Ericson, you've never sunk your capital in *wine?*"

"He has, my friend, he has," said Lyfing. He shook a leonine, mournful head. " 'Sunk' is hardly the word for it. 'Scuttled' would be better."

The business part of the meeting in the hide merchant's Southwark hall was over. A motion to increase pensions for widows of members dying in the course of their business had been approved and a resolution taken to protest the latest import taxes. Now, in the pause between the official business and the refreshments, members and guests had set aside formality in favour of professional gossip. One of the functions of the guild was to be a mart for news, and no one pretended otherwise. Rolf, after a year's absence, was as eager for gossip as the rest and not now impatient for the refreshments, having eaten at home first. In any case, the sorrowful faces of his colleagues as they considered his cargo of wine were enough to ruin both palate and appetite.

"What's the matter with wine?" he demanded. "It was healthy enough when I left."

"You left a year ago," said Edmund. "Have you seen no changes since you landed?"

Rolf rubbed a hand over his jaw, clean-shaven since a recent sojourn in Normandy, where shaving was the fashion. He liked to fit in with his surroundings. Before he left England, the fashion had been appearing there as well. But he hadn't seen a single bare male face since he got home. And there were the revived laws against exporting horses, and the clerk's suspicion of a possible foreigner . . . and here came Edmund's servers with mead barrels; not a drop of wine to be seen. When he left England, it would have been a normal alternative at such a gathering.

"A few things," he said cautiously. "But . . ." Certainly neither guile nor merriment could be seen on any of the serious faces round the table. "Tell me," he said.

Another guest, a reeve from someone's Sussex estate, up in London to sell a wagonload of iron ingots and oxhides for his lord, said: "The Godwins came home and that pushed the Normans out of favour, see? He and they was always opposites, like."

"I heard about *that*," said Rolf. "France isn't Vinland. I heard about Champart leaving the country . . ." They all grinned. ". . . and I saw Godwin's ships in the Thames only today. But what has that to do with my wine?"

"You didn't see *Godwin's* ships this morning," Edmund told him gravely. "Wessex vessels, yes. But not Godwin's. Godwin is dead."

"Dead?" said Rolf blankly.

They let the news penetrate, understanding its shock value. It was like being told that the Thames had stopped flowing. Rolf was thirty-seven and he had been less than two when Godwin became Earl of Wessex. To Rolf's generation, the name Godwin was a synonym for Wessex. And to Rolf himself . . .

"I'm sorry," said Edmund, though not quite without malice, for despite a long business association with Rolf, he had never really learned to like him. "You were connected with him, I believe?"

"Hardly that," said Rolf. "My brother-in-law is—or was." He turned to Lyfing. "You'll have heard of my brother-in-law. His name's Brand Woodcutter. He was Godwin's man and Harold Godwinson's friend, once."

"Ay, ay, we know the tale. Brand's sister had a son by one of the Godwinsons. The eldest, Sweyn, was it not?" Lyfing laughed, throwing back his head. "Which might have caused less comment had the lady not been an abbess at the time. What a man, that Sweyn! So, in the end, the Woodcutter betrayed the truth of Gildenford to King Edward, and Godwin and his house were cast into exile. Well, who can blame the Woodcutter?"

"It wasn't revenge," said Rolf. "And he tried to make some amends. He lent Godwin a man of his, a housecarle called Odi Pathfinder, to do some service to help Godwin win home again. Odi is still with the Godwin house, I believe. But I don't talk of Brand much."

"No, defending him would be bad for business," said Lyfing.

He might be built like an ox but his sharp grey eyes were not bovine. "And now you wish to talk about your wine cargo instead, yes?"

"Very much so! Not a word that has been said explains what is wrong with it!"

"Well, it's simple," said Edmund. "Wine is out of fashion. It's a foreign, Frenchified drink, Master Rolf. Today we drink the liquors our fathers did, honey-mead and ale. Just as we wear beards."

"But I still don't see . . ."

"It started when Godwin came back," said Edmund, "though at first it wasn't so marked, for while Godwin lived there was still discord between him and the king, and the king clung on to his Norman courtiers. They weren't all thrown out with Champart. But when Godwin died . . ."

"When *did* he die?"

"Two months back, at Easter. He collapsed at the Easter Feast and died four days later. Harold Godwinson is Earl of Wessex in his father's stead, now, and it's said that though the king doesn't quite trust any Godwin, he has nothing much against Harold, and Harold is useful. In fact, Harold practically administers the realm. The king does little in public life now. He spends most of his time, by all accounts, studying plans for this new cathedral he wants to build—he once took an oath to go on pilgrimage, it seems, and then couldn't go, so this is his offering in place of it. He relies on Earl Harold for nearly everything else. On top of that, the other earls like Harold. Even Alfgar does—for the good reason that he's got East Anglia back since Harold took over Wessex. Result: the tide for the Norman influence has ebbed over the horizon. Harold is everyone's favourite. A lot more of the Norman courtiers have gone home, and if the Norman duke is still the nominated heir no one mentions it. And French fashions have vanished from England, and French wine goes cheap for lack of takers."

"The market should pick up if you can wait," Lyfing interposed encouragingly. "The drop in price ought to bring buyers along soon."

"And I'll have to sell at a loss," Rolf retorted. A chill was settling in his stomach. When he had entered this hall tonight it was with the sure tread of a man who knows where he is going and expects to get there. Now . . .

"Harold's the queen's brother and all," the reeve from Sussex was saying. "If the king and his lady get no children—and they've never got none in all these years—by the old customs, Earl Harold'd be a likely atheling. And most folk'd like that, I reckon."

"And Duke William?" Rolf said, pulling himself together. It was not good to parade financial disaster before one's peers.

"Ah," the Sussex man agreed. "He's Atheling, so they say. But for how long?"

"That," chipped in a corn dealer, "is what we're all wondering, and that includes Earl Harold, in my view. He's started a horse-breeding programme, for bigger horses, so as to get the English housecarles fighting on horseback, did you know? He says it's because the Welsh are troublesome along the Marches and new methods of warfare must be tried, but we all think . . ."

"The Normans fight on horseback," said a man who had sailed in the previous day with a shipload of pine masts and Scandinavian furs. "We reckon Harold's got it in mind that one day we'll be at war with William."

Talk became general, and political. The mead was followed by cold meats. Small, private conversations took place under cover of the general babble. Edmund, who proposed to buy the Sussex reeve's oxhides, beat the price down by two pence and arranged for the corn dealer to witness the transaction afterwards. Rolf tried to interest himself in listening to them. Lyfing watched him thoughtfully. Then he said into Rolf's ear: "Is all your cargo wine, my friend? At the Port Reeve's office, surely I heard you say . . . ?"

"There's some silk and silver tableware too," said Rolf listlessly. He was calculating in his head. If he sold a little land as well, might he get together enough—just enough—to back another voyage? He thought grimly that he wouldn't, not unless he rowed the ship singlehanded. "The silk I shall mostly sell to Earl Alfgar's lady, Lady Alveva," he said with false cheerfulness. "I bought it for her. Oh, I've recovered from worse reverses. All merchanting has a gamble in it." He achieved a smile.

"So you don't fear . . . a little gambling?"

Rolf turned to study Lyfing and found the big man's bright, narrowed gaze fixed on him intently. "It depends on the nature of the gamble," he said. "The odds, for instance. And the stake."

"The stake is your thanehood, is it not? Your ambition is

known, Rolf Ericson. To finance three successful voyages will make
a merchant into a thane. Your father dreamed of it but never succeeded in it. You dream of it still. I knew you by repute, before
today, as you knew me. As for the odds, they're in your favour. The
only risk is lack of discretion. Does your tongue wag?"

"Not to its own danger," said Rolf warily.

"Your—silk and silver, was it?—will bring in some profit in
silver coin. And no doubt you have some reserves somewhere. Even
the wine can be sold for *something*. You can get some silver together."

"Yes. But not enough to buy a cargo and go overseas again."

"What if that silver could be made to grow until it *would* take
you overseas again? Are you narrowminded? I too must take care."

"Horses?" hazarded Rolf.

"No," said Lyfing regretfully. "Too hard to get away with these
days."

Rolf watched him curiously. Once, years ago, Rolf had been
captured by pirates. Among them had been many men like this: big,
aggressive, lawless.

"Well, do you want to hear my proposal?" Lyfing asked. "And
I—can I be sure of your silence, even if you . . . choose to let the
chance pass by?"

Rolf thought about it. Of the dream which had cheated his father but should not, he was determined, cheat himself. Of its near-
ness two hours ago and its remoteness now. Of greater sinners than
himself, like Sweyn Godwinson who had seduced an abbess and
committed murder but died shriven all the same, a pilgrim who had
set foot in Jerusalem. One could always buy one's way out of guilt.
He nodded. "You may be sure of my silence," he said, and raised in-
terrogative brows at Lyfing.

His father's son in more ways than he knew, he had just given
history a nudge on his own account but he did not realise it any
more than his father had on that day in Dover. Any more than Earl
Harold of Wessex knew it now, or Gruffyd of North Wales, or the
unfortunate Earl Alfgar.

"That man Lyfing Thorkellson," said the Sussex reeve to Edmund as
Rolf left with Lyfing after the meeting, "what does he deal in? Livestock?"

Edmund grunted disapprovingly. "You didn't know? No, how

could you? Well, he's said to deal in a lot of things, some of them questionable. Livestock's included, yes, of one sort and another. Some of it does have four legs as a matter of fact. But . . ."

"But . . . ?"

"He brought horses in," said Edmund, "but he isn't taking horses out. Well, we all keep thralls. But mostly we keep them always and they're part of the household. Lyfing's different. He'll sail soon, I hear, with a cargo for the Moorish coast that won't be bullocks or ponies. Oh, they're mostly criminals, of course, men who've killed and can't pay the weregild. But I don't like to hear of men and women sold like animals, and that's the truth. Slaves, my friend. Lyfing deals in slaves."

3 ⚬ *Marriage, without Love*

Wulfhild, born in a thrall's round hut at Saxmundham, to a thrall woman who belonged to Earl Harold's wife, was scarcely the companion Lady Alveva would normally choose for her daughter. She had allowed it for three reasons. The first was that if Wulfhild's mother was a thrall, her father, according to her owner, Lady Eadgyth, was not. Lady Eadgyth said that she had sat with the child's mother when the woman was dying and been told that Wulfhild's other parent was a freeborn man of dignity. It had occurred to Alveva and her husband, from various pieces of evidence, that he might well be a very exalted person indeed. Which made a difference.

The second reason was their daughter Aldith's passionate attachment to her small friend. This would not have been a point in Wulfhild's favour on its own, but it became so when allied to the third reason, which was that Wulfhild was not only presentable but steady, and steadiness was a quality that Aldith sadly lacked.

Aldith was a puzzle to her parents. Her two small brothers were far less trouble. Fair and blue-eyed, much as Alfgar had been at their age, they were predictable, noisy, and not unduly sensitive. Very like them too had been the younger daughter who had died of marsh fever during their first winter in the East Anglian fenland. But Aldith . . . One could work out that the crinkly brown hair with the auburn lights; and the dark brown eyes came from Alveva's Norman side, as did the small bones and the fine skin, though it was fairer than Alveva's. But the saints alone—if the saints were involved at all and not, as Alveva had once grimly commented, the minions of the other party—knew who was responsible for that passionate nature, that dogged and inconvenient loyalty which at times adhered to the most unexpected objects. The household still paled at the memory of Aldith at the age of six, screaming like a soul in damnation when her favourite doll was confiscated for some childish misdemeanor. That time, Alveva had refused to yield. For the space of three days Aldith must do without her wretched, scruffy doll, she decreed, and for three days Aldith did. While for three days—and nights—the rest of the household did without sleep. It was possible that this hideous memory also had something to do with Alveva's surrender over Wulfhild, though Alveva herself denied that.

Wulfhild's arrival in their lives was the direct result of Earl Harold's departure into exile. The new-made Earl Alfgar's family moved for a while into one of the earl's halls on the coast, at Aldeburgh, only a few miles from the Saxmundham estate where Earl Harold's wife still lived. She had not been exiled with her husband. Alveva, impelled by a mixture of curiosity and a moderately genuine wish to see if Eadgyth was in need, visited her. She took Aldith. The child, when not directly under her mother's eye, was for ever getting into mischief and had become too good at evading her nurse. Alveva and Alfgar had already talked of getting her a companion, ". . . the right kind of girl, who will be a good influence."

At Saxmundham, nine-year-old Aldith played with six-year-old Wulfhild, and Alveva did not protest, being under the impression that Wulfhild was one of Lady Eadgyth's brood. By the time she discovered otherwise, it was too late. Aldith had become attached and her protests at being parted from her new friend were earsplitting.

"How in the world," Alveva demanded exasperatedly, "does a thrall child come to have a name like Wulfhild? That's a name for a lady."

"She had no name at all when we brought her into the hall," said Eadgyth composedly. She was not in need and had recognised the curiosity element in Alveva's errand of mercy. Her courtesy to her visitor was somewhat distant. "Her mother used to call her Little One or Brat, according to the mood she was in. We gave her a name befitting a freeman's daughter."

"You're sure she is a freeman's daughter?"

"So her mother said. The dying rarely lie."

Alveva took her daughter home, Aldith's sobs notwithstanding, and talked to Alfgar.

"You say the child seemed good for Aldith?" he asked, "and kept her quiet and occupied?"

"Yes. They sat on the hearth with one of the dogs, and this girl Wulfhild was telling her stories about the dog. The child's very young, of course, but in some ways she behaved as though she were older than Aldith. And then, there's this question of her father."

"You think he was . . . ?"

"It's possible. She's treated like a daughter of the house and there are those remarkable blue eyes. When you see them, you'll know what I mean."

"But would Lady Eadgyth have taken the child in, in that case?"

"She might," said Alveva, with a touch of contempt. "She is mad for Harold, they say. If he wished it—yes, she might."

"Well, let the child come," said Alfgar. "If Lady Eadgyth will manumit her, that is. She must be made free, if she is to be a companion to Aldith. We can still push her into the kitchens if she's a bad influence."

Lady Eadgyth was compliant. It was a chance for the child, she said. Wulfhild accepted the change philosophically. As Alveva had said, she was old for her age. Peasant-bred children often were. She was certainly far more levelheaded than Aldith, who was three years her senior. If she found the change painful, from the haphazard hall of Lady Eadgyth, always full of noise and children, to the controlled and dignified household of Lady Alveva, she did not show it. Alveva, after a time, decided that the move had been wise. Wulfhild steadied Aldith. During the upheaval when Earl Harold came back to England and the household had to leave East Anglia and live with Alfgar's father, she kept Aldith out of mischief and encouraged her to help her mother. During the second upheaval, when Harold had taken over Wessex and they all moved back again, it was Wulfhild who explained it all to Aldith and cheered her when she grew tired and fretful on the journey. She was much better at it than the nurse was, and this gave Alveva's nerves a rest.

Today, however, Aldith's were the nerves that were being lacerated. Alveva had been scathing about her insufficient efforts to burnish the silver, and when Alveva was scathing, blisters rose on

Aldith's spirit and tears rose in her eyes. Alveva observed the tears and discerned the presence of the blisters, but without pity. The child had had her way over Wulfhild, but now, all the more, Alveva must use a firm hand in other matters. Aldith must be trained for a worthy marriage and fulfil her destiny as her mother had. Alveva prided herself on her excellent performance as the wife of Earl Alfgar, and should he die before she did, she would be a most correct and mournful widow. Both wifehood and widowhood would be polished performances and no more, but to Alveva that was normal. Marriage was a business transaction, an exchange of domestic and bodily service on the woman's part for protection and a roof and children. Love was a minstrels' fiction.

It was far more necessary, Alveva considered, that Aldith should clean her future husband's silver properly than that she should love him.

"When you're married, with your own hall, you must know how to do every single thing in it better than any servant. What is set before guests must be flawless—*flawless*, do you understand?" Alveva lifted a silver mirror with distinct traces of tarnish round the rim, and shook it in her daughter's face. "This would make your hall a byword for slovenliness! And this!" She seized on a large Byzantine bowl with black marks in the engraved cross pattern. "What have you to say about this? You are lazy and careless. I want all this work done to perfection before you go out-of-doors, do you hear?"

She left Aldith unsupervised to finish it, walking away with upright carriage and firm tread, certain that she would be obeyed, whether present or not. Wulfhild, who had been loitering on the other side of an alcove curtain, emerged, smiled at her young mistress, and took the bowl from her. Wulfhild subdued the silver in a quarter of the time it would have taken Aldith, and said: "What shall we do now? Shall we go to the dovecot?"

The dovecot was a favourite place with both of them. Aldith liked it because no one ever looked for her there; it was a way of escape from her mother and her nurse. Wulfhild liked it because the boy who looked after it was a friend of hers, and because she was fond of the warm, powdery doves and enjoyed hearing stories of their ways. But it was not, after all, to be their refuge today. Alveva was in a mood for giving instruction, and she had left them only because her sharp ears had heard the sounds of arrivals at the gate.

She whisked back into the hall just as they were about to slip out of it, and stopped them.

"Now where are you going?"

"Only into the courtyard, Mother," said Aldith timidly.

"What for? There's nothing in the courtyard but a great many geese and a midden. Is that silver done? Let me look. Yes, that's better. I think you know how to clean silver, now. Very well, having cleaned it, you can learn to value it. A merchant has arrived with some to sell, and lengths of silk too. Sit over here and listen while I talk to him. You too, Wulfhild." She turned as footsteps entered the hall, and smiled graciously. "Ah, there you are, Rolf Ericson. May I present my daughter?"

"East Anglia is a remarkable place," said Rolf Ericson. He smiled at the two little girls sitting so solemnly next to Lady Alveva. "Do you like the fens?" he asked them. He was never sure what to say to children, but a certain way to the goodwill of most customers was to be nice to their young. At least Alveva had made it clear from the start which was her daughter and which the mere servant. It was possible to make mistakes over that sort of thing. He was careful to look at Aldith as he spoke.

Aldith hesitated, glanced at her mother, understood that she was to answer, and said: "I like them very much, only they're so wet."

"They certainly are," said Lady Alveva with a sigh. "The children get marsh fever in winter and the walls sweat all the time. People die young here. The damp rots their bones."

Rolf had made his sale. Lady Alveva, though exacting, was a customer worth saving good merchandise for. He thought she probably knew the precise value of every pearl in the bunches that tasselled her girdle and swung to and fro above the violet silk of her overtunic. Throughout the transaction, which had embraced silver spoons and bowls from the eastern Mediterranean, as well as the bespoken silk from much further east than that, she had expounded on her knowledge in detail, for her daughter's benefit. Aldith had attended with almost painful earnestness. The poor child would probably be put through a catechism about it tomorrow. But for himself he was content. He only regretted he hadn't more to offer Lady Alveva. If he had, he might have offset the disaster of the Burgundian wine, and avoided the unpalatable methods of recouping to which he had been forced. He thought of the other transactions which had taken place between his departure from London and his arrival in Thetford, of the unpleasant meeting with the unpleasant persons in that doubtful deep-forest tryst, and of the necessary further meeting that lay ahead, after he had finished his selling tour and obtained sufficient silver coin. Then he decided to stop thinking about it. It was too late to retreat now. He was pledged. He jerked his attention back to the wetness of East Anglia.

"One always has to come by ship," he commented. "Never overland. The swamps are too dangerous. You're almost cut off from the rest of England, here. I had heard you were in Aldeburgh, you know, and when I got there and found you were in Thetford after all, I had to come round the coast and up the river to reach you—though as the crow flies, Thetford would be much nearer overland. Except that you can hardly call it land!"

"We should have been at Aldeburgh," said Alveva rather waspishly, "but there was a storm and a freak tide and the salt water got into the wells. The local folk went inland and billetted themselves on friends with river water till the wells got back to normal, and we embarked our own household and sailed here."

"It was exciting," said Aldith. "We had to pack up all in a hurry, and send someone for water-skins from an inland farm."

"It was a nuisance!" Alveva snapped.

The hall door opened, to admit Earl Alfgar. He paused in the doorway to pat a hound which had gone up to greet him, and beyond him they had a view of the gate, still open, and of Rolf's ship moored on the Little Ouse river beyond. The marshes lay on the other side of the river and mists hung over them, shot with red from the setting sun. The hangings of Thetford Hall were always damp to the touch and rotted quickly. The bed linen needed airing every day.

Alfgar, the hound at his side, walked over to them. He was a square-built man with tight yellow curls and round, slightly protuberant blue eyes. "Master Rolf Ericson?" he said. "I heard you were here. You've come from Normandy, I believe. What news do you bring?"

The talk played round Normandy for a while, though some-

what unproductively. Rolf discovered that he had left just too soon
to know the answers to his host's enquiries.

No, he had not seen the Lady Alveva's brother, William Malet,
though he had visited the Norman court with his wares. No, unluckily he had not been there when the news of Godwin's death came,
and so he couldn't say what the Normans thought of it. He felt he
was a disappointment to them and tried a carefully chosen opinion in
lieu of facts.

"I doubt if the duke was pleased by Godwin's reinstatement. So
he must have been glad to hear of his death."

"There's much to be said for the duke as Atheling," Alfgar
remarked. "He's a tried ruler and can bring a sound succession. His
duchess had a son in less than a year of marriage. It would be a pity
if the Godwins made King Edward change his mind."

"What can he change it to?" asked Alveva, shrugging. "He'll
hardly nominate a Godwin—under the law he could, but I can't
imagine him doing it after his quarrel with Earl Godwin—and who
else is there? He has no children, his nephew Ralph of Hereford has
refused, and surely the nephew they say lives in Hungary won't be
interested."

Alfgar chuckled. "We're prejudiced, Master Rolf. My brother-
in-law is so close to the Duke of Normandy that naturally my wife
hopes to see the duke made king one day. Earls and merchants alike,
we both have to cultivate the right people, eh, Ericson?"

"Ah," said Rolf, leaning forward. "Now . . . cultivating people. There's someone I want to find. Last time I was in Thetford I
saw some exceptionally fine woollen cloth in a market and I can sell
that in Normandy if I can find who makes it. I heard a man called
Redwald mentioned as owning the weaving sheds, but I don't know
who he is. Do you?"

"Redwald? He's a thane of mine. His estate and weaving sheds
are only five miles off. You'll need a flat-bottomed boat and a guide
to get there, but I can supply those. You want to visit him?"

"Yes. Not immediately, but when I'm on my way back to the
coast to sail again in a month or two. Will he take payment in silver,
by the way?"

"Oh, certainly. Most men will these days. We pay in coin ourselves, as you know." Alfgar waved dismissively at the two children,

who rose, curtsied, and retired to join their nurse, who was waiting to take them to bed. The Earl of East Anglia leant back and yawned, one cross-gartered calf resting on the other. "Master Rolf," he said, "you've not mentioned the one thing we're all eager to hear about. Pure curiosity, I admit, but did you see your own brother-in-law while you were in Normandy? Brand Woodcutter?"

He had known it would come. It invariably did. These noble customers could be very affable. They'd give you a respectable guesthouse and treat you like a kinsman but they thought they had the right to ask the most impertinent questions, and if you didn't answer, you could lose custom. And this question was hard to answer: it was like keeping one's footing on a ship's deck in a gale. It was not possible to speak of Brand Woodcutter without openly or tacitly taking sides about him, and Rolf did not know which side to take. On the one hand he wished to speak well of Brand, for Brand had married his sister and once he himself had owed his life to Brand; Brand had rescued him from those pirates. On the other hand he mustn't offend his listeners, and a man who had betrayed his lord as Brand had betrayed Godwin was an outlaw in most men's eyes. "I saw him briefly," he said cautiously. "He's prospering in the duke's service, I understand."

He wished he didn't feel that Alveva and Alfgar asked questions like that purely for the pleasure of embarrassing him.

"That man," said Alveva as they walked across the darkening courtyard to their own sleepinghouse, "climbs like a cat."

They had seen their guest to the door of his guesthouse, as good hosts should, and were returning from it. The sleeping chambers all stood apart from the main hall, neat, thatched, wooden buildings with one good bedchamber in each and a small outer chamber for servants, all tapestry-hung and warmed with iron braziers.

"He's not the only one," said Alfgar sweetly. "Some live in hopes of a new king one day and rich preferment for her family when the crown goes on his head. Pots and kettles. You know the proverb."

Alveva glanced at him sidelong. Even in this light she could see that his eyelids were lowered, curtaining his eyes behind white lashes. He did that when he was angry. Her lips tightened. "I thought you felt the same. I should like to see you lord of a major earldom one day, yes. East Anglia isn't that."

"My sweet, ambitious little wife," said Alfgar. "I know it isn't. And it's too damp for you. Yes, I would like a greater estate one day. But I am not longing for King Edward—or failing him, my father—to die so that I can get one. My father and the king must both feel quite chilly when you look at them."

"Your father's never liked me, anyway," said Alveva shortly, and truthfully. Leofric of Mercia disliked foreigners. Only the size of her dowry had made Alveva's Norman father acceptable to him. His silent criticism whenever Alveva spoke in her French accent had annoyed her since the day she met him.

But it had been a mistake to show it now. She felt the jerk in Alfgar's mind and said placatingly: "It is not a matter of longing for anyone's death. It is a matter of wanting recognition, of wanting a worthwhile earldom in your own right. You were angry when you lost East Anglia, before Godwin died. Weren't you? Well, why not? It's natural, my love."

"Love?" Alfgar stopped short. "Love? That's one thing you know nothing about, my dear wife. For all I know, you dislike me as much as you dislike my father. You're equally polite to us both. I wonder if anyone could ever win your love? And if so, how?" Without warning, his fist came up. Alveva sprang back too late. The courtyard was puddled with recent rain. Alfgar watched coldly as she scrambled up, pearl girdle-ends dripping with dark water and mudstains on the violet silk.

She stood out of arm's reach. "You're bitter because you've never won the position you want and so you vent your temper on me, and accuse me of thinking what *you* are thinking, all the time. I shall sleep in my bower tonight."

The worst of Alveva, Alfgar thought, as she walked away with her small, neat head carried high, was that the bitch so frequently was right.

4 ❊ Cavalry, without Horses

The prelates, Earl Harold of Wessex decided, were completely wrong about the nature of Hell.

He wiped the drizzle and sweat from his face and wheeled his horse, Stormcock, to face the men on the practice ground again. Hell was not, he told himself exasperatedly, a lake of fire. It was an expanse of autumn mud just outside the city of London, with a strong west wind blowing rain squalls across it, and the task of forging a cavalry out of this inexpert squad of men mounted on small, wiry, obstinate ponies which twisted catlike out of line and shied, from pure devilment, at the straw targets when their riders tried to cast javelins. They had had three consecutive hours of it, the sixth day running, with filthy weather nearly every day. He was beginning to fear that the whole enterprise was a mistake.

It was quite true that something must be done about the Welsh. The uneasy peace which had held during the early part of the year had broken lately with fresh raids across the border. The chain of Norman-style castles which Earl Ralph of Hereford had built along his boundaries was proving to be a mere defensive measure. For the pursuit and capture of the raiders, the garrisons weren't mobile enough. The border farmers, shaking impotent fists at the mountains and surveying their depleted herds, had cause for complaint and it was possible that mounted forces might combat Gruffyd ap Llewellyn's technique of lightning swoops. And with the experience gained in such warfare, the cavalry would be equipped to deal with other . . . possible . . . foes in the future. The men whom Harold was trying to train included many thanes from the Welsh Marches, but there were East Anglians and Northumbrians as well.

He had not enlarged on the nature of the possible future enemies, though he knew these had been guessed at. They were bound to be. It was obvious enough that neither East Anglia nor Northumbria was likely to need mounted soldiers on its borders in the near future. The chief enemy in East Anglia was the sea, and although Northumbria had the Scots, they were quiet just now. Siward of Northumbria was harbouring an exiled Scottish prince who could be used as either hostage or ambassador according to circumstances and who had proved his worth in both capacities. That left the Normans. But it was better not to talk openly of the Normans as prospective foes. Not while King Edward still regretted his departed Norman friends and the Duke of Normandy still remained, nominally, the Atheling. Better, the Earl of Wessex had decided, to say nothing, and be prepared.

He assembled the line of men for another charge, expounding on the previous effort's mistakes as he did so. When they were drawn up in front of him, the inadequate nature of their mounts annoyed him all over again. There were only a smattering of horses like his Stormcock, tall and well-bred, with Barbary blood and a built-in instinct to cooperate with a rider. Stormcock had been overspirited as a colt, but with maturity had grown marvellously manageable. A hundred years wouldn't make most of these tough, cussed little ponies manageable in that fashion. And for shortage of anything better, many chief thanes had to make do with ponies. Even Earl Alfgar, who had arrived with a good horse, had had to revert to a pony when his first mount went lame. Alfgar had already said candidly that he would gladly see the brute slaughtered for hound meat.

Harold drew aside, winding his curved horn. The line surged forward while he sat still and watched. It thundered towards the targets, at which the men were to hurl their spears before veering away. In a ditch beyond the targets crouched a line of Earl Harold's housecarles, whose orders were to leap out and shout war cries as the riders approached, in order to accustom the ponies to battle noises. They were to duck back into the trench in time to dodge the javelins. The weapons were blunt and the housecarles both armoured and spry, but there had already been several accidents. It wasn't satisfactory. At this rate, the Marches would get their cavalry while Wessex was denuded of any defending forces at all. Nor were the imitation battle noises really convincing. The housecarles were showing an understandable tendency to duck too soon.

In the line, one of the ponies was giving trouble. It belonged to a Northumbrian, a member of the same redheaded clan which had been noisy at the disastrous Easter Feast, a man called Ulf. He had a hirsute piebald pony with huge yellow teeth and a bad temper. It had lunged, a wicked head with flattened ears snaking out, to rake the crest of Earl Alfgar's mount. The latter squealed, whirled, and lashed out, and Alfgar kept his seat with evident difficulty. His mouth opened in curses aimed at Ulf and the piebald, and both men's spears went wide. Harold raised his horn and sounded the call to get back in line.

It was the more maddening because it was so nearly right. You could see, when the horsemen moved forward, javelins swinging back to the throwing position, aimed at the enemy's collective straw heart, what it could be like. It could be like reaping corn, the scything down of an opposing army. If only men and beasts could be trained to the precision that was needed. It was possible that the inexpertness of the men was making the ponies worse. If he could get the men sufficiently trained . . .

On the next charge, the error was undoubtedly human and not equine. Specifically, it was Ulf's. He cast too soon, and awkwardly, frightening his mount. It plunged. The spear went wild, singing past Alfgar's head to take the tip off his mount's ear. Alfgar's pony became an earthquake, bucketing crabwise across the line of other frustrated javelin throwers, whose angry cries rose in protest as they tried to avoid him. The luckless Earl of East Anglia was borne clear of the row of targets and out to the open ground beyond, over which his pony proceeded to bolt. Alfgar could be seen dragging vainly on the near-side rein, trying to haul the animal in a circle, and being defeated by its iron mouth and its girder of a neck. "Poor old Alfgar," said Thane Ulf as Harold rode wrathfully up to him. "My apologies, Earl Harold. I did not set yon pony running on purpose. Just our Alfgar's luck, that's all it was."

Briefly, in the midst of his exasperation, the Earl of Wessex grinned.

Alfgar, knees clamped tight on the saddle in the effort to stay in it, took a less humorous view of his luck. They were hurtling amid marsh and brambles straight towards Tyburn Stream, beyond which the king's hall and the rising new cathedral were set. Worse, on a track which crossed their path and led to a ford over the stream, a new obstacle had now appeared: an ox-cart and an escort of horsemen. Materials for the abbey, no doubt. If this fool of a pony would neither turn nor slow down, it would crash into them headlong. He yelled in warning and redoubled his wrenching at the reins. The pony saw the obstacle at the last moment and instantaneously stopped. Its head went down and its forefeet dug into the earth and the soaking grass received its rider.

He sat up slowly. The mild horned heads of the ox team gazed at him, snorting enquiringly. He shifted his gaze and looked straight into the eyes of King Edward.

The king these days was oftener with his architects than with his Witan. Today he had taken a personal interest in his cathedral to the extent of riding out to inspect a consignment of timber beams himself. He sat grey-cloaked in the rain, amusement in his face. "Earl Alfgar at my feet! A very proper place for a subject, but that ground is wet. Please get up." His voice was gently, but definitely, mocking. "May I ask what you are doing?"

"Military exercises." Alfgar rose. One of the royal escort led his pony up to him and expressionlessly handed him the reins. He brushed mud and brambles off himself. "The art of warfare on horseback," he explained, and elaborated.

Edward listened thoughtfully, while in the distance the horn spoke again and another shower of javelins showed briefly in the air. A dip in the ground hid the horsemen themselves.

"I see," said Edward at length. "We knew nothing of this." Alfgar detected anger in the cool voice. "It is . . . most impressive."

"We begin, I think, to see what could be done." Harold scanned the men crowded into the whitewashed stone room. It was one of the lesser buildings of Edward's London palace. It had a small dais, benches, a stone-flagged floor, and was persistently cold. Coming in from the practice, they had all thrown cloaks over their armour.

Perched on the edge of the dais table, helmet off and corn-coloured hair plastered flat to his scalp from the sweat of exertion, Harold grinned at them. "Does anyone here *not* think mounted fighting is possible, now?"

"It's possible," said Alfgar from the front rank. "We know that. The Normans do it. But is it possible with these damned ponies?" Heartfelt agreement rose round him. Encouraged, he enlarged. "They are too small and too bloody wilful." Under his cloak were green grass-stains on his mail. The mockery in Edward's voice had considerably rasped his self-esteem.

Harold nodded, as the affirming murmur died away. "I know. Horses are the problem. In Normandy they've not only got far more Barb and part-Barb stock, they've also bred them selectively for stamina and temperament over many generations. It will take another two decades at least to produce a reasonable number of horses of the right type for England. But meanwhile we must make do with what we have. Some of you do have horses of the right sort at stud. In three years a few good mounts will start to be available. We may be able to import . . ."

"If we can't be mounted properly for years, this whole scheme is a waste of time," said the red-haired Thane Ulf roundly.

His relatives nodded their heads wisely, a patch of sagacious flame on the lefthand side of the hall. The clan was here in force: Ulf, his carrotty father, and two equally colourful uncles. The younger uncle, another thane, by the name of Gospatric, was not much older than Ulf and they behaved as if they were brothers. "Ulf is in the right of it," Gospatric said loudly, now.

"Listen," said Harold, "if you can learn to fight riding the ponies, by the time you get real destriers you'll be the most irresistible force in the world. And remember, we haven't been training long. The ponies may turn out better than we hoped. The Romans used ponies for battle . . ."

"That was in chariots," said another Northumbrian, a thin young man with a bleached look as if he had been left out in the sun, which in Northumbria was unlikely. "Who wants to be Boadicea?" he enquired.

Harold pounded on the table and the laughter stopped. "Let me remind you, Thane Gamel," he said to the bleached one, "that they're also used—ridden—for warfare by the Hungarian Magyars. When they first came to Hungary as roaming hordes, the Magyars were famed as the most dangerous warriors ever known, *because* their ponies were small and handy, not in spite of it. Well, ours are small and handy too. Granted they've not been bred to the business for centuries. But I can tell you this: half of the horse is the rider! Properly trained, properly ridden, our ponies may surprise us yet!"

"And in what way will they surprise you, I wonder, Earl Harold?" said King Edward with enormous interest.

No one had heard him enter. Coming late to kingship, he had never accepted the convention that kings should move everywhere accompanied and be announced at every entrance. He had slipped in at a side door, alone, unnoticed. He now walked to the dais, where Harold at once drew forward a chair for him. "I missed the earlier part of the debate," said Edward. "Will somebody briefly describe it?"

Harold did so, while Edward took the chair he was offered, and listened. He removed his gloves, wet from riding in the rain, and tossed them on to the table. At the end of the exposition he said: "I knew of your plans to create a cavalry, of course. I agreed at the last Witan Council, I think, that some new tactic is needed against the Welsh. But that your proposals were so . . . large-scale . . . and embraced so many parts of the country far removed from Wales . . . I did not learn until today. I watched the last half-hour of your practice, from a distance. I see that you understand the business."

"I was instructed in it by your nephew Earl Ralph, my lord." Harold had heard the edge on Edward's voice but judged it wise to pretend he had not. "As I have said, our chief difficulty is getting mounts. I have tried to import Norman destriers but . . ."

"My cousin of Normandy forbade the sale. Yes, I had heard something about that." Edward was not using the royal speech form, but referred to himself as "I," as he would in private. One tended to forget that the king and Earl Harold were actually brothers-in-law. Yet despite the intimate form, temper was present under the surface.

"I did try to smuggle some across," Harold said with regret. "A man called Thorkellson thought he might manage it. But he failed me."

"If the man you mean is Lyfing Thorkellson, he has been outlawed," said Edward. "On the recommendation of Bishop Aldred of Worcester. Aldred objects to slave trading and your Thorkellson was in that business. He won't be seen in England again, with or without

Norman destriers. That need not puzzle you. But what puzzles me," said Edward in the deceptively mild tone which those who knew him recognised as a warning signal, "is what you want all this cavalry for. Your plans far outreach the Marches, that's evident. Yet the only other people I can think of likely to be involved in such fighting are the Normans. Who are not our enemies."

"Gruffyd ap Llewellyn," said Harold quietly, "should not be underestimated. He's becoming a power in Wales. The Marches may demand more than we expect."

"Indeed? You'll forgive me, Earl Harold," said Edward, his voice rising a little, "but I can't help doubting if Gruffyd is really the only foe you have in mind. I imagine my cousin of Normandy doubts it too—or he wouldn't refuse to sell his horses." The hall became very quiet. "After all," said Edward benignly, "a well-defended Welsh border will be much to Duke William's advantage one day, as he knows. It was he who first suggested the chain of castles we have raised there. He must have doubts indeed about the use to which those horses might be put."

"My lord," said Harold tiredly, "if only you would trust me."

He actually was tired; it showed in little crow's-feet round the vivid eyes, in the slackened set of the big shoulders. It was more than physical. His voice betrayed it too, the weariness of a man troubled by chronic sickness or an old wound.

"And you suppose I don't trust you, Harold?" Edward's brows rose.

Harold was silent, visibly considering his reply. When he made it, it was with the air of one who lays a stake on a gambling table. "My lord, you did not trust my father, though he served you as well as he knew how. Do you still think of me only as his son?"

The hall waited, quite motionless.

Edward, also, considered his answer. "It will depend on you," he said finally. "On this question of the cavalry, I still await your full explanation."

"It concerns William of Normandy, as you surmise," said Harold steadily. "I should like to open my mind to you, here, before this company. But if I do, even with my hand on a rood, will you believe me?"

"Don't be a fool, Harold." Edward was suddenly testy. "Say what you have to say. I shall listen."

"Some of it won't please you. But it's the truth."

"Very well. Let me hear it."

With one palm pressed flat on the table to discharge the tension in his body, and the other hand hooked in his belt to keep it from clenching, Harold began: "My lord, I am willing to accept, serve, and follow any man you choose as heir. As far as I am concerned, should William of Normandy inherit in my lifetime, I would uphold him . . ."

"You're years younger than I am, Harold. 'When' he inherits, you mean."

"When he inherits, then. And my fellow earls would mostly agree with me. But we, the earls, are only a few. I tell you, sire, we can't command the loyalties of all our followers, of all our thanes." He shot a swift glance at the many thanes in the audience, and more than one head fractionally nodded. "The Londoners," he said, "have shown their views on the Norman influence very clearly. Robert Champart would have lost his life, had he stayed. Your nephew Earl Ralph could tell you that his Marcher castles have made the local people angry even though they were built for their protection. If William lands in England to claim the crown, there may be war. If there is war, I will not fight for William against my own. It seems to me that we must be prepared for a day when he comes . . . as an enemy. I warned you you might not like what I told you."

"And whom do you suggest I name instead of William, Earl Harold?" Edward asked tightly. "My nephew Ralph has already refused. Do you mean to offer yourself, as my wife's brother and my chief earl? Is that what you're hinting?"

Anger showed in Harold's eyes, but with an effort those close to him could see he kept it out of his voice. "No, my lord, it is not. A moment ago I spoke to this assembly of the Magyar horsemen. There's something else in Magyar-land besides fine riders. Your half-brother's younger son, Edward Edmundson, is there. We have heard he has a place at court there and is thought an able man. We know he's married to a princess and has a son of his own to follow him. And there are troubles in those lands now that might make it worth his while to come to England. Ask him to come, sire. Give us an Edward Atheling."

Edward's face had grown less cold. "Edward Edmundson . . ." he said musingly.

"If the king desires it, I will seek him out myself," Harold said.

Edward rose, gathering up his gloves. "The matter is worth some thought. I shall give it some. But you, Earl Harold, will not leave England now and nor will any other earl of mine. I've another task in hand. A full Witan Council is about to be called, but I may as well forewarn you: the constant uproar on the Welsh borders makes me feel I should like a friendly ruler in Scotland. I propose to put one there. Siward of Northumbria has an exiled Scottish prince in his house. I want you and Siward to lead a campaign to put the crown of Scotland on young Malcolm's head. You won't be requiring cavalry."

5 ✳ Northumbria, without an Earl

On the backgammon board between Alfgar and Alveva, a piece clicked as it was moved. The brazier by the table settled with a soft rustle and the attendant thrall rose quietly to replenish it, before sinking back into her corner to doze until wanted again. The lamps flickered in a February draught which had found its way through all the defences of wooden walls and hangings in the apartment. "So Siward's dead," said Alveva consideringly, her eyes upon the board.

The news, borne by a messenger who also bore a summons to a Witan meeting in two months' time, had arrived the day before but till now they had not discussed it. They had looked after the messenger, pursued their thoughts within themselves, and waited for the natural moment to speak. It had come.

"I suppose," said Alveva, "that the Witan will decide who takes over Northumbria. His only son is a mere child."

The campaign to enthrone Malcolm of Scotland had taken place. The purpose was achieved by summer, 1054. Siward of Northumbria was in the forefront, enjoying it all, fighting battles bloody enough to rejoice even his Viking heart. But his elder son Osbern had fought at his side, and Osbern had died. "A tree with no leaves," Siward had said, envisaging himself if he were to lose his son. A good metaphor, for when he saw Osbern's body carried from the field he looked, men said, like a stricken oak, gnarled and mighty still, but stark, the sap destroyed. In the next January he took a chill and within days he was dead too. He left a wife, an infant son, and a wild, stormy earldom with no lord.

"It's an opportunity," said Alfgar, as one who agrees with a statement already made. "Though you might not like Northumbria."

He had visited it once, for a wedding. He remembered bleak hills that rolled in orderly waves like a gigantic, petrified sea, and a sky which persistently wept, and a hardy, hospitable people who, for all their open-handedness to guests, carried weapons to hall, kept their own customs—in particular, the blood feud—in the face of all the king's ordinances, and were as proud and intransigent as Lucifer. The place was almost a kingdom in its own right. It was known to be hard to rule. But it conferred great lustre on the man who held it.

"As Earl of Northumbria," said Alveva, "you'd be any man's equal—your father's, or Earl Harold's. I don't suppose it's any more uncomfortable to live in than the fens. It couldn't be."

Alfgar thought privately that it probably could, but they would worry about that later. New hopes, kindled by the news of Siward's death, were being fanned to a bright burning by his wife's encouragement. In Northumbria, indeed, he would be any man's equal. And he would be it in his own right, not because he was his father's son, or brother-in-law to Normandy's friend.

"I need the support of the chief thanes. There's time to get a messenger north, I think. I'll invite some of them to stop at Thetford on their way to the Witan. Most will sail down the east coast—I expect some would call here, anyway. I may need to buy their favour."

"Can we afford it?"

"Oh yes. The treasure-house is well filled. Thane Redwald has just paid his dues and he paid in silver coin again this year. Now, silver coin's rare in the north. They'll appreciate it."

"The merchant Ericson bought up all Redwald's wool cloth, I imagine," said Alveva. "Redwald used to pay his dues in cloth. A pity he didn't let us have a few lengths; Aldith needs new clothes. She grows so fast. Time goes very quickly. It's the Year of Our Lord One Thousand and Fifty-five, and I'm thirty-two. I'm beginning to feel old. Do I look old?"

From Alveva, this was nearly flirtatiousness. It was a long time since she had used that tone of voice to him and a long time since he had felt it worth the effort to push through her aloofness. He picked up the end of one of her glossy black braids. Her dark, lovely hair had been the first thing he noticed about her when he saw her that first time at a Christmas Feast in Chester, when she was visiting an English kinsman. It had made him urge the match in the face of his father's objections to her Norman blood.

"I'm bored with backgammon," he essayed. Alveva swept up the pieces at once and dropped them into their box. She made a dismissive gesture at the thrall.

She almost certainly wouldn't like Northumbria, Alfgar thought. But for the moment the prospect had pleased her and her dark eyes were kind. She smelt quite delightful, of rosewater.

"It's a gift from Archbishop Stigand," said Edith, laying down the thick book and turning the leaves to show the illuminations of red and blue and gold leaf inside. "Bede's *Ecclesiastical History.*"

Edward, who was resting on his bed, as he sometimes did now after hunting, sat up and smiled. "It's magnificent," he said.

The chamber was simple, even austere. The narrow straw pallet crackled as Edward moved. Edith was welcome to come in and out of the room but she would never again share the royal bed. It was a monk's pallet now. She had accustomed herself to that.

"Did you ask him to send it?" Edward enquired.

"Yes . . . At least, I suggested it. I had heard him praise the work of some of his manuscript makers and I thought you would like to see an example."

"You're a good wife," said Edward unexpectedly. He sat on the edge of the pallet, long hands hanging down between his knees, and considered her gravely. "Edith, you are not to think I don't . . . realise what a curious marriage ours is. It must be a difficult one for you. I mean . . . your parents were so unlike us."

"I should have made a nun, had God so willed it," said Edith reassuringly and with partial truth, at least. She would have made an even better mother but God had not willed that, either.

"You're a good woman. I wish I could do something to show how I value you. Is there anything I can do, Edith? Something . . ." He hesitated but then went determinedly on. ". . . for one of your family, for instance? A gift? Lands? Some . . . some office?"

"I'm fond of my brother Tostig," said Edith after a pause. "He often seems overshadowed by Harold, and he has no worthwhile possessions of his own. I'd like to do something for Tostig, yes."

"Would you?" said Edward. "Then please, suggest what you would like."

From the tall, narrow windows on the eastern side of the king's London hall, bars of bright light were thrown across the wide flagged floor and the white wooden table in the middle. A fire burned briskly in a round stone hearth towards one end, to counteract the airstreams from those same tall windows. But the sun had some power now that spring was coming. The Witan would meet in comfort.

A "Witenagemot" was a word like a large tent. It could be cast over any gathering of the king and his chief men, be it Edward with two picked earls and a bishop, or Edward with all his earls, both archbishops, a dozen ordinary bishops, and thirty-five thanes, including fifteen members of the Royal Bodyguard—which was the case today.

The thanes of the Royal Bodyguard, Wessex men for the most part, had their own bench at the Witan, and their followers formed a large portion of the extensive hall guard of ordinary housecarles who lined the walls. The air was full of muted, ceremonious activity. Clerks sharpened quills and rustled parchments, and the guards saluted arrivals with raised spears. Only the guards bore arms, however. It was long since there had been any unseemly outbursts at a Witan Council; Edward's ascetic, unimpassioned personality discouraged such things. But the habit of taking precautions lingered and even the Bodyguard were here today as Council members. They had left their swords outside and they were bareheaded, their helmets with the golden insignias resting on their knees.

Some of the older men among the guard, who recalled the days of Edward's stormier predecessors, when blades were sometimes drawn in council or heads punched in ardent dispute, somewhat regretted the change.

"I wonder, will it be as dull as usual?" one of Harold's housecarles murmured to his neighbour. He nudged the neighbour in the ribs. "You can remember some lively times, I reckon. Born in Scandinavia, weren't you? I've heard their Thing Meetings can be a riot."

"No, very orderly as a rule," said the neighbour. "In the open air, that's the only difference. But just as dull." He yawned. He was a large, fair, amiable man whose essential good nature never spoiled his enjoyment of a good fight. The yawn brought him an admonishing elbow from the man on the other side.

"Stop that, Odi, or you'll set us all off. And you're both wrong; I've heard some good gossip. Thought you'd have heard it, being who you are. Brand Woodcutter's man, seconded in person to help the Godwin family. You ought to have ears in all high places."

"I'll pull your ears clean off in a minute," said Odi with perfect good-humour. "I was the only man the Woodcutter had with him, that time, and because I was his man, no one thought I'd be taking messages for the Godwins. That's all. I don't know any more about what goes on in high places than you do."

"They say the Woodcutter's done well for himself in Normandy," said the first man. "Lucky for him, considering what he . . ."

"Watch your tone." Odi Pathfinder's voice was less affable. "The Woodcutter's all right." He turned his head to address his other neighbour. "What's this gossip you've heard?"

"They're saying that a pack of Northumbrian thanes called at Thetford on the way south and that Earl Alfgar practically sank their ships with the weight of expensive gifts and bags of silver. And they're saying that . . ."

The Chief Clerk's gavel came down on the table and talking was cut short. "The Witan will stand," said the Chief Clerk, "for the opening prayer."

With a scrape of wood on stone, the assembly rose. It was crowded. There were only two empty seats. Bishop Aldred of Worcester was on the Continent, following instructions to make contact with the Hungarian court, and Siward was in his grave. It was to Siward's place that all eyes kept turning.

Archbishop Stigand of Canterbury pronounced the opening prayer, sowing it thickly with petitions that all decisions might be taken with God's guidance. The Chief Clerk raised his gavel again as the Witan sat, and looked at Edward. Edward nodded. "Item one. The choice of a successor to the earldom of Northumbria, formerly held by Earl Siward, now deceased, may God have mercy on his soul . . ."

The eyes of the Witan were on Edward and Edward for the moment was avoiding them. It was clear that he found it hard to speak. Different as he and Siward had been, they had also been friends. A curious friendship, an attraction of opposites. Edward the scholarly, Edward the pious—and Siward the Viking, the warrior, the pagan.

On his deathbed, Siward had grieved that he was not dying in battle, because only those who had so perished had entrance to Valhalla, and in his last days it was Valhalla that he turned to for hope, not to the Christian heaven. At the end he had staggered, delirious, from his bed and with threats and wild gestures forced his servants to arm him. Wheezing for breath while the sweat poured from his body, he dragged his huge battle-axe from the wall and somehow—only God, or Odin, knew how a man so sick had the strength—he raised it over his head and swung it and brought it down in a flash of blue-edged steel on a bench. The bench shattered and Siward's heart with it. He had died armed and brandishing his axe and perhaps Odin would take the will as substitute for the deed, his wife declared.

And when Edward, pious Edward, heard of it, he only said: "That was Siward, God rest him." Now, faced with Siward's empty seat and the task of replacing him, Edward could not speak.

They waited, and the king commanded himself. He raised his eyes and met theirs.

"This appointment is not easy to make," he said.

He studied them. He considered in particular the Northumbrians: Thane Ulf and Ulf's ginger kinsmen, and Thane Gamel, son of Orm, with his bleached hair and his bony, ivory-coloured countenance. Turning from them, he examined the Godwins—his chief earl, Harold of Wessex, and Harold's brothers Tostig and Gyrth —and then Alfgar. Alfgar had gone pink. "Earl Siward," said the king seriously, "has only one surviving son, Waltheof, aged ten. The boy is his proper heir but we also have to consider the well-being of Northumbria. It's a big territory and wild and remote."

He paused, again looking hard at the Northumbrians. Even in their best clothes and their best manners they always seemed less predictable than anyone else. Their beards were more tangled, their fur cloaks hairier, their ornaments more barbaric. They never sank into the background. The rest of the Witan, following Edward's gaze, appeared to be noticing these characteristics too.

"An earl in Northumbria," said Edward, "can't quickly call on help from the Crown if trouble breaks out. It's hardly a fair inheritance for a boy so young, even if he has competent protectors. Yes, Thane Gamel?"

"Protectors never are satisfactory, anyway," said Gamel, in his dry voice. "There are always rivals and they squabble over the young heir. Young heirs have vanished in the scrimmage before now. Normandy saw enough of that when her duke was a boy. Nearly murdered he was, himself, more than once. Woke up one morning in his guardian's bed and found his guardian stabbed beside him, in mistake for himself. We want none of that in Northumbria. We want no minorities, my lord. Northumbria needs a well-seasoned man."

Alfgar turned pinker still. At the lower end of the table, where Tostig and Gyrth Godwinson had seats by virtue of being Harold's brothers, though they were not themselves earls, Gyrth whispered: "Now, would that describe Alfgar, would you say?" and Tostig's eyes danced.

Thane Ulf caught Edward's eye and the king pointed to him. The red-haired thane stood up. "I'm charged with a message to the Witan from the boy's mother, Earl Siward's widow." He had a broad accent, reminiscent of Siward's own. "She knows he's too young to take on Northumbria and she fears for him, like Thane Gamel here. She wants his interests guarded but not that way. What she says is, he's nobbut ten now, but come six or seven years time when he's grown, can some other provision be made for him? He's an earl's son and there's nought wrong with him but youth. It's not just to leave him landless because he weren't born soon enough, but the lands needn't be Northumbrian."

Assent was murmured round the table. Edward considered, hands loosely clasped on the table before him.

"The suggestion seems proper," he said at length. A clerk interpreted a twitch of the king's head and dipped a quill. "When you return north, Thane Ulf, take word to Siward's lady to bring or send her son to finish his education here at our court. When he reaches a suitable age, we will provide for him." When the scribbling quill had caught up, the king added: "That seems to decide who shall not inherit Northumbria. But we still have to decide on who shall. Any name put forward by the thanes of the earldom will of course be considered. We also have a name to suggest ourselves." He looked his enquiry at the northern thanes. They said nothing.

The silence lasted some time. As it went on, Alfgar's body grew rigid and his eyes turned restlessly to first one Northumbrian face and then another. They did not look at him. His right hand, lying on the table edge, took a hard grip on it.

"So," said Edward briskly, "since no one has any names to offer, you had better consider ours. The house of Godwin has served us well of late. We propose therefore to elevate Tostig Godwinson. Will you rise and be seen, Tostig, please?"

Tostig, his vigorous, snub-nosed face aglow with pleasure, stood up. He had known of the proposal in advance and was dressed for it, violet over tawny, with a garnet-studded mantle clasp the size of a small plate. Thick gold ringed his sturdy forearms. The hands resting on bench-back and belt were padded with muscle. He looked the part of an earl already, as if he had been designed for it on a drawing-board.

Alfgar had dressed for the occasion too, but his red cloak did not suit his florid skin and his tightly curled hair was always too bushy to be neat. He stared at Tostig with loathing.

"Tostig," said the king formally, "has acted as Earl Harold's right hand in East Anglia and Wessex and is the son of an earl. His wife is Judith, daughter of the Count of Flanders, a very noble connection. He has a claim to the charge of an earldom. Tostig Godwinson, are you willing to undertake this task?"

"I'm willing," said Tostig. He grinned at the Northumbrians. "And able, I believe."

Alfgar's round blue eyes had gone shiny with rage. His glance hooked itself on to Ulf's face and then Gamel's. Their expressions were enigmatic. Ulf's father, Dolfin, whispered something to the rest of the clan, and Ulf's young uncle, Gospatric, laughed. Alfgar's mouth tightened.

He went on staring fixedly at Gamel Ormson. Visibly, he willed the fair man to speak. Gamel transferred his own gaze to the ceiling. The other Northumbrians were now watching Gamel as

well. They too seemed to expect him to say something. He appeared
to make up his mind, and raised a hand. Edward pointed to him.

"I and my fellow Northumbrians," said Gamel, his voice drier
than ever, "think that one other person may be interested in Northumbria." Alfgar let go the table edge and his face became wary. "I
mean Earl Alfgar of East Anglia," said the bleached man. He did not
smile. "He is, of course, experienced as an earl and is the son of
Leofric." He bowed towards Leofric, who did not respond.

Leofric too was aware of something wrong. Among the housecarles round the walls, attention sharpened. They were trained to
sense incipient conflict, and it was here.

"My lord Alfgar invited myself and my fellow thanes to his hall
on our journey here," Gamel said. "He made us welcome and gave
us presents. Very rich presents."

"Do I understand, Thane Gamel," said Edward impatiently,
"that you wish to offer Earl Alfgar as a candidate? Or are you accus-
ing him of something? I can't make out where all this is leading."

"By your leave, sire, I'll make it clear. From the hospitality and
gifts and certain things that Earl Alfgar said, we understood that he
sought our support in Northumbria."

"It's not a crime, Gamel," said Harold coolly.

"I'd agree with you there, but for one thing," Gamel said. He
reached under his cloak and drew out a heavy leather bag. "The
gifts," he said, "were of jewellery and saddlery and weapons and silver. Silver coin. This is my share of the coin."

He rose and tossed the bag on to the table. "There are ten
smaller bags in there, a pound's weight in each." The faces round
the table expressed complete noncomprehension. "If you take a
pound's weight of coin in accredited silver," said Gamel grimly,
"and count the coins, and then count those, you'll find some interesting differences in two of the bags. Likewise in one given to Thane
Ulf and in one given to Thane Gospatric." He turned to Alfgar and
looked at him contemptuously. "You tried to bribe us with adulter-
ated coin! One of my bags has twenty more coins to the pound than
it should have. What do you think we are? So wild and ignorant in
the north that we can't use a pair of scales? Hm? And you think we
want you as earl?"

The blood flooded Alfgar's face. His father saw it and gripped his elbow, but Alfgar wrenched his arm away. He strode from his place, feeling for his sword, which was not there. Reaching Gamel, he raised his fist instead and drove it into the Northumbrian's face.

Gamel swore savagely, in Danish, and his own fist shot out in reply. They grappled, swayed, and fell to the floor in a rolling, pummelling, hoarsely shouting heap. Those who were in the way moved hastily out of it and round the hall the housecarles, bright-eyed with delight because this was an exciting Witan after all, a real old-fashioned one, let out a unanimous growl of encouragement. Earl Leofric looked appalled and Harold furious. Edward rose to his feet, white with anger, and the golden fleurs-de-lys of his crown sent forth dazzling flashes of reflected sunlight as he moved. *"Guard!"* roared the king.

The guards who took Alfgar and Gamel away to bestow them, barred in, in their respective guesthouses, performed their task with zeal and also with speed. The council chamber, for once, was worth hurrying back to. But matters had moved swiftly even in that short time. When the returning housecarles stepped across the threshold, it was into a hall humming like an upset wasps' nest with new possibilities of violence.

It was Leofric who was in need of restraint this time. Harold of Wessex and Ralph of Hereford were one on each side of him, each gripping an arm, both talking at once. The old earl was trying to shake clenched fists at the king and he was also, shockingly, crying. Archbishop Stigand was leaning across the table and trying to talk to him, looking almost equally distressed. The other archbishop, Cynsige of York, a mild-mannered man of great piety but little forcefulness, was expostulating helplessly with the king. Edward sat in cold contemplation of the far distance and ignored him. Tostig was in a huddle with the Northumbrian thanes, his new colleagues. The guards took their places again without attempting to report. No one had time for that now.

Edward turned at last and spoke, shortly, to Cynsige. The archbishop stepped back, with a gesture of despair. The king jerked his head at the Chief Clerk and the gavel was used. No one took any notice. The king snatched the gavel up himself and hammered the table vindictively, scarring the pinewood. Quiet fell.

"Sit down!" Edward ordered. "In your places, all of you! You too, Earl Leofric. I appreciate your distress on your son's behalf. I forgive it, and the immoderate language and menacing gestures you have used towards us. But before God, you have had your say now. Do you rule this country, or do I? I have made my mind up."

He paused to let them settle and also to recover his own breath. Having done so, he went on more levelly: "It is not acceptable to us that bad coin should be passed in this realm. There is too much of this. Merchants are the usual culprits. They give good silver to the coiners, who keep some in payment and mix the rest with base metal and stamp it into coins with false dies. They give back to the merchant what looks like more than he gave in the first place. Those who are caught lose their right hands, but the evil still goes on. Out of belief that Earl Alfgar did not know the silver was bad, and out of consideration for the loyalty of his house in the past, Leofric, we shall spare him that. But he is cast out of his former earldom of East Anglia from this day onwards, and out of the realm of England. Let him find his fortune somewhere else. If he is not dishonest, he is a fool, for the silver must have come to him from someone and most men are wise enough to check the number of coins to the pound when they receive such monies."

"My lord . . ." Harold began in tones of protest.

"You have also had your say, Harold of Wessex. I respect *your* honesty. I never thought I should say that to any of the house of Wessex, but I say it now. We had a quarrel with your father. We have none with you. Nor with your brothers. We have promoted Tostig Godwinson today. Now we are pleased to promote Gyrth Godwinson also, to be Earl of East Anglia in place of the former Earl Alfgar. Gyrth Godwinson, rise and be seen by the thanes of East Anglia."

The East Anglian thanes, none of whom had greatly cared for Alfgar, signified acceptance with raised right hands, as Gyrth stood up, rather unhappily.

"Surrounded by Godwins," Leofric said bitterly, "is that how you want it, my lord? What's my son done, beyond cultivate friends like any man of ambition, and forget to count the coins in a paltry bag of silver, like a usurer! Is that worth casting him out of the country for? He won't swallow this tamely, and nor will I."

"Is that another threat, Earl Leofric?" asked Edward with courteous and apparently academic interest.

"No, my lord, it is not." The earl rose, unbidden. His square face was deeply lined with hurt. "The loyalty of my house is as it always was, sire. But if my son didn't struggle against this unjust ruling, he'd be no son of mine. I'm going now to break the news to him. Someone must—and who better than his father? I shan't take up arms against you for him, my lord. But if he takes up arms on his own account, I shan't go to war against him, either. I'll tell him that I hope that in your wisdom and mercy, you'll reinstate him in time to come, for I believe that you will. Maybe that hope will save you a battle or two. It's the best I can do for either of you."

"We shall not reinstate him," said Edward. "It would be best not to give him false hopes in return for his false silver, Leofric."

"As you wish, my lord," said Leofric, and stumped out, taking with him a dignity which at that moment far outclassed the king's.

Edward, however, seemed unconscious of it. He nodded coldly to the Chief Clerk and the gavel crashed on to the table again, ending the subject of Alfgar as if it had never been and introducing a new item.

". . . A report from the messenger sent by Bishop Aldred, who has been abroad seeking to communicate with Edward Edmundson in Hungary."

"Ah yes," said Edward. "Bring him in." He addressed the Witan, as the ushers called for the messenger. "Not good news, I regret to say. Aldred could not get in touch with Hungary. There was a rebellion in the way. He is on his way back. But I understand that the report contains promising information on the character of Edward Edmundson himself and I propose to ask the Witan's agreement to reopening the negotiations at some more auspicious time . . ."

"The Godwinsons seem to be in favour today," murmured Tostig contentedly to Harold. "Elevation for me and for Gyrth, and a compliment for you . . . And the seeking out of Edward Edmundson was your idea first, was it not?"

"We're being given a chance," Harold said. He sat with his muscular, gold-ringed arms folded across his chest, the posture of a man who awaits events, and does not exclude attack from the possibilities. "We now have to justify it," he said softly. "And we shall have some troubled times in which to do so, make no mistake, my brother. Northumbria is not a sinecure. And Alfgar, although he is a nitwit, is not a nithing. He will fight against his banishment—just as we did."

"I wonder where he'll go?" Tostig hazarded. Bishop Aldred's messenger, a young priest, took his place at the table and somebody muttered: "Shush."

"More to the point, what will he do?" Harold remarked. "Although I can guess."

Tostig raised an eyebrow at him, as the priest cleared his throat.

"I'd go and find a friend," Harold said under his breath. "Probably in the form of a nice, reliable, longstanding enemy. I'd look for support among England's ancient foes. Norway, perhaps. Or Wales. If I were Alfgar, I think I should try Gruffyd."

6 ✠ Battle, without Fighting

From the place where Alfgar and his curious mixture of supporters waited, Hereford was a far-off smoke stain. Only the cathedral tower and the crenellated castle keep could be identified. Between lay common land, bounded to the south by a river and to the
north by a straggling elm wood, dark green leaves patched with
yellow against the smooth, cool blue of a fine October sky. Recent
rain had made the grass brilliant. It was like an arena set for a sport-
ing event.

In Mercia, when Alfgar was a boy, his father had marked festival days with such events. There would be mock duels and archery
contests and horse fights, and all the local populace would come.
There were stalls round the field selling gewgaws or hot pasties or
ale. In today's arena the stalls were missing and so was the populace.
The populace was inside the walls of Hereford, along with its sheep
and cattle. At first word of the horde advancing out of the Black
Mountains of Wales, they had fled.

Let them. Hereford wouldn't withstand a force like this for
long. Alfgar surveyed his supporters with pleasure. He had gone
into exile with only twenty men; he had returned with fifteen hundred. He had five hundred Irish Vikings, gathered up in Dublin,
and nearly a thousand Welshmen with Gruffyd ap Llewellyn of
Wales to lead them. The Vikings, who had friendly relations with
the Welsh, had advised him to try Gruffyd, and Gruffyd had proved
to be all that a man in search of friends could hope.

The Vikings were here for the plunder, and Gruffyd was here

to extend his boundaries eastward and also for the pure joy of provoking his traditional foes, the English. It was Gruffyd's idea that Hereford should be the first objective. It contained the first of the Norman-style castles to be built along the border, and Gruffyd did not like those castles.

Gruffyd walked towards Alfgar, along the waiting line of men. The thickset Welshman's bright brown eyes were full of enjoyment. He jerked a thumb at the distant town. "Man, they think they're safe in there," he said. "Scuttled like coneys, they did, the scouts say, when they saw us coming. They'll wish they'd scuttled out of the trap, indeed, instead of into it, before sunset." He spoke English, heavily accented and with weird grammatical distortions, but fluently.

The Viking leader came up, adjusting his helmet. "They're coming."

They strained their eyes. At the far end of the open land was movement, a line of something, dark below and glittery above. It resolved itself as they watched. Horsemen, with bright spears and banners, approaching slowly. "Ralph of Hereford's banner is there," Alfgar said.

"And half the other border castellans with him." Gruffyd spat on a broad thumb and rubbed at a dull patch on his belt buckle. "All the rats in *one* trap. Hah!" He took his horn from his belt. Alfgar did the same.

He wanted the battle now. He had hoped to avoid it, at first; there had been a dawn meeting, an attempt to make terms. He and Gruffyd and Gruffyd's two half brothers had ridden to a halfway point to meet Ralph of Hereford and his fellow castellans. But the terms included the reinstatement of Alfgar and the ceding of extensive English lands to Gruffyd, and Ralph said he had no authority to make such gifts and wouldn't if he had, and rode away. Gruffyd and the Viking leader were pleased. Where would the fun be without any fighting? they said. And Alfgar, remembering how Ralph had looked at him as if he were a stranger, a foreigner with no right in England, shook with sick anger, and hoped to have Ralph's head.

"They're in sight. There, where the land rises. Get ready." Leofwin Godwinson, trotting his horse back from a cautious forward reconnaissance, drew up by Ralph of Hereford.

His voice was taut. More was at stake today than only a battle between the English and an invader, or Edward and a renegade, more even than the defence of Hereford—though God knew these were enough. Today the cavalry which Earl Ralph and Earl Harold had painstakingly put together over the last three years would be tested in the field. He wished that Harold were here. But the alarm had come too suddenly. Harold and the king were in London when the first news came of a Welsh mustering, and they could not yet be nearer than Gloucester. "We have forces enough, I think," Earl Ralph had said, though with a trace of doubt in his amiable round face. "We shall manage. We must." Leofwin, himself in Hereford only by chance, on a hunting visit, hoped they would.

Earl Ralph had raised his voice. He was out in front, standing in his stirrups, trying to make himself heard to as many of the men as he could. His voice did not have great carrying power: like the rest of him it was pleasant but slightly ineffectual. Most people said he had been right to refuse to be Edward's heir. "Remember!" he shouted, "they won't expect a mounted charge—or at least they've never faced one before! Surprise is on our side. You all understand what you have to do! I shall ride with the first line; Leofwin God-winson and his men will follow me. After him . . ."

The reiteration of prepared plans went on. The chargers fidgeted. Most were ponies, still, with only the leaders and a handful of their better-off followers on horses of any size. In the distance, a horn spoke faintly. Ralph's head twitched round. "To your stations!"

He lifted his own horn, swinging his horse to face the enemy. A Hereford thane on a restless grey pony half started forward, and checked his mount with an effort, to await the releasing command. It came. Leofwin, holding his own line back until Ralph's were well on their way, sent a prayer after them. This had never been done on English soil before. It had been planned and rehearsed and dreamed of, but now, in this moment, it was still a breathless innovation and a gamble.

But they did have the power of surprise. As his own line set off, he saw it working. His own steed was tall, and the lift of the land ahead permitted him to see the foe over the first wave of riders. He saw an initial foot charge down the slope waver and falter; heard, far away, an urgent horn note echoed by another, commanding the enemy forces to stand, close up, form a shield wall. He saw the ragged line of attackers coalesce into that traditional defensive tactic. It was all as they had foreseen in practice. It would be all right.

Ahead, the first line had become untidy. There was too much variation in the quality of the mounts. The man on the grey pony was going ahead too fast; the creature had a surprising turn of speed, in spite of its short legs. Well, it would be the end of him, but that needn't affect the rest of the charge. It might even do good! The sight of him was tempting the men in the shield wall. Before Leofwin's happy gaze, the embattled enemy at one place broke ranks. A few men ran out to meet the oncoming lone rider, unable to resist the opportunity to kill. The lone man raised his javelin and cast and one of the enemy fell, tumbling on to his back. Leofwin caught a momentary glimpse of him, a fallen figure miniatured by distance, with sticklike arms and legs jerking and the javelin sticking up. He saw the figure tear the javelin out. He was nearer by then. He saw the blood spout up.

It took the oncoming grey pony in the face.

The grey head was suddenly dyed scarlet. The pony screamed, its appalled, flaring nostrils taking in the reek. Its ancestral memories, which told it that blood was the smell of death, of wolf and lion, awoke. It reared and whirled, throwing its rider, and plunged back towards the onrushing ranks of Earl Ralph's charge. Beyond it, the first yell of anger from the Welsh and the Vikings changed to a shriek of triumph. The pony, saddle empty and stirrups flailing, crashed into its fellows, bringing with it the twin stenches of fresh blood and panic.

Panic had been only just under the surface with most of the ponies, in any case. The clashing shields and battle cries of the real battlefield were louder and more menacing than anything the house-carles on the practice field had managed, and the sense of danger in their riders' bodies had passed into the animals. Gasping, shaken with horror as if with a phantom spear in his middle, Leofwin saw the line in front of him break up in a crazy confusion of kicking and rearing, saw the ponies spin round, skidding, charging back on his own line. Grass spurted from the bolting feet. Then his and Ralph's lines were entangled and the world dissolved into a nightmare of white-ringed eyes and tossing equine heads, of the squeals of terrified horses, and the screams from the men who threshed, thrown and trampled, under the frightened hooves.

First astounded, then disbelieving, then hilarious, Alfgar and

Gruffyd and their warriors watched it happen. Wide-eyed and open-mouthed, they heard Ralph's horn blare and blare again in the order to charge, and they heard it fade away as Ralph's own destrier, infected by the fear all round it, although a seasoned warhorse, laid back its ears and galloped its rider willy-nilly from the field. Men flung from suddenly untenable saddles fell like leaves in an autumn gale. Those who somehow kept their seats went perforce where their ponies did. Swearing, shouting, hauling on mouths suddenly impervious to the fiercest application of muscle and bit, baleless and redeless, they were swept from the battle, over the horizon and out of sight.

And the Vikings and the Welsh, dashing tears of laughter from their eyes, gripped their weapons hard and raced over the grass to the littered forms of the unhorsed. Some had already been kicked senseless or trodden to death. Those who had not were lives for the taking.

After that, the victors took Hereford.

The news reached Gloucester just after noon, carried from ridge to ridge by a series of beacons, always kept ready in case of grave emergency on the border. This disaster more than qualified. The column of smoke in the distance galvanised the court. Harold, already preparing to ride to Hereford with reinforcements, bellowed orders that jarred every man who was walking about his duties into a run. Edward ordered a force of the Royal Guard to join him. Harold galloped out of Gloucester with five hundred men behind him, and had crossed the twenty-five miles to Hereford, following the line of the beacons, before dusk.

A cloud of dark vapour hung over Hereford, and a smell of burning came towards them on a northwest wind. The castle gate, south of the river, stood wide and they rode straight in. Bodies lay huddled and small in the courtyard: castle servants who had tried to resist. Some clutched staves or knives still in their stiff hands. Harold spurred his horse straight up the steps into the hall. The steward and some of the other servants had been sitting down to eat when the foe arrived. The table was strewn with the remnants of the meal, and seats were overturned. There were more bodies on the floor, collapsed over the benches and one—an old thrall with wounds in his back—lay halfway up the steps to the upper chamber. None of

Ralph's family, mercifully, were here; he must have sent them away beforehand. But his steward had been his friend, Harold remembered The place had been stripped of valuables. Hangings were torn down and chests lay tossed about with lids flung open. He stayed only long enough to be sure that among the bodies none still lived, and then clattered down the steps again, and away, to lead his men over the river into Hereford.

In the town was more confusion. The raiders had gone, having seized a wealth of booty and captives and kindled the houses for fun. Ash still smouldered where wooden buildings had stood. Survivors stumbled about in the smoke with buckets of water from river or well. Others wandered, weeping or stunned witless or frantically crying the names of lost relatives who did not reply.

A woman, old, lined, with faded hair escaping her torn veil, caught at Harold's bridle and he stopped of necessity. "I came too late, mother. I know it. I am sorry."

"My son," she said, "they took my son. For a slave. He was seventeen. Who'll draw my water and cut wood for me now, or dig our strip in the fields? He ran out with his knife but they knocked it away . . . They laughed, said he was strong and too good to kill, he'd make a stout thrall. They took my Osric. He could read and write, even, and he never let the miller cheat us. Oh, get him back for me! Get him back!"

"If I can, I will," said Harold, knowing he couldn't. He took a ring from his hand. "Sell this, it'll feed you and a servant to care for you, for a long time. Now let me go, mother. I've much to do."

He rode on, his anger burning in him as if Gruffyd's brands had made a fire in his stomach. On the steps of the cathedral was more carnage. Seven priests had died there, defending the House of God and its treasures. He left his horse this time and went in on foot, stepping over the dead as reverently as he might. The church, like the castle, had been stripped. The altar was desecrated, furnishings tossed about and the things of no value hacked and torn.

One rood, of ivory and silver, had escaped the marauders because it was hung too high for them to reach. "O God," he said, standing below it, "let me avenge this. One day."

His anger was not, he found, chiefly against Alfgar. That puzzled him at first. He thought about it, gazing at the rood. Then he remembered how he himself had ravaged his own lands when he was fighting to return from exile. He might well, had he been Alfgar, have sought Gruffyd's aid. He might well have sought Satan's, he thought grimly. When a man was desperate, and wild with rage at what seemed to him an injustice, he might do all manner of things and be forgiven for it.

But Alfgar was one thing. Gruffyd himself was another. Gruffyd had no business here and no business to let himself be involved in Alfgar's affairs. "O God," Harold prayed aloud, "let Gruffyd ap Llewellyn pay for this with his own blood, and let me have the shedding of it!"

"This is no laughing matter," said Earl Harold sternly. He studied the faces in Edward's Gloucester council chamber, his own face bleak. So also was Edward's. Harold was conscious that the king did not want to look at him. Ralph of Hereford was obviously acutely conscious of the same thing. Ralph would meet no one's eyes at all. The cavalry experiment had been essentially his and Harold's.

But one or two thanes who had not been at Hereford, notably those infernal Northumbrians Gamel, Ulf, and Gospatric, were showing unmistakable signs of suppressed merriment. The mental picture conjured up by the news, of the fine new mounted forces presenting a vista of retreating tails to the foe, of Earl Ralph hurtling ignominiously at full gallop off the battlefield, while still sounding the order to charge, was too much for their composure. Their eyes had a sparkle which was by no means pure outrage. Harold turned a cold countenance to them.

"When I was earl in East Anglia," he said, "I went to a funeral, of a thane who had been a friend of mine for many years. It was January. The weather had been wet for weeks and the ground was marshy, and when the grave was dug it had to be lined with planks to keep it from caving in before the coffin could be lowered. When the priest was reciting the committal, the earth gave way under him and he fell into the grave. We had to haul him out before he could finish." He let the muffled chuckles subside. "Yes, it was funny. But my friend was still dead. His wife was still widowed and his children still cried for him. On Hereford field more than five hundred men were killed, who remain dead." His voice strengthened. "And then came the sacking of the city. Priests and clergy slaughtered. Citizens killed or seized as slaves. Treasures snatched by a rabble of savages. If anyone can find humour in this, I can't. On the field of

Hereford we left one—just one—of the enemy dead. Laugh? I feel ill, my friends, ill and ready to die myself of shame!"

A thane who had been at Hereford and was not laughing, said: "The ponies needed more training—to noise and bloodshed. That was the trouble."

"When a cavalry force opposes a force on foot," Ralph said wearily, "the unmounted army usually keeps within its shield wall. Then one can hurl spears from a distance, in over the shields, and veer away ready for the men behind you to cast too. We had trained expecting warfare of that sort and . . ."

From the head of the table, Edward spoke. "Next time, we must remember to tell the enemy all these things before the fighting starts. Then the battle may go according to plan. I agree, I see little point in developing the idea of mounted warfare any further. It was an interesting experiment but it has failed. However, we can discuss that later. For the moment, Alfgar and Gruffyd are in possession of the Hereford district. They can't be left there. What is to be done?"

"I was never in favour of exiling Alfgar," Harold said. "If it were only Alfgar, I should say that we should negotiate . . ."

"After the sacking of Hereford?" asked Edward, his voice chilly.

"My lord," said Harold, "I think that was mostly Gruffyd's doing. Oh yes, Alfgar brought him there. But when a man has been cast out of his home, he's liable to do wild things. Having got Gruffyd—I gather that some of his forces were Viking but most were Gruffyd's Welshmen—to Hereford, I doubt if Alfgar could control him. Alfgar . . ."

"Bloody good thing he never tried to rule Northumbria, if he can't keep one miserable Welshman in order!" the thane from Hereford remarked.

Harold glanced at him. "You may be right. I did not, if you remember, suggest that he should be given the rule of Northumbria. Only that he should not have been thrown out of East Anglia. Gruffyd is our real foe, not Alfgar. Gruffyd has been an invader in the past and will be again in time to come, without any help from Alfgar. Gruffyd is the enemy."

"Well, Harold." The king contemplated his chief magnate. "And what do you propose that we do about him? Our trust, as I believe you would have it, is in you."

7 ✖ *Peace, without Honour*

"My lord!" said the Earl of Mercia imperatively. "Wake up! *Wake up*! My lord . . . *Harold*!"

He was half asleep himself, having tumbled his elderly bones hurriedly from bed to shake the younger man awake. Harold roused with a thankful jerk, blinking up into Leofric's face. The pages, whose youthful slumber was deeper than Leofric's, sat up blearily on their pallets, and guards' feet clattered outside. "It's all right," Leofric said as the guards plunged through the doorway. "Earl Harold was riding the night mare." To the pages he said: "So you boys are awake at last? Will you snore through the Day of Judgement, I wonder? Get some hot water. It's time we were up, anyway." When they had gone, he sat down on the end of Harold's bed. "I thought you were being murdered in your sleep. What was it?"

"Gruffyd, of course," said Harold.

They were in a guesthouse belonging to a thane near the River Severn ferry crossing to South Wales. There was not much space and their milling retinues had had to be content with tents outside. It was daybreak and a thin grey light crept through a half-open shutter. Outside there was a piping of birdsong.

Harold ran a hand through a damp confusion of gold hair. "How sane the daylight is," he remarked.

"What do you mean by 'Gruffyd, of course'?" asked Leofric.

The Earl of Wessex reached for his clothes. "We've been chasing Gruffyd in and out and up and down his damnable mountains for months and never caught him, haven't we?" he said. "I'd swear he's in league with the Little People the legends say haunt his beastly

72

domains. We never get a glimpse of him. But mists come down when we're miles from base and we lose ten men down a ravine one week, and seven more from exposure the next, caught all night on a mountainside in a cloud. We post enough guards round the camp to keep out a mouse . . . and in the night, fire breaks out in the wood-stack and in the uproar someone releases all the headropes in the horse lines—which were not in danger—and stampedes the horses. In the morning, half the men have nothing to ride and when those who have go after the truants, they can't find them and seventeen of those men don't come back either. When at last there is a battle—and I wasn't there; if I had been I'd have sought that Celtic devil out and killed him, by the Beard of Odin I would!—he smashes us. He kills a dozen good thanes and the Bishop of Hereford, who was a friend of mine, and goes off laughing. And you wonder that I dream of him?"

Roughly, Harold yanked on his hose. "I see him, night after night, swollen to a giant and playing peekaboo round his blasted mountains, thumbing his nose at me." The pages came back with steaming ewers and Harold began on irritable, rapid ablutions. "Why else do you think I joined you in getting the king to agree to make peace when they offered it? What else is there to do that leaves any of us with a shred of dignity?"

"You told Edward," said Leofric heavily, "that it was because my son had not deserved his exile and that you wished to see him reinstated and that your brother Gyrth had agreed to give back East Anglia. For which I was grateful to you both; I had not expected it. You said also that while Alfgar remained an exile he was Gruffyd's excuse for committing excesses, that the alliance would be better broken."

"They're reasons too," said Harold, "and valid ones. Alfgar should not in my opinion have been banished, you know that. I don't call him an enemy. My enemy is Gruffyd. *Gruffyd.* The king once complimented me on my loyalty and ability, and now Gruffyd is calling that ability in question. He's been too much for me. So I make peace, amongst other things, to save my face. I would rather have killed Gruffyd first and then negotiated for Alfgar's return. But I couldn't kill Gruffyd. Do you think I like admitting it? I helped you urge the king to respond to this peace offer, but do you think my heart is in it?"

Leofric's hands, with their wrinkled knuckles and age-mottled backs, shook a little. He was growing old. If the king or Harold jibbed now at the peace terms, he might not see his son again. He was afraid of this young, powerful, golden, angry Godwinson. "What is your heart in, then?" he asked.

Harold tossed his used towel aside and dragged his shirt on. "I want to succeed. I want to prove to the king that I and my family are loyal to him, and able to show our loyalty by destroying his enemies. I don't call Alfgar such an enemy. But Gruffyd is a foe to the realm of England and to me personally. My heart, Leofric, is in cutting off Gruffyd's head and impaling it on a spear as a trophy. Do I make myself plain?"

"It would not be proper," said King Edward with good-humoured inflexibility, "for us to cross the Severn to treat with your lord. It was he who challenged our boundaries, not the other way about. It is he and his ally Alfgar who now sue for peace. They must cross to meet us. They will be honourably received."

A pavilion had been pitched near the shore of the estuary, because the house where they had stayed at Aust stood back a mile from the water. Here the emissaries had been received, with ceremony, for Prince Gruffyd himself was expected. But Gruffyd had not come.

Edward had prepared his terms: a friendship pact with Gruffyd and the wiping out of all old quarrels, reinstatement for Alfgar, and the gift of a narrow strip of border lands to Gruffyd, lands he already occupied. But Gruffyd would almost certainly haggle. Peace could not be concluded until the two royal gentlemen had discussed it in person, and in the interests of strict equality between them, the place of discussion should be halfway between their respective encampments. It was unfortunate that the halfway point should be in the middle of the Severn estuary, for the middle of the estuary, and on a rough, windy day at that, was to put it mildly an unsuitable venue for such a conference. Hence the arrival of a deputation inviting Edward to cross. And Edward was shaking his head at it.

The deputation was appropriately high-ranking. One of Gruffyd's half brothers led it, Prince Rhiwallon, a gorgeously clad young man with a head fiercer than Thane Ulf's. With him was a great deep-chested mountain of a man who was introduced as Lord Berddig, aristocrat, Chief Bard to the Welsh court, and one of Gruffyd's dearest friends. Alfgar was represented by a thane who had followed him to exile. The estuary crossing had been bad and the thane looked ill. But he refused a seat, saying that to sit in King Edward's presence would be impolite, and now stood with the rest, respectfully bareheaded, before King Edward to hear his reply to their message.

Bishop Aldred of Worcester, home at last from his unsuccessful Continental mission, glanced rapidly from king to deputation and snapped his fingers at a group of waiting pages. "Wine or mead, Prince Rhiwallon? Lord Berddig? Thane Redwald? The mead is brewed from clover honey and the wine I brought back from Germany myself. It's back in fashion since the bottom dropped out of the market and the price went down to nothing . . ."

The atmosphere remained unsoftened. Prince Rhiwallon took a goblet but did not attempt to drink from it. "My lord," he said to Edward, "it is true my brother is suing for peace. But not in defeat. In magnanimity."

"And because Alfgar's homesick," said Edward. "We're quite ready to fight on if it's necessary, I assure you."

"We are," Harold agreed.

Aldred, who had his own reasons to further the peace, exchanged glances with Leofric.

"We have given our answer," said Edward. "Drink, and go in peace. I wish you a better crossing than the one you had when you came." Thane Redwald smiled wanly.

When the emissaries took their leave, there was a new spark in Harold's eyes, but Earl Leofric looked at no one and would not go down to the shore.

After the boat had been seen off, they found him still standing in the pavilion, staring down into the depths of a full drinking horn, too dispirited to taste it. Harold walked brusquely up to him and put a hand under Leofric's, pushing the horn up to the old earl's lips. "They'll be back," he said roughly. "They *want* this peace—or Alfgar does. Much more than I do."

The boat returned in the afternoon, through a wind fresher than before. Thane Redwald had to be helped ashore and his face nearly matched Prince Rhiwallon's grass-green cloak. The deputation stood once more in a row in front of Edward, and Lord Berddig presented his master's compliments.

"He sends his compliments, but withholds himself?" said Edward.

"My lord," said Prince Rhiwallon, "Prince Gruffyd cannot accept your hospitality, though he regrets this. But it would harm his standing as the senior king."

Leofric closed his eyes. Harold's brows drew down. Aldred took half a step forward as if ready to intervene. Edward was momentarily taken aback but his voice was lightly amused when, after a pause, he spoke. "As the what?" he asked. "Wales is half the size of England, even though Gruffyd I know now claims it all. Equals I might concede," said Edward, "since rulers all hold a like responsibility for their people and are all the deputies of God. But that the ruler of Wales should claim to be senior to the king of England . . . Come, come."

"Certain facts bear my brother's argument out," said Rhiwallon calmly. "He is the lineal descendant of men who once ruled all England and Scotland, as well as Wales. They won these lands by strength from the giants long ago."

"No doubt. And I am the lineal descendant of men who conquered England from Gruffyd's forebears, thus proving themselves superior to both the giants *and* Gruffyd's ancestors!" Edward, having teetered visibly between outrage and laughter, had decided to settle for wit. The deputation looked nonplussed.

Leofric opened his eyes. "My lord," he said desperately, "if the envoys might withdraw for a little . . ."

Edward nodded and the deputation was led out of earshot. "What is it, Leofric? A special plea for your son?"

"It would be natural, wouldn't it?" said Leofric frankly. He rested an obstinately tremulous hand on the back of Edward's chair, to steady it. "But it's not only my son, my lord. Bishop Aldred will bear me out. There's the folk of the Marches. Exposed to attack and no way to fight back. Bishop Aldred, isn't it so?"

"It is." The bishop, a sturdy, quiet man with a jet-black tonsure encircling his round head, and tranquil, mature brown eyes, supported him. "I saw Earl Ralph of Hereford on my way here, and he agrees. If he were here and not sick in bed, he would say it for me.

If there's no peace made, the people of the Marches will go to the slaughter like their own sheep. This is not the time, my lord, for squabbling over *where* the peace is made. It is the time for making it." His eyes rested briefly and quellingly on Harold, whose expression was set.

"What are you suggesting, the two of you?" Edward enquired.

"That you should meet this Welshman, here or on the other side of the Severn. What does it matter, damn it all?" said Leofric.

"Harold?" Edward asked.

Harold took a deep breath, and then let it out again in an exasperated snort. "We've tried to fight Gruffyd and failed," he said distastefully. "A time may come—I pray—when the story is otherwise, but it hasn't come yet. Until it does . . . yes, very well. If a way can be found to cross the Severn with some semblance of dignity, then"—he could not help grimacing—"in view of what Bishop Aldred says, it had best be crossed."

The bishop considered him with approval. "In respect of crossing the Severn with dignity, as Earl Harold puts it," he said, "I've a suggestion. Let us argue the peace terms out through the envoys first and cross only when agreement has been reached. That would be much less of a surrender."

"Gruffyd won't agree to the terms easily," said Edward. "I know his mettle. There will be a long, hard bargaining before we reach agreement."

"And we shall end by giving more than we offer to start with," said the bishop. "Then let us begin from that point. Let us alter the terms. That should shorten the argument."

"Alter the terms to what?" said Leofric and Harold together.

"Do you mean buy Gruffyd off with treasure?" asked Edward sourly. "As my father used to buy off the Vikings? They always came back for more."

"Not treasure," said Aldred. "Make him swear fealty to you . . ."

"*Swear fealty?*" Edward's snort of laughter exploded through the pavilion. "*Gruffyd?*"

". . . as," continued Aldred imperturbably, "your viceroy for the lands which he has seized this year along the Marches. All of them, not only the strip you have already suggested. Make him your liege man, sworn to keep the peace in those lands on your behalf, to protect them from the tribesmen—his own tribesmen—in the west, and to remain peacefully within the borders on the east."

"Confirm Gruffyd in what he's snatched—in all of it?" shouted Harold. "What are you talking about?"

"The lives of the border folk, Harold!" Aldred retorted. "I suggest that Gruffyd and Alfgar be separated from their alliance with each other and bound in friendship, both of them, directly to the king. Can't you understand?"

Leofric was frowning over the idea. "Gruffyd's likely to protect the border lands better than we can," he said gloomily. "Thieves catch other thieves very neatly. They know all the tricks."

"It means taking lands from Earl Ralph," Harold insisted.

"Lands already virtually lost," Aldred reminded him. "Also, Earl Ralph wants the peace. His wishes should be respected. He may be on his deathbed. His breath was rasping his lungs like a blade on a whetstone when I saw him."

"But . . ." Red patches had appeared on Harold's bronzed skin and he had started to pace the pavilion. ". . . it's making Gruffyd a present of everything he's stolen! After Hereford! It's unthinkable." He halted in front of Edward. Edward, one hand caressing his chin, his mind turned inwards, said nothing. But he was thinking the unthinkable; they could all see that. "A strip along the border was bad enough," said Harold, addressing the pavilion in general. "I understand we must give something. But not this, not everything he's seized by force, *not after Hereford* . . . I say no!"

"Can you think of a better way to save the border, Harold?" Edward asked quietly, looking up at last. "Have you shown us one?" Harold went white. "Bishop Aldred, we think the envoys should put these proposals to their principal. Have them recalled, please." Outside, the wind rose again and buffeted the walls of the tent. "The person I feel sorry for," said Edward, "is that poor man Thane Redwald. He'll be ill again, going back in this. Let us hope the weather is calmer when *we* cross. It should be an interesting meeting. Gruffyd, by the tone of his messages, is an interesting man. I quite look forward to seeing him."

Silently, as he arranged his features into a suitable smile of welcome with which to greet the returning envoys, Harold of Wessex looked forward to killing him.

8 ✖ *Future, with Prospects*

They crossed the estuary next day in fair weather, the water sweetly sparkling and the gilded figurehead of the ship dazzling in the sun. Figures in brightly coloured clothes stood on the shore to watch them come, a crimson-clad man standing forward of the rest, hands on hips and feet apart, the red cloak held wide by his jutting elbows. When they were within hail, he suddenly cast off his cloak and forged through the water to meet them, pausing when it was thigh-deep, his splendid tunic callously dabbled in the brine. Harold and King Edward, side by side, looked over the gunwale into a black-bearded face with merry, simian, round brown eyes set a little close, and before he announced himself they knew that this was Gruffyd.

The eyes, intelligently, took in Earl Leofric's years, Earl Harold's challenge, Bishop Aldred's office, and King Edward's dignity. "Gruffyd of Wales, I am," their owner said, in a voice nearly as deep as Berddig's, but more heavily accented, "and it seems to me it belittles us both to let you come all this way to meet me and I take not one step to meet you. My apologies, King Edward, and my thanks for your courtesy, and now my amends. Get on my back and I'll carry you ashore, and level the score between us. Take my hand!"

It was not possible to refuse. Edward laid his long fingered white hand in the square brown one waiting for it, and yielded himself to Gruffyd's broad velvet back. "To the coast of Wales, Prince Gruffyd!" he instructed gravely.

"Gruffyd," remarked Leofric as the Welshman began his bur-
dened journey to the beach, "has charm."

"Too bloody much," Harold muttered.

The treaty was concluded, formally, in a great tent hot under the
untempered sun. Gruffyd had sworn his fealty once already, unof-
ficially, at the moment when he brought Edward ashore and, having
set him down, turned at once to kneel dripping on the sand before
him. ("Mummer!" muttered Harold under his breath.) He repeated
the act before the English witnesses, dry-clad and with a clerk at
hand to set down for Edward's signature the terms of the treaty, the
trade agreement which was Gruffyd's addition to the terms offered—he had haggled as expected—and the names and boundaries
of the lands the prince would hold as Edward's viceroy. Harold
watched the performance, silent, resentful, and smiling determinedly.

Joylessly, he heard the swearing away of valuable taxes, and of
whole segments of Cheshire, Shropshire, and Herefordshire. Several
villages whose entire revenues had once been Edward's went with
them, while Edward sat and nodded in consent. Even Kington, a
village whose very name protested its ownership, passed under
Gruffyd's sway unquestioned. At the end of it they went out to sit
on benches in the open, while the tent was prepared for a feast, and
made conversation.

Alfgar, now once more Earl of East Anglia, was present, but
inclined, like Harold, to be silent. He was thinner than he used to
be, with a line between his pollen-coloured eyebrows. "No need for
such a gloomy face, man," Gruffyd growled at him, noticing it as
they took their seats. "You'll be home within days. Your family's
waiting at Aust, I hear. You'll see your sons again tonight. I'm sending two hound pups with you for them, dogs they can rear and train
themselves. Will they like that? It's what my own boys would like."

Harold forced himself to speak. To sit dumb would be as rude
and noticeable as to utter insults. "You have sons, Prince Gruffyd?
Is your wife living?"

"No, dead these many years, poor *merched*—lass, I mean." Gruf-
fyd shook his head. "Not that she was my wife, strictly speaking.
Strictly speaking, she was Hywel ab Edwin's—an old foe of mine in
South Wales. I rescued her from him fifteen years back, when I was

at war with him. He got away alive that time . . ." Gruffyd's voice was full of regret. "So I couldn't marry her, and before I managed to kill him, three years later, she was dead. But . . ."

"You *rescued* a wife from her husband?" Edward interposed, more than faintly shocked. He looked at Gruffyd as if the Welshman were an exotic animal, a camelopard or a griffin. Patently Edward, alternately delighted and astounded by Gruffyd, did not know what to make of him.

"Man, you didn't know Hywel! He was one of your merchants of mournfulness. Thought laughter an offence to God. At feasts he'd only stay an hour for show and make up for it by fasting all the day before and most of the day after and making his wife fast too. Thirteen she was when she was wed to the miserable sod, and when I picked her up and put her on my saddle she weighed no more than a child of ten. She'd had a year of him and him complaining he'd got no heir from her. He used to feed his hound bitches, look you! A shame it never occurred to him to feed his wife. I told her not to be frightened, that I knew a princess when I saw one, and by next morning the only thing she feared was that he'd come and get her back." Gruffyd sighed. "But in the end I was no better for her than he was. She was as beautiful as an angel, with long black hair, and I'm flesh and blood, no spirit." Edward still looked bemused. "I gave her two sons in two years and the second was her last battlefield, little thing as she was. But she was happy with me while it lasted."

"So your boys are growing up now," said Edward eventually into the silence. "You are fortunate to have them. Greatly blessed."

"More than a carnal devil like me deserves, you're thinking, maybe," said Gruffyd. "But we can't all have your piety, King Edward. We may wish it, but it's a gift God sends to few. In granting it to you, he has greatly blessed you too."

Edward very nearly bridled and Harold clenched an anguished right hand. Gruffyd was wooing the king, wooing him blatantly, as if Edward were a girl, wanting Edward to love him. And therefore to distrust his own best friends?

But the courtesies must be maintained. "You have no daughters, then, Prince Gruffyd?" said Harold conversationally.

"No, to my sorrow. You've a daughter, haven't you, Alfgar? You have scarcely spoken of your family, in all our time together, but you mentioned a daughter once, I think."

"I've two," said Alfgar. "It would have been three but one died of fever. The fenland mists breed it. But the other two thrive, I hear. One is a baby I've never seen . . . Lucia . . ."

"The mother's part Norman," put in Leofric disparagingly. "These fancy names are fashionable over there."

". . . and the other is fourteen now. She has a good English name. Aldith, we call her."

"Pretty?" asked Gruffyd.

"I don't know . . . She's got brown hair with a dash of red in it, and a dash of the temperament to go with it, her mother says."

Gruffyd chuckled. "I know that red streak. Temperament? That's the sign of the passionate lover to come. Is she promised?"

"Not yet."

"Very wise. Let her grow up first. She'll live the longer and it's best for children to keep their mother. My boys feel the lack of one, but I've had no wish to marry since Bronwen died. At least with the boys and my brothers I have heirs. We're a healthy family, happily."

"To have heirs is a great relief," Edward agreed seriously.

"Ah yes, you would know about that." Gruffyd nodded. "But I heard that the matter was settled? A nephew has been sent for from Hungary, has he not? Has he come yet?"

"We never reached him," said Bishop Aldred. "I was the envoy. We couldn't get past the Magyar rebellion that was going on at the time. Though we've heard that things are quieter now, and we hope to renew the attempt. We shall have an atheling in England by this time next year, I trust."

"Ah. And what," said Gruffyd with enormous interest, "will the Duke of Normandy do when this Hungarian atheling comes home to be your heir? He was heir once, was he not? And he has hostages from the house of Godwin in his court."

"He has," said Harold, "but they are treated as guests."

The agreeable smell of roasting meat and baking fish drifted through the air. They all stirred, restless and hungry from the long business session and the fresh sea wind.

"The land was in confusion when Duke William was named," Edward said. "My nephew is a closer relative. The duke will know that. William's an able ruler, but he would come as a Norman—to make England a new Normandy. My nephew, I trust, will come to make himself an Englishman. Indeed, I shan't make him my heir till

I've seen him and I am satisfied. I don't buy horses without riding them first."

"Bishop Aldred will know the way to Hungary blindfold by the time he's been there and back twice," Gruffyd commented with amusement.

"I shan't send Aldred this time," Edward said. Surprise flickered across the bishop's face. "You'll approve the reasons," the king said to him. "I've another task for you. Since the Bishop of Hereford is dead"—he gave Gruffyd one quick, sideways glance—" I want you to be Bishop of Hereford as well as Worcester for a while." He smiled his familiar, thin-lipped, gracious smile, taking in Aldred, Harold, Gruffyd, and Alfgar simultaneously. "Bishop Aldred is accustomed to the Welsh as neighbours and will, I think, perform this office most ably."

"King Edward," said Gruffyd, leaning back and gazing at the king with candid admiration, "it's an equal pleasure, it is, to be either your adversary or your friend. When Bishop Aldred took the field against the Welsh in years gone by, we called him the Battling Bishop. It is a compliment I am paying you, my lord bishop. I admire a good warrior. We are all friends here now, though we have fought in the past and the Bishop of Hereford lies among the dead. But if I may ask, if you are not to go to Hungary, who is?"

"I thought of sending Earl Harold," said Edward.

"I should be honoured," said Harold. Relief was running in his veins, warmer than the wine. It was all right. Edward had seen through this Welsh mountebank. Yes, Gruffyd had won territory. But perhaps the peace on the border was worth the price. Aldred had been placed as watchdog. And on the credit side again, Alfgar was now divided from Gruffyd and would come home, where he ought to be. It was all right. Edward knew better than to trust Gruffyd. And one day he, Earl Harold, would rid his king of that persuasive Welshman for ever.

It did occur to him to wonder why Earl Alfgar did not look happier about his long-sought reinstatement, but it didn't strike him as important.

Alfgar's moroseness had a simple cause. He had gone into exile without seeing his wife before he went. During his battle to get out of exile, he had had little time to think of her. But now that his return home was imminent, the fact that home and Alveva were inextricably linked was something to keep him wakeful at night—and not with joyous expectation.

When the reunion came, it was as bad as he had feared, though not in the way he had feared. He had looked for recriminations and bitter reminders of lost hopes. But Alveva's greeting at Aust was formal, conventionally gracious. Only her eyes betrayed her thoughts. He found that it was worse to see them than to hear them spoken out. They set off by sea for Thetford, accompanied by unuttered accusations like swords in the sheath. One hoped they would rust with disuse. But knowing Alveva, he doubted it.

They travelled by stages round the south and east coasts, towards Norfolk. The equinoctial storms had begun and they had to put in several times to escape bad weather. Passing Aldeburgh on a pouring wet afternoon, they put in again, but found the place deserted. Alveva, with memories of recent gales and high tides and vivid recollections of what these things could achieve at Aldeburgh, sent Wulfhild through the downpour to investigate. Wulfhild drew water from the well, tasted it, and came back making faces. They had the alternative, which Alfgar gingerly suggested, of going inland to Saxmundham, which was surrounded by what in East Anglia passed for hills and never experienced this nuisance. But Lady Eadgyth was at Saxmundham and Lady Eadgyth, Alveva indicated meaningly, was not someone she wished to cultivate just now. "Her husband Harold was once exiled, and she might sympathise, and sympathy I cannot stand. We reembark."

They lodged more successfully that night in one of Alfgar's smaller halls, at Dunwich, and the next day dawned bright. But the weather closed down anew as they set out. They sailed dismally on, while the baby Lucia, wrapped in a blanket, alternately cried and was seasick. She had to be constantly handed between her nurse, her mother, Aldith, and Wulfhild, none of whom were in much better case on the short, choppy seas. The small boys, Edwin and Morcar, mercifully were not sick, but they whimpered at the cold and wet and made Alveva impatient, and her sharp voice presently made them tearful.

The boat with its lugubrious passengers came safely to the port of Lynn and the mouth of the Ouse at last, and the tossing stopped. But the rain still fell and when, two days later, they at last finished the river journey and came in sight of Thetford Hall, it was like arriving at the gate of Heaven. The hearth fire in the hall was bright and there was a smell of cooking: the boat had been sighted from a distance.

The thankfulness of homecoming soaked into Alfgar along with the heat of the fire, as he stood by the blaze and let his garments steam. For the first time, his spirits made a cautious attempt to rise. Surely after living with her father-in-law for nearly a year, Alveva would appreciate her own home now. Surely the outlook was improving . . . But his hopes sank when in their apartment that night, after the children had been sent to bed, he covertly examined Alveva's face and saw no relenting there. She had already raised her voice angrily to order the children in the adjoining chamber to be quiet. Excited by their return, they had begun a noisy game instead of going to sleep, with Aldith and Wulfhild as bad as the boys and the nurse unable to silence them. But at the edge on Alveva's voice as she shouted through the wall, stillness fell instantly. Alfgar knew that edge.

Now Alveva was inspecting with fastidious dislike a mantle on which rain, sea water, and Lucia's *mal de mer* had wrought irrevocable havoc. "Our clothes look like patchwork costumes for jesters," she said disdainfully. "We sent you every penny we could, while you were away. We've had nothing new for a year."

"I shall provide new clothes as soon as I can," said Alfgar shortly. "I was glad of the money. Thank you. It helped me to hire the Irish Vikings."

"Yes. It got East Anglia back for us, at least," Alveva said acidly. She rose to fasten a rattling shutter, peering out as she did so on to the rainswept river. "Ugh! What a place! Four of the serving men are down with the fever, the steward tells me, and from the ache in my bones I'm afraid of getting it myself. If we don't lose another child from it, it will be a miracle."

Here it came. At last.

Alveva fed the brazier, rubbing chilblained fingers. She dragged a sheepskin from a pile in the corner and put it across her lap as she sat down. "It was Thane Redwald's silver that was bad, wasn't it?" she said. "Was that why he went into exile with you? How did it happen? And why have you let him come back with you? What will you do with him now? He lost you Northumbria."

"He didn't know the silver was bad," said Alfgar. "He knew it was his, yes. It was still in the leather bags he'd put it in when he paid it to me. When Gamel brought them out, he recognised them. But he gave the silver to me in good faith, Alveva. Thane Redwald thought it was sound. He says he knows which coffer of his it came from; it's one where he keeps the proceeds in silver from sales of cloth. He admits that he takes payment by coin count, not by weight, and that he doesn't check the number of coins to the pound weight. I shall do nothing to Redwald, Alveva. He showed me his loyalty when he came with me into banishment."

"If he knows all that," said Alveva tartly, "possibly he knows who paid *him* the silver. Does he?"

"According to Redwald, our friend Rolf Ericson. Who is now Thane Rolf Ericson, I hear! Apparently, about two years before Redwald passed that silver on to me, Ericson became a chief buyer of his cloth, and is the only one who pays by coin. The rest pay in kind. I can believe it, you know. I know that not long after Rolf began buying that cloth, he backed a voyage and behaved as a well-off man, although he'd had a disastrous venture over wine just before. Rolf is our man, if we do anything to anyone. I have considered it. But I had to get home first."

"Yes. Home to East Anglia. Alfgar, how can you be so obtuse? *Considered* it, indeed! Don't you see what that bad silver's done?"

"Of course I do." Alfgar was amazed. "It was done to me."

"You've been exiled," said Alveva angrily, "and had to make war to get back. You're practically a blood brother now to the Welsh and the Vikings, enemies to King Edward and all the dear Godwinsons. William will never be king in England now and Tostig Godwinson has Northumbria. We may as well get used to living in this freezing swamp for the rest of our lives. With your history of brotherly attachment to the principal foes of the realm, do you think you'll even inherit Mercia?"

Alfgar's mouth dropped open. Whatever other hopes were dashed, Mercia at least remained, the earldom he would one day inherit from Leofric. In exile he had thought at times: If my father dies now, they may recall me. And now Alveva was saying . . .

"Who said this to you?" he demanded.

"I thought it out for myself. On the way here, in that damnable boat."

Alfgar's head dropped into his hands. He wanted to be angry, to shout at her and shake her, but he knew that she might well be right. Her train of thought was abominably plausible. He thought of the sniggers of his fellow Witan members if the day came when Mercia fell vacant and he was passed over, he who had once aspired to Northumbria. The only pallid hope now, he supposed dejectedly, lay in the failure of Earl Harold's mission to Hungary. If the king's nephew did not come to England, William of Normandy might have his chance again.

"If only," said Alveva, as if she had heard his thoughts, "this man Edward Edmundson were not coming. People are calling him Atheling already." She poked the brazier viciously. "Apparently the rebellion over there is quite ended. What we need," said Alveva, "is an emissary with a dagger."

He looked to see if she was serious and saw that she was, and that this too she had worked out beforehand. It was he who had read her mind, not the reverse. "We'd risk too much," he said.

"One must risk something. Look what we may lose, if this atheling comes. All hope of *all* advancement. A future, a lifetime, of this!" Alveva huddled her sheepskin more closely round her. "We need a loyal man," she said, "not known to belong to us, or else someone we can bribe or threaten. Someone competent to travel."

Words echoed in Alfgar's head, from a dramatic Easter Feast, three years before: " 'Men,' " Alfgar said, " 'will pretend to much to save their lives . . .' And I should think some men would do much to save their right hands. We know the right man, Alveva." He lowered his voice. "It sounds to me just like Rolf Ericson."

In the chapel of Rouen Castle, the man who had once been Brand Woodcutter knelt alone.

Godwin's eldest son had given him the name of Woodcutter, because of Brand's stolid style of swordsmanship, which Sweyn Godwinson said reminded him of a woodcutter chopping down trees. Yet he had learned skill with that sword, and Earl Godwin had taught it to him. Later, Harold Godwinson had become his friend. He remembered them as he knelt by the altar, his hands clasped on the hilt of the new sword Duke William had given him the day before. Incense burned nearby, filling the air with its disturbing sweetness, and on the altar the candle flames quivered in convection currents, so that shadows raced and fled over the thick pillars and the rounded roof of stone. It was a place built for endurance. He would think of that presently, as the night deepened and his vigil lay heavy on his eyes, and if any humorously inclined young squires crept into the chapel and made spook noises, he would not attend to them. Tomorrow he would be a knight, in the service of Duke William.

It was unsuitable, the duke said, that the man who was guardian to two noble hostages, the son and grandson of Godwin of Wessex, should be without any rank of his own. All the more so, considering that one of the hostages was actually Brand's nephew: Hakon Sweynson, son of that Sweyn who had named him the Woodcutter and of Brand's sister, the renegade abbess.

So tomorrow he would be one of that elite of mounted warriors, each equipped with horse and armour and a landholding to keep himself, who were the chief followers and supporters of the duke and each of his barons. He was very fortunate, he knew. He, a foreigner and an outcast from his own country, had made his way in Normandy, beyond all expectation. He wondered if he would ever see England again.

He might, perhaps, if Duke William ever inherited it. One day . . .

THE COMING OF
THE ATHELING
1057 A.D.

1 ❄ *Journey Ahead*

The fair, stoop-shouldered man seated at the long wooden table compared the book and the slate before him, was dissatisfied, wiped the slate and began again, copying laboriously like a schoolboy. Ornate and beautiful, imitated from the lovely illuminated vellum primer his mother had given him long ago, the letters appeared one by one: A, B, C . . .

He was forty years old and his mother had been dead for twenty years. She had taught him English, written and spoken, but he had made little use of either and they had rusted. He had never needed them before. His wife was Hungarian, his position that of Magyar noble and landowner. Hungary was his home and her court his career. His life had changed little even when his wife, Agatha's, family were flung off the throne by a rival. Agatha was more interested in matters spiritual than in politics temporal, and was content to accept the new King Andrew. Her husband followed her example. And King Andrew, amiably enough, was willing to accept their friendship.

Until the war with Germany broke out. And until the news arrived from England.

The first English messengers never actually came in person, but a rumour of them reached Hungary. After that, Edward and Agatha began to think. While they thought, the surrounding world grew stormier, as rebellion seethed against the German emperor's claims to be overlord of Hungary. And King Andrew's manner cooled towards them, for Agatha was not only related to his predecessor; she was also half German.

Then in swift succession came the emperor's illness, a lull in the fighting, and at last the emperor's death—and peace . . . for a while, at least. Soon after, another messenger from England came, and reached them this time. He bore a letter from Earl Harold of Wessex, waiting in Cologne. It asked how interested Edward Exile would be in a future at the English court, and offered a personal visit from Earl Harold if Edward thought the invitation worth discussing.

The first person with whom it had to be discussed, however, was King Andrew.

"We're not enemies," Andrew had said, striding about the small tower room where he received privileged guests. He was an active, restless man. He had taken power, not inherited it, and the royal techniques of remoteness and immobility were not his. He was a Magyar to the last springy hair on his black head. He had the flat nose, the broad cheekbones, the black eyes, and the short sturdy legs, a little bandy from much riding, which were the hallmarks of his race. A nomad tent would have suited him quite as well as a palace, even though his forebears had abandoned tents some generations back. "I've no complaint against you. I wish you well, not ill," he said.

Edward waited. The letter lay on the table between them. They had had to get it read to them by its bearer. Andrew could not read and Edward could make out only a few of the English letters. Only the cuneiform writing of the Magyars made sense to him now.

Andrew suddenly took his arm and led him to where a great silver mirror hung, between two slit windows, in the rough, unhung stone wall. "What a contrast we are, eh?" They looked at themselves: the one short and dark and Mongoloid; the other thin, long-boned, mousey-fair, fragile by comparison. Very fragile in some ways. Edward passed over half the dishes at banquets. Andrew could stomach anything, no matter how high, tough, spiced, or undercooked, and sometimes made fun of the Exile's dyspeptic nature.

"You've lived with us," said Andrew. "Worked, fought, ridden with us. But you're not a Magyar. You're a Frank. Your wife's half Frank and your children are fair. Let me advise you."

"I welcome your advice."

Andrew laughed. His teeth were brown and in laughter his

mouth was like a dark cavern. "That's my stiff Edward. Well, why waste time over it? My advice is: Go. You've more future there than here. They'll make you heir to England, I expect. Here anything could happen. There'll be more war with Germany one day and a lot of feeling against the Franks. You could end up dead one way or another, fighting for us or against us, in a quarrel that's not yours. You'd be best out of it and so would your family."

"You want that war," said Edward thoughtfully.

"What else are men for?" asked Andrew, in a reasonable voice.

"Books and hawks and husbandry, perhaps? I'll fight to defend myself, but not for pleasure. Only as a task."

"In that case," said Andrew candidly, "this is no place for you. Go home, Englishman. Hungary is not your home."

"That's the trouble," said Edward with a sigh. "It is."

But with Andrew, advice was an order in a soft glove. So here Edward sat on the eve of his departure, in the sunlit upper room of the palisaded wooden house which was his home on his chief estate, tracing his way through the English alphabet, henceforth the only lettering he would use. He was learning to speak the tongue again, too, though slowly. His children, with an English-speaking priest as tutor, had already outdistanced him. Well, children were adaptable. Their minds held new impressions like damp sand. His own felt dry and gritty, unable to hold anything. Go home, Andrew had said. But *this* was home: Hungary, with its plains and its dark, tree-clad mountains and horse herds grazing by the Danube, its bitter winters and drought-stricken summers, its forests full of bears and its legends of werewolves. Even the Magyars felt to him like his own people, however different from him they might look. He put down his charcoal and rubbed his beaky profile consideringly. It was as well that Agatha and the children all took after their Frankish relatives. They would fit in better in England . . . But he would miss the Magyar faces.

The door latch clicked and Agatha entered, dressed in the old clothes she used for charity visiting, and carrying a basket. She didn't like, she said, to flaunt her worldly good fortune in the faces of those who lacked it. She was yellow-haired and pale with a long chin and a high-bridged nose; the Magyar strain showed only in the flatness of the bone under the eye sockets, which gave her face an air of impassivity. "Are you still working? My dear, you'll have clerks enough to do your writing for you in England. And whatever is that on your nose?"

Edward fingered his nose and examined the result. "Charcoal. I must wash. I see you've been feeding the poor for the last time."

"I took meat jelly and eggs to the sick people in the hamlet, yes. I hope the new overlord keeps up my charities."

"The English messengers tell me the peasants live better there than they do here," Edward said. "And the climate is milder. But there won't be any mountains or plains to speak of. Where are the children?"

"Christina's in the chapel, offering candles for our safe journey. Margaret's trying to comfort Edgar. He's crying about leaving his dogs behind."

"Leaving his . . . !" Edward gathered up book and slate with a hasty movement. "We're not fugitives! We're going with a train of riders and wagons and packhorses and God knows what else. I'm taking all my hawks. Oh, it's been my fault. Too much to do; I didn't explain to him properly. Of course he can bring his dogs. I'll tell him myself." He went out, tutting.

He felt for Edgar. They were leaving enough behind already, in the land and the people and the language they had always called theirs, and the daily, beloved routines of a lifetime. Whatever could be taken—from the bed he had himself been born in at the Polish court and which had been given to his mother as a present, to Agatha's jewelled book of saints' lives and Edgar's adored dogs— would go with them.

In Cologne, the Emperor of Germany had chosen to use the archbishop's establishment as his headquarters while housing Harold's retinue and receiving Edward Edmundson's.

The archbishop's establishment was much bigger than his cathedral. The cathedral was a modest affair, and they were always talking of building a new one. The palace, on the other hand, was vast and sprawling. It had started out as a castlelike building with towers and walls and courtyards. But it had grown, until the keep and the battlemented walls were merely a core amid a welter of less aggressive buildings, of which many were timber. Ways had been made into the central area so that now, despite the thick walls with the passages and chambers burrowed into them, it was no more secure than the outer part.

Its capacity was useful. It could shelter the court of the twelve-year-old Emperor Henry (chief nobles, lesser nobles, wives, children, clerks, servants, and the eternally shifting population of petitioners, merchants, guests, and gatecrashers that went with them), the separate but equally huge households of the regents, Archbishop Herman and Agnes the Queen Mother, and the entourage of Harold Earl of Wessex, waiting there for Edward Edmundson to come . . . But because of its casual construction, and because of the very ability to stand crowding which had made the Emperor choose it, it made Harold Earl of Wessex nervous.

Once, twenty years ago, he had ridden with his father to escort Alfred Atheling into England and the Atheling that time hadn't survived the encounter. This one wasn't, Harold told himself, going to run risks. And risks might well exist. It was being said that William of Normandy was not pleased with the news of Harold's embassy, and there was a whisper abroad that an attempt against the Atheling might be made. In which case, he must be guarded.

And how did you guard him, in this great honeycomb of a palace, swarming with the energetic populations of four households? Harold regarded them with a lacklustre gaze: butlers and stewards as dignified as potentates, scuttling scullions and subservient slaves, gold-festooned gallants and persuasive men selling things, a mass of faces among which some would appear once and never again, to be replaced by others. God alone knew how many smiling, courteous countenances hid secret hatreds or debts or sins by which their owners might be manipulated, and God alone knew how many more such men might live among the clustered houses of the town outside, or ply along the river that passed the building's feet. It was a terrifying task.

The speed of the Atheling's response had been bewildering. His reception had had to be planned too quickly for comfort. The first exploratory letter brought not an invitation to advance into Hungary but an unequivocal acceptance of the English proposals and an estimated date of arrival in Cologne, in late spring, 1057.

"He hasn't even stopped to think!" Harold exclaimed, amazed.

The boy emperor, Henry, older than his years as children of

high estate often were, forced into maturity by their dedicated up-bringing, said: "The Magyar king wants to be rid of him. He wants an all-Magyar court. The Atheling's a Frank and his lady's worse—she's part Frank and linked to the old king. It isn't so much that Edward Edmundson wants to come, as that King Andrew's sending him."

The boy was probably right. He understood his business well already, Harold thought, dismounting in the main courtyard on a hot afternoon. The court was paved with white stone, which shone achingly in the sun. But it was not as quiet as it usually was at this sleepy hour. Two ponies of an unfamiliar breed were being rubbed down, tied to their stable doors, and servants were hurrying about. Something was afoot. He watched with interest, until the unloading of a palpitating basket from the back of a mule demanded his professional attention.

"Careful with that or she'll damage her plumage. No, I'll take charge of her, myself. She's a gift for Edward Edmundson."

"And Edward Edmundson will be here inside two hours, my lord!" A thane of his suite came hurrying among the horses, his manner flustered and thankful both at once. "What a blessing you're back. We went after you but you must have missed the riders. Out-riders from Edward's train came in this morning. There are their ponies. He's nearly here."

"So soon?" Harold was startled. He laughed. "It certainly is as well I'm back. It wouldn't have looked polite if I wasn't here to greet him. Well, I got the hawk just in time, it seems."

"In good condition?"

"Yes. And fully grown. A late-migrating passage hawk, female. There's no gift like a new bird no one else has spoiled." He took up the basket as tenderly as a cradle. Within it something thumped and scratched. "Hush, my pretty. You'll hurt your lovely tail. I spent most of yesterday," he said to the thane, "crouched behind a fishing net threaded with sprigs of heather and hung over a pair of rocks to look like a heathery bank, with the sun hammering at the back of my neck, waiting for her to come and eat the bait pigeon. I almost gave up today; thought she'd travelled on. I could hardly believe my luck when she came down to the bait and I pulled the noose tight round her feet. Let's take her to the mews."

The mews was partitioned at one end to make a small room where new birds could be kept in solitude while they settled down.

The building was wooden, standing on its own in the courtyard, and inside it seemed dark after the sunlight. Two windows with shutters folded back made a pair of brilliant rectangles in the wall. Through them one could see the steps to the main hall, and the entrance to a tower. Harold set the basket down in a corner, out of the light. He took a pair of gauntlets from a shelf. "Let's look at her."

The emperor's own falconer came quietly in as they were un-packing the hawk. He stood back tactfully until they had her secured to her perch, and then stepped forward to help admire her. She was panting and furious, wings wildly beating and tail feathers, as Harold had foretold, in a discouraging mess, but she was unques-tionably a beauty. "Superb, isn't she?" said Harold proudly. "In per-fect condition, once she's tidied up."

"She is," said the thane delicately, "but if I might say so, my lord, the same applies to you. You look a little dishevelled too. And time is going. Could I suggest . . . ?"

"Better with not so many people round her," suggested the fal-coner gruffly, in the court German, which was close enough to En-glish to be understandable, with an effort.

Harold considered his brown hunting tunic and dusty boots and laughed. "Very well."

His personal chambers occupied two floors of a tower. A nar-row spiral stair led from the ground to serve both. Edward Edmund-son when he came would have similar but bigger quarters in another tower. Harold approved, since the single precipitous stair was easy to guard. He reviewed the precautions he had taken for Edward's safety as he went up to his own apartments. He then began to wonder if he had taken precautions enough for himself. His quarters appeared to be on fire.

Then he saw that the curling vapours that drifted to meet him were steam, not smoke, and betokened nothing more sinister than a bath. He walked in to find not only his own servants but also two valets and a barber whom he recognised as part of the royal house-hold waiting with deferential determination round a steaming tub in mid-floor. The barber's young assistant was setting out combs and soaps and razors and nail files on a small table, and one of the valets was struggling with the stopper of a rock crystal phial. "I had a bath two days ago," said Harold protestingly.

"My lord the Emperor was sure, sir, that you would wish a full

toilet before Edward Atheling's arrival," said the senior of the
two royal valets politely. They had all begun to think of Edward as
the Atheling, though he was still unofficial. The second valet deftly
thrust a stool behind Harold's knees in a virtually irresistible invitation to sit down, and his own attendants looked annoyed. He
drooped an eyelid at them in a reassuring ghost of a wink. The senior valet took the now unstoppered phial from his colleague's hand,
sniffed at it, and advanced upon the bath.

"What's that?" demanded Harold, as his boots were removed.

"Rosewater, sir."

"Take it away! Save it for the Atheling's lady. I'll have a bath if
you insist, but I refuse to be perfumed like a flower garden!"

"Very well, sir," said the valet without arguing and began
smoothly to disrobe him. He stepped into the bath and what seemed
like a dozen pairs of hands instantly began applying soap.

"Thane Rolf Ericson, Merchant of London," announced a very
youthful page, suddenly appearing in the doorway.

"Don't be a fool, boy!" snapped the barber, testing his utensils
under the still-jealous eye of Harold's usual attendant. "Tell him to
wait. Can't you see my lord is in his bath?"

"My lord may be in his bath," said Harold, "but he isn't yet
drowned. I can speak for myself." The usual attendant grinned. "I
used to know Thane Rolf well. Bring him in, boy."

He peered through the wreathing steam as Rolf followed the
page in, across the wet floor, to a point where he was fully visible. A
plumper Rolf than of old, with a definite stomach on him, and thick
marten trimming on his cloak, and gemmed buckles and brooches all
over him, which said "thane" to all who cared to look.

"What brings you here?" Harold enquired. "Come to make a
killing out of Edward Edmundson, have you? I'm glad to see . . .
Good God, man!" said Harold, rising without warning, his soapy
body sliding eel-like through his ministers' grasp. "What is it? Have
you seen a ghost?" A monstrous idea invaded the earl's mind and
was reflected in his horrified eyes. "You haven't brought news about
Edward Edmundson, have you? Has something happened to him?"

Seated, sipping wine, Rolf regained his natural colour. "I've no news
of Edward Edmundson," he said, and Harold exhaled a thankful
breath. "I called with . . . goods to show him, as you thought, and

when I heard he wasn't yet here I thought of calling on you . . I'm sorry . . ." Nervously he drew out a small box of cinnamon from his pouch and put a pinch in the wine, moving jerkily. After a moment he had got his stammer under control. "I thought of asking you for an introduction to him," he said.

Harold, now dried and wrapped up, seated himself and surrendered once more to his flock of beauticians. In tones compounded equally of kindness and command, he said: "Something is wrong. Tell me."

"I met someone from Normandy on my way here," Rolf said wretchedly. "A minstrel boy from Rouen. He had news for me."

"News from Normandy?" Harold was alert.

"Yes. He told me, not knowing who I was. My sister Hild is dead."

The breath went out of Harold in another secret sigh of relief. Hild. Nothing to do with Norman plots against the Atheling. Thank God for that. But he said gently: "I remember her very well. I'm sorry, Rolf."

Hild, Rolf's sister . . . Wife of that Brand Woodcutter who had betrayed the Godwin family. When the final break with Godwin came, King Edward had taken hostages from among the younger members of the earl's house. One had been Godwin's own youngest son. The other was Hakon, Godwin's grandson, the child sired by Sweyn Godwinson on his seduced abbess. Because Brand was brother to that abbess and so Hakon's uncle, the hostages were billeted with Brand and Hild. When Edward passed his hostages on to William of Normandy, as pledges that William was now the accredited heir, Brand and Hild had been passed on with them, partly to get them out of England, where they were an embarrassment, and partly to care for little Hakon Sweynson, who would thus have familiar faces round him as he started his new life. He and young Wulfnoth Godwinson were still in Normandy. A new thought clutched at Harold. Were they in danger? But he held back his questions for a moment. Rolf was upset about his sister—odd that Rolf, not an affectionate man, should care so much for a sister he hadn't seen in years, but all the more admirable for that—and enquiries must be phrased with tact. "What did she die of?" he asked. "Sickness?"

"Yes, a fever, the scarlet fever they call it."

"I've heard of it. It's contagious. Was there an epidemic? Forgive me—but did you hear if my brother and nephew were well?"

"As far as I know," Rolf said. "Ivon—that's the minstrel boy—mentioned them, yes. Your brother Wulfnoth is going in for religion, and Hakon is to be a knight. They hadn't taken the fever when Ivon left Normandy, I think."

The boys were safe, then. A weapon in William's hands but not being used. It occurred to him suddenly to wonder what he would do if William were to send him secret word: *Destroy Edward Edmundson or I will destroy your kinsmen.* But no, William wouldn't be so foolish, or so crude. He too had a credit to maintain. Let a whisper of such a threat get to King Edward's ears and the Pope would hear of it next, and William had suffered from papal disapproval already. He had married in the face of it and found it expensive. No, if William struck it wouldn't be that way. It would be in the dark, through the secret assassin.

"Brand must be grieving badly," he said.

Rolf looked surprised and Harold smiled. "You can talk to me about Brand," he said. "My mother always said that in his place she'd have done as he did. And my wife has a kindness for him. He was in love with her once." Harold's tone was reminiscent. "She has a good memory for a compliment. She talked me out of wanting to slit Brand's throat. How is he? Do you know?"

"He's been made a knight," said Rolf. He was calmer. "The duke told him it was unsuitable for the guardian of a noble hostage and relative like his nephew Hakon to be anything else. Ivon Minstrel actually heard him say it; it was in the open hall. He said that Brand had a knack with mounted fighting that shouldn't go to waste."

Harold thought briefly of the men whose knack with mounted fighting was going to waste in England for lack of horses and royal encouragement. He let himself be positioned for the trimming and tidying of his beard. "I'll arrange a Mass for Hild's soul," he said kindly. "You'll feel better then."

"I've no other relatives," said Rolf. "Even away in Normandy, she was still someone . . . a sister. I married, you know, when I first became a thane, but she died too, while I was away on a voyage. Bad meat, the physician said . . ."

"What goods do you have to offer Edward Edmundson?" asked Harold quickly, hearing Rolf's voice shake again. "And have you found anything in Cologne worth taking back to England?"

"Glassware," said Rolf, a little distractedly. "They make it with a green tint here, very unusual. Something to do with the pinewood ash they use. I've brought cloaks and tunics of English cut, and gold and silver embroidery for Edward Atheling and his family . . ."

A trumpet sounded stridently on the walls, not six yards from the window. The barber lifted his hand quickly away from Harold's face and said reprovingly: "Now, my lord, I wouldn't want to nick your ear."

"The Atheling's been sighted, I think," said Harold, angry at his own nervousness. The barber renewed his grip on his captive's head and patiently scraped at the surplus growth near the temples. "I feel helpless like this," said the Earl of Wessex. "A perfect victim for assassination." If you didn't joke about it, you'd dream of it at night, the way he'd dreamed of Gruffyd, and still did at times. He rolled his eyes sideways. "You look shocked, Rolf. I know what you're thinking. The last time a Godwin met an atheling, there was tragedy. But not this time, Rolf, not this time."

"To be assassinated where you are now, sir," the barber said solemnly, "would need the connivance of myself, my assistant, the royal valets, your own attendants, and the guard outside the door. If I wanted to kill anyone, I should use poison, or else catch him alone. Could you tilt your head back a little more, please?"

2 ✹ *The Journey Begins*

The most painful part of the journey was the first, through Hungary. Every mile brought one more loved landmark which must now be looked on for the last time. They did not pretend about that. They would never come back. The stretch of pasture where as a boy Edward had flown his first hawk, in company with his long-dead elder brother; the friend's house where they had passed last Christmas, snowballing each other on the way back from Christmas-morning Mass, and afterwards skating on the frozen Danube till they smelt meat cooking at the fires on the banks, and glided in with a roar of bone blades on ice to eat juicy collops straight off the toasting forks; the mountain spur which Edward's nurse had once told him was a witch miraculously petrified by the prayers of a saint . . . one by one all slipped over the horizon into eternity. Edward was glad to reach strange country, which had no power to hurt.

He did not think Agatha minded as he did. His wife often spoke of Heaven as if it were a real, if distant, place—like Cathay, for instance—and more than that, as if it were home. All mortal places were simply inns along the road, to her. Their seven-year-old daughter, Christina, seemed to have her mother's attitudes already and Edgar at five was too small to understand fully what was happening. Once assured he could take his beloved dogs, he asked no more. Only Margaret, mature for eight years old, shared at all her father's grief. He saw tears in her eyes once or twice when they passed some familiar object. "They say England is beautiful and peaceful," he said once, trying to comfort her.

"And we shall be welcomed there," she said, and he realised, touched, that she in turn wanted to comfort him.

Their train, royally vast at the start, swelled still more as they went on. Such large parties were cloaks of safety for other wayfarers, who would join them if possible, and whose right to do so was accepted. Before they were out of Hungary a party of pilgrims, going home to Germany after visiting Hungary's shrine of St. Stephen, had attached themselves, and before they were a day across the border a troupe of itinerant entertainers had hailed them. During the next week they acquired successively a party of nuns (bound from Vienna to Linz to form a daughter house for their convent), a merchant with a mule train of furs and a band of tough-looking henchmen, and a private family going to a wedding, who had already hitched themselves on to the merchant. The latter was called Osbeorn and he was a black-haired, light-eyed Dane who had once lived in England and turned out to possess good English. Hearing of Edward's struggles with the language, he at once offered to help and was invited to ride at Edward's side. Edward welcomed the diversion. It kept him from thinking too much of the home he had left.

Their route followed the Danube towards its mountain source while the ranges rose on either hand, and then led deep among the passes and over the watershed until they came down to Frankfurt Town and the Rhine Valley beyond. Six weeks it would take to reach Cologne, the messengers had said. They stayed in abbeys and castles and inns, the overflow camping out or finding lodgings where they could. Once they halted for a day to have the horses' shoes checked, and another time because Edward's uncertain digestion had failed to cope with a spicy local stew which he had tried to eat to please his host. Usually his own cooks prepared his food but now and then hosts were overhospitable or touchy. He wondered what English food was like.

On the Rhine they embarked, horses and all, on wide flat-bottomed barges to finish the journey by water. On the final morning, two riders on fast mounts were put ashore and sent galloping ahead to announce them. As the afternoon lengthened, the river, running oil-smooth through its widening vale as the highlands fell back to east and west, bore them in sight of the cathedral and palace of Cologne. The boatmen, backs swinging to a faster stroke, sang as they drove and thrust with the oars, and a horn sounded beyond the city walls. The tops of the walls were dotted with spectators. A portcullis water-gate rose as they neared it and they passed under it to a landing stage before a gatehouse arch. Here, grouped under the arch, long ceremonial mantles gracefully draped from their shoulders and coiled at their feet, sweating stealthily under the velvets and furs because the weather was warm, stood the boy king Henry, his mother Queen Agnes, Archbishop Herman, and a wide-shouldered, golden man with high cheekbones and brilliant blue eyes whose description had been given to the Atheling beforehand—who could only be Harold of Wessex and who looked worried.

"I never saw so much soldiery in one fortress before," Edward said to Harold, "not even during the rebellion."

The feast of welcome, a considerable ordeal for Edward Edmundson, was over. He had not actually disgraced himself. Agatha had contrived to warn the kitchens that there were some foods her husband could not eat, and of other dishes he had managed to consume enough to be polite. The emperor's cuisine relied heavily on oil and spices, it seemed. Now, in their private apartment, Agatha was quietly mulling some wine, with cinnamon and ginger in it, over a brazier to settle her husband's stomach. These, she had already explained to an anxious Harold, were two of the few flavourings which would benefit him. He sat near her, looking somewhat pale.

"Are you sure you're not ill, my lord?" Harold asked.

"No, it's only indigestion. The food at the feast was rich, as my wife says. It's nothing. No one's poisoned me, if that's what you mean. Am I the reason for the garrison?"

Harold studied him. A scholarly man, not unlike his namesake and half uncle, Edward of England. A courteous man, since he had struggled with food that disagreed with him, to please the boy king who was so obviously proud of his lavish feast. Lady Agatha too was a woman one could approve of. She was dressed suitably for the wife of a future king of England, in blue silk with gold embroidery and a delightful veil covered in gold-thread stars, but her face was that of a loving, worried wife. He liked them both. But the Atheling, clearly, was not physically strong. How good were his nerves, in the face of danger?

At least, judging by the question he had asked, he seemed to have some consciousness of that danger already, which was helpful as it was the subject Harold had come here to discuss. "Tell me," said Harold obliquely, "what do you know of events in England in your lifetime?"

"Will you not sit down?" Edward asked, waving at a carved stool like the one he himself occupied. Harold sat. "I imagine I know most of it. Which events exactly do you mean?" the Atheling asked. He found that, largely due to Osbeorn's coaching, he could talk to Harold quite well, if slowly.

"Your uncle, King Edward, was once an exile like yourself," said Harold with brevity. "His brother was exiled with him. That brother journeyed to England and . . . my father met him and permitted his arrest by the king of the time. My father was an honest man. But he lost his reputation over that. I have that reputation to redeem. I have to bring you home safely."

"And will it be difficult?"

Edward's voice was even, his face a little quizzical. His wife looked up from the brazier, where she was heating the wine. She had understood and her face was grave. In her thick accent she said: "Norman William?"

"I see. You do understand," said Harold, with some relief.

"He'd hardly welcome my intrusion," Edward said dryly. "You need not tread so delicately. Is an attempt on me probable?"

"I don't know. But yes, you are the cause of the big garrison. You may find your guards a nuisance at times. But I prefer to take no chances."

"Life wasn't always safe in Hungary," said Edward mildly. "I hope not to disgrace you."

He was shrewd, Harold thought. Aloud he said: "You can only disgrace me in one way. By failing to remain safe in my care. I congratulate you on your English, by the way."

"You must congratulate Osbeorn for that. He worked very hard on the journey to instruct me. I left Hungary very awkward in your tongue."

"Osbeorn?"

"A fur merchant," said Agatha. "He has business in the palace. We met him on the road. He walks with Edward after dining, every evening. He will come soon."

"He has lived in England. He told me many things about it," added Edward. "Is it true that French is spoken at court there? Will I need to learn French too?"

He hoped with all his heart that he would not. Another language to learn, at his age, was another language too many. Exhaustion swept over him, even as he asked the question. He had a desperate longing for home. But he would never go home again, and as if exile from it and strange tongues were not enough, he was apparently journeying into danger. Well, it was no surprise. Even in Hungary it was said that the young Duke William had a strong will and a long arm.

"You can take your time over learning French. It is spoken at court—King Edward was reared in Normandy. But English will do just as well," said Harold. Another subject was uppermost in his mind. "This man Osbeorn . . ." he began.

Agatha, turning from the brazier with a sweep of her skirt over the rushes, handed the mulled wine to Edward. "Here he is," she said.

There was a tapping on the open door. Harold turned and saw in the doorway a dark, burly man with light eyes. "May I enter?" said the new arrival. His English had a northern intonation. "I am expected, yes?"

"This," said Edward Edmundson, "is Osbeorn."

"My lord Edward was good enough to give my mule train the protection of his retinue," said Osbeorn. "I have helped him with his English and he does me the honour to say we are friends. I have come to learn if he is better. I heard you were unwell after the feast, my lord . . . We were engaged, Earl Harold, to walk together tonight and practise conversation."

"Guarded?" Harold demanded.

"Two guards always attend us," Edward Edmundson told him.

"I'm glad to hear it. I'm glad too that I can speak openly to you, that you understand the position. I hear that you have cooks of your own with you. I take it that you can trust them . . . ?"

"Certainly."

"Good. I will arrange that they and only they prepare your food. Your digestive weakness will be an excuse. Please don't misunderstand me when I say I'm grateful for it . . . It means I can make this arrangement without offending Henry. I also insist that you never leave your rooms, for any purpose . . . I mean *any* purpose"—Edward grinned and Harold momentarily responded—"without two guards to accompany you." The earl grew serious again. "I am responsible for your safety. I mean to discharge that responsibility."

"Naturally I will do as you ask," said Edward, sipping his posset. "But isn't it a little overdone? I may have a bad digestion, but I'm not breakable otherwise. I can use a sword, or a knife, or my hands, to some effect, I promise you. Must I sleep in my armour too?" His eyes crinkled in another smile and slid amusedly to his wife. An affectionate spouse, Harold thought with appreciation. In this respect, not at all like his austere uncle. On the contrary, an improvement.

"You need not go as far as that," he said, and they all laughed. "And now," said Harold, "if you feel well enough to walk, will you forgo your English lesson and walk with me? Master Osbeorn may come too, of course, if you wish. I have a gift for you in the mews, my lord, a fine haggard goshawk. I heard you liked the sport and were interested in hawkmastery. It's a favourite pastime of mine, as it happens. One day I hope to write a book about it . . ."

3 ❊ Journey into Danger

"Lamplighting time," said Edward Edmundson, softly, to the bird which clutched savagely at his gauntlet. The glove was unavoidable when training a hawk. Later, when she had learned to treat his arm as her natural perch, he could abandon it. Carefully, with his spare hand, he lit the oil lamps in the corners of the small mews room. As each wick kindled, a mellow glow rose round it, imparting a warmer tinge to the goshawk's breast, brown streaks on golden buff. The man moved slowly, so as not to startle the hawk, and also to safeguard his own energies. It was the second night of the vigil.

He and Harold had passed from cautious courtesy to genuine friendship in one stride when in the mews Edward revealed himself a hawkmaster as ardent as Harold's heart could desire. Five minutes after that they quarrelled, with all the freedom of the long-acquainted. Edward, like Harold, saw no pleasure in flying a hawk he hadn't trained himself. He was to spend a fortnight at Cologne and saw no reason why he should not use some of it to begin his new possession's education. He wanted to take the long watch during which a hawk was kept awake day and night, until at last the bird from sheer exhaustion accepted the man's arm as a place to eat and sleep, and gave up trying to hurl itself away from him. "My falconer can finish her after that," Edward said, "though I shall carry her sometimes on the journey. But the first watch is mine."

"No," said Harold flatly. "It means being alone with her for something like three days and nights. I cannot allow it."

"I realise your responsibility," said the Atheling. "I also respect it. Nevertheless, I am a man and not a baby. Furthermore, in England, I shall be at least declared an earl's equal and possibly the official heir, which will put me above you. If I say I intend to watch this hawk, by what right do you say you 'cannot allow it'?"

"The right of a man whose name may be smeared if harm comes to you."

"If that happens," Edward pointed out, "I shall probably be dead. Do you think I don't care for my own safety?"

They glared at each other and the hawk sensed their warring wills and plunged from her perch, wings wildly beating. They withdrew to argue in the courtyard.

"The mews stands separate." Edward pointed to it. "It can be ringed with guards. Fill the courtyard with them! Put them in the main mews room. Just let me and the hawk have the little compartment at the end. That's all!"

Harold lost the argument. The young king proved anxious to please his guest and supported Edward. By all means. But certainly. Guards should be posted as my lord Edward suggested. It would be perfectly safe. What was the difficulty, Lord Harold?

So here Edward was, with two days and a night of it behind him, as dark came down softly for the second time. It was a hard vigil, for the hawk was full grown, and very wild. But such vigils were the most satisfying in the end, like a hard-fought duel. In this he could find escape for his troubled mind. Between his lost homeland and the unknown challenge of his new one, his spirit felt as though it were being crushed in pincers. Alone in the mews with his hawk, he found a place to pause and breathe.

A guard coughed outside and the hawk bated for approximately the ninetieth time. And for approximately the ninetieth time he lifted her back, teasing her breast feathers and offering her a titbit of partridge. She was in beautiful fettle now. They had straightened her tail feathers by dipping them in hot water, and once tidied her plumage proved healthy and undamaged. She was a prize.

He wished the courtyard noises would stop. The watching hawkmaster, himself forced to do without sleep—for three nights on end as often as not—always, curiously, wanted other people to settle down in the evening and leave him to his task. But the palace was restless far into the night. Servants came and went with flagons and brooms. Stray individuals slipped across courtyards bound for assig-

nations or reresuppers with friends. Harold might curse the throng
of hangers-on but he could do little about them; he himself had asked
for lodgings for Thane Rolf Ericson and his men, and Rolf had included the minstrel boy, Ivon. After that, Harold could hardly protest when Edward wanted accommodation for the travelling entertainers who, he said, amused him. Osbeorn the fur merchant already
had the entree, since Queen Agnes was interested in his wares, and
no objection, therefore, could be made to him either. Similar arguments applied to the other constituents of the motley palace horde.
Edward, strolling to the open mews window, spared a sympathetic
thought for the Earl of Wessex.

The entertainers were crossing the courtyard, arm in arm and
laughing. They stopped by a small open-fronted hay barn and began
to practise somersaults on the hay. Whoops and merriment echoed
and the hawk panicked again. Edward soothed her patiently. In the
palace, one narrow black slit after another turned to dull gold as
lights were kindled inside. The stars emerged in the dimming sky
and the shadows under the palace walls were deep and black. He
controlled, firmly, a yawn.

The tumblers went indoors at last. Silence fell. He caressed the
talons of the hawk to wake her, as she seemed drowsy. Annoyed,
she beat her wings and one of the lamps went out.

It had been burning low and needed fresh oil. There was no
harm in setting her on the wooden perch for a few moments while he
used both hands to see to it. He poured in the oil, set the jar down
on a stool by the window, and went to light a taper from another
lamp. As he moved from the window, he heard behind him the
swish and flurry of the hawk diving from her perch again, and
clicked his tongue. It was bad to leave her hanging from her jesses,
but he must finish this first. He turned round with his lit taper
shielded in the curve of his palm, and stood still, unbelieving.

The hawk, a-dangle at the end of her white leather jesses,
swung slowly to and fro, a dead weight on the thongs. She was not a
hawk any more. She was a sad bundle of spoilt plumage, with blood
running sluggishly over her breast and her beak gaping open, and an
arrow, still slightly vibrant, transfixing her dead body.

When the alarm sounded, with a blare of horns and a babble of
shouting, Harold was falling asleep. He was out of his bed headlong

and scrambling into his clothes in a single convulsive movement. Around him, his men were doing the same. Someone lit a torch. By its light he yanked on his boots, jammed a helmet on his head, seized his sword, and ran.

The Atheling stood outside the mews, surrounded by a gesticulating crowd. Torches and lanterns jigged dementedly all over the courtyard as the palace spilled affrighted inhabitants into the open. "In here," said Edward curtly, catching sight of Harold, and flung open the door of the mews. "It was meant for me. You were right," he said.

Harold took the dead, spoilt hawk into his hands. "Through the window?"

"Yes. I was lighting a lamp. I was by the window for a moment and then I moved away. Just in time. I was a target, I suppose."

Harold looked out of the window. It was a rectangle, not a slit. A man standing by it, in lamplight, would indeed make a target. The courtyard was full of guards. But what of that, to an archer in a hidden vantage point?

What vantage point?

He scanned the view. The battlemented wall on the far side . . . too far and too well policed. To the right . . . no, too close and too high. He found himself looking at a tower which swelled from the right-hand wall, not many yards away. From there? From a window? First or second storey, perhaps?

His men had followed him and were crowding at the door. Archbishop Herman was outside, tall and thin and vinegary with alarm, demanding to know what had happened. "Edward Atheling will tell you," said Harold shortly, pushing his way out. "Guard him!" Then he shouldered his way out of the crowd and ran once more.

At the tower's foot a sentry stopped him, but lowered his spear on seeing who it was. "Who has come through since the alarm sounded?" Harold barked. But the man's guttural answer was unintelligible. He was a peasant who knew only his local dialect. Pushing him aside, Harold snatched the torch from the bracket above the arch, and strode in.

The ground level was slave quarters. Pallets, pushed aside after a frightened exodus, and a smell of sweaty humanity greeted him. Two scared bondmen and a girl were still there, peering at him fearfully. The arrow hadn't come from here. He made for the steps.

The next floor was empty of humankind. Store rooms, apparently. Jars of oil and wine and meal sacks in the first. The second smelt of damp stone and disuse and was a junk room. The torch threw its smoky light over rusting bits of armour, dented helms, a broken table, a chest—he kicked up the lid—containing old clothes and threadbare tapestries. He turned to the narrow window overlooking the courtyard. He could see the mews window, still bright with lamplight. The angle was right. He stooped, holding the torch low. The floor was dusty and his own footprints were there. So were those of someone else. Someone had lately stood by this window. This was the place.

But the archer was gone, leaving no other traces. Seeking a way out of the tower he took a wrong turning and emerged into the adjoining courtyard instead, through a door which had been left unguarded because the Atheling was elsewhere. To escape, the archer need never have passed the sentry. Harold damned his own shortsightedness. He plunged back into the tower, in search of the door by which he had entered.

The crowd was clearing and the Atheling, escorted by the archbishop and surrounded by guards, was disappearing through the door to his own quarters. Harold, as he stepped out into the right courtyard this time, observed it with relief. He set out briskly towards Edward Edmundson's tower.

He was passing close to the hay barn when his foot struck a loose object on the ground, which slid and scraped on the paving. He moved the torch to illuminate it, and picked the object up. It was a commonplace article enough, a box of turned wood. Every household had one. Most had more than one. The housewife kept one on a handy shelf; the soldier, the hunter carried one in his pack. They were rarely found, however, in the vicinity of hay barns. He was still standing, idly considering the thing, when one of his thanes, with two housecarles, came hurrying, flambeaux held high, to challenge him.

"Sorry, my lord!" said the thane as the light fell on Harold's face. "I didn't see it was you. We saw someone wandering about alone with a torch, near the hay, and . . ."

Mutely, Harold held out the box. The thane grunted and with great care played light over the surrounding ground and the piled bales of hay. It was bundled into convenient quantities and tied with thongs. Or should have been. Two or three bundles had had their thongs cut, and had been spread out loosely. And . . .

"Here's the flints," said the thane, crouching to pick them up from close beside the hay. "No sign of the steel, but here's the flints from that tinderbox." He nodded towards the scattered hay. "It'd burn faster, loose. Arson, sir?"

"I think so," said Harold grimly. He stood silent a moment, remembering.

The campaign against Gruffyd. A fire one night in the woodpile and the scramble to put it out. The loosing of the horses under cover of the disturbance. A good ruse and a very old one, too. If this barn burst suddenly into flames, what would happen?

It needed little imagination. There would be uproar. Men would rush for buckets. Since the stable was nearby—much nearer than the horse lines had been to that woodpile—people would run to free the horses, officially this time. The horses would be frightened, stampeding, squealing and kicking all over the courtyard. The Atheling . . . would put the hawk in her basket and come out of the mews. The guards would be there, but in the flickering light and the confusion . . . a hand on the Atheling's arm, a voice saying: "This way, sir!" And then the Atheling hustled into the shadows and the knife or the club coming out from a cloak's concealment. The body might not be found till daylight.

"An accomplice for the archer?" suggested the thane. "Only, if so, why wasn't there a fire?" His thoughts, evidently, had followed the same path as Harold's.

"He was interrupted, perhaps," said Harold. "Challenged, as you challenged me."

"I was on duty, sir," one of the housecarles said, "not twenty yards from this barn. No one was challenged. It was black dark here, sir. Ten men could have been prowling round it and we wouldn't see them. No moonlight, even. The wall casts a shadow. He'd start his fire and slip away into the dark in seconds. He'd be gone before the alarm was raised."

"But something startled him," said Harold. "He dropped the tinder box and abandoned it."

"As if . . ." said his thane slowly, "the arrow and the outcry it caused were what disturbed him."

They began to walk, slowly, thoughtfully, on across the courtyard. "But in that case," said Harold, "he wasn't expecting the
arrow. So he wasn't an accomplice."

In that case, in other words, there were two separate hunters,
not just one, on Edward Edmundson's spoor.

"God's Teeth!" Harold whispered to himself in the midnight
courtyard, as his stomach contracted and froze.

It was a nightmare. It was all the worse because not a fragment of a
reason could be found to link any individual with either archer or
fire-raiser. The entertainers had been seen in the hay barn earlier but
were accounted for later on; they were billeted in the main hall,
where, a number of people said unanimously and bitterly, they had
been present in force from nightfall onwards. Far from being out ig-
niting hay barns, they had been making pests of themselves by
strumming instruments and practising falls when others wanted to
sleep. Harold, mindful that the minstrel Ivon came from Normandy,
enquired into his whereabouts, but sixteen members of Archbishop
Herman's household insisted that when the outcry began, Ivon had
been halfway through a chanson about the Emperor Charlemagne.
Ivon himself was furious at being questioned. He considered it tan-
tamount to an accusation. He came, he said, of good birth and his
family did not conduct their affairs by shooting unarmed men at
midnight, nor yet by setting fire to things, either. He was a good-
looking, athletic young man with thick fair hair and, surprisingly,
dark brown eyes. His indignation rang with conviction. Even without the sixteen witnesses, Harold would have believed him.

There were no grounds for suspecting anyone else at all, though
numerous persons admitted that they had been wandering about, to
the kitchen to cadge snacks, to the slave quarters to be agreeable to
the bondswomen or—in the case of the merchant Osbeorn and his
men—to guard the room that held their merchandise, because of
recent pilferage. The room had direct access through a trapdoor to a
water channel that flowed under the masonry and led to the river.
They thought the thieves had come that way. "This place is like a
rabbit warren!" said Earl Harold in disgust, and turned his attention
to the Atheling's future safety instead, with a thoroughness which
considerably irked the Atheling.

"I'm willing," said Edward, "to ride in the middle of a pack of guards and wear armour on the road, but there are limits. I *must* take part in the emperor's hunting parties, and attend the amusements he arranges for me. The same will apply when we get to Flanders and join Count Baldwin's court. For the love of heaven, Harold! You want to guard your reputation—what about mine? I thought I was supposed to impress the English. What will they think if I arrive wrapped up in fleeces like a consignment of Thane Rolf's glassware? Allow me some dignity, please!"

Harold considered him with a mixture of exasperation and approval. "You'll make a fine king one day," he said, "if you live long enough."

4 ❊ *Journey on Horseback*

The Count of Flanders stood in an equivocal relationship to Edward Atheling and the anxious Earl of Wessex. One of his daughters was married to Harold's brother Tostig and the other to William of Normandy, which was, in these circumstances, awkward. Harold, explaining his wishes in the matter of security, when the journey to Flanders had been nervously but safely accomplished, candidly pointed out the awkwardness. "I think we must cut our visit as short as we can," he finished.

Baldwin of Flanders raised his eyebrows in urbane horror and decided to be scandalised.

"My dear Harold, I admire both my sons-in-law, but I shouldn't dream of allowing my guests to be murdered to oblige either of them. So what awkwardness do you mean? Consider my garrison your own." He took Harold's arm and led him on to the walls of the St. Omer residence. They surveyed the prospect before them, of flat wide country where spinney and pasture mingled in the foreground and a river wound, to where dark green forest closed the distances. A strong west wind chased cloud shadows over the landscape. "With this wind you can't sail yet," he pointed out, "and in any case I expect your brother Tostig to bring Judith on a visit almost any moment. You won't want to miss them, surely? Come, Harold. Edward Edmundson is as safe here as in London and I want you both to enjoy your stay. I have a gift for Edmundson, by the way. A very fine horse. I hear he's no mean horseman."

"Brought up among the Magyars. They can ride before they can walk."

"Exactly. And I'd like to see him on Redfire. Surely he'll want to hunt?"

"I've no doubt of it," said Harold bitterly. "He likes hawking, too."

More perilous, watchful delay. As the days wore on to the end of the first week in Flanders, he began to perceive clearly what at first he had only sensed by instinct: that, in a stay of any length anywhere, a routine naturally formed itself. And in the victim's routine lay the assassin's opportunity.

The afternoon was warm under hazy sunlight, the blustery west wind having dropped at last. The game was mostly asleep, except where Baldwin's hounds had cut a swathe of disturbance through the forest. There was hunting on most days: the court must eat and the guests be amused. And Edward Edmundson, Atheling-presumptive of England, was a most important guest . . .

Thane Rolf Ericson, spurring his horse at speed along a thin, all but invisible forest track, was not unusual in riding solitary. The participants of a hunt tended to get scattered as the day wore on. But anyone watching him would have wondered why, although he was pressing his horse onwards regardless of undergrowth and rivulet, he did not turn towards the noise of questing hounds to his right. They might also have wondered why he looked so frightened. His face was more that of the pursued than a pursuer.

Rolf was more than frightened. He was terrified.

The vacuum of dread in his stomach was exacerbated by hunger, for he had scarcely eaten in three days, as the moment approached when his plan must become reality or fail. He hadn't slept much, either. He was tremulous with lack of food and sleep, and his fear was the worse for it. What if his hand shook?

It mustn't shake, not now. Not after all this patient preparation. For days he had dogged the Atheling at a distance, especially in the hunt, waiting his chance and seeing that chance bit by bit take shape as habits formed and showed themselves. At least once in every hunt, the Atheling's headstrong young horse, Redfire, would outpace his escort. His rider probably connived at it; Harold had complained to that effect. But Edward continued to mislay his guards and there were certain stretches of track where he was especially liable to do it. Having shed his escort, he would then, as often as not, finish the day alone. He had followed this programme today.

Rolf, who now knew the local topography by heart, was cutting a corner—flat out—to intercept his quarry. He reached the place he had chosen, steered his horse into a clump of elm, and loosened a shaft in his quiver. Yes, his hand was shaky. He tried to steady it. There was nothing to fear. This lurking place was safe. The track was in front and the river would protect him from approach from the rear. It would soon, he told himself, be over. His first scheme of using poison had failed because of the Atheling's determined adherence to his own cooks, and the first attempt with a bow had missed. But this time, he promised himself, he would succeed.

One swift shot and then away, back to St. Omer. He would circle and come in from an innocent direction. If he fulfilled his task, Alfgar would keep silent on the false coin passed to Thane Redwald. He, Rolf, would keep his thanehood and his right hand. He knew he was risking his life to defend these things, but he saw no alternative. For the thousandth time he tested his plan in his mind, looking for flaws, and for the thousandth time travelled within himself the weary closed circle of argument which brought him face-to-face each time with the ugly conviction that, to survive, he must kill the Atheling and escape. Fail to do either, and the consequences would be unthinkable. He felt, mundanely, sick.

He'd nearly given himself away to Harold, that first day in Cologne. He blessed, not his sister's death, but the grief of it because it had given him a reason to be distraught. He had come to Cologne and latterly to St. Omer, looking at their towers as if they were the waiting gallows. If he were caught, he would knife himself. In his heart he damned the merchant of Bristol, Lyfing Thorkellson, who had introduced him to the coiners, and so brought him here.

Hoofbeats. Moving at an easy canter. His stomach fell into space. A glint of burnished red hide and silver-mounted saddlery showed among the trees to his right. He stiffened. Edward Edmundson had fifty yards to live. Just ahead, the track was in clear view and easy bowshot. When Edward reached *that* place . . . Rolf's hands sweated, levelling the shaft. It wouldn't be hard. He was a good shot and the man wasn't riding too fast . . . Draw the bow . . . here he was . . . yes . . . *now*!

The message from brain to hand, to loose the shaft, was already on its way when he heard the other hoofbeats.

It was too late to check the arrow but not too late to shake it. It sprang away weaving, lacking force. It struck the Atheling in the ribs, more or less where it was meant to, but without the power to penetrate the chain mail under Edward's tunic. It bounced off.

Redfire saw it strike, and plunged. The rider saw and felt it, and gave his horse the spur. Redfire leapt forward and straight into the mile-consuming gallop which had made Baldwin pick him from a whole stud to be a gift for a prince. Sick and trembling, Rolf watched them go. Then he turned his own horse and saw behind him the owners of those other hoofbeats. They had drawn up in a semi-circle between him and the river he had thought was his protection. Five horsemen. And five more men on foot. All were helmeted, all were armed. His muscles went slack with fear.

One of the horsemen rode forward. He halted almost nose-to-nose with Rolf's mount and spoke, and his voice was familiar. So was the face behind the nosepiece of the helmet, even though the only visible strand of hair was, surprisingly, black.

"You stupid, wantwit, interfering, incompetent blockhead!" said Lyfing Thorkellson, Merchant of Bristol, otherwise known as Osbeorn.

"I'm perfectly well!" Edward Edmundson repeated wrathfully, freeing himself from his wife's ministrations and pacing restively across the chamber. His half-stripped body was lean and white, except for a round, bluish beginning of a bruise on the leftmost side of his ribs. "The skin isn't even broken. Don't make such a to-do!"

"To-do! Is that what you call it?" Harold's face was patched with red above his golden beard, and his blue eyes were glassy with anger. "After what happened in Cologne, you still call it that? How many more arrows will have to be shot at you before you take them seriously, I wonder?"

"I do take them seriously!" snapped Edward. "I wouldn't have been wearing mail otherwise. And it saved me, didn't it?"

"The arrow wouldn't have been shot at all if you'd been with your guards as you should have been!" retorted the Earl of Wessex. "No one would have dared."

"You and your horse," Lady Agatha agreed gently, seated beside the table which bore the bowl of warm water and the salves her husband had rejected, "have been outrunning your guards every day, my dear." There was an appeal in her voice.

"Redfire is too fast for them," said Edward defensively.

"With your experience of horsemanship," Harold barked, "you could surely control him?"

"I feel sure," said Edward obstinately, "that whoever it is won't try again now."

"Why are you sure? They might think the third time was bound to be lucky," said Count Baldwin, arriving unannounced and still in his brown hunting dress. This was a measure of his concern, since it was his custom to change immediately on his return, no matter what urgent business awaited him. His fleshy face was unwontedly lined and his eyes were anxious. "What can I say?" he asked. "That this should happen in *my* court, while you were under *my* protection, is horrifying, horrifying! There is no chance of accident? Earl Harold . . . ?"

"None," said Harold heavily.

The count sat down. "Would Normandy be responsible?"

"Most likely." Harold shrugged. "More than one hand may be at work, but one is probably Normandy, yes. My lord count, I think you'll be glad to see us out of Flanders now, since Duke William is your kinsman. Now do you see what I meant by an awkward situation? And since the west wind has dropped . . ."

"Ah yes, the west wind." The count greeted a change of subject with relief. "Before it dropped, it brought some ships to Flanders. The news met me as I came in from the hunt."

"News?"

"Guests, I should say. Your brother Tostig has ridden in. Well," said Baldwin, thankful to have something cheerful to say, "you'll have time to talk to him before you leave. You're free to do so. I shall put the enquiries you want in hand. And I shan't myself leave Edward Edmundson's side till you come back."

5 ❊ *Adjournments*

He was willing to leave the Atheling and the search for the Atheling's would-be killers to Baldwin for an hour, largely because he was angry with Edward. A respite, from Edward's obstinacy and the blank search for faceless foes, was welcome. When the time came, he would willingly do homage to Edward as the new king. Meanwhile, he wished wholeheartedly that Edward had stayed in Hungary or been fetched by someone else, or had just a little more healthy timidity. He longed, ardently, for the day when Edward's safety would cease to be his responsibility.

He stepped over the threshold of Tostig's chamber, with relief. He stopped short.

"Oh come," said Tostig bracingly, "it isn't as bad as that."

Harold flung himself down on the nearest bench and linked his hands behind his head. The Atheling, it appeared, was not the only person to be assailed of late. "What on earth is the matter with your face?" he asked.

Tostig's freckled, snub-nosed countenance, normally noted for its candid expression and symmetrical jawline, had undergone a sinister transformation. The jaw was lopsided, on account of a large, dull purple swelling on the left. The remains of what had recently been a superb black eye added to the villainous air. A cut on the right cheekbone bore signs of stitching and would scar. Tostig grinned, and there was a tooth missing.

"I went to a wedding," he said, as if this were sufficient explanation.

"And the bride ale proved many men's bale, yours included?" his brother hazarded.

"It was a Northumbrian wedding."

"And as you're Earl of Northumbria, your presence was an honour. Is it a fine old northern custom to hammer in the faces of the chief guests?"

Tostig chuckled, perching himself on a window seat. "The ale hadn't much to do with it. The real trouble was that the bride had spots."

Harold sighed, pulled a dagger meditatively out of its sheath and began to examine the edge of it.

"One *could* say that the bride's chief handmaid caused it all—don't stab at the bench like that, Harold, you'll spoil the dagger and damage Baldwin's property. I'm not playing games. It's all true, and not as funny as you think, either. You recall Thane Gamel?"

"A skinny, bleached-out man with a sarcastic voice? Yes."

"The groom was his cousin and Gamel had arranged a match for him with a well-dowered girl from the other side of Northumbria, a connection of the Dolfin clan—that redheaded tribe, remember? But Gamel hadn't seen her beforehand and neither had the groom, and when she arrived for the wedding she turned out to be spotty and the groom was difficult."

"He refused to go on with it?" Such an insult would be serious anywhere and above all in the proud and touchy north.

"No, we talked him into going through with it. He was being extremely foolish," said Tostig austerely. "Girls of seventeen often have spots. Judith says *she* did. They soon clear up. She was a good girl otherwise. Pretty, fair hair and plenty of spirit. Too much as it turned out. The vows were taken without any incident, but after that we had the feast and at the feast there were more eyes on the chief handmaid than on the bride. She was a bonny lass, I grant you. Irish blood. Black hair in long thick braids and sparkling blue eyes and . . ."

"You're getting a Northumbrian accent."

". . . halfway through the feast, the groom started blowing kisses to the handmaid and the bride got angry. They quarrelled in undertones at first and then she slapped him."

"I'm not surprised."

"He went to hit her back but her brother caught his arm." Tostig's face remained bland but strong emotions seethed below the surface. "So the groom hit the brother and there they were, on their feet, fighting. The bride and the handmaid were fighting too, by then, pulling each other's hair. Then the bride's father and the groom's mother joined in. He told her to keep out of it and called her an old cow, and she threw a loaf of bread at him . . ."

Harold crossed his arms and gripped his ribs hard.

". . . then someone, I don't know who, flung a basin of cream in the mother's face and after that things got exciting." Reminiscently he touched his plum-hued eye. "It was only half serious at first. People were laughing and fighting with food, not blades. Ribs of beef and bowls of sauce and what not. The bride's father jumped on the table. But he's a big man and it gave way, and that made Gamel angry because he was sitting on it, cross-legged, pelting people with meat pasties. When he picked himself out of the wreckage he was furious and he snatched up a mackerel . . ."

Harold put his face in his hands and groaned.

". . . and laid about him with it. He caught me with it. I think it was an accident, but then I got angry too and pushed his face into the crust of a venison pie and then . . ."

Harold raised a mirth-streaked face from his hands, looked at Tostig, and suddenly sobered. "Yes? And then?"

"Everyone got angry," said Tostig sombrely. "It went over the edge. Fists and knives. That's when I got this." He put a hand to the scar on his cheekbone. "Then someone knocked a torch out of its bracket, and the end of it was that the hall burned down. There were ten dead men when it was all over and any amount of wounding. Then, next day, I hanged four more men because I'd seen them strike to kill. Two from each family. One was the bridegroom. I'd have spared him if his wife had pleaded for him, but she said I was welcome, she could find a better man than one who'd insulted her on their marriage day. Now the two houses are feuding with each other and declaring feuds against me. Gamel's house and Dolfin's. The Northumbrians," said Tostig harshly, "are a pack of savages."

Harold, all laughter gone, said: "Be advised and don't try to civilise them too fast. You won't change Northumbria single-handed in your lifetime. Siward rode them on an easy rein and it worked. Remember him."

"Siward was hardly civilised himself!" Tostig scowled. "While I ride them 'on an easy rein,' as you put it, murder and lawlessness go unchecked. It's time they learned to behave. I took the lands of the executed men and I've raised the taxes. If they want to act like barbarians, they can pay for the privilege. Well!"—he stopped glowering and shook himself—"that's my history. What about yours? I hear you've had an eventful journey. What's the new atheling like?"

"I take it," said Lyfing Thorkellson with venom, "that it was you who tried to shoot Edward Edmundson that night in Cologne as well? Well, was it? What's the matter? Lost your tongue?"

Rolf stood, in the midst of a threatening circle, in a forest clearing a mile downstream of the place where they had seized him. Lyfing had simply grabbed his bridle and brought him there. The men on foot had had a boat nearby, and followed in it. The scene of the attack on Edward was clearly not a healthy place to linger.

The atmosphere was ominous but not, Rolf's numbed perceptions had gradually realised, precisely murderous. For one thing it seemed that he and Lyfing had interests in common. "Yes," he said warily. "Yes, it was."

"Interfering," Lyfing had called him . . . He took heart from that. He waited.

"Who's paying you?" demanded Lyfing. Rolf hesitated and the pseudo–fur merchant erupted. "God's Teeth, if I'd known you were about the same business, much trouble could I have saved, hiding from you. I've avoided you since Cologne, because you knew me . . ."

"Osbeorn," Rolf agreed. "You are Osbeorn, the merchant friend of the Atheling. You're also Lyfing Thorkellson."

"I am. I changed my sleeping quarters and ate meals in the town to keep away from you. And now—*now*, may Odin hunt your soul to hell and leave it there—twice you have tripped me! We'd have had him off from his horse and halfway downriver to the sea by now but for you. In Cologne we were to fire the hay barn and hustle him away in the confusion, straight to our storeroom and through the trap door to a boat underneath it. Trailed him, I have, getting into his confidence, since he crossed the Hungarian border! And now, twice, you—I repeat, who's paying you?"

Annoyance, rising up in Rolf, did duty instead of courage. "No one, except with silence!" Lyfing glared at him from under dark, dyed brows. He found it in him to return the glare. "That light-weight silver brought me here. Your damned silver! Your nice oblig-ing coiners in the forest! Some of it got into Alfgar of East Anglia's hands and he traced it to me."

"Oho! Yes, I heard of the coinage for which Alfgar was flung out of England. So yours it was?" Lyfing stopped scowling, threw back his head, and laughed. "And he wants his revenge and he wants William crowned as well! Yes, I see!"

"If you hadn't been there today," said Rolf, "I shouldn't have missed. I'm a good shot. I only missed in Cologne because he moved just as the arrow left the bow. If you'd kept back today, he'd have been dead by now and we should all be happy."

"You misunderstand . . . I shouldn't," said Lyfing.

"Then why—what . . . ?" Rolf stammered, frightened anew, bewildered.

"I was not there to kill him," Lyfing explained. "Only to see that he was not acclaimed in England. Or rather . . . I could kill if I so wished. But I had a better plan."

It had been an extraordinary interview, that secretive meeting in the tiny round room in a tower in Rouen Castle. He hadn't even known who had summoned him. The man who sought him out was a man-at-arms of Rouen, plain of dress and economical of speech. A type with which Lyfing was familiar enough; he employed it. A type which obeyed orders unquestioningly, priding itself on loyalty. Lyf-ing was wanted—or someone of his kind—to undertake a commis-sion, the man had said briefly. He knew no more than that and had obviously been told to withhold his principal's name. Lyfing, follow-ing him up the dim, twisting staircase with its narrow, wedge-shaped steps, did not waste his breath on questions. Besides, he thought he had deduced the principal's identity.

He had deduced wrong. The person sitting composedly in the little room was neither Duke William nor his seneschal, William Fitz-Osbern, who often represented him. It was a woman: tiny, fair-haired, fragile, and intimidating.

In his guttural but serviceable French he said: "Lyfing Thorkell-son at your service, madame. I speak, do I not, to the Duchess Ma-tilda?"

Matilda inclined her head in agreement. She had the kind of face commonly called heart-shaped, wide across the forehead, pointed at the chin. When she spoke or smiled she showed perfect teeth, white and even and small. Her face would have been piquant, had her eyes had been less pale and cold.

"I have a commission for you," she said in her clear, pretty voice. "It is dangerous and difficult. Some might call it lawless. It will also be richly rewarded. You are on a list that I have, Messer Lyfing, of men reputed to be interested in dangerous and . . . lawless adventures that are worth their while."

"Have I the option of refusing?" asked Lyfing with interest.

"Yes. But not the option of speaking of this talk outside this room, except to such agents as you need, if you accept."

"I understand. What is the commission?"

"The English king has sent to Hungary to fetch his nephew, Edward FitzEdmund, to England to be heir in my husband's stead. See that it does not happen."

"Let me have my orders clear," Lyfing said. "You wish me to kill Edward FitzEdmund?"

"If necessary. It probably is necessary. If you can think of a way to prevent the nomination without killing him, of course, do so. Remove him," said Matilda calmly, "to Heaven or Ultima Thule. Either will do, as long as he doesn't come back. But do it before, not after, he is named officially as atheling. If that declaration is made in England, your reward will be halved even if he dies the same day. My husband at present holds the title of atheling. His grasp on it would be lessened if his place were usurped, though it be only for an hour."

"The price?"

"Land. Treasure." Matilda went into details. She was prepared, it seemed, to pay the market price for her requirements and she had accurately assessed both the difficulty and the danger.

"The man has a family, including a small son," said Lyfing. "Do you want the boy removed as well?"

There was a silence. For the first time Matilda hesitated. She tapped slender, polished fingertips on her chair arm. "He's . . . five?" she said. "Not a great menace. No one will nominate a child that age. The English aren't as stupid as that. No. Leave him."

"Very well. I can't promise success."

"No success, no reward."

"And I am not compelled to kill him, if there is another way to dispose of him?"

"Quite," said Matilda, displaying no curiosity about alternative schemes to assassination.

Lyfing grinned, his twin drives of adventurousness and avarice now powerfully active. "I accept," he said.

And now . . .

"If you don't want him dead, what do you want?" Rolf asked curiously.

"You've forgotten," said Lyfing, "or perhaps you never knew. I deal in slaves."

With the introduction of commerce into the conversation, Rolf was at home again. "But how could you make a slave of him?" he protested. "Whoever bought him would free him and be rewarded for it."

"It would depend on the buyer. I meant—I mean—to take him south. Down the coast of Europe to infidel Spain. To three different caliphs I know who would buy and be proud of a slave so illustrious and never dream of freeing him. They need no rewards. They could buy England, if King Edward felt like selling it."

"You deal regularly . . . with infidels?"

"I am a merchant," said Lyfing. "I sell to those who will buy."

"But *infidels*! One can't . . ."

"One can. I do. I worship Thor and Odin, when I wish to worship, which is rarely." Standing over Rolf, under an oak bough in which small birds incongruously twittered, he considered the smaller man unamiably. "I must make new plans now. It is hard. I cannot hope to seize the Atheling now before he reaches England. I must stave his nomination off when he lands—that I can do, I think, for a while. Until I make a new chance to take him. I have ideas in my mind. But there is you. Well, you are in this against your will, yes? Even, you could say it is my fault, for bringing you into the silver game?"

"Yes!" said Rolf.

"Then let me make amends. Leave him to me. But don't interfere again. I don't want him dead. I want double price for him, one from my employer and one from the man who buys Edward." He patted his dagger hilt and Rolf's eyes warily followed his hand. "If Edward vanishes, Earl Alfgar will not complain, I think? I will do your work for you. Only," said Lyfing, in a pleasant and conversational tone of voice, "if you spoil my plans again, sooner or later I shall kill you."

6 ⚔ Journey's End

To Edward Edmundson the first sight of England was a relief. For months—and it felt like years—he had had to imagine it, to throw his mind ahead into the unknown. Now, at last, he saw for himself.

First impressions, as they sailed up the wide, tidal Thames, were confused. Flat marshy land, disentangling itself only slowly from the sea. Then drier ground and habitations, mostly wooden and without defences beyond an occasional ditch and palisade. There were castles on the borders of Wales, Harold told him, but none here. Between the settlements lay meads and forests; trees grew overhanging the banks for miles at a time, so thick that backwaters might appear only as fleeting gleams through a latticework of boughs. The foilage was green to excess and the sky above was variable, the sun often hidden although it was summer.

London appeared through a drizzle and his first view of it was discouraging. A wooden bridge with water swirling under the piers. A muddle of buildings, stone and wood, and a glimpse of a street with balconied houses. Wharves. Then a landing place on the north bank, before a great whitewashed stone building set amid marshy surroundings, which Harold said was the London palace of King Edward.

The hall was garlanded, with thyme and rosemary strewn among the bulrushes on the floor. A phalanx of dignitaries awaited them . . . Two archbishops and numerous ordinary bishops. Earl Harold's brothers Gyrth and Leofwin. A series of respectful thanes.

Another earl, Alfgar of East Anglia, with a curious watchfulness in his round blue eyes. The constituents, Edward knew, of the Witenagemot, which would sit in council on the question of his official nomination as atheling. King Edward himself was not there. They had known that before they left Flanders. He had been held up by a dispute ("Already!" growled Harold when he heard of it) over the new trading agreements with the Welsh. He would come within a day or two, Archbishop Stigand of Canterbury said. Meanwhile . . .

There were several ladies to meet. Edward greeted Alfgar's wife, Alveva; dark, petite—and a perfect shrew, he suspected. From her he turned to a tall, dignified woman, Harold's mother, Countess Gytha. Her calm face bore the lines of life and death as a tomb might carry an inscription. You guessed without being told that she was a widow who had loved her husband, and a mother who had lost a child. Then, with a blare of trumpets and a graceful stepping back of all lesser persons, came Queen Edith, wife to the king and sister to Harold. The Atheling was astonished to see as she welcomed him that, although only in her thirties, she resembled her mother not only in her features and fair colouring but in the stillness and remoteness of her face. She was childless, he knew, and the marriage was said to be in name only. He wondered what sort of man his uncle was, that his wife should look like that.

Too much to take in; it was too confusing, too bemusing. He was glad, when the feast of welcome was over, to be shown to his own apartments, and glad to walk by the river with Osbeorn and the obligatory guards, and ask questions about England privately, not to exhibit his ignorance. The depths of that ignorance had grown increasingly obvious to him since he left Flanders. In one respect especially.

"Till I came to Flanders I had never seen the sea," he said, watching the ships on the river. "And till I sailed for England, I was never afloat on it. But here, ships are part of life."

"An English king is expected to command forces at sea," Osbeorn agreed. "I have two vessels here. My big trader, the *Bristol Maiden*, and a little ship I bought last year, my *Swan*. The *Swan* is easy to handle. If you wish, you shall sail her and I will instruct you. I had it in mind to suggest something of the sort."

"I should be most grateful," said the Atheling.

"The smallpox?" demanded Earl Harold. He had been summoned from his breakfast by an insistent message that the merchant Osbeorn wanted to see him on a matter concerning Edward Edmundson. He was not pleased at the disturbance, but Osbeorn's information was more disturbing still. "Are you certain?"

"I think I'm right, my lord. The man—one of my followers for many years—complained of feeling ill on the voyage. He was lending a hand at the oars and had to be relieved. Unfortunately, he was rowing in my lord Edward's ship. And I believe that my lord has not had the disease."

"Oh, dear Christ!" said Harold, turning away. His heavy shoulders were rigid under the cloth of his tunic, straining it. "If anything happens *now* . . . !"

"I believe my lord the king has not had it, either," said Osbeorn. "Myself, I have."

"So have I. As a small child."

"It is not for me to give orders," said Osbeorn deprecatingly. "But if my lord Edward Edmundson is carrying the sickness, he is both in peril and a peril to others. Should he not keep apart from others till we know? The king, perhaps . . ."

"Had better not meet him yet? Oh yes, I suppose so," said Harold worriedly.

The Atheling's rooms were linked to the main hall by a short covered passage. His quarters were a small hall in their own right, with a sleeping chamber above and a wide room below big enough to hold a hundred guests in comfort. Its tall windows overlooked the river, and the Thames cast mother-of-pearl reflections on the whitened stone walls. Only one wall was tapestried. Once, they had all been hung, but some years before, a visiting embassy from Iceland had used the rooms while the hangings were down for repair, and had waved away apologies, saying they liked the river light on the stone. Since then, the effect had been kept.

Entering the apartment on the second day of Edward's sojourn there, Harold thought the effect chilly. The weather was grey and there were too few people to generate a sense of cheer. The Atheling was keeping his quarantine strictly. His wife and daughter Margaret were there because they had had the illness; his son and his other daughter had been quartered elsewhere. Various attendants and guards who had had it were there. The merchant Osbeorn was present and Thane Rolf Ericson; both were safe. Ivon the Minstrel, whose young face did indeed show faint traces of pocking, and who had stayed with the Atheling's train since Cologne, had come tonight to make music. There was no one else.

Edward had eaten earlier and this small gathering was a brief, convivial aftermath before he took his evening exercise, walking by the river or sailing on it in Osbeorn's *Swan*. He came to greet Harold, who scanned his host's face anxiously. The Atheling looked pale, Harold thought. He followed Edward to where Lady Agatha, helped by Margaret, was dispensing wine herself, in silver cups.

"Plain or spiced?" she asked. It was a little joke between her and Harold that Harold, who would eat high beef smothered in onions without a tremor, detested alien tastes in his wine, while Edward of the uncertain digestion liked spices in his.

"Plain," he said, taking the cup with a bow. He thought once again what a charming woman she was, though too passive perhaps. He remembered his Eadgyth's rioting sunset hair and her alive green eyes and wondered how soon he could visit her again. He asked Edward: "Is all well?"

"As yet," said Edward. "But I'm not weakly as far as most illnesses go. I've had a touch of my old gastric trouble, but nothing more. I rode out this morning. And tonight, if the sky clears, which Osbeorn says it will, I am going out on his ship on the river for a navigation lesson. Oh, with six guards and just two of Osbeorn's men; nothing to be alarmed about, my lord earl! Osbeorn has shown me how his lode needle works and pointed out some of the star constellations he uses for navigation, and now I am to try steering to a course. I find his ship quite simple to manage. His big vessel, the *Bristol Maiden*, would be harder, I imagine. I must say I'd like to try her," said Edward thoughtfully, "but she's sailed on a voyage. She left yesterday. I must learn about ships, you know, if I am ever to rule England." He nursed his wine, swirling it in the cup. "I think the minstrel is about to play. He's trying a Magyar lyre tonight. I brought it from ho . . . Hungary. I must remind him how to . . ." He drifted away.

"Your wife does not come to court, Earl Harold?" Lady Agatha asked. "This cup is for Thane Rolf, Margaret. Take it to him."

"Eadgyth and I were only able to marry on the understanding

that she shouldn't come to court. My sister was marrying the king at that time and Eadgyth was not as well-born as my parents thought proper. Her family wanted us to marry according to the old rites, without a priest, and my parents encouraged that. I think they hoped I should set her aside one day and marry somebody more splendid. But they came to love her in the end."

"Yet she doesn't come with you even now? Surely she could by this time?"

"We have five children and she says she would rather stay at home with them. I think . . . she was hurt, and now doesn't want to come among people who were once told she wasn't good enough. But it may change one day. I shall want my elder children to come to court eventually.

"Is she beautiful?" asked Margaret, rejoining them. Her wide-set, dark grey eyes appraised him with a child's frankness. "She ought to be," said Margaret candidly, "because you're so handsome."

"Margaret!" Lady Agatha gathered herself, scandalised, to express reproof. But the Atheling called his daughter's name, and Margaret, with an impish glance, slipped away again. "She's a dear child," said Agatha, "but her tongue is far too free."

"Better that than too timid," Harold said, laughing, and they fell into a discussion on child rearing, while across the room Margaret chattered to her father and Ivon, and Thane Rolf Ericson joined them. Ivon tuned his Hungarian lyre, and in the room the talking died down. Subsiding, it isolated and made plain the fact that outside in the passageway a violent altercation was in progress.

A French voice was the centre of the uproar. It was demanding admittance, in execrable English with a strong Gallic intonation. A frosty, impeccable major-domo's voice was heard answering, inform-ing it that French was spoken here. It then broke into a pure if sten-torian mother tongue. It was going to be let in, it said, and no one would keep it out. Boots grated and pikes clashed outside in evident contradiction, and the voice swore colourfully. In the Atheling's room, people glanced doubtfully at each other. Rolf Ericson and the Atheling put their wine down on a nearby table, as if preparing for some kind of action. Harold strode towards the door.

Flinging it open, he discovered a striking tableau in the passage. A massive man of some rank, judging by his costly belt clasp and shoulder brooch, but mailed beneath his mantle and clutching a helmet under his arm, stood fuming and red-faced on the other side of two determined guards. The major-domo and a cluster of anxious servants closed the far end of the passage.

The man, who had the burly good looks of a well-bred ox, clearly had the appropriate muscle as well. The sight of the open door encouraged him to use it. He clapped his helmet on to his thick grey hair, seized the two guards by the scruffs of their necks, crashed their heads together, and flung them apart. Through the gap thus created he charged head down. The stricken housecarles recovered and leapt after him, grabbing his arms as he was about to rush headlong on Harold. Harold, who had automatically taken hold of the doorposts to either side, and braced himself for the onslaught, stared into the man's face.

"Where are you going?" he asked in French. Speaking past the stranger, and in English, he added, to the guards: "You gentlemen seem to need more training in anticipation. I shall arrange it." He switched back to French. "Your name, business, and credentials, sir? We admit no one to Edward Edmundson's apartments without them. From your manner, I doubt if you have any."

The stranger's bulging brown eyes took in Harold's curling, shoulder-length hair and elegant garments and visibly labelled him effete. "And who might you be, may I ask? And who," he added rhetorically, "is anyone to keep a man from his son?"

"From his . . . Who *are* you, sir?"

The stranger ignored him. He could not physically escape the guards and plunge past Harold, but his eyes had become fixed on something in the room behind the earl, and now he raised his voice to a still louder roar. *"Ivon! Come here!"*

Harold, still gripping the doorposts, twisted his head round. The minstrel, Ivon, was standing in mid-floor, lyre in hand, scowling savagely. He was a sturdy young man and now, in anger, a resemblance to the muscle-bound stranger could be seen. Ivon had the same jaw, the same wide-sprung nostrils, and although his eyes were deep-set, they were of the selfsame brown.

The scowl was for his father's benefit. "I will not!"

"You'll do as you're told, you impudent cub!" The big man changed his pitch to speak to Harold. *"That's* my son. Ran away from his home and inheritance, and his chance of knighthood, to walk the roads like a common jongleur, all because he cared for his lyre more than his warhorse, the young fool! There's a place waiting for him at the Norman court and he throws it away, can you credit it? *Ivon! Will* you come here?"

"You smashed my lyre," said Ivon. He looked down at the one in his hands, recognised it as the Magyar instrument, put it down on a stool, and picked up his own, holding it as though it were a weapon. "I spent all I had to get another. You won't smash this. I'll break your head open first, father or no father!"

His parent seemed more soothed than enraged by this filial sentiment. "My boy," he informed Ivon, "the day you prove to me you're capable of breaking anyone's head open, I'll be thankful." His voice became a bellow again. "I've come to take you home and by the Elbow of God I *will* take you home! I've not trailed you over half Christendom to be said no to now! Let me *get* at him!"

He lunged unsuccessfully. Harold barred his way and said to Ivon: "Are you this man's son?"

"Yes," said Ivon sullenly. He saw that Harold was waiting for more. "He says I didn't want to be a knight. Well, I do. But I want to be a minstrel too, and he sneered at me and broke my lyre. If I can't have my lyre I won't have a knighthood. And I *will* break anyone's skull who tries to force me." His shoulders went back. "In England, all the greatest men can play and sing. And in Wales, bards are the highest aristocrats in the land. It's not unmanly." He looked at Harold. "Are you going to hand me to him?"

"What will you do if I do?" Harold asked.

"Fight!"

"Can you, I wonder?" jeered his father.

"I told you!" shouted Ivon. "I'm going to be a minstrel. Try and stop me and I've said what I'll do. Helmet and all!"

"Well!" said his father. He relaxed, with an impatient jerk of his head at the guards who still held him, and at a nod from Harold they let him go. "Big talk from a little cub. If I thought you could do that, my boy, maybe we could bargain, eh?"

Edward, who had not come forward to join in the argument, although the room was his, but who instead had sat down on a handy bench to wait while someone translated the French speech for him, had now had the situation explained by Rolf. Without rising, he called: "Make it a bet. If the boy can cleave a stuffed helmet with a sword, he is free to be a minstrel. Then he can go home and be a knight as well."

Harold translated this for Ivon's father. The big man listened, thought, and then nodded vehemently. He pulled off his helmet and threw it into the room. "Let me see him split that with a sword. Give him a blade, someone! If he can do it, I'll keep my hands off his lyre. Nasty twanging noise; can't tell one sound from another, myself. Maybe he'll have the goodness to twang it out of my hearing, that's all. Right, Ivon! Let's see you perform!"

Everyone in the room gathered round, interested. Lady Agatha looked mildly disapproving, but nevertheless came with them. Little Margaret was excited and her mother let her run forward to see better. Osbeorn, leaning against the wall with arms folded, was grinning. A guard offered a sword, and another stuffed the helmet with straw and rushes scooped up from the floor, and sent a servant to fetch some old rags to wad in after the straw. The result was a fair facsimile of a helmet with a head inside. Ivon put down his lyre and tried the balance of the sword. He swung it experimentally, and competently.

"Well," said his father provokingly from the doorway. "We're waiting."

The young man pointedly ignored him. He raised the blade.

He was unhappy with the feel of it and lowered it, to start again. The second time he had found his grip. The sword rose high above the boy's fair head and came down with a powerful sweep aided by its own weight. It smote the helmet accurately in the middle, on the exact apex of its conical top. It was an extremely difficult blow to achieve and they all knew it. The helmet's metal cracked and sparked. It gave. The sword's descent stopped with the blade halfway between top and base of the helm. Had anyone been wearing it, his brain would have been cut in two.

There was a burst of cheering. Ivon, rather red with exertion, picked up the helm and tossed it to his father's feet. He handed the sword back to its owner and stood, thumbs hooked into belt and head thrown back. "Well? Is it agreed? I will be knight *and* jongleur? You promise . . . ? Unless you promise, I won't come."

"I'll promise." His father surveyed him. "I promised before you did it, boy, and keeping oaths is a knight's duty." He picked up the remains of the helmet and as he straightened, sheer delighted pride burst out of him. His roar made them all jump. "I didn't think you had it in you, you young devil! Iron-Cleaver, that's your name now! Young Ivon Iron-Cleaver! *Now* will you come home?"

Ivon let go of his belt. He walked towards his father and, for the first time, smiled.

They went away, amicably. Harold saw them back to the main hall and, returning, shut the apartment door thankfully. He turned to the Atheling, an amused comment on his lips. Edward was still sitting on his bench. But not just sitting. He was bent double, holding his stomach with anguished hands, and when he raised his face it was waxen-coloured, and his eyes were black with pain.

Long after sunset, the king's chamber still glowed with lamplight. King Edward, who had paused outside his city at the first warning of smallpox, had entered his palace at last. With Queen Edith he knelt in prayer before a little altar in his room. Harold entered softly, unannounced because the tired servants were sleeping in the outer chamber. He waited and, presently, their prayer done, the royal pair rose with silently questioning faces. He shook his head.

"No hope?" Edward asked.

"The physician says not. He's had the last rites. It isn't smallpox, certainly, but no one knows what it is instead. It could be a malady sent by God or a poison given by man, but if it's poison no one knows how it was given. The Lady Agatha says her husband has eaten nothing except food shared with others for a matter of days . . ."

"There was wine on the evening he fell ill," said Edith. "And he had guests, not all of them people we know well."

Harold shook his head again, and obeyed King Edward's sign to sit down. He was heavy-eyed. He had hardly slept since Edward Atheling sickened, three nights since. "His wife Lady Agatha served everyone the wine," Harold said. "There was nothing wrong with it. No one else is sick—except that Lady Agatha is ill with grief."

Of grief there had been much. Lady Agatha had suffered with her husband, every dreadful step of the way, her religion for once failing to console her. She had watched while despite all the purges and prayers, the charms and fomentations, the abdominal pains steadily worsened and the sufferer's stomach swelled. His temperature had risen to a raging fever that consumed his strength. Now his wife waited by him as his breath began to rattle and he lay in a stupor, dreaming his last hours away. Death was written on his face for anyone to read who knew that alphabet, and Lady Agatha, poor soul, knew it. Bitterly, Harold said: "To have brought him so far, in safety, for this! He'd have suffered less if that arrow in Cologne had killed him."

"You did your best," said Edward. "No one blames you, Harold. Tostig is here, did you know?"

"No. For the Council, I suppose? The Council we need not hold now."

"Yes." Edward sat, hands on knees. In the yellow light, the long fingers and the fine-boned face resembled old ivory. His mantle fell round his feet in pools of ruby and indigo shadow. Even exhausted, even grieving, Edward kept his royalty. Even though he was losing far more than a nephew, and knew it. He was losing his kingdom's future tonight. "I wish to see him," he said. "Just once."

"I told them you might. They're trying to clean him. They'll send word when he's ready. I've a piece of news of my own, although I don't understand what it means. The man who was supposed to be sick with smallpox, who began all this. He has never been ill at all."

Edward and Edith looked bewildered.

"A man of mine saw him swimming in the river this morning. He's sure it was the man Osbeorn meant. He remembered him being relieved of his oar."

"I don't see . . . What does the merchant Osbeorn say?" Edward asked.

"Unfortunately," said Harold with irritation, "my man Odi, who is not very clever, called out in surprise and the swimmer knew he had been recognised. When I sent for Osbeorn, he wasn't to be found and his ship had gone. I sent after him but he was a tide ahead of me and I doubt he'll be caught. I must say . . . " He shook his head yet again, as one who gives up trying to guess a riddle. "There have been attempts on Lord Edward. We know that. I would say that Osbeorn was part of such an attempt. There was some talk of Lord Edward going aboard Osbeorn's big vessel soon. He wanted to go; I was against it. Rightly, I now suspect. But if so, Osbeorn has fled disappointed. I think no one had a hand in this but God himself. I have a feeling that we shall never know."

Someone scratched at the door. A voice whispered: "Sire! My lord Harold! The physician says he is near the end."

They went out softly, crossing the great hall, where they picked their way among off-duty housecarles and thralls lying on pallets and snoring in the weak moonlight, and on through the passage to the Atheling's apartment. Archbishop Stigand of Canterbury and Bishop Aldred of Worcester were already there. Tostig and Earl Alfgar came in quietly on the heels of the king; Tostig and Harold briefly acknowledged each other.

In the sick man's upper room was more lamplight and a brazier sprinkled with aromatic herbs. But it could not drown the sour smell of disease; the air was heavy with it. Lady Agatha sat beside Bishop Aldred and they were intoning together in low voices over their beads. The Atheling's children were huddled on the floor in a corner. Only Margaret quite understood what was happening and she sat with her eyes fixed on her father, while tears rolled steadily down her white face. The physician sat at the bedside, watching the sunken countenance. Edward Edmundson lay still, except that his eyes were half open and now and then the eyelids flickered. The dry rasp of his breath scraped the nerves like grit.

Edith went at once to comfort Agatha, but the others drew near to the bedside. King Edward stood by the physician, looking down, curiously, gravely, at the face of the nephew he had never seen before and would not see again. Harold glanced at him quickly, sideways, and remembered once watching a man bid goodbye to a daughter who was sailing to Denmark to marry there. On that man's face, as the ship drew away from the shore, had been the same accepting desolation.

"Time is very short," the physician said. "He's past all feeling."

As if in refutation, the Atheling stirred and muttered. The physician leaned over him and moistened the cracked lips with a wet cloth. The muttering increased and the eyes opened. Harold said: "What is it? My lord?"

Edward Edmundson did not answer. He heard Harold speak and wanted to reply, but could not remember what he wished to say. In his ears the roaring of his own breath had blended with the roar of bone blades across the frozen Danube as he glided in towards the bank, where his friends were waiting.

Harold saw the glare of death enter the Atheling's eyes and himself reached out to draw the eyelids down. He turned to the king, and then took his gaze away from the grief in Edward's face. He moved instead to speak to Tostig. Tostig's expression shocked him. Tostig's freckled, pugnacious countenance showed the thing he had feared to find in Edward's. Tostig's blue eyes were marble-hard with suspicion.

In Rouen Castle, in his wife's bower, William of Normandy stood with arms folded on his crimson-clad chest and considered his duchess. His attitude would have alarmed most people, but Matilda continued her embroidery with serenity. The tip of a small pink tongue showed between her lips as she concentrated on a particularly technical stitch.

"And so," she said, repeating the words he had just uttered, "Edward Edmundson is dead. But that's a reason for rejoicing, my dear, surely?"

"You're fencing with me. Was your emissary Lyfing Thorkellson?"

"If I have removed Edward Edmundson from your path, as I think you're suggesting, you should be pleased," said Matilda. "You want to remain England's heir, do you not? Why do you say Thorkellson?"

"Shortly after the news broke that ambassadors had set out again from England to Hungary, you summoned Thorkellson here and had a meeting with him. After which he left Rouen. Now, when news comes of Edmundson's death, Thorkellson reappears and has another private talk with you and has now ridden off to take possession of a large estate in southern Normandy, ceded to him by you. Not much happens in my court without my knowledge, Matilda, my love. All comings and goings are told to me, in the end. Well?"

Matilda sighed and laid down her work. "I did it for you. The first time the English were more secret and I missed my chance then. But I prepared a plan to be ready, in case they tried again. They did. For you and our children, William, that's why I acted. A woman cannot go to war to fight her husband's enemies. She must use other weapons."

"Poison," said William gratingly. "An ugly choice of weapon."

Matilda, though twenty inches shorter than he was, looked into his black eyes with the boldness of an equal. "Mutilation is no prettier," she said. "How many lost their hands and feet at Alençon, because they had insulted you?"

He unfolded his arms and put his hands on her shoulders, pulling her to her feet. "So that's your shield, is it? Listen to me, Matilda. What orders did you give about the child, Edgar, who came to England with his father?"

"Edgar is still alive."

"I know. *But what orders did you give?*" He shook her.

"That he was—let me answer!—not to be harmed." He released her and she sat down again, straightening a disarranged headdress. "He's hardly dangerous, at five," she said. "And one doesn't make war on children."

"I don't," said the Duke of Normandy. "I'm not so certain about you."

Matilda smiled, lifting her needle. "I'm a mother myself."

"Cats make good mothers," William remarked. He sat down opposite her. "You often remind me of a lovable little cat, my pretty Mald—claws and all. But they only love their own young; no one else's. You know, do you not, that I will never harm, or let you harm, a child of Edgar's age? You were wise not to. That's why you didn't, I hope. I wasn't much older than he is—seven, I think—when my enemies tried to murder me. I remember it too well."

Matilda smiled again, with infinite tenderness towards this one touching weakness in her otherwise all-steel husband.

"I'm not ungrateful," William said with a trace of mockery. "Provided you confine your activities to adult enemies—yours and mine. I trust you won't forget that our interests are identical?"

"*William!*" Matilda sounded shocked. "I love you."

"Just as well . . . for you. What substance did Thorkellson use, do you know?"

"He didn't," said Matilda, unexpectedly, needle darting.

"What do you mean?"

"I mean he didn't poison Edmundson. He meant, apparently, to kidnap him and sell him to the Spanish Moors. He wanted double payment, once from me and once from them. He was teaching Edward to sail and had arranged for him to sail himself into an ambush waiting in a Thames backwater." Matilda smiled. "It was a carefully prepared plot." Head on one side, she examined her equally carefully prepared embroidery design. "He'd staved off official recognition of him as Atheling by putting him in quarantine for nonexistent smallpox. Very clever. But someone got to Edward first and killed him."

"Lyfing told you this himself?"

"Lyfing came to me and looked straight at me and said: 'My lady, the Atheling Edward is dead. May I claim my reward?' They have their own honesty, these fjord-men. He told me no lies. I knew of the Atheling's death already and I had the treasure and the land charters at hand. I wondered what he meant by that careful phrase, so I said: 'If the man is disposed of—and I know that he is—these are yours.' Then I gave them to him and then I asked for the details. 'It sounds as if you didn't do the killing yourself. Don't be afraid to tell me. The agreement was that you should be paid if the Atheling were removed without being declared the official heir. This has happened, so the payment is yours.' Then he told me the rest. He was glad to relieve his feelings, I think. He was very very angry," said Matilda.

Passing through the hall on his way out, Duke William paused near the hearth fire, where a stocky, black-haired knight and a handsome, ginger-haired squire were setting out a backgammon game to play before dinner. "Sir Brand, and Hakon Sweynson. Quintain practice finished for the day?"

"My nephew will soon be scoring higher than I am," Brand Woodcutter said, rising.

"Good." William studied them, his dark hawk-face apparently seeking something in their expressions that he did not find. "You have not heard the English news? Concerning Edward Edmundson? No. Well, Sir Brand, in your homeland, Edward Edmundson, who might have been the Atheling, is dead. Are you ever homesick, Brand?"

"Sometimes," said Brand after a short hesitation.

"You may see your home again yet," William told him, with a flash of teeth in a sudden, lupine grin, as he walked on.

Part

III

THE MARRIAGE
OF ALDITH
1058–1063 A.D.

1 ✷ The Loving Cup

"We're ready. Load the mules," Alveva said to the thralls, and they stepped towards the piles of baggage near the door of the hall: ironbound and padlocked chests, leather sacks with mouths drawn tight and knotted, hampers strapped shut, and last-minute recollections rolled up in discarded tapestries and tied with thongs. The three new chests standing apart were the transportable portion of Aldith's dowry. The nontransportable part was represented by a roll of vellum in Alfgar's saddlebag, on which the revenues of three estates were ceded to his daughter's future husband.

The dowry chests were taken out first. Aldith, as they were borne away, had a blinding moment of fear as if something irreversible had happened. "Sit down till the horses are ready," Alveva said.

They sat on a settle, Aldith stiff and nervous in her brand-new clothes, hands clasped tightly on her lap. "We shan't have much chance for private talk after today," said Alveva.

She studied her daughter. Aldith was a credit to her upbringing after all, she decided. The girl sat straight and had ceased to answer back. Her skin was good and her hair had responded well to the shampoo of mashed radish and privet which made the most of the red lights in it (an attempt to turn Aldith blond with elder bark and egg yolk and saffron hadn't gone well, but fortunately it had washed out). "I hope," said Alveva, "that you understand how lucky you are. You will marry a prince, and be styled Princess of All Wales. If God is good, you'll found a line of rulers. I've tried to teach you about the responsibilities of a great man's wife. I hope you'll justify my efforts."

"I'll try, Mother." Aldith found herself wishing that since they must go, they could go now. The hall, with half its contents stored away or else being loaded on to mules, had an odd, hollow echo; it was telling her to go, that home was home no longer. But her mother was still talking.

Alveva was unaware of the hectoring note in her voice. The girl seemed abstracted, and she wanted her to take in this last exhortation. "Your principal duties will be to have children and order your husband's house . . . Even Queen Edith weaves cloth for the king to wear. Set an example of piety and charity. If people ask you to take their petitions to Prince Gruffyd, do so if it's suitable, but learn to tell the difference between good and bad causes and convince him of your good sense. Never trouble him with foolish appeals. Never be demanding, or jealous, and . . . Are you listening?"

"Yes, Mother." One couldn't call this hall home, exactly. Earl Leofric was not long dead and they had only recently come to Mercia. Her father had been allowed to inherit, though the Witan had argued over it by all accounts. This Chester hall was still comparatively strange. It wouldn't be too hard to part from it. But she must part from her family too. Thank the saints that Wulfhild was coming with her. She wouldn't be alone with the stranger Prince Gruffyd.

". . . If you are wise you will smile at his lesser amusements. Think of the wife of Harald Hardraada of Norway. When she could not give him a son, she urged him to take a second wife and even found one for him. Now the two wives live in friendship."

"Yes, Mother."

"Don't be misled by the songs of love the bards sing at the wedding. The Welsh are emotional. Men rarely love women as the poets pretend. Don't expect it. Be dutiful and faithful and that will be enough. Your position as princess is unassailable, if you do as I have taught you."

"Yes, Mother," Aldith repeated, looking terrified. Outside, hooves clattered on flagstones and a horse whinnied. It was time.

If only, she thought, the unknown Gruffyd would prove to be not too dreadful. She felt unready, like a child called from play to its bed before the sun has gone down far enough. And the bed in this case held more than an order to sleep. Wulfhild, who seemed to know about it—she had certainly been on close terms with the dove boy at Thetford—said there was nothing to fear. But other women told lurid tales sometimes. Alveva, appealed to for reassurance, had merely shrugged and said: "All women go through it except nuns. We all survive." Which was hardly helpful.

"There we are!" said Alfgar heartily as they emerged into the courtyard, and the big man, Lord Berddig, whom Gruffyd had sent to fetch his bride, gave her a broad smile. This was a happy day for them. She was setting out to seal the friendship between Gruffyd and her father, and, according to Earl Alfgar, to secure peace on the Welsh frontier in the process. It was his task, he had said. Ralph of Hereford was dead; it was for Mercia to settle the Marches now. Alveva had said ominously that she hoped the Witan would see it in that light, and not just as an alliance with an enemy. But she didn't press the point because the lure of a prince for a son-in-law was too great.

What, Aldith wondered, was Gruffyd really like? Would he see her only as a political convenience, as her parents did? Would she be happier with him than she had been at home?

Probably not.

They travelled steadily throughout the day, on good roads. It was April and there had been rain, but strong winds had dried the ground. One night had to be spent on the way and they sheltered in the guesthouse of an abbey on a hillside in what Lord Berddig said was actually North Wales. In the morning, Aldith pattered barefoot to look from the window of the little stone room, pushing back the shutters to see out. A segment of rolling land greeted her, with a rumour of mountains beyond. She had never seen real mountains. Berddig, yesterday, had said she would come to love them. The air was sweet and had a new tang in it. The scent of Wales, she told herself.

Outside, two women thralls, carrying milk pails, went by. Their voices rose, lilting. They were speaking Welsh. She had heard it spoken by Berddig's escort, but they were foreign men travelling in England. These women were using their own tongue in their own land. It was she who was the foreigner here. It struck her that this was changing now, that henceforth Wales was her country and that the Welsh language must become hers also.

With a shock, as of cold water closing over a diver, she remembered that by tonight she would have met the man who would rule her life, and that tomorrow, whatever he was like, she would be married to him. She turned from the window and saw Wulfhild waiting, armed with brush and towels and clothing.

"It's bright but it's cold. You'll want your cloak," said Wulfhild, and the familiar, flat East Anglian accent brought the safe world back again. Once more, Aldith felt a surge of gratitude that Wulfhild would be with her in the days to come.

Berddig rode at her side as they set out again, and talked to her of Wales, and of the household she was to join, addressing her kindly from what seemed like an immense height. She had the impression of a round face very high and far away and topping a mighty bulk like a moon rising over one of the mountains he had talked about yesterday. It was his great depth of chest and lungs that gave him his resonant voice and had helped to make him the greatest bard in Wales. His horse was probably the biggest in the principality, and even so it looked overburdened. But she noticed that he often stroked it and spoke to it. When he did so, he used Welsh. Shyly, she asked him what it meant. "I shall have to learn," she said.

"It's not a simple tongue," he told her. "But you are right. If you learn a phrase or two, you will compliment Prince Gruffyd and warm his people to you. You're young enough to learn it quickly; in a few years it will be natural to you. Shall we try a little? This long valley we're riding through, we call it a *cwm*. And that meadow there where the sheep and the lambs are, that's a *dol*. The wood up there on the *bryn*—I mean the hill—the wood is *coed*. Say them."

Aldith said them, with the wrong pronunciation. He repeated them and she tried again, more successfully, and laughed at the small triumph. When she laughed, her small, tense, heart-shaped face brightened, and the warm brown eyes glowed.

She would come to life in time, Berddig thought, watching her. Once safely removed from that mother of hers. "The music is in your voice already," he said. "Ours is a speech full of music. Listen." He rolled out a complete Welsh sentence, unintelligible to her, but with such a ring to its tuneful syllables that she turned her face upwards in wonder.

"What . . . did it mean?" she asked.

Berddig smiled down at her. "It was a message that Prince

Gruffyd wished me to give you, out of anyone else's hearing—which you never were, yesterday. He said I was to tell you: in your beauty and your youth, he bids you welcome to Wales and to his heart and he prays to Mary the Mother of God that in both you will find joy without bounds to it, or end."

"Oh!" said Aldith. She added: "It's like something from a minstrel's song."

"My master is a fine minstrel, you will find."

It was past noon when they came in sight of Rhuddlan Fort ("*Caer*," said Berddig, "is the word for fort"). A narrow path led through a beech grove where the branches arched above, their dark pattern misted now in the first young foliage. Emerging, the path wound on through marshland, and ahead of them the ground rose in a long slope up to a crest crowned by stout walls, a mix of wooden palisades and stone. Gruffyd might not like the Norman castles on his borders, but he was prepared to learn from them. To the left a river flowed and they glimpsed new stone walling leading down the hill to the water, and a landing place at the foot. But the path went straight to the great main gate, which stood open, revealing more buildings beyond it, timber and stone, round huts and gable-ended houses, roofs of thatch and slate. Flags and banners were hung round the entrance, a festive frame of colour.

The escort leader sounded his horn and was answered from within, and a stream of horsemen came galloping out of the gate. They encircled the approaching riders, spiralled in and cut Berddig and Aldith deftly off from the rest. Berddig, who had apparently expected it, laughed and put a hand on her pony's bridle. "Are you ready?"

"For . . . what?"

"To meet your future husband."

"My mother said . . ."

"Prince Gruffyd rules here and he said I was to bring you to him and no other. So . . . are you ready?"

Aldith nodded, helplessly. Berddig took the reins from her hands and drew them over the pony's head, taking full control. He threw his head back and roared a command. Then with hands and voice and spurs he lifted both their steeds into a gallop and the escort galloped with them, closing them round and only falling back as the wide-set gate hurtled up. Berddig and Aldith dashed through it side by side, his great steed loping easily with its long stride, her pony at full stretch, its four small hooves beating double time. Within, the enclosure was big enough to house a small town, and in a sense it did, so many were the buildings there. But chief of all was a great hall that overshadowed the rest and stood in the centre of them. The door of this stood open too and steps of dark grey slate led up to it. An avenue of staring, laughing, cheering people, a blur of faces as Aldith was swept by, led up to the steps; and on the topmost step, a man was waiting.

She was not aware of him till they halted, suddenly, dramatically, at the very foot of the steps, their mounts' hindquarters sliding under them. It was fortunate, thought Aldith breathlessly, and with a nervous desire to giggle, that she could ride. How undignified to arrive in one's bridegroom's residence headfirst. Then she looked up, and there was her bridegroom.

The first impression was not physical but mental: the emanation of power. It informed the whole man, being present in the strong, stocky build, in the mind that lit the deep-set brown eyes, even in his choice of garments—in the crimson tunic and the purple mantle. She took in that most of his face was hidden by a mass of black beard and that his nose was flattened, and wondered if these features were appealing or repulsive, but had no time to decide. Berddig was out of his saddle and holding his hand to her.

She descended unsteadily and someone took away the horses. She shook out her skirts, kilted for easier riding and now badly creased and mud-splashed, and began to murmur something about her disarray, but was calmly ignored by Berddig. He took her hand again, and holding it aloft as if it were a trophy, began to lead her up the steps. She went of necessity, careful not to stumble, groping in her mind for the Welsh phrase of greeting he had taught her. Berddig bowed deeply and handed her firmly forward as they reached the top. "My lord, Prince Gruffyd, I present to you the Lady Aldith of Mercia."

Her Welsh had fled with the wind of the gallop, she found, but she attempted to curtsey to Gruffyd. She failed because he took her hand away from Berddig and pulled her towards him instead. She found herself folded to a very broad and muscular chest, with Gruffyd's lips pressing warmly on her own. "My lady Aldith!" he said, as he drew back at last. His voice was nearly as deep as Berddig's. "My lady of Mercia. Welcome to Wales, my darling."

Gently, politely, hot to the lobes of her ears and the line of her dishevelled hair, now escaping from its decent veil, Aldith eased herself backwards out of his grasp. She remembered to smile and she said in English: "Thank you, my lord. I am happy to be in Wales." The rest of the cavalcade had caught up now, and somewhere behind her she could hear her mother's voice. Alveva would certainly be watching. She managed, at last, to achieve the curtsey.

Under the deerskins and the great sleek marten rug of Gruffyd's state bed, Aldith waited, watching the moon through a window left unshuttered, and wondered what would befall her before the moon had passed out of sight.

She was not as frightened as she had expected to be because Gruffyd, an experienced man, had spent a good deal of time with her throughout today, and during the previous afternoon after her dramatic arrival. But her mother and the women had made such a to-do over the preparations for tonight. The vows and the feasting had been nothing compared to the elaborate, now-let's-get-to-business ritual which followed. What seemed like dozens of women—her own, Alveva's, and some new Welsh ones (who were, she gathered, the ladies who attended on the wives of Gruffyd's brothers)—had brushed her hair and sponged her skin with rosewater and pushed back the cuticles of her nails and all but embalmed her in well-meant but hair-raising advice. Now she was alone, her skin warm from the hot water but her stomach cold. Only, she felt that Gruffyd's unperfumed masculinity might be a relief after all that too-feminine ceremony. She hoped he would not be too long.

He arrived roaring with laughter at some joke made by his companions, but although exalted, he was much less drunk than they were. He barred the door efficiently in their faces. Outside, they began a noisy song. "It's well that in Welsh it is, the salacious devils," he said. "Best you shouldn't understand it. Well, Aldith, my little love, we are here at last. Long it is I have waited for you, since your father first told me of his lovely daughter, on the banks of the Severn two endless years ago."

He tossed off his loose robe and she saw him for the first time. His body was hard and heavy with muscle and thatched on chest and stomach with thick dark hair. This was intriguing and Aldith, as he came and sat down on the bed, and put his arms round her, hesitantly combed it with a finger before deciding that her mother would not approve of this. She then desisted, despite his amused permission to go on.

He sensed her nervousness and began to talk to her again in his reassuring rumble. "This is just an ordinary thing, Aldith. Thousands on thousands of couples are settling for the night, everywhere, blowing candles out and lying down together. Come. There's some in bond huts and some in great houses. There's some too weary with toil to do much more than take comfort in each other's warmth, and sleep. There's some who've been wed so long that it's all an old song and they're lying in the dark and gossiping. There're some who've quarrelled and they've turned their backs to each other and they're lying listening, each hoping the other will weaken and put out a hand. And there's some like us, who'll be lovers tonight and maybe set a flame to a new life before dawn. Would you not like to do that, little Aldith?"

The moment had to come, and be passed through. Aldith alternately watched the curved, carved ceiling beams and Gruffyd's face, taut with gathering joy, above her. His was a mask of a face, she thought, the eyes glazed, not focused on her at all, but on secret sensations of his own, which she did not share.

There was nothing, after all, to fear. There seemed very little to enjoy, either. After all the long dread and anticipation and the incredible, protracted grooming that had gone before, there was . . . nothing.

Gruffyd knew it. He came back from his secret place of delight to scan her face concernedly, seeking some answering delight there, in vain. But: "You're young yet and I still strange to you. It will come," he said kindly, before they slept.

"This is an outrage," said Harold of Wessex, not loudly, but with enormous passion. His forehead was flushed.

It had taken the news of the marriage two weeks to get to King Edward at Gloucester and it took another ten days to convene a quorum for a Witenagemot. Now they were gathered: Harold and Tostig, Gyrth Godwinson, once more Earl of East Anglia, and his brother Leofwin, recently raised to be Earl of Kent. The death of

Ralph of Hereford had brought changes. Mercia had swelled to swallow most of Ralph's lands and Wessex to engulf the rest. In return for the growth of Wessex in the west, Harold had yielded up the easternmost end of his earldom to Leofwin. There were five earldoms in England now and the Godwinsons held four of them; and the fifth earl, Alfgar, was not here.

Harold, considering the council table, wondered if Edward felt beleaguered.

He gave no sign of it, if so. He sat with assurance at the table head, flanked by his chief prelates. In contrast to the angry Harold, the king's face was still, giving no clue to his thoughts.

Dissent was voiced by Aldred Bishop of Worcester. "The marriage could be thought good in some ways," he said. "It may help to keep the border quiet."

"We already have an agreement with Gruffyd which was meant to do that," said Leofwin coldly.

"I could believe that Gruffyd's intentions were peaceful, if I could believe that Gruffyd were to be trusted a yard," Tostig said. "But I don't happen to believe either. He's crafty and two-faced—a typical Celt. That man Brand Woodcutter had Welsh blood, I recall. They're all natural enemies to England. If war breaks out along the border, which side will Alfgar take now?'

"They've been allies once already," said Harold grimly. "Alfgar *may* be hoping to do us all a service by making the Welsh into our in-laws. He may also be strengthening his own arm for his own glory. At a guess, I should say the latter."

Tostig nodded. He and Harold had met rarely since the Atheling's death, but when they did meet they could cooperate as brother earls at least. Gytha had achieved that.

"You dislike Gruffyd, Harold," Edward said. "With good reason, I know, but yours is a private grievance. Your brother ranges himself beside you, which I am glad to see—I had heard that you had quarrelled, and it rejoices me to see that your difference is settled." Both their faces grew warm. "But lacking your personal grievance," Edward said, "I must make my choice on other grounds. Bishop Aldred has put a point of view. There is sense in it."

"You have met Gruffyd, my lord," said Harold. "Do *you* trust him?"

Edward laid his hands flat, palms down, on the table and

smiled, the austere curving of a closed mouth that in him was the equivalent of another man's broad grin. "I do not," he said. Softly Harold let his lungs exhale a pent-up breath. "I might agree," said Edward, turning towards the bishop, "with Aldred that to bond Gruffyd by marriage to England could help preserve peace. But I can't, Aldred, accept that Alfgar's house is the one for such a bonding. Nor would I accept a marriage between Gruffyd and any English house at all, if it took place without my consent." He changed without warning to the royal plural. "We propose therefore that until a suitable regent be chosen for Mercia, on behalf of the infant Edwin, Harold and Tostig Godwinson divide the administration of the earldom of Mercia between them, and that Alfgar be once more deposed and banished." He pointed a hand at one of the clerks who waited, as at all Witan Councils, to record decisions. "Note it. You will draw up the appropriate documents after this meeting."

He looked round the table, apparently searching for approval and faintly surprised by the silence. Even the well-trained clerk hesitated infinitesimally before dipping his quill. When he did start to write, the scratching pen broke the hush like the scrabbling of a gigantic mouse, and the clerk turned pink with embarrassment.

But the hush was of amazement, not protest. Presently, Harold voiced the amazement. "My lord, if you do that, until a protector is appointed for Mercia you will have every earldom in the land in the hands of us Godwinsons. Is that your wish?"

"What a gambler with words you are, Harold," said Edward lightly. It was impossible to tell from his eyes or his voice whether he was in earnest or not. "You and your brothers are the only men now in the realm with the background and experience for such work. Where else I shall find a regent for Mercia I can't as yet imagine. I have no choice that I can see." There was a fractional pause. Then he smiled again. "Rest assured, Harold, that I have accepted you all as my brothers for a long time now. And a man needs brothers. Without them, one is lonely." He sensed that the hush was still wary, and it seemed that until that moment, he had not seen the full meaning of his own words. He said, and now they knew that he meant it: "I am serious. That was not a reference to . . . the past."

2 ❊ The Wine of Enchantment

"I was born . . ." said Gruffyd. "You're laughing but it's the usual way to start out in life, and if I'm to tell you the story of my life it's at the beginning I should start. I was the eldest born of my mother's first marriage and next to me was a sister. Then my father died and my mother entered a humbler union with my stepfather, of whom we grew fond in time. My half brothers were born of that marriage."

Aldith looked attentive but puzzled. They had been talking of her father's exile and she had been distressed. Gruffyd, comfortingly, said it might not be for long. But the Irish Vikings had refused to help her father this time and she didn't see what made him so sure. And now, instead of explaining himself, Gruffyd had begun on his autobiography. It made her smile, but chiefly with surprise.

They stood cloaked against the upland wind, looking over the outer wall of a Snowdonian hunting lodge. They were so high that below them the mists made a white ocean in which mountain peaks were afloat. Gruffyd was still talking.

"My sister died at twenty-two and it was a mercy perhaps, for she had a tongue on her like a woodsman's saw and a terrible life she'd have led any husband. But I owe her something. Drove me out of the house, she did, one icy New Year's Eve, saying I was a lazy good-for-nothing and timid . . ."

"Timid?" said Aldith, jolted into comment by the sheer absurdity of it.

"As a boy I'd no interest in feats of arms. A warm hearth and

155

the songs of bards and food and good wine, that's all I cared for. My eldest son Maredudd is the same. I hope he'll take after his Da when he grows up too. But to go on. My sister nagged me so hard that night I could get no peace by the fire, so out I went. It was a night to look for omens, being New Year, so I thought I'd find one for me. Low-hearted, she'd made me feel. There's ten thousand ways to divine the future on New Year's Eve and I chose an easy one. I put my ear to the crack of a wattle and daub house wall and listened to the talk inside."

"Were they talking about you?"

"Not they. They were cooks boiling up meat in a cauldron and one complained that there was one piece of meat that kept bobbing to the top however often he pushed it down. I took that for my omen. From now on, I said, that will be me, the one who can't be kept down, who won't do what others choose but does as he likes for himself. And the weird thing, Aldith, is that that's how it's proved. That day I came into my manhood. And after a while, into the lordship of all Wales."

Aldith was beginning to be interested. "How?"

"I was born of the north Welsh royal line, though some of my forebears were careless and all their unions weren't legal But I thought: what of it? There is young William declared Duke of Normandy, and his parents never wed. So I went to war against the man who held the north in those days and killed him and drove away his son. And it's because of that son, Aldith, my love, that the King of Dublin won't send men to help your father. Now we're married, to help your father is to help me. The son went to Ireland. He's a sulky, silent brute called Cynan—Berddig once went to Ireland too and met him—and a few years back he married the Irish king's daughter and he's been digging himself in with them ever since. He's got a big say now in their affairs, indeed he has, and if he says no soldiers for Alfgar—well, no soldiers it is." Gruffyd leaned his elbows on the wall, and his eyes, looking at her over the hunch of his shoulder, were laughing. "Only you despair too soon. I am a name to reckon with in some places, if not in Ireland now. I took the south of Wales too in the end, remember. There are other Vikings, the original ones, the fjord-men of Norway, and they'll come if a leader like Gruffyd ap Llewellyn calls. Your father has sailed for Norway. I heard yesterday. He'll be home in Mercia before the year is out.

So, no more sorrow, my *merched*, my lass. This is still our honeymoon."

"It was because of the marriage that he was exiled at all," said Aldith sadly.

"He wished the marriage made. And I don't wish it unmade. Do you?"

Aldith looked not at him, but down to the vapours of the valley, which sunlight and breeze were now dispersing in misty swirls and coils. "No," she said shyly at last. "No, I don't wish that."

It was true. Once the dreaded introduction to the obligations of the marriage bed was over, the sense of liberation from Alveva had been almost heady. She who had once been compelled to say yes and no in agreement now said yes and no in command. It was to her that the steward came, asking which guesthouse should be allotted at Rhuddlan to the easily offended visiting nobles from Deheubarth (as she must learn to call South Wales). It was she who chose the wine to be served to Lord Dafid of Conwy Valley, another touchy one, and with a discerning palate at that. And when in the evening they left the hall, even the wives of Gruffyd's half brothers, the Princes Rhiwallon and Bleddyn, must walk behind her, though they were older than she. Nervously at first, but with increasing confidence as her first timid orders were not only accepted but approved, she took control of her domains.

Well . . . some control. There were limits. It was a shock on her first day to see Saxons among the bondmen. Some of the Welsh were fair—Dafid of Conwy was—but their faces were different in cast from these unmistakeable English. She learned that many were not thralls born but were captives from raids, and she also learned that nothing could be done for them. One, a young man who had been taken from Hereford when her father and Gruffyd sacked it, appealed to her but she was powerless.

"My captives are the gems in my coronet, *merched*. What do you care? You have thralls at home as Saxon as these, and not all bondborn, either. Don't men and their kin get sold to pay their debts in England? Some of my thralls—and that boy Osric is one—eat better and sleep softer here than they ever did as free men. If you want a bondman freed as a token of my goodwill, you shall have one. But not a captive. You can free that cousin of mine who helps the Rhuddlan cowman . . ."

"Your *cousin?*"

"I had an uncle who was a devil among the bondwomen. You'll see a good few in the slaves' quarters who look like me. This one does. Free him."

For lack of alternative, Aldith accepted. She was a princess. But not the prince.

But that was a small shadow, and the only one. She had wondered, when told that she must take lessons in the Welsh tongue and the history of Wales, that these might constitute another, but it wasn't so. Between Alveva's stern instruction in household skills and Berddig's tonic ideas of tuition there was no comparison. He taught through songs and poems and tales; study became entertainment. She had already heard some of Gruffyd's life story from him. Her husband, it seemed, was a man of prowess in battle and magnanimity to the conquered. He had conquered both the north and south of Wales, as he said, and though the tale of exiled Cynan was new to her, she already knew that a descendant of the southern ruling house still lived as a landowner in his ancestral kingdom, and flourished. "Though God knows Caradoc stirs up his nobles at times," said Berddig, "and one day Prince Gruffyd will lose patience with him. I say the south, but you must learn to call it Deheubarth. Say it after me . . . No, no, you have lost the lilt. Let us try it in a song instead . . ." And the lesson turned to music once again.

Wales was full of music. In Mercia, a bard was a servant. But here minstrelsy was the prerogative of birth; men served their apprenticeship to arms and music simultaneously and with equal seriousness. Lord Berddig was Bard Teulu, Court Poet, with trained minstrels under him and a professional status which almost outdid his status as a lord of lands. When as part of the marriage festivities, Gruffyd had bidden her to present the prizes at a bardic contest given in her honour, he had explained carefully that this was a great honour, which she must not undervalue.

She had enjoyed it. The bards sang of war and love and hunting and past heroes of Wales. Songs of battles between the Welsh and the English were not given, although one young and tactless minstrel did attempt to play the Lament for Cynddylan, which commemorated an English victory over the Welsh more than a century ago. He had meant to compliment Aldith's ancestors, but Berddig stopped him in the middle of the first stanza with a cuff on the head. In Wales, people were considerate of her feelings.

Standing now beside Gruffyd, she thought she could learn to love Wales. It was less stiff than at home. Used to the rigid status divisions of her father's hall, she had been first astonished and then enchanted to see Gruffyd's petitioners accosting him haphazard as he came from Mass or set out hunting. Official audiences there certainly were, but no one seemed to feel constrained to see him only then. He had been known to settle an inheritance dispute in the forge, giving judgement with his arms crossed on the back of a horse, or adjudicate at one of the extraordinary civil divorce settlements of Wales while sitting in the armoury and holding the blue-sharp edge of a sword to the light.

No, it would not be hard to love Wales. Nor would it be hard to love . . . but her thoughts stopped short of the word "Gruffyd." Her mother had warned her, had she not? She did not wish the marriage unmade. But with two dispossessed heirs to the two halves of his kingdom at large, Gruffyd might well regret that his bride, who should have brought him the friendship of a powerful Mercian earl, had done nothing of the sort because the earl had now lost Mercia.

The mists, uncoiling in the breeze, made enigmatic shapes below, as enigmatic as Gruffyd's thoughts. He put his arm about her and it was firm and warm, but she could not feel his mind through it. He said: "It's quiet here. There's glad I am I left my brothers and their quarrels—we are dear to each other, my brothers and I, but never do we cease to wrangle—and brought you to this mountain eyrie of mine. Worn out you were in Rhuddlan with all the turmoil of the wedding. I saw it. So I brought you here with Berddig to play lovesongs for us, not that I can't play them myself. But he does it better. There will never be such a minstrel again, Aldith. When he touches a harp, the cool notes spray out from his fingers as if he had set them free, not made them . . . The weather is clearing. I can see Llanberis hamlet down there now; the mists are blowing away. I hope it stays fair for a while . . . I must ride south soon."

"Ride south?"

"The nobles of Deheubarth," he said, "including the man Caradoc, are at their complaining again. They dislike the laws I made when I became lord of the south . . . God's Teeth! Laws for their own protection and well-being, look you! They are disputing with each other in ways I have not sanctioned, with weapons and not words. Will you stay here till I come back? You can choose. If you would like to go back to Rhuddlan, you shall. Or I have a big hall you've not yet seen, right beside Mount Snowdon, and there's fine hawking to be had there on the slopes of the mountain, and you can ride and gather wild flowers by the lake at Snowdon's foot. I must leave in four days. I've called the parties to council in the south in one week's time. So—tell me what you wish."

If there was trouble in the south, he wouldn't want to expose her to risk. She must not assume that he was simply weary of her company. She must not be sensitive. She considered his question. She did not want to go to yet another strange place, and Rhuddlan with its whirl of unfamiliar faces had indeed been tiring. But she liked this mountain lodge.

"May I stay here?" she asked. "Will you be gone long?" she added. It might be a relief to be alone for a while, in charge of this modest establishment and no longer on duty with wifely words and smiles and gestures of affection, which must never be allowed to be more than duty. Yet she must be careful not to seem pleased that he was going away. Aldith sighed. Marriage was very complicated.

"Two weeks or three," Gruffyd said easily. "I'll send you news. Lord Berddig will be here and my son Maredudd will stay too. Your maid Wulfhild will keep you company."

"Yes, indeed," said Aldith brightly. "I shall find plenty to do. I had thought of replanting the herb garden behind this house. There's no coltsfoot in it, I notice, or horehound either, and we must have that for winter coughs. In fact, I shouldn't let this dry morning pass and do no work there. I shall fetch Wulfhild and we'll begin at once. My lord, excuse me!" She slid out of his arm, curtseyed gracefully and hastily, and went away. Presently he heard her in the house, summoning Wulfhild to work. There was little of the feckless child left in Aldith, he thought, regretfully.

He was still thinking it when Berddig found him by the wall a few minutes later. The minstrel eyed his lord quizzically. "God's Instep, man, why do you look so mournful? Did they put gall in your breakfast porridge?"

"I am not mournful. You have too much imagination."

"I have not, at that." Berddig shook his head and leant on the wall beside Gruffyd, breathing deeply of the euphoric mountain air. "It'll take time to set the little one free of her mother's solemn spell," he said. "Even the lass Wulfhild, who is not much more than a child, cannot play in peace. She and your son Maredudd were racing a pair of snails on the floor of the hall just now, and my lady Aldith is still of an age to join them. But no, she must call Wulfhild from the game, and take her out to the garden, and set them both to work." He considered, and then addressed the drop of rocks and grass below, where they fell steeply to the far-off valley. "Try a counter-spell, man," he advised. "Whether you believe the old legends or not, the talk of them might stir the soul in her. Try the Cwmanog."

The day before he was to ride south, Gruffyd came on his wife in the herb garden. Three bondmen, under her direction, were digging over a place where grass and bindweed had taken unsanctioned control, and in a patch already cleared and turned Wulfhild was sowing horehound. Aldith had even, apparently, commandeered his son Maredudd's help; Maredudd was lending a hand with the horehound, intent on it, his shock of black hair falling into his bright, sea-coloured eyes, as he knelt beside Wulfhild. Aldith herself was industriously plying a hoe.

"What a vision of industry." Gruffyd's voice was not wholly approving. "But since when has the wife of the Welsh ruler needed to toil like a labourer in the garden? Leave Wulfhild in charge here, Aldith, my love. You can stay too, Maredudd, the work will be good for you. I want to ride with my wife. Alone."

He said alone and he meant alone. They went without an escort and they took winding hill paths, descending slowly, till they reached a deep valley where a river splashed and rattled along a bed littered with grey boulders. Alders overhung the banks and stunted oak clung to the hillsides. A narrow path ran by the water and this they followed, going upstream. Gruffyd led the way. He would not say where they were going, but she sensed a clear purpose in him. Presently the sides of the glen closed in and the valley bent sharply to the left. Here the path crossed by a ford and the entrance to the crossing was a dark arch under the trees. The sky was shut away.

Gruffyd pressed on, crouching to avoid low branches. On the opposite side of the ford, the path continued along the other bank. The glen was climbing now and the water brawled in its steep channel, bounding over little falls and hurtling in eddies round obstructive stones, and its sound was flung to and fro and multiplied under the roof of leaves.

Involuntarily, Aldith glanced back. The bend hid all view of the open places behind them. Left and right, before and behind and overhead, the laden boughs and the rocky slopes surrounded them and the river's voice made walls of sound that shut them in. She turned again and found that Gruffyd had paused, and that there was room to ride up beside him. He spoke, or shouted, to be heard above the river. "I saw you look back! Why?"

"I felt that the trees were watching me!" Aldith called into his ear. "That we were strangers here!" Her own words surprised her. "But where," she cried, "is 'here'?"

The round brown eyes danced. "The very soul of my land is here, my sweetheart! This is the Cwmanog!"

"Cwm . . . ? That's a valley! But what . . . ?"

"Cwmanog is the Glen of the Immortal Ones!" He was leaning from his saddle to speak into her ear now. "They live here! You are right, we are strangers, for we're mortal! But we're not at journey's end yet! Come!"

They had to dismount and leave the horses tethered before they reached the head of the valley. Here path and river separated and the path climbed alone above the water, which now rushed between sheer grey walls of rock. Gruffyd strode on, sure-footed. Behind him, Aldith grew breathless. Then the path turned sharply round a rocky mass, and she halted, gasping.

They were on a flat rock platform. A cliff soared beside them, with ferns and grasses in its crevices, and there was a smell of wet stone and foliage. Below, far below, was a deep pool. A little sunlight found its way there and dragonflies with bright bodies glittered in the shaft. But the stillness of the pool was the aftermath of violence, for the pool was fed by a waterfall, pouring over the edge of the cliff. Aldith looked up and her head reeled. Two, three, maybe four or five hundred feet, the cliff wall rose and the straight white stream fell without hindrance to thunder into the gorge below. The noise was a steady, sonorous roar.

"Sit down!" shouted Gruffyd, gesturing.

They sat. The white fall fascinated her. It must be moving swiftly, very swiftly, yet like sea breakers seen from a distance it looked motionless. Gruffyd was talking into her ear again.

"There is a legend in the Cwmanog. I've never tried it out. But today I thought . . . perhaps today I will. If you are brave enough to try it with me!"

She put her question into her expression. *Brave enough?* Did he want them to dive into the pool? That wouldn't be brave. It would be suicidal. She waited.

"They say," Gruffyd explained, "that if you cast a stone into this pool and, as you do it, speak in your soul to the Immortal Ones and ask them to grant you your heart's desire, they will do it."

"But why do you have to be brave?"

"Because they do not give their services for nothing, and because they have no feelings of their own, so they do not care for yours. They are cold and fair and know nothing of terror or bloodshed or tears. They'll grant your wish and take your payment! There was a woman came here once and asked for a child. Ten years wed she'd been, and no child. Within a year she had a son and he grew up fine and strong and quarrelled with his father, her husband, and slew him!"

"That's a horrible story!"

Gruffyd reached to where grasses and moss grew on the cliff in a patch of stony earth, and felt for a stone. He sat bouncing it on his palm. "They drive a hard bargain but they don't cheat! I dare you!" He looked at her sidelong, still playing with the stone.

"It's pagan! The priest would forbid it!"

"Priests don't come here, my bird! They let the Cwmanog alone!"

"Is there something you want so much, you'd dare this to get it?"

She did not understand the expression on Gruffyd's face. It seemed that she had said something to hurt him, yet he was not angry. His eyes were kind and a little sad. A travelling entertainer had come to Thetford once, bringing with him a queer little animal called a monkey. It had a half-human face and round brown eyes in which that same sadness lurked. She thought it was because the creature felt itself to be akin to humankind yet shut out for ever from their world. But from what was Gruffyd, conqueror of all Wales, shut out?

"I cannot tell you what my wish is!" he told her. "It may not be spoken till it is granted. You must keep your secret too!"

"Mine?"

"Yes, yours! We'll dare the legend of Cwmanog together or not at all! Well, Aldith? Do we cast our stones together? Or not?"

"Always do as your husband tells you," her mother had enjoined Alveva could hardly have envisaged this, this unholy gambling game in a haunted glen, with the white waterfall roaring out of the sky and the pool as deep as death below, and the iridescent dragonflies like bright needles, stitching the darkness to the light. There was madness here, a sense of presences who would bend you to their will. Or perhaps the madness and the will were Gruffyd's. If so, she had caught it. She would do as he asked and not be afraid.

She groped for a stone and found one and they stood up and he put his arm round her. They cast their stones together. Up here, one couldn't hear the plops. But there were two small splashes in the pool and two rings of ripples widening slowly outwards, and overlapping, before the water was quiet again. She turned to Gruffyd and the sadness was gone from his eyes. They were merry.

"The path climbs higher," he said, "and there's a safe place with moss and sweet grasses to lie on, and if I put my cloak down it won't be damp. You'll remember it all your life, my little Aldith, the day we made love in the early summer, within sound of the waters of the Cwmanog."

Ten days later, one evening as she was lying down, Aldith was seized with unaccountable, violent nausea. Another ten days and she told Wulfhild rather doubtfully that she might be with child. In two more weeks Gruffyd was back from the south and she told him that she was sure. He roared with delighted laughter and hugged her and took her to Rhuddlan the very next day, to hold a feast of rejoicing. They were still there when, less than a fortnight later, Earl Alfgar, ex-Mercia, arrived by way of the River Clwyd. He was accompanied by a large, blond, powerful young man whom he introduced as a son of Harald Hardraada of Norway, and by a dozen shiploads of Vikings, adventurers rounded up from Norway and the Orkneys and the Hebrides, come for the sport and the booty that might be won in the process of putting Alfgar back into power in Mercia.

Gruffyd said he would join in with the greatest of pleasure. He wasn't at all averse to pulling Harold's nose again, he said.

3 ※ Cup of Poison

"One day," said Harold to his wife Eadgyth, in a voice deceptively dispassionate, "I will, oh, I *will* grind Gruffyd ap Llewellyn's bones for flour and all the Welsh shall eat of the loaves I bake from it."

"What made you say that now?" enquired Eadgyth. She pushed up his tunic and clicked her tongue. "Take that off. And your shirt." Having got them off, she examined the damaged flesh beneath. There were six deep scratches and a number of unpleasant talon punctures. There was a vicious tear in the right forearm, too. She dusted her hands clean of flour, having been called from baking, and dipped a cloth into the hot water basin at her side.

"The flour on your hands," Harold said. "I think of Gruffyd nearly all the time, anyway. He haunts me. I wish I was a falconer instead of an earl. Life would be more peaceful."

"If it didn't end before time with blood poisoning," said Eadgyth, dabbing. "What happened?"

"That half-trained goshawk went for me when I was untangling his jesses. That water's hot!"

"I've got to clean it. I wish you'd wear armour when you train hawks! Some of these marks will scar." Eadgyth knelt, regardless of the straw on her skirts, to see better. "I'd have thought the man whose bones you want to grind would be Alfgar. He started it. And what about Magnus Haraldson and his gang of berserkers?"

"They're professional pirates, that's all." Harold shrugged off the Norwegian Vikings as impersonal perils, like storms at sea. "And as for Alfgar . . . he was once Earl of Mercia. I've been exiled myself and fought back, and lopped heads doing it. I don't blame him for fighting back. But I do blame Edward for letting him win— and letting Gruffyd win along with him." He spoke irritably. "Edward lost his nerve and bought the onslaught off. Danegeld, no less! Just as his father did before him. He's getting old, Eadgyth. Treasure for the Vikings, his earldom back for Alfgar—and for Gruffyd, a hearty laugh at our expense. Damn Gruffyd!"

Eadgyth applied unguent and said soothingly: "Gruffyd's a long way off. This is Saxmundham, my home and therefore yours." A spatter of rain on the thatch above made them glance up. "What a terrible August."

Harold laughed and let her coax him. Saxmundham Hall was a comforting place. In the rain outside, sky and fen would be blending now in universal wetness while harvesters ran swearing for cover and forlorn, dripping cattle sought the lee of farm buildings. If the August of 1058 produced a harvest fit to be called one at all, it would be a wonder. But in the hall a fire crackled cheerfully, heavy hangings muffled draughts, and a thrall was already going round with tapers to kindle a torch or two against the gloom. Eadgyth's children were tumbling happily at the other end of the hall, playing at sieges with a pile of benches as the fort. Children were always underfoot in this house; those of the thralls and servants as well as Eadgyth's. Harold liked it. It was like his boyhood home in Winchester, where Gytha had added another infant to the strength every year or two and one negotiated the main hall stepping over dogs and babies impartially.

Released at last from Eadgyth's ministrations, he pulled a table to him and pensively began to sharpen a quill. "I've been a sorry failure in the mews today. I think I'll write about how one should handle hawks, instead of demonstrating how one shouldn't. It's harder to write a book than I thought, Eadgyth. I keep forgetting things and having to go back to put them in." He began to turn over a pile of battered parchment leaves. Parchment was costly, but it could be scraped clean and reused and he was making his first rough draft on such sheets. Later he would make a fair copy on new ones. "I shall conquer Gruffyd one day," he said, dipping the quill, "just as I shall finish this book one day. I must wait my time. How long has our time been, Eadgyth? Since I brought you here?"

Eadgyth, who had waved a thrall into the kitchen to take over the baking, found a stool and picked a pair of her eldest son's hose out of the mending basket. "What *does* that boy Godwin do with his clothes? I'm thirty-five now, Harold." She counted on her fingers, dropping the damaged hose in her lap. "Fourteen years. I'm getting an old woman, love. No waist to be seen."

"Your hair would still set fire to a city. Or a man." Harold chuckled. "You set fire to poor Brand Woodcutter, didn't you? Eadgyth, you were a wicked wench. How could you treat him so badly?"

"You," said Eadgyth with tranquil unrepentance, taking up her needle, "were treating me badly. Only by flirting with him and making a tryst with him in your hearing could I get you to the point."

"And then I stepped in and you left him waiting in vain." He wrote two lines slowly and sat back to think them over. But went on talking instead. "Eadgyth, if I hadn't stopped you that night, would you have gone to Brand?"

"Yes. I might even have married him." Eadgyth turned a hose leg inside out.

"He was a good man," Harold said thoughtfully. "Braver than I am, I've come to think."

"I always liked him," Eadgyth agreed, "in spite of what he did to you all. He tried to put it right afterwards. That was why he sent his man Odi to be a messenger between your father and you. He minded what he'd done. I could see what made him do it, too. But why do you say braver?"

"I can't explain in words how to mend a hawk's tail feathers if they break," said Harold discontentedly. He scratched out what he had written. "I'll have to draw a picture . . . He was brave *because* of what he did to us, I think. He knew the truth about Gildenford. He knew my father betrayed Alfred Atheling. And he knew that Queen Emma was innocent. On one side of him was my father, to whom he owed all that he was, and to whom he had sworn secrecy. On the other side of him was Lady Emma. Not a nice woman . . ."

"No," agreed Eadgyth. "Not very."

". . . but innocent and accused. And old and sick and crying because no one would believe her. Brand made his choice. I should have chosen otherwise and kept my oath, but sometimes I wonder . . . what my reasons would have been."

"I don't understand that."

"I wonder," said Harold slowly, "if I would have kept faith because I thought it right, or because I feared to be called oath-breaker, feared to be an outcast? I think Brand broke his word knowing what its cost would be, but thinking it was right. Yes, I feel that . . . Though I sometimes think that if I came face to face with him, even now, I might well kill him at once! I don't know what I'd do. A divided loyalty is an ugly thing. What is it like, I wonder, to take an oath, which is a sacred thing, and be made to break it?"

"Cadell, you are lying," said the woman with the snapping black eyes, the hooked nose, and the incipient moustache. She turned to Gruffyd, presiding from his dais, his fingers for some reason closed convulsively on the arm-ends of his chair. "Never in seven whole years, never mind about less three days, have I shared his couch with him, the dog! A fine thing it would be if I had," cried the woman Gwenllian, "considering that that red-haired slut from Blaenau was on it already with him!"

Gruffyd recognised from the ensuing pause that it was now for him to speak. He must attend. On the far side of the hall, five minutes since, he had seen one of the bondmen—it was that sulky young Saxon, Osric—slouch in and tug at Wulfhild's sleeve, and Wulfhild had dropped her spindle and run. And he was sure, almost sure, that from the direction of Aldith's bower, he had heard a commotion. Feet, a door slamming, women's voices . . .

But this was a complex case. He shifted his gaze to the male half of the pair petitioning for divorce: the so-called liar, Cadell. Cadell was big and fleshy and scowling and only too ready to pick up the challenge his estranged spouse had hurled at him.

"Red-haired slut, is it? If I ever looked at a woman across the width of a river in flood, that makes her my mistress according to you, you jealous cow! And what of that shepherd, all muscles and good looks, you cast your eyes on? Once you get free of me, will you go after him? Well, he's welcome to you and your condescension!"

"*Condescension!*" shrieked his wife. "Oh yes, now we're at the heart of it. Always you've thrown that at me, so you have! My dowry and my cowyll gift between them add up to more than you've got or ever will have, you lazy brute; and my family's kin, what's more, to great folk in Deheubarth and to Lord Dafid of the Conwy

Valley here, and never have I heard the last of it! Jealous, am I? You're not jealous, then, oh no!"

"*Quiet!*" Gruffyd exploded. The door at the end of the hall had opened as someone came in, and the sound of female voices in the distance became momentarily clear. "You both know the law," he said. "If man and wife have not shared a bed in seven years all but three days, they may be declared free to remarry. The woman takes her dowry, her morning gift, and her personal possessions. The man takes the rest. But if they have lain together even once in all that time, their goods are divided equally. It seems, Gwenllian, that you will do better in the first case than the second and you swear that indeed you have not slept with your man in seven years. But he swears to the contrary. Now, do either of you wish to reconsider your oath-taking?"

Passionately, in furious antiphony, the pair averred that they did not. Cadell further declared, bawling over the top of Gwenllian's protests, that he had witnesses, and pointed dramatically to the audience, which included not only household guards and servants attached to Gruffyd, but other petitioners, and petitioners' kin and friends. A man came forward who was so plainly Cadell's brother that Gruffyd did not trouble to ask him his identity. Cadell, however, supplied the information unasked.

"This is Rhys, my brother, and six years back in the time when the Conwy flooded he stayed in my house three nights when he couldn't get home across the river. Rhys, say what you saw!"

"The first night I slept at my brother's house," said Rhys, "the two were separate, yes. Her up in the loft room and him on a pallet by the fireside, same as me. But the second night he said he was sick of being barred out by his wife as if he were nothing under his own roof and he went up the ladder and she didn't throw him down it."

"I wouldn't shame him before his own brother," said Gwenllian with arctic dignity. "But he slept on the old straw mattress up there and not with me."

". . . and later, I heard them laughing up there . . ."

"That's a foul, dirty lie! You've hated me, Rhys, since I turned you down before I wed your brother . . ."

"And a lucky escape I had of it too!" said her brother-in-law with energy. "But you and Cadell were together that night and the next till you quarrelled again and you flung out of your place to your sister's house, and I'll swear on the Rood to it and no fear of the fine for perjury. You'd best fear it yourself, woman!"

"Gwenllian, what witness have you to swear to your side of it?" Gruffyd demanded.

"I've not spent every night for seven years in company. Is not that the point?" Gwenllian was smouldering. "Even my sister is dead, God rest her soul, who could tell you what I told her when I ran to her for shelter—when I told her how this man who is my husband, God help me, has insulted and ill-used me. I have no witnesses. How can I have?"

Beyond the door, still open, a woman scurried across Gruffyd's line of vision with a steaming bowl, followed by another clutching linen. "Then in default of further evidence," he said, "I find it proven that you and Cadell did indeed bed together since the seven years began and that the goods must be divided according to custom. Half the land to each. The farm implements to him and the household goods to you. And of the rest, you must make two heaps of equal value and he shall take which he likes. And I will have an accounting of the value of your share, for there is, as Rhys says, a fine for perjury . . ."

He stopped, drowned out. Gwenllian had burst into violent speech. On a less distracting occasion he might have admired such an agile gift of invective. As it was, he couldn't be bothered with it, or her. He jerked his head and the guards closed in. "Take them to their house and see that the goods are split fairly. Bring me details."

Gwenllian, twisting to shout over her shoulder to him as she was removed, screamed: "I won't forget! I've powerful kin and I'm no perjurer! And Cadell's a liar and Rhys is worse! I'm cousin to . . ."

Her voice died away as she was hauled out. Gruffyd turned to his brother Rhiwallon, standing at his side. "Take over, Rhiwallon. I give you full authority. I've business elsewhere."

"I know. Aldith," said Rhiwallon, half teasing and half compassionate.

Gruffyd shook off the grip of the audience chamber with a physical movement like a dog ridding itself of water, and strode out of the hall. At the door of Aldith's bower he knocked for admittance. A woman's bower was her own domain, an institution which indignant wives sometimes used as a weapon against erring spouses, who might find themselves shut out, pending peace negotiations. Gwenllian had done something of the sort, with the upper room in her house.

But Aldith had never barred him out. There was a barrier this time, but it wasn't hers.

It was Alveva's.

He had sent for Alveva to come from Mercia, thinking that Aldith was young and might be frightened and that her mother would help her. He had already begun to regret it. Alveva clearly considered her daughter still a child under her control, while he, Gruffyd, was an outsider who had done his duty in siring the baby his wife now carried, and henceforth would be best out of the way. When Alveva urged him to stop worrying and go hunting, her voice had a ring of impatience which annoyed him. She had reduced him to stallion status and he resented it.

And here was Alveva, blocking his entrance. He could only get in by thrusting her aside, which would be rude. But from within came a small, disquieting whimpering which tugged at him. "Is that Aldith?" he asked brusquely.

"Aldith is quite all right and in safe hands," said his mother-in-law repressively. "Come, now. You're a father twice over already."

He was. And Bronwen had died of the second. "How long will . . . ?"

"Soon. The pains started early this morning and matters are now moving quickly. Everything is normal."

Wulfhild appeared at Alveva's shoulder. "My lady!" she said, on a note of urgency. The small sounds escalated into a wailing which made his scalp prickle and twisted up his stomach.

"I'm coming," said Alveva. "My lord, go and rest. I shall call you as soon as there is news. Don't be anxious."

She shut the door on him without pausing to see him go, and he heard her feet retreat briskly, tap tap tap, on the other side. He turned wretchedly away. He could have sat by Aldith and let her clutch his hand, couldn't he? What did they think he was going to do? Faint? Him? Gruffyd ap Llewellyn, veteran of battlefields? Women!

His dark-haired brother, Bleddyn, met him as he walked towards his own quarters, and began what Gruffyd considered an ill-timed protest about the judgement on Gwenllian. "I think she may appeal, and it's my opinion and Rhiwallon's too that she has cause; Cadell and Rhys have the faces of liars to our minds, and brothers they are when all's said and done." Bleddyn held up two fingers jammed tight together.

"And brothers you and Rhiwallon are, when all's said and done, and for ever making common cause against me. Get out of my way!" He brushed past Bleddyn and walked rapidly to his chamber. Berddig was there. He was playing dice with Berddig, a restless game with many silent pauses, when Alveva was announced, and he sprang up, dropping the dice. "Is it . . . ?"

"Your wife is well," said Alveva, hands linked at her middle, over a stained white apron. "Your child is well too. But I have to tell you that although healthy and properly formed . . ."

" 'Although healthy and properly formed'? What else is there to go wrong, woman?" He could have shaken her. "Green all over, is it? Or with a full set of teeth?"

"Of course not. But I have to tell you that it's a daughter."

"But that," cried Gruffyd, bounding forward to embrace the astonished Alveva, "is wonderful!"

"Your husband's an odd man," Alveva said.

Aldith peered at the baby she was nursing. The child, now firmly attached to her mother's nipple, had stopped crying. She was sucking contentedly with her transparent blue eyes shut. They would darken later, Alveva said. The tuft on top of the small head was jet black. Gruffyd had held her, marvelling at her. Her name should be Nest, he'd declared. It was a name he liked and had been saving for his first daughter. He had approved Aldith's unfashionable wish to be her own wet-nurse. He had pressed lavish gifts on every woman who was present at the birth, and had now gone to bespeak a feast for his court. He was aglow with joy. Alveva was flabbergasted.

"He was *pleased* to have a daughter," she explained to Aldith.

"He told me once," said Aldith, "that with two sons nearly grown, who never stopped arguing with him, he'd like a little girl this time if I could manage it." She had been surprised but relieved to hear that.

"I'm very glad, for your sake," Alveva said. "But I still advise you to have a boy next time. No man's patience lasts for ever. They like sons, all of them, at heart."

"It's hardly a thing I can control," said Aldith shortly. She held Nest closer. She was glad Nest's father was pleased with her. Indeed, had he not been, she, Aldith, would have had something to say about it. She had not expected, never dreamed of, the surge of love and tenderness and protectiveness that flooded through her when she held Nest for the first time, and she looked down into the miniature, shawl-framed face. Now, because her mother seemed to think Nest less than perfect, she eyed her mother askance.

Alveva did not notice. She was examining a pair of unfinished slippers, a man's size, on the stool at the bedside. The pattern was of entwined gold-thread dragons on a scarlet ground. The work was admirable—delicate and symmetrical as the patterning of frost on glass. "Are these for Gruffyd?"

"Yes, to go with his scarlet robe with dragons on it."

"Well, Aldith, I'm pleased with you. You have learned what I tried to teach you. I hear good reports of you here in Rhuddlan. You've been of help to some of the people, I believe."

"Oh, a little. I arranged for an old woman to have a pension, and found a foster home for an orphan. I couldn't get freedom for a Saxon thrall here, though. I tried, but Gruffyd refused. I don't think the thrall believed me. He looks the other way now when he sees me. It's one of the things Gruffyd's not reasonable about."

"There are always dozens of things men aren't reasonable about," said Alveva tartly. "Being unreasonable is a masculine gift." She studied her daughter searchingly. "How is it with you otherwise? I must go home soon. Your father is not well these days; he came home weary from his exile, and since then he has ailed a lot. If I can advise you in any way, tell me now."

Aldith thought about it, shifting her arm under Nest's sleepy weight. She was not sure that she wished to confide in her mother. They had never been close; now the gap was widening. But Wulfhild was the only other person she was near enough to ask, and Wulfhild here was no help; she seemed to think it didn't matter. But perhaps Wulfhild's partner or partners (one had certainly been the dove boy at Thetford, and Aldith suspected that Maredudd had now replaced him, but preferred not to enquire too closely) were not the same as Gruffyd.

She said: "There's something I don't understand."

"You can tell me. I'm your mother."

"When we lie together," Aldith said slowly, "he thinks . . . I should feel what he feels. But I don't know what that is. It's neither here nor there with me. All the time, he waits and watches for a sign from me. And I don't understand what it is he *wants!*"

"Oh, is that all?" Alveva looked amused. "You'll just have to act. It's quite simple. Men are very peculiar. Give them the sun and the moon and they'll cry for the stars as well. All you have to do is this . . ."

4 ❧ Cup of Rue

"A mountain house is a good lookout," Wulfhild said. "We'll see them coming a long way off."

Aldith craned over the low wall of the Llanberis lodge, as if trying to see past the bend of the zigzag track below. "Yes. I like the mountain country. Do you?"

Wulfhild examined the rugged distances thoughtfully. Her expression changed little. It rarely did. "No, not much."

"Why? Are you homesick?"

"N . . . no. But Wales is so . . . foreign."

"It's my land now," Aldith said. "Wulfhild, if you're unhappy here . . ."

"I'm not unhappy," said Wulfhild, definitely and with the air of one who closes a door. It was never any use trying to probe Wulfhild's emotions. Either she had none to speak of, or she guarded them too well. Her peasant childhood was the cause, perhaps. Peasants couldn't afford fine feelings. "There are horsemen below," she said.

It was a brilliant May afternoon, the air washed by early rain and left to sparkle when the sun came out. It was a year since Aldith and Gruffyd had ridden to the Cwmanog; and behind the lodge, carefully tended by a hand-picked thrall, the coltsfoot and horehound were flourishing. Early this morning, Aldith had gathered coltsfoot, and bay and rosemary too, for the venison that would welcome Gruffyd home from Deheubarth. And down there in the valley, now, the spear points of his escort were glinting. "Half an hour," Aldith said, estimating the distance. "I wonder if he'll think Nest has grown?"

"Well, she has," said Wulfhild. "He hasn't seen her since she was a month old, and she's three months now. They grow fast at that age." She glanced to where the baby lay asleep in the wheeled, out-of-doors cradle which Maredudd and his brother, Idwal, had made for their half-sister.

Aldith stepped back from the wall. "I must go and see that the dinner's in order. I'm not sure the cook understood how much honey to put in the cakes and . . ."

"He ought to," said Wulfhild, "or he wouldn't be in charge of Prince Gruffyd's kitchen, not even in a hunting lodge. He can be trusted. Come to your bower. You should be making yourself ready, not worrying about honey cakes."

When the procession, which was slowed down by mules and waggons and took longer than the predicted half-hour to arrive, eventually reached the lodge gate, Aldith was ready in the way that Wulfhild considered right. Wulfhild had worked hard. The red lights in her mistress's hair had been burnished to combustion point and cunningly arranged so that a shining wave escaped from the green, silver-embroidered veiling round Aldith's head. Her long underskirt was of amber silk and the overtunic was of green and silver like the veil. Wulfhild had also striven hard with Aldith's eyebrows, plucking them into shape.

"Your own could do with it more than mine," Aldith said, laughing at Wulfhild's heavy brows.

"I haven't got a husband," said Wulfhild severely.

Gruffyd leapt out of his saddle and embraced his wife with an enthusiasm which justified all the toil of presentation. "My lovely Aldith! Supple as a sapling! I've been trying to massage the stiff necks of the damned Deheubarth nobles for weeks. What a blessed improvement on them you are, my love."

"Whatever are all these waggons and pack mules for?" asked Aldith. "Did you plunder the nobles because you were cross with their stiff necks?"

"No, no! We'd be at war with them by now if I had. No, I made a quick visit to the eastern Marches before I came home, to a village called Kington. Used to be in Mercia, but it came to me when your father won back from exile the first time . . ."

"I remember," Aldith said.

"Its May Day dues were ready, so I picked them up myself as a homecoming gift for you. There are wool bales there, wine casks, cattle hides, cured pork, and iron ingots—all yours to use or dispose of as you like. As a matter of fact, that village once belonged to King Edward, so you can call the revenues a real royal gift."

"What a generous present!" said Aldith, appreciatively.

They went into the hall, where apple boughs burned sweetly and the floor was strewn with fresh yellow straw which the hounds had not as yet had time to infuse with dogginess. Gruffyd's companions tramped in after him: Berddig, majestic as ever; Prince Rhiwallon, typically gorgeous in garments of turquoise and tawny; dark-haired Prince Bleddyn in more sombre clothes. Gruffyd, in moments of disenchantment with them, had been heard to call the latter two the Kingfisher and the Crow.

The steward came to greet the returning travellers, and respectful hands collected cloaks and gloves. The arrivals crowded round the hearth in a cheerful bass flurry of laughter and Welsh talk. They were disputing as they often did; Aldith understood enough of the cascading speech to know that. But it was good-humoured this time. She had seen Gruffyd and Rhiwallon roll on the floor pummelling each other at times, when it was not. And if Bleddyn was calmer than Rhiwallon, with arguments more reasonable, that very reasonableness at times maddened Gruffyd. On one memorable occasion, when wrangling about the likely numbers of men in the English border garrisons, he had flung a hammer at Bleddyn's head. "And your aim is as bad as your arithmetic," said Bleddyn, infuriatingly unmoved as the missile sailed past his ear; and they hadn't spoken to each other for the next three days.

But the talk now was of Deheubarth, and the latest grumbles of the dispossessed Caradoc, a subject on which they were in comparative accord. Aldith sat near Gruffyd, hands folded round her knees, following as best she could. Presently, the topic of Caradoc exhausted, he turned to her and asked her in Welsh how she had passed the two months of his absence. She managed to answer in the same tongue, albeit slowly and with grammatical errors.

"I've cared for Nest. She grows fast and her voice with her. I've made a gift for you, to give you later. I've arranged a feast, and taught the cook new dishes. I was not idle."

Gruffyd laughed. She thought he looked tired. "You never are. I know that."

"Oh, and we have new hangings in our bedchamber. But I did not waste the old ones. I put them . . ."

"My love," said Gruffyd, stretching back in the chair in which he was letting saddle-weary bones gratefully collapse, "never mind about the old ones. I can carry the expense even if you gave them to the poor or burnt them for fuel. I'm sure you found something appropriate to do with them. Did you miss me, *merched*?"

Aldith, drawing breath for further recitals of domestic activities, stopped short. "Oh yes, of course!"

Gruffyd grinned. "I'm glad to hear it."

"I started them before Nest was born," Aldith said. "I hope they fit. I used your old blue ones as a model. The soles are doeskin."

The May sunset shone fierily through the unshuttered window of the bedchamber, adding a new dimension of colour to the red-and-gold slippers Aldith was fitting to Gruffyd's feet. The sky in the west was a sheet of flame, with mountains standing stark against it. A nightingale had begun to sing somewhere, its notes falling as purely as the notes of Berddig's harp had fallen by the hearthside after the feast.

"They fit to perfection," said Gruffyd, and leant down, his red bedrobe and its golden dragons stretched taut over his broad shoulders, to take her face in his square brown hands. "What a little beaver it is. All this trouble for my common old feet with their big knuckles."

Aldith smiled. "But that sort of trouble is my proper business. Will you walk in them?"

He rose and went to shutter the window. She watched him, taking pleasure in his strongly knit and compact form, awaiting his return with serenity. She had listened carefully to her mother's instructions. This time, when she felt that urgent, questing body of his asking its persistent questions, she would know the answers.

So his anger, not twenty minutes later, was doubly terrifying, so utterly was it the reverse of the expected. It was as if the sunset had turned to real fire and set the thatch alight. She did not even recognise it as anger at first. When he flung himself away from her she thought he had overbalanced. Then she saw his face, and her own grew stiff with fear.

"It's just a task, isn't it?" he said. He said it at first in Welsh and she, paralysed with horror, visibly failed to understand him. So he repeated it in English. He spoke through his teeth. "Just a task. *Just another duty*! Like embroidering slippers and changing the hangings and cutting up honey cakes to look like stags!"

Aldith's mouth opened and shook. But she could think of nothing to answer, because the accusation made no sense.

"You look like a trapped hare, waiting for the jug," he said scornfully, and thrust his feet down to the floor. He reached for his old blue slippers. "Don't be afraid. I wouldn't hurt anything so pathetic and bewildered and dutiful!"

Aldith struggled to wipe the fright off her face and to some extent succeeded. "What are you talking about?"

He swung round to face her again. "By the Face of God, don't you know? You were pretending, weren't you? Acting! Making a fool of me. Who told you to fool me? Who told you to pretend?"

Anger came to Aldith's rescue. A temper occasionally served instead of courage, she had learnt that long ago. "There's no need to insult me! You can save your abuse! I wanted to please you. Since when was that a crime?"

"And you thought *that* would please me? That . . . that *performance*? The act that whores in harbour taverns put on for their clients?"

"I wouldn't," said Aldith with furious dignity, "know how whores in harbour taverns—or anywhere else—please their clients. You do, obviously!"

Gruffyd seized her shoulders. "Who told you to do it? *Who*?"

Aldith glared at him. Her anger now was like a fire in her stomach, sending up waves of heat to enflame her brain. She put a foot on his chest and shoved with all her might and he lost his grip and lurched backwards. "I asked my mother's advice!" she shouted.

"Your *mother*—that man-hating bitch—yes, that explains it!"

"My mother," said Aldith, proceeding from the torrid to the glacial in a single sentence, "taught me my duty."

"God's Teeth! *Duty*!" He snatched up his robe. "I'll leave you. You'll want Nest in here to feed her. It won't look odd if I sleep elsewhere." Tying his girdle, he added a parting volley, his eyes round and hard. "Duty isn't the universe, didn't you know? You order my house but who ordered it before you came? Any of my stewards could do it without you, and maybe better. Embroider my slippers? If I crook my little finger I can have an army of embroidresses fighting for the privilege, and every woman of them more gifted at it than you. And I don't need you to guide me in tactful acts of charity either, and I don't need secondhand imitations of love!"

"Then what *do* you need?" demanded Aldith, sitting upright, her feet curled beside her on the bed and her hands tightly clasped.

"Oh God, what's the use? If you had it to give, I wouldn't have to ask for it, would I now? Good night, Aldith. If you find it hard to sleep, try thinking."

"If you'd simply tell me . . ."

He paused, hand on door latch. The anger was dying out of his eyes. "I'm in my forties," he said. "And you . . . I forget, so housewifely and earnest you are . . . that you're so young. Seventeen, isn't it? How can I burden you with demands you can't understand, even? I want the moon, Aldith, and the sun and the stars and the firmament they're set in, and it isn't fair. Not fair to you, I mean. I did hope—for that we went to the Cwmanog—but . . ."

"Went to the Cwmanog?" said Aldith. She had got used to making an effort to understand Welsh, but when even English became unintelligible it was as though the ground underfoot had turned to water. The only lucid part of Gruffyd's sentence seemed to be a confirmation of her mother's statement that men wanted the stars as well as the sun and the moon. Except that Gruffyd appeared to think this a reasonable desire. She wanted to cry with despair. How could one ever build a life with a man who talked such nonsense?

"I've half a mind to go again and chuck an iron ingot or two in their bloody pool," said Gruffyd, with what she dimly recognised as a species of battlefield humour. "They hate iron. My revenge it'd be, for not keeping their bargain. It isn't your fault, Aldith. I'm not angry now. Sleep well."

In the morning he rode away again. He had work to do, he said, along the Marches. He would come back, he said. Eventually.

5 ✵ Cup of Sorrow

Aldith adjusted the angle of the silver mirror she held before her face. She held out a hand and Wulfhild put the eyebrow tweezers into it. Aldith looked after her own eyebrows now that she had learned the art. Comb, veil, and pins were already in place. There were guests to impress at Rhuddlan this evening.

The silver mirror gave a soft and wavery reflection, but it was clear enough to show the difference between the girl who had come to Rhuddlan for her wedding and the young woman who sat here four years later. An adult face looked from the mirror now, the wonder gone from the brown eyes and the dewiness gone from the mouth. There was command in this face and the mouth was strongly cut, lips a little compressed. Sometimes, not too happily, Aldith recognised her mother in that face. She knew she looked older than twenty.

Feet pattered, accompanied by a flutter of feminine voices. "Now, now, Nest, my chicken, you mustn't run into your mother's room and not knock, not even you. There's naughty now!"

"Daddy coming!" announced Nest triumphantly, evading her nurse's grasp and darting to Aldith to climb on her lap. The nurse, Myfanwy, middle-aged and a believer in propriety, clucked in disapproval.

Eiluned, the rotund, merry little woman who was the much-petted wife of Prince Bleddyn, had come in with Myfanwy. "A messenger has come," she said in slow Welsh. Aldith still preferred to be

181

addressed without haste. "He had a tired horse. Muddy it was and foam on its flanks."

"Nice *gwyn* horse," said Nest happily. She was mastering the art of bilingual speech but with little sign of awareness that it *was* bilingual.

They would have to separate the languages for her soon, Gruffyd said, but he never did anything about it beyond laughing helplessly at his daughter's mixed-up sentences, and singing lullabies to her with the lines in alternate languages, to Aldith's exasperation. "Nice *white* horse, dear," she corrected Nest patiently, and straightened the veil anew. She wished to do Gruffyd credit at the feast.

He had returned six weeks after that sudden, angry departure to the Marches. They had gone on together, carefully, not quarrelling again. Alveva had been right in one thing: failing treachery or infidelity, Aldith's position as princess was unassailable. They resumed their marriage bonds, with no more pretence at passion from her, or demands for it from him. Gingerly, they shaped a new relationship. They discussed affairs of the realm, the education of Nest. The escapades of Wulfhild and Maredudd, who were now constant companions, provided subjects for laughter. These two had invented a new pastime, of abstracting pigeons from the dovecot, riding out with them, and seeing whose bird got home first. Some never arrived at all, which annoyed the dovecot keeper. "How's the feud between Wulfhild and the dove-keeper?" Gruffyd would say, returning from a journey. It was possible, he and Aldith found, to keep their conversations smooth and continuous without ever touching on themselves.

In time, although their unions were not now frequent, Aldith became pregnant again and this time bore a boy. Alveva—not on this occasion called on to assist—sent gifts and congratulations. Six months later both the baby and Nest fell ill with bronchial coughs. The horehound that Aldith was so insistent should be grown at Llanberis cured Nest. But little Llewellyn, who had ailed from birth, succumbed. Gruffyd comforted his wife, saying he had two fine sons already and that Aldith at least had Nest, and she was glad of his gentleness. They could have other children. Gruffyd was a good husband, she thought. She was fortunate. Marriage was a comfortable estate after all, now that the queer volcanic disturbances of its early days had ceased.

So it was a calm and gracious Aldith, an epitome of the well-bred wife, who put down the mirror and rose as Gruffyd entered in his daughter's wake. He came straight to her, nodding only briefly to the other ladies. His face was grave; Aldith saw it and checked her smile of welcome. He lifted Nest up, greeted her perfunctorily, and handed her to Myfanwy. "Leave us," he said to the gathering in general.

"What is it?" Aldith asked as they went out.

"I'm sorry," said Gruffyd. "Seat yourself. A messenger rode in from Mercia a short time ago . . ."

"Eiluned saw him."

"How does one find soft words for bad news? Your father, Earl Alfgar, is dead."

Grief, Aldith found, was unpredictable. She hadn't seen her father for more than two years and she had never been very close to him, any more than she was to her mother. But now she didn't know what to do with a world in which he was not. She knelt in the chapel as the warm June evening closed in, and could not even find words to pray for him, so impossible it was to think that he was dead.

A soft step heralded Wulfhild's coming. "Is the feast over?" Aldith asked.

She need not attend it, Gruffyd had said. So she had come here instead. She wished to be alone and had sent Wulfhild to the hall to eat her own dinner. Since Wulfhild had now reappeared, the banquet must be finished. It must be late.

"I've made you a tisane," said Wulfhild, offering the steaming cup she held. "It's herbs, not wine. It won't make you drowsy if you want to keep vigil all night. Shall I stay with you? Prince Gruffyd wouldn't want you to stay here all night alone."

Aldith nodded. She sipped the tisane, which was warm and aromatic; it cleared her head. She saw that the sky beyond the slit windows was dimming and the corners of the little stone chapel were vanishing into shadow. She finished the tisane and knelt once more. Wulfhild knelt with her.

"I can't imagine him . . . dead," Aldith said presently.

"It happens. My mother died. I couldn't understand it, either, at first. Lady Eadgyth took me to say goodbye to her and I couldn't understand why she wouldn't open her eyes or speak to me. But it happens."

"Yes." It did. Death was a commonplace. It could strike anyone at any time. You could be healthy one day, feverish the next, and dead on the third. It had been so with her father, Gruffyd said. A short illness, such as he had often had during the last few years. But this time it had worsened suddenly, and now her father had gone into nowhere and she couldn't believe it.

Perhaps he hadn't gone into nowhere. It might be worse than that.

They said the dead went to Heaven or at least, unless they had been very wicked, to purgatory, to cleanse themselves enough to enter the company of the saints and angels. But some, the greatest sinners, went to the fires of Hell. "I hope he isn't . . ." she began hesitantly, and for the first time since Gruffyd had brought the news, the tears welled up in her. "I must pray for him, Wulfhild, I must ask the saints to intercede. He wasn't . . . wasn't a very good man. Did you know that?"

"He was a brave one," said Wulfhild. Her blue eyes regarded her mistress kindly. Wulfhild, with those eyes and the high cheekbones, must have Viking blood somewhere, Aldith thought. She would honour a valiant man, good or not. "He fought well to restore himself from exile," Wulfhild said. "You can be proud of that."

"I am. I didn't mean . . . He was my father and it makes no difference to me whether he was good or not. But God might care."

"I never had a father," Wulfhild stated, "or if I have, he's never acknowledged me. So I don't know how one feels. But why do you say he wasn't a good man? He was kind to me."

Aldith wiped her eyes. "It's because . . . Wulfhild, the reason why I want to stay here all night is because of something he once did. If I tell you, will you pray for him too?"

"I'll pray for him, anyway. Don't tell me more, unless you wish to."

But Aldith did wish to. The silence and the deepening night outside the candlelit chapel had made it a place for confidences, as if it were a confessional. She needed to talk. She needed to talk of her father. And since she spoke of him at all, she must speak of the thing that hurt her most in his death, that made her fear for him in the hereafter. "He had something to do with Edward Edmundson's death," she whispered. "I overheard. I was in the next room and the wall was thin. It was at Thetford, the night he returned from exile, the first time. You were there too but not by the wall . . . I think he sent a man to . . . kill the Atheling. It was someone he could force to go, something to do with that false silver that caused his exile in the first place. He got the silver from Thane Redwald, but he'd found out who passed it to Redwald in the first place. Poor Redwald!" Aldith smiled tremulously. "He wanted to be modern and accept silver for his goods, but he was never really used to handling coin. So few people ever paid him in it. People say that Edward Edmundson died of illness, but I know what I overheard. And I know my father wanted William of Normandy to be Atheling too, because my mother is Norman and my uncle important at the Norman court. Now do you see why he needs our prayers?"

"Shall we tell a rosary for him? Together?"

Their voices murmured on. Outside, a wind rose and the altar candles smoked and streamed. At midnight, they heard the outer door creak. Aldith turned.

Gruffyd, still in the velvet and garnets of his banquet dress, came quietly across the flag-stoned floor towards the altar. "Eiluned said you were still here."

With consideration, he had removed the grosser traces of what had probably been a bibulous feast. There was wine on his breath, but his head had been in cold water. The black hair was as flat to the scalp as if painted there. "Are you staying through the night?"

"Yes. You don't object?"

"By no means. But shall I watch with you? Wulfhild can go to her bed."

Aldith hesitated. Wulfhild remained quiet. "You have an audience in the morning," Aldith said to her husband at length. "I cannot ask you to stay awake all night. Wulfhild will take care of me. But thank you."

"I would comfort you if I could, but what words can do that?" Gruffyd said.

"None," said Aldith. "No words can make him be alive again. He's dead and now there is nothing I can do except keep the vigil and pray for his soul. He wasn't . . ." But no. The confidence she could give to her childhood friend she could not give to this man who was in so many ways still a stranger. She amended the phrase. ". . . he wasn't anything but a good father to me. I loved him."

"Goodnight," said Gruffyd gently. And still treading very softly, he went out.

The sparrow hawk, Harold wrote, in the slow, detailed calligraphy his old priest-tutor had taught him long ago, *most frequently kills on the wing but can also be caught with bait.* He raised his eyes to the evidence, the beautiful female sparrow hawk on the perch at his side. She was not big, but she regularly caught larks, and sometimes larger game, for his table and he was as proud of her as he was of any of his bigger hawks, his goshawks and his peregrine and the great gerfalcon that an Icelandic nobleman had given him. He dipped his quill again and wondered what it would really be like to be a hawkmaster with only his mews to worry about, instead of an earldom; or, to be a clerk, to whom calamity was a blotted piece of vellum instead of a lost battle. It might well, he thought, be extraordinarily restful.

His apartment in the king's Gloucester residence was quiet. A young page, permanently tired as these boys often were from rising at dawn and running errands all day, dozed in a corner, technically on duty. But his other servants had leave and were probably dicing or gossiping with their friends. It was July, but disagreeable. A low, greyish-yellow sky lay on the hills and a muggy drizzle persistently ran from it. But the bad weather at least gave him an excuse to work at his slowly growing treatise. Ten minutes later, the sound of Tostig's voice was an interruption.

He didn't show it, however. Not with Tostig. The chill that had fallen between them when Edward Atheling died had been more or less dispersed by Gytha, certainly. "Tostig, don't be an *utter* fool!" she said indignantly when Tostig unwisely voiced his doubts, and he had ceased from voicing them. But, for his mother's sake if not his own, Harold had since then judged it wise to cultivate Tostig a little.

He raised his head, therefore, at his brother's entrance. "What brings you here?" He couldn't resist an oblique criticism. "I thought you were bound for Northumbria soon?"

"Edith asked me to stay longer."

"Who controls your wild thanes while you hunt with the court?"

"They control each other," said Tostig. Square and jaunty in blue and saffron, thick yellow hair bright as topaz in the dull afternoon, he looked very much alive and equal to any number of turbulent earldoms or truculent thanes. "I have a nephew of Thane Gamel's here at court with me, and Thane Gospatric as well, in person. Gamel and Gospatric were causing much of the trouble in my earldom. Control them, and the trouble subsides. The ones left behind keep watch on each other for fear of getting dragged into fighting which might make me injure their relatives here. Gospatric is holding a bear-baiting in his quarters now. Coming?"

"In his guesthouse?" Harold shouted with laughter. "If he's got a bear and a pack of dogs and an audience all jammed in there, the walls will burst. Why doesn't he bring the bear to the hall, where we can all see the fun in comfort?"

"The king's in the hall with half a dozen prelates and the plans of the West Minster, discussing completion dates. He won't allow interruptions. What's that you're doing?"

"Writing a treatise on hawks." He turned over the pile of parchment leaves. "Trying to get things in order . . . I must rewrite this bit about studying the habits of hawks before trying to catch them. I want to put in examples, of real hawks that were caught after being observed beforehand."

"You've more patience than I have. I couldn't sit down for hours with a pen like you and I don't much enjoy catching and training hawks, either. Takes too long."

"It's like outwitting an enemy, in a way," said Harold thoughtfully. "Except that you don't want to kill the hawk . . . I must use those words in the book, I think. Now, if I could have watched Gruffyd as I did my sparrow hawk, and got to understand him as I did her, I might have brought that gentleman down to my fist long ago. Maybe I will yet."

"Gruffyd," said Tostig consideringly, finding this a topic more engrossing than authorship or the training of hawks. He whistled a few notes of a popular war song and wandered about the room, picking objects up and putting them down, as if thinking. "Since Aldred was made Archbishop of York two years ago," he said, "he hasn't had much time to look after the Marches. Bishop Wulfstan of Worcester is a very saintly man but not much use with a sword. Aldred is worried about what will happen now that Alfgar's dead. He told Edward that, not long ago. The king agreed, but he didn't suggest doing anything about it. What do you think?"

"That Gruffyd is an enemy and always was and always will be, and that you're right. Alfgar was a check who is now gone. Gruffyd respected his father-in-law's territory, but Edwin Alfgarson may be less of a restraint. Edwin's only in his teens; he's never been Gruffyd's friend as his father was, and may not be close to his sister either. It's getting very dark in here."

Tostig glanced at the sleeping page and moved to wake him, but Harold shook his head. The Earl of Wessex rose and went quietly to kindle a torch himself. He struck flint and lit a taper, and the flame of it illuminated his features from below, showing the strong nose, etching the prominent cheekbones, and making dark pits of eye sockets and nostrils. It was a face withdrawn into thought. "I should like to pay Gruffyd's bill before it gets any longer," he said, and touched the flame to a torch waiting in its bracket.

"Settle an old quarrel?" Tostig looked at his brother as light sprang up in the room. "Attack without provocation?"

"We can't do that." Harold sat down again. "But . . . ."

They stared at each other, struck by the same thought at the same time, as if telepathically. "You say you wished you could catch Gruffyd by watching his habits, as you would with a hawk. But you must have learned something about him over the years. Surely . . ."

"You mean learned exactly what, other than taking up arms openly, might irritate him?"

"Yes. And if we were ready beforehand . . ."

"For instance," said Harold, laying down the spent taper, "there were some things not specifically mentioned when we gave the border lands to Gruffyd in 1056. He has interpreted them as he likes. Suppose we challenged his interpretation?"

"Tell me," said Tostig, "exactly what you have in mind."

It would require Edward's consent. Others of the Witan would have to be consulted too. But few had cared for Edward's surrender over Alfgar's reinstatement. More people regarded Gruffyd as a menace than thought of him as a good neighbour. It shouldn't be hard to convince them.

They sought Edward out when he had finished with his prelates. It was one of those moments, for Harold, when a familiar face is suddenly, briefly, seen anew as if it were a stranger's countenance. He looked at Edward's pale and hollowed features, the fragility of the long bones and spare body, the transparency of the white skin, and saw that the king, indeed, was growing old. He wouldn't take overmuch persuading, either.

The most remarkable features of campaign preparation, Aldith considered, were the uproar and the smells it generated.

Rhuddlan, as an erupting Gruffyd made ready to show the impertinent English to whom the revenues of the village of Kington now rightfully belonged, had become a nightmare of noise and noisesomeness. The regular forge was working from dawn to nightfall, augmented by half a dozen temporary ones, that armour might be fashioned and horses shod and sword blades tempered, and all day long the air shuddered to the clang of hammers and the wheeze of bellows, to the hiss of water on white-hot metal and the neighing and clattering and shouting of horses and men. Nor was there one corner left which was pleasing to the nose. Smoke from the furnaces. Scorching horn. The appalling reek of boiling glue from the small army of fletchers who lived in tents behind the chapel, tipping arrows and fitting flight feathers to bushel after bushel of shafts. Leather and horse flesh and urgency. The nostril-distending scent of war.

Not that Aldith or her ladies had much time to brood. They had work to do too. Meat must be salted and packed in barrels, cheeses packed likewise, poultry bought and cooped ready to travel on muleback with the army. Grain must be ground and flour sacks filled. For folded hands there was no time.

Besides, she had to make it clear whose side she was on. Gruffyd's target was Mercia.

It was an easier choice than she expected. Daughter of an earl, reared to understand the eternal shifting and manoeuvring for power which were an earl's existence, she knew why Gruffyd was going to war. She knew he could not do otherwise.

It was a shame that the start of this dispute had spoilt that happy day in August . . .

The end of August, it had been, and they were in Rhuddlan as they were now. It was a blue, sunny morning, with Gruffyd in the hall preparing to go hunting and playing with Nest, both at once. He was sitting in his chair, with one foot stuck out for his man to cross-garter his leggings, caressing a hound with one hand, bouncing

Nest on his knee, and singing her a hunting song that was also a game, which she adored:

"When your father hunted the land,
"Spear on shoulder, club in hand,
"Thus his speedy dogs he'd teach:
"Giff gaff catch her, catch her, fetch!"

On the last line he tossed Nest up with his spare hand and caught her with the appropriate words. Aldith laughed at them, and Berddig, already dressed for the hunt, said: "That was first sung four hundred years ago. I wonder who'll sing it when we hold the minstrels' contest I'm planning for next year? Someone always does sing it, at every bards' gathering." And then a page ran in, and said there was an English thane to see Gruffyd.

"Oh yes, bring him in. Let him share the hunt if he likes," said Gruffyd cheerfully. But a moment later he saw, they all saw, that the thane, gold-ornamented and dressed to impress, had an escort of twenty full-armed men, and was not smiling as he crossed the hall; and the hall grew very still.

The thane brought a rolled parchment with King Edward's seal swinging from it. He bowed and presented it. Gruffyd undid it, frowning. He read it carefully to the end. Then he rolled up the parchment, kicked away the man who was still working on his leggings, and struck the royal messenger across the face with the message.

The swinging seal scored the thane's forehead and behind him his escort jerked, making a concerted move towards its weapons. But he snapped: "Stand!" And they stood, unwilling but obedient, like hounds forbidden the scent. The thane bowed again, insultingly, and turned without speaking and went.

They heard departing horses. And in the hall, brandishing the royal message as if it were a burning brand, Gruffyd bellowed commands. The message, he shouted, stated that henceforth the dues of Kington village were to revert to King Edward, that indeed they had never been anyone else's, that Gruffyd's administration of the land as Edward's vassal did not alter that, although King Edward would graciously . . . "God's Teeth, what big-heartedness! Big as a needle point!" yelled Gruffyd . . . would not demand repayment of the back-dated dues in the six years since 1056.

Gruffyd, with his sons and Berddig and three hundred men, was in the saddle and riding for Kington in an hour.

They came back empty-handed and beside themselves. Three hundred or three, it made no difference. Harold had got there first, skilfully timing his descent. The end-of-summer dues, the grain and honey and fat bull calves, were already over the English border.

"And this," Gruffyd thundered to his gathered nobles in the hall, "I will not stomach! I hold Kington and have done homage for it and what it produces is mine! And," he added, more thoughtfully, "there are certain trade agreements, too, which the English have tried to twist to their advantage. I would have let that pass . . . but not now or there'll be no end to it!" He paced the hall, thinking aloud. "Kington is a Mercian village, or was. The Mercian nobles knew of this and permitted it, since Harold rode through their lands to get there. Very well. The easiest town of Mercia to reach from here is Chester. I shall take back the value of the Kington revenues from Chester, and that with addition for interest. If the English turn thieves, I shall turn usurer." He looked to where his wife, Aldith, sat with Wulfhild at her side. He met her eyes and for a moment spoke to her only. "My apologies, Aldith, that my sword must be unsheathed in Mercia. Choose now if you will be Lady of Mercia or Lady of Wales, for by God you cannot be both. Which is it to be?"

"I am Lady of Wales," said Aldith and said it without even stopping to think. But within minutes, the hidden workings of her own mind were made plain to her, because Gruffyd repeated them aloud for her. For if Aldith was not against him, others were and he had to answer them.

"Would it not be better," said Rhiwallon, surprisingly for that impulsive redhead, "to send a formal protest to King Edward? There may be a mistake."

"I have sent a protest," said Gruffyd coldly. "Across the messenger's forehead. I doubt if Edward will heed it. The sacking of Chester may be more effective."

"Yes," said Bleddyn soberly, "it could bring the might of England over our borders in revenge. Let us think about it first."

Aldith looked at the brothers in astonishment. But Gruffyd looked at them with fury. He marched over to them and stood, arms akimbo, glaring at them. "God's Teeth, what is it you want me to do? Mistakes, you talk about mistakes! A pity you were not with me when I rode to Kington! There's no mistake. Earl Harold was laughing at me all the time he was in that village, they tell me. The terms of the treaty with Edward are plain. This is an encroachment and unless I resist there will be another and another till I must fight or dwindle, and no man worthy of the name will dwindle and say nothing! What is it, the two of you? Afraid?"

Rhiwallon turned crimson but held his temper in. "Suicide," he said with commendable coolness, "is a sin."

"*Suicide!*"

"Chester lies deep in Mercia and it is strong," said Bleddyn, although a chorus in support of Gruffyd had started among the other nobles, including Berddig, who was staring at the brothers with a shocked expression as if they were leaking sawdust. "We risk getting cut off. Remember, the English may expect an attack. I agree with Rhiwallon: we must think first. This may be a ploy to tempt us to rashness. Don't look so scandalised, my lord Berddig. Do you want this crazy venture? I thought you were all afire with your latest minstrels' contest and sending invitations out to half Christendom. That's all gone, if we go to war with Mercia."

"Another time will do for that," retorted Berddig. "If my lord goes to war, I go with him."

"If you've no thought for the people of Wales," said another voice, supporting the brothers, "what of the lady Aldith? She has declared for you as a good wife should, but Mercian she is for all that and her brother is Earl of Mercia now. For her sake, man, hold back!"

Gruffyd gave Aldith a quick, permissive glance. She accepted the permission and answered Dafid of Conwy herself. "My brother should not have allowed Earl Harold access into Kington. I am with my husband in this."

"Thank you, my dear," said Gruffyd. "See, Dafid of Conwy? She is not timid like you." He stood with feet apart, rocking from heels to toes, arms now folded. His round eyes were fixed on Dafid and Dafid had gone white at the insult. He was as fair and angular as Gruffyd was dark and stocky; they looked as if they were born to be opposites. "Tell me," said Gruffyd sweetly. "If I let this provocation go on, what sort of a husband would my wife have then? A skulking nithing, indeed to goodness, afraid to defend his rights and soon with none to defend, I should think. What place in the world would she have then? Tell me that!"

"This is improper!" said Bleddyn with energy. "The lady Aldith has spoken in her husband's support. She is not to be used as a tool, Dafid. But Rhiwallon has the right of it. Send an embassy to King Edward, my lord. There are channels . . ."

"Channels! And what will come floating through them but oily talk that means nothing? Will ships bearing my dues from Kington sail to me on them, I wonder?" He turned to the rest of his nobles, drew his sword and pointed it at the rafters. "Who comes to Chester with me? Do I have to go alone? Answer me!"

Six, ten, a dozen, twenty swords were drawn in reply and a score of voices roared that he should have company. Triumphant, he laughed at the objectors. "There's your answer, my handsome brothers, my *cautious* Dafid! Now will you change your minds?"

"Even you," said Dafid grimly, "aren't infallible, my lord. I never sued you in the matter of Gwenllian my kinswoman, though that was an error of judgement and one that should shame you . . ."

"What the devil has Gwenllian to do with the revenues of Kington?"

"Nothing," said the fair man, "except as proof that you are not always perfect in the choices you make, my lord."

It was unfortunate for Dafid that compared to Gruffyd's rumbling bass, his voice was thin. It made his arguments sound weak too. Gruffyd bellowed at him and Dafid's protests were lost. "Words, Dafid, nothing but words. A word shield to hide your shrinking ladylike soul, that's frightened of the fight! Get out of my hall, Dafid, faint-heartedness is catching. I don't want an epidemic of it here. And you, Rhiwallon and Bleddyn, go with him or else come with me. Make up your minds!"

Dafid's pallor, already deep enough, became terrifying, the whiteness of a shock and anger so deep that a man in their grip might equally faint or kill. He went out of the hall, walking slowly and mechanically, like a toy whose limbs are moved by strings.

Berddig, watching him go, said: "It was a mistake to taunt him, I think. He is not timid."

Gruffyd did not appear even to hear. He had apparently forgotten Dafid at once and had turned to glower again at his brothers. Rhiwallon glowered back and burst out. "The trouble with you, Gruffyd, is that you always think if you can shout the loudest that makes you right! It doesn't! People can talk sense who don't have great strong lungs to bawl it with."

"There's nothing wrong with your lungs, you red-headed bull-roarer, damn you!"

"No, there's not, but it was Dafid I meant. Sense he was talking and you called him timid, in temper, and he's not a man who forgives. He's an enemy now for the rest of your life. And if you tell me and Bleddyn here that we're faint-hearted too, you'll have two more! Go to Mercia if you want! But don't ask us to ride with you and don't call us frightened either or we'll ram the lie down your throat on a point. If you go to Mercia, Gruffyd ap Llewellyn, you're a hot-headed *fool*!"

"You and Bleddyn," said Gruffyd, no longer shouting, but in a soft, dangerous voice like the pad of a stalking lion, "may withdraw, as I said."

But there were enough left, for the Mercian adventure.

At the moment of departure, she was in the courtyard, handing the stirrup cup to Gruffyd. Berddig was beside him on a massive horse, swearing softly at the weight of his armour. "We shall come back soon," the minstrel said. "And I shall call the minstrels of all the world to come and they shall play for Prince Gruffyd and yourself, my lady, and we shall forget the war."

"And I shall bring mule-loads of spoil to lay at your feet," said Gruffyd, kindly also.

Aldith stood at Wulfhild's side and watched them go, the leaders with their standards in front, then the long snaking column of horsemen, and last of all the clumsy tail of supply waggons and mules. As the column passed out of sight, Aldith said: "We shall hear from them regularly, of course. I believe Maredudd is in charge of that. I expect you'll miss Maredudd."

"Yes, a little," said Wulfhild. She did not ask her mistress if Aldith would miss Gruffyd. For one thing, such a question was rude. For another, Wulfhild suspected that Aldith herself did not know the answer.

6 ❊ *Winter Wine*

When the army had gone, one could feel the emptiness. Aldith, waking at the sixth successive cock-light, lay and listened to it.

Sounds there were. Her women round her breathed evenly. Birds sang for the dawn: thrush, finch, piping blackbird, and urchin crow. A dog barked. A cock crowed and was answered by another, further off. And in the hall someone was rousing the bondfolk, and a pail clanked on its way to the byre.

But as far as Aldith was concerned, this might well prove to be the sixth consecutive day of utter silence. Maredudd had promised messages but none had come. The Welsh force had vanished over the eastern horizon and might never have existed.

Wulfhild's head lifted from its pallet. She yawned and sat up. Wulfhild was an early riser, a habit going back to her childhood, when the first light summoned the thralls out to draw water and begin the daylong toil of grinding corn and tending the beasts.

"There's no hurry," said Aldith, "and if we get up too soon it only makes the day seem longer."

"There may be news today," said Wulfhild sturdily, and reached for her robe.

It was, indeed, time that there was news. Throughout the morning Mass, Aldith tried to pray for the Welsh and for Gruffyd but found that instead of praying she was persistently thinking about them, which wasn't the same thing. Her mind was attuned to the outer world. As she knelt and stood and received the sacrament and smelt the incense, she was listening. Every sudden noise made her startle: a cackling from the geese in the courtyard, a clatter of wings in the dovecot, the whinny of a horse. A banging door and a shout just outside the chapel made her blood race, and when the rite was ended she went out faster than was seemly.

Wulfhild was there, impatient, a small piece of parchment in her hand. Wulfhild rarely attended Mass, which Aldith usually deplored. But today she was glad. "It's come!" said Wulfhild, and thrust it at her.

It had been hastily written but the hand was certainly that of Maredudd. Aldith's own hand trembled as she read it out, sharing it with Wulfhild. "Returning. Chester too strong. Some booty but many losses. Father and many others wounded. Important make ready to care for them. M."

Those of her women who had been in the chapel with her had come out and crowded round. The nurse Myfanwy, holding Nest by the hand, spoke first. Myfanwy was old enough to remember a number of other wars, vividly. "He says make ready, my lady. That means preparations to nurse wounded men. Hot water we'll need, ready in cauldrons, and the fire well stoked. And pallets we'll want in the hall, and linen and ointments."

Aldith pulled herself together. "It doesn't say how many are hurt or when they'll come. We must be ready for the worst, at the soonest." How badly was Gruffyd injured? "Myfanwy, Wulfhild, come with me to the hall. Gladys, go to the kitchens and see the three big cauldrons put on to boil immediately. Angharad, go to the herb garden and get nettle tops and all-heal and sage and balm, plenty of them. Hurry!"

At least activity kept you from brooding. If the front of your mind was humming with present necessities, you couldn't hear the frightened muttering at the back of it. Pallets must be set in rows on the hall floor. Gruffyd's own chamber must be got ready. The water in the kitchen must be kept hot but not allowed to boil wastefully away. White linen, such as old bed linen and napkins, tablecloths and shifts, must be pulled out of chests and cut up for bandages. Herbs must be boiled, wine jars and salt fetched from store, mouldy bread—a most valuable constituent in poultices—must be collected. There was always some in a big store-room and Aldith ordered a further dozen loaves to be cut open and put in the steamy kitchens to acquire mould as soon as possible. If by the blessing of God they weren't needed, they might still be eaten.

The hall at Rhuddlan went the height of the building for half its length but over the other half was an upper chamber with a slatted wooden stair leading to it. It was useful, a handy second reception room for important guests, or for private talk, and when the house was crowded those not important enough to have first claim on a guesthouse, but too important to be quartered haphazard in the hall, could sleep there. Now Aldith ordered most of the furniture from the hall to be taken there; the upper room should do duty for the ordinary life of the household while the hall proper was a hospital. Some spare medical supplies were put up there too, near the stairs. In the intervals, she sent members of the thin household guard which had remained at Rhuddlan to survey the country for the first sign of the returning army. She wondered if it might come pursued, and sent word that the people of the hamlet could come within the palisade if they wished, with their animals, and camp behind the hall.

The late-afternoon meal was eaten as usual. It would help no one if they all grew weak with hunger, but it was a hasty, nervous, ill-cooked meal. Aldith found herself forcing food down, all but choking on it, and constantly wiping damp hands. She left the table early.

A mild, clear September dusk was falling, in a babble of starlings and a cawing of jackdaws as they flew to roost in the beechwood. As Wulfhild joined her in the courtyard, Aldith said: "The birds make too much noise. I can't hear myself think."

"We're not listening for thoughts," said Wulfhild. She stood still, head cocked. "I *can* hear something," she said slowly, "that isn't birds . . . I think. Listen. Isn't that a horn?"

They waited, tense, straining. The sound was repeated.

"It's our scouts!" said Aldith.

It came a third time, a long note and a short. "No pursuit," said Wulfhild, relieved. "That is the signal you agreed, isn't it, for no pursuit?"

"Yes. Thank God. We can set the gates wide and open the river gate as well. We'll order it now."

The army came both by land and by river; someone had

thought of commandeering barges to give the wounded a smoother journey on the last leg home. There were stretchers on board.

They did not carry only wounded. When the first stretchers were brought from the river and across the courtyard, crowded now and strident with men and horses and shouted orders crossing in midair, it was seen that some of them bore motionless burdens and were wholly shrouded. Aldith, kneeling by the first wounded man to need her help, bit her lip as a cloth-covered form, looking shrunken, too small to be a man, was carried past. But a moment later even that seemed less ugly than some of the living burdens that followed, that moved and moaned and tossed tormented limbs under wrappings splashed with blood. Soon she and all her women were stained with it as they went from pallet to pallet with their remedies, trying not to cry because tears only stopped you from seeing what you were at. After a time, even grief and revulsion ceased. Aldith poulticed and washed and bound, recited prayers and charms, and let her fingers be crushed in the clutch of agony, as if she had known no other world. The succession of the wounded seemed endless, a nightmare with no waking.

Gruffyd, and his sons, and Berddig, were not among either the wounded or the well.

She asked for them repeatedly, but the answers were vague. One man said yes, Prince Gruffyd was hurt, it was young Maredudd who organised the last stand to protect the retreat of the wounded. "Mules and carts we used and as many left on the field, God help them, as we got away. In a dozen places at once, the boy Maredudd was." Another man, feverish, his hot body shuddering against her as she tried to hold his arm-stump steady for a dressing, muttered, "Dead, dead," no matter what name was spoken to him. A third, not wounded, helping her with those who were, said: "He was alive when I last saw him. He'll be all right, don't be afraid, my lady." His tones were so consciously soothing that her stomach heaved with alarm.

But Wulfhild's voice called her back to present urgencies and she forced herself to attend. "Run out of linen? But we must have some more . . . there's some in the upper room. Oh, come with me!"

She hurried away, leaving her last patient in the care of her helper. Mounting the stairs, she saw that more stretchers were coming in. Oh God, when would it end? Would the supplies be enough? There was Maredudd, at last; he was lending a hand with the injured, so he must himself be all right. He would know where his father was; in a minute she would ask him. The linen first. "The chest was at the top of the stairs here, Wulfhild . . . Oh dear Saints, where's it gone? I *know* I had it put here . . ."

It had been pushed aside in some scramble for other necessities. They found it in a corner and threw back the lid, dragging out the old sheets it contained. Wulfhild sped off with an armful. Aldith shut the lid and followed. From the top of the stairs she looked down on a hall so crowded now with pallets and stretchers there was hardly room to walk between them. She must arrange for more straw pallets, and the dead must be taken somewhere else, to leave room for the living. Hurrying down, ready with instructions, she was impeded by Maredudd and his brother, Idwal, trying to find a space for one of the biers.

"Oh, not here, Maredudd, I think the dead must be put in the chapel. There's no room. Yes, well, put it down for a moment but . . ."

They lowered it, awkwardly, because Maredudd was taller than Idwal and they found it hard to move in unison. The red cloth covering the dead man's face slipped aside, and it was Gruffyd.

She thrust Maredudd aside, dropping the linen she carried, and knelt by the bier.

Under the ripple of smoky torchlight, the chief light in the hall as the sun went down, Gruffyd lay with closed eyes. With one closed eye. The other side of his face was a ruin, where a broad-headed arrow had smashed into the bone. But on the sound side, the blue-black hair and beard were as they had always been and the texture of the skin was as familiar to her as her own. If the one round, deep-set eye was shut, the black, strong brow was not to be mistaken. She drew the cloth back further and exposed the hands, folded over the silent heart. She made to lift one but it was cold and heavy like stone and would not move. A pain, destructive, clenching, began in the pit of her stomach.

She had prayed for his safe return but, she thought wildly, only half her spirit had gone out in that prayer, for the rest had been listening for news. So only half the prayer had been granted. He had returned, but not safely.

The pain grew and swelled. It found its way out of her like the coming forth of a child. She did not realise at first that it was her own voice, crying Gruffyd's name. She clung to the bier with both hands though people were trying to drag her away. Wulfhild was saying: "My lady! My lady!" Maredudd was tugging at her arm. Berddig had come from somewhere; he was facing her across the bier, his large face white and urgent, and he seemed to want her to stand up. She resisted them all. Until, from behind her, Gruffyd spoke her name.

"But who," she asked frantically, grasping hands that were warm and flexible and could answer her grip, "is that on the stretcher?"

"That, God rest his soul in Heaven, for he proved a brave fighter, is my poor bond-born cousin that I freed for you on our wedding. He'd have lived longer as a thrall, poor sod. But he died quick and singing a great battle song so maybe he won't need all these tears. Hush now. I don't need them, either. It's all over and I'm safe."

"That's what they're for, for the end of the terror. You're alive and I thought you were dead. Don't stop me crying, Gruffyd, I must cry. I thought it was you on that bier. I heard you were hurt. I thought you had died of it. I th . . . thought you were dead."

"I was hurt. I got an arrow through the upper arm. Here." He moved to show her the bulge of the padding. "But it's healing. I put wild carrot leaves on it; you should make them plant some in that herb garden of yours. Better than all your nettle tops and what not."

Aldith touched the padding and measured the distance to his chest. A few inches to one side and it would have entered his lung. "So near . . ." she said. "You make light of it. But it was so near."

Gruffyd's face altered, grew serious, and—was it possible?—doubtful. It was the face of a man about to ask a question that frightened him. Frightened him? Gruffyd?

"What is it?" she asked.

He said, in a private voice, as if they stood alone on a mountain instead of in the aftermath of battle, with the sounds of loss and pain all round them and tossing forms and crimsoned water in makeshift basins: "Did you care—as much as that, Aldith? Is it true?"

"Care? You've never been out of my thoughts for a day, or a minute. I've been so afraid for you. I love you so much."

"I thought I was too old for you. You were such a child, and I a seasoned man. I envied Maredudd for being nearer to you in age. I would have been jealous, only he seemed to like Wulfhild better."

Aldith laughed. "They've been lovers, on and off, since we came to Wales."

"*Have* they?" Gruffyd suddenly shot upright on the pelt-strewn couch. "But she hasn't . . . she's never . . ."

"She says there are ways not to conceive if you don't want to."

"Thank the saints for that! I thought for a moment I'd bred a son who wasn't all there. Don't give me such frights. The English spears were bad enough. Chased back from Chester we were, Aldith, chased like deer before a hound pack . . ."

"Don't think about it."

"I can't forget it. Never in my life before have I fled from a foe . . ."

"It brought you here."

"Yes." He lay down again and was quieted. "Aldith, what can I do to please you now? That bondman you wanted me to free, when first we were married, that Hereford boy . . ."

"Osric."

"Yes, Osric. He shall go free if you still want it, Aldith. He shall have his manumission and set out for his home in the morning. It is your second cowyll, your morning gift for your marriage made anew."

"It must be past midnight. We ought to be too tired to stay awake."

"We are drinking at a magic fountain, the source of all vitality. Aldith . . ."

"Yes?"

"When we went to the Cwmanog that day . . . you remember?"

"Of course."

"We made wishes. I wished for this. That I should have you love me. I thought they'd cheated me, the Immortal Ones. But they haven't failed me, after all."

"My wish was the same, the other way round. I wanted your love, too."

"You . . . ? But afterwards?"

"That was a strange place and a strange day. Afterwards it

seemed unreal, foolish, nothing to do with daily life. My mother told me . . ."

"No, no, Aldith! Darling. Not your mother. Not tonight."

"But it seems our wishes were heard after all. Only . . . didn't you say they charge for them?"

"They do. But all lovers pay a price in the end. We are mortal. Soon or late, we will be separated. Whatever happens now, we were together before we were apart. That we have for ever. Don't be afraid."

"I'm not afraid of anything tonight."

"How quiet it is."

"Dawn's near. I can smell it. There's mist in it; the winter won't be long. Aldith, dear love, why did it take you four years to say 'I love you'?"

"I didn't know it myself. You could have asked."

"God help me, I was afraid of the answer."

"I would have said yes."

"Yes, yes, you would have *said* it. But how would you have said it? Dutifully, to please me? If you had said it and not meant it, that would be worse than not to hear it at all. Say it again."

"I love you. From the heart. But Gruffyd . . ."

"Yes? But? What 'buts' are there tonight?"

"Should we be so happy? Those other men in the hall, the dead and the ones who are hurt, and may die too . . . How can we be so happy while they're lying there like that?"

"Someone is always lying somewhere like that. But happiness goes on. We may be on our own deathbeds next. Let us possess our heritage while we have it still. We are each other's realms, let us explore them, that no hill or valley be unknown to us, no precious vein untraced, no forest left without paths. This is your sceptre, hard and straight. Receive it. And here on these twin mountains will I raise my citadels of joy, Aldith, daughter of Mercia, Lady of Wales."

When the debris of war had been cleared away, by the time the wounded were healing or lost and the worst of the mourning was done, autumn had come and gone and Rhuddlan was making ready for Christmas.

Aldith entered now on an enchanted time. Her mother had never foreshadowed this; had not, Aldith thought compassionately, believed in it. Yet it had happened. All the passionate attachments for which she had been condemned as a child had been the tuning of the instrument for this, that she should become the harp on which Gruffyd should make melody.

Not that there were no sombre notes in that melody, but then, as Gruffyd said, in this imperfect world there were bound to be some. There was a risk of English reprisals. Rumour had come that the English, not content with winning a battle, were planning a counterattack. Rhuddlan had to be put into a state of defence. Also, the quarrel between Gruffyd and his brothers remained unhealed. They would not come to Rhuddlan for Christmas.

"But we'll do well enough without them," Gruffyd said blithely. "We'll have guests and merrymaking enough. Maybe they'll come next year when Berddig holds his great bards' gathering at last. Rhiwallon is wild for good music; he'll never keep away from that."

There were indeed plenty of guests for Christmas, enough even to fret the host and hostess, who still greatly desired to spend time alone together. On the afternoon of the seventh feast day, they slipped away.

"Two hours we'll have," said Gruffyd as they slid downstream in a small boat, "and Berddig shall entertain the company. We'll moor below the beech grove and walk in there. It's dry."

It was a still afternoon, mild for midwinter, the sky covered with thin cloud and a pale December sun shining diffusedly through it. The boles of the beeches were smooth, silvery or green with moss, slim pillars in a hall whose roof was intricately patterned with branches and whose floor was soft brown leaf mould. Their feet made no sound. It was not a season for birdsong, but some living things of the woods were abroad, encouraged out of retreat by the luminescent sky. A squirrel peered at them, bright-eyed, from the fork of a tree before it skittered up to the safe higher boughs, keeping the trunk between itself and the humans; and under a dry, tangled bush at the side of the path some tiny mouse creature scuttled for shelter, disturbed by the sound of their voices.

They talked of the Christmas feast and Berddig's forthcoming trial of minstrelsy. But presently they fell silent and passed through the grove without speaking any more, until they came to the edge of it. There, with one accord, they halted. They stood still, close together, and looked.

"It's a day of magic," said Gruffyd in his deep voice. "The kind of day that never comes when you try to make it be. The kind of day that is given, once or twice in a lifetime, for us to remember until we die. Look at the sky."

For the sky was all shining now, from horizon to horizon, a vast inverted bowl of burnished silver. It encircled them and the distant hall and the river and the wood at their backs, and within that circle they stood alone, the only man and the only woman in the world. The winter air was sweet and cold to taste, pale wine in a cup of silver. They felt for each others' hands, not able to take their eyes from that sky, not able to draw back from the enchantment.

They stood handfasted for what might have been a minute, or an hour. Until Gruffyd at last said: "Let us go. Before the light dims. Before we see the spell disperse." And with him she turned back into the wood.

They returned to their boat and came to the hall by the river entrance. As they stepped into the courtyard, Berddig came striding across it to meet them. His face sent all memory of wonder flying from their minds. He was pale and angry and even before he spoke, a horn sounded a warning note and men ran from the hall. "We have had word from one of the outposts!" he cried. "Five minutes ago. We were sending out to find you! Harold of Wessex is in Wales, making for Rhuddlan, with an army!"

7 ✖ The Treacherous Brewing

"What I want to know," said Harold murderously, "and what no one can tell me, is *how did they know* . . . ? *Who* warned them and *how* did he get here before us? It was a lightning swoop at an unlikely season and still, *still*, they are warned and escape down the Clywd ahead of me. And me with no ships to follow them!"

In the last sentence his voice sank from a roar to a growl. He had begun by addressing his lieutenants and ended in communion with himself. Communion, and a visibly hardening resolution. Next time, the impression came strongly over, there would be ships. Next time, there would be something to meet anything Gruffyd did, even if he grew wings and flew away on them.

They stood, Harold, his brother Gyrth, and their thanes, and stared at the unsatisfactory devastation of Rhuddlan. It was unsatisfactory because, although Rhuddlan was burning and the wooden buildings within its walls were sending up their smoke like a great black tree, Gruffyd was gone. When the attackers rode in, the Welshman's masts were already thin sticks on the seaward horizon of the river. The village was ablaze, and hot sparks floated on the wind, but the villagers too were gone. They had presumably fled into the hills with their stock. The hamlet had been fired without a blade raised in its defence. Harold hoped that Gruffyd would see the smoke from his ship and know it for what it was. But that hope was a very poor substitute for Gruffyd's head.

"We camp here," said Harold, "and search the district. *Someone* outsped us to get here. From within our own camp, maybe. I want to know who. Whomever we find, we question."

But the first informant to arrive brought a quite different kind of intelligence, and he was no shivering, reluctant shepherd or husbandman of the region, needing an interpreter to make himself understood, but a strapping towheaded lad who came of his own free will out of the January wind and rain. The guard who brought him to Harold was puzzled by him.

"Can't make him out, sir. Asked for you by name, he did, Harold Earl of Wessex, he said. He looks all English and says he is, but he talks singsong like they do. Says he knows something you'd find useful. He's very civil and dressed decent and he's sopping wet as well. He's drying off by our brazier till we know what to do with him."

"Bring him in," said Harold. Another brazier stood in the middle of the tent. "He can finish drying off in here."

He glanced across the table at Gyrth as the housecarle went out. Gyrth raised copper-brown eyebrows in enquiry. Of all the Godwin boys, only Gyrth had inherited Godwin's colouring, or Godwin's exceptionally expressive features. Harold read the question at once.

"I'll interrogate anyone with news, myself. I want no well-meant muddle-headed sifting of information before I hear it." He leant on the table, palms on the edges of the map spread there, faded lines on old parchment. "God's Teeth, what a country! You can't get from anywhere to anywhere in a straight line. You can be two miles from where you're going as the crow flies, and twenty-seven miles from it on a pony. If you're lucky!"

"Osric of Hereford, my lord," said the guard, reappearing.

As reported, the newcomer was wet through. He stood by the brazier and steamed. He was in his early twenties; big-boned, with very blue eyes in a face weather-roughened to a deep dull pink. His fingers were mauve with cold. Gyrth pushed a wine flask at him. "Thank you, sir," he said, and Gyrth barked: "You say you're from Hereford. You don't sound like it."

The young man's eyes sparked. "I've been in Wales since Hereford was sacked," he said. He spoke evenly, almost humbly, but anger was there, a deep undercurrent. "I was taken there a prisoner," he said. "They said I'd make a good strong slave, me, a freeman of Hereford City. Learnt my letters, I had, and how to make tallies and calculate, and they made a thrall of me. I've been in Wales and talking Welsh by order for seven years. That's what makes me sound like them, sir. I'll lose it, in time."

"So you were seized and made a thrall," said Harold. "Did you escape?"

"I was freed, sir. I was lucky, maybe." Osric said it with a twist to his mouth at the word "lucky," as if his luck had been an apple with a maggotty core. "I wasn't sold off at Bristol to God knows where, like some. I was kept at Gruffyd's court with an iron collar on like an animal. He had a lot of captured slaves there like me." Osric stared into the brazier, and spoke out of his memories. "I had to draw water for his royal Welsh baths. And lug wood about for his hearth and comb the burrs from his bloody hounds and unload his mules and sweep their dung up. He used to say thralls in his hall were well off, and sneer that at home as freemen half of us slept with the cattle. So we did, sir, true enough. In my Hereford house we slept on one side of the place with the byre across the passage and when it was cold we'd go and snuggle in with the cow. We slept with the cattle, right enough. But in Gruffyd's hall, we *were* the cattle!"

Gyrth moved impatiently, but Harold's fractional headshake checked him. "Go on," said Harold.

"When he married his English princess I asked her to get me my freedom," said Osric. "But she couldn't, or said she couldn't. I dunno." He wiped his mouth and set the flask down. "But last autumn I was set free. Just like that. It makes no sense, none of it. But anyhow it happened, and they gave me a set of new wool clothes and another to change into, and cut the iron off my neck and gave me a parchment saying my freedom was given me—*given* me, by them that had no right to take it from me to start with! And I had to kneel and kiss Gruffyd's great hairy fist in gratitude before I left. Bah!"

"And what brings you here now?" Gyrth broke out.

"Sorry, sir," Osric recollected himself. "I know you want to hear what I can tell, not what happened to me, but . . ."

"Oh, but we do want to know what happened to you," Harold said. "If only to tell the tale to those who might think well of Gruffyd through not knowing enough about him. Finish your tale."

"I went back to Hereford, sir. I'd left my mother there. She was old; I was born when she was late for childbearing, but I lived and those before me didn't. But when I got there she'd died too. I heard you'd given her something to help her, that she'd seen you after the sack. I was grateful. So I thought when I heard you were marching on Wales that I'd follow you. I set out to walk after you." He spread his hands above the bright charcoal and a smile, boyish and carefree, suddenly transformed his sullen face. "More like swim it's been, these last two days. But the fact is, sir, I picked up Welsh in Gruffyd's court. When you're a slave, believe me, you *have* to learn what orders mean. I was mostly at Rhuddlan, where Gruffyd's important men would come, and they'd talk in front of thralls as if we were deaf or idiots. Well, I heard a lot, one time and another."

"Such as?" Gyrth leaned forward.

"There's a good few folk in Wales," said Osric, "north and south, some with good blood and great lands and big fat treasure hoards, who aren't Gruffyd's friends. And there's a few more who're fair-weather friends and no more. If they thought he was running they'd join the hound pack. And I can name names. Is that of interest?"

Harold leant back, to throw his voice past Osric, and shouted. When the guard came in, he said: "Fetch my clerk."

"Can you use a sword?" he asked Osric while they waited.

"As much as any freeman can. But I've not got one. Someone had stolen my father's, when I got home. It was like coming back from the dead. Everyone I knew was used to me being gone. I was an embarrassment."

Gyrth laughed. "I'll find you a place with one of my thanes, and a sword to go with it, if you want."

The clerk came in. "I want those names you say you can tell us, Osric," Harold said. "The clerk will write them down."

"Some we probably know already," Gyrth observed. "There's a man called Caradoc in the south, a descendant of the old royal house there. He's no friend to Gruffyd, I fancy."

"You're right, sir. But there's six nobles of Deheubarth as well as him, that you might not know about. They've made more trouble for Gruffyd at times than he has." He turned to the clerk and began on a list. "Awful jaw-cracking names they've got," he said apologetically, as the clerk muttered over them, "but they've all got their father's names attached. Shouldn't be too hard to find 'em." He plodded slowly through the six. "Then in the north. Dafid of Conwy.

He was against the raid into Mercia and he don't like Gruffyd much anyhow. Gruffyd made a bad judgement against a kinswoman of his . . . *and* she's kin to two of the Deheubarth men as well." He looked at Harold. "They're touchy, sir. They're all touchy. But fair terms . . ."

"Might make them persuadable," Harold agreed. "Any more?"

"Some more in the north who might swing with the wind." Osric embarked on another set of improbable syllables. "And then," he said as the clerk rested his quill and gazed disbelievingly at the extraordinary nomenclature it had written, "there's Cynan ap Iago."

"Cynan . . . a survivor of the old northern house that Gruffyd defeated," said Gyrth thoughtfully. "He's in Ireland."

"And no friend to Gruffyd, and since he married into the Irish court, the Irish king's no friend to Gruffyd, either," said Osric. "I've heard plenty of talk about that."

"Tell me," said Harold, changing the subject, "who warned Gruffyd we were coming to Rhuddlan? Do you know?"

"No, sir. Was he warned? I've come from Hereford."

"And did you, in Wales, learn anything of the paths from one place to another? We've a map, but it's not very helpful."

"I can't read a map, sir. But I know the paths around Rhuddlan and to and from the big hall near Snowdon. Some are only open in summer."

"That might be very useful," Harold said.

When the boy had gone, to make friends among the men and rediscover what he once knew of swordsmanship, the two Godwinsons sat on in the tent and considered.

"An embassy to Cynan, as soon as the seas are navigable, Gyrth. We want half a dozen thanes of good standing. The Irish court is very dignified."

"And sea reinforcements. Gruffyd must have patrols of some sort, but we must break through them if necessary." Gyrth crossed ankle over knee and gazed at the ridgepole of the tent as if reading his inspiration from it. "If a land army entered Wales from the English side—Tostig might cooperate—and closed on Gruffyd while a sea force came in from the west, we should have him like a hot coal in a pair of pincers . . . And if among his own nobles there were some who had not openly declared for us, but were in secret on our side and ready to answer our call when needed . . ."

"And," said Harold, with a smile so predatory that it almost frightened his brother, "if we also had a handful of men who could pass for Welsh but had their hearts in England—mixed-blood folk from the borders, perhaps, who could go about in Wales and say what they were told to say . . . I've heard news of a great bards' gathering to be held this spring. There'll be many strangers wandering through the country. They'd cause no comment. Yes, I think, Gyrth, we might have Gruffyd this time."

The second useful informant arrived precisely half an hour later. He was a messenger from the Princes Bleddyn and Rhiwallon, jointly. The letter he bore was in beautiful English on beautiful vellum in beautiful black lettering. The brother princes did not desire to take part in any war against their half brother Gruffyd. But in present circumstances, nor did they wish to take up arms on his behalf. If they could be assured of remaining unmolested on their estates, they would undertake to stay there until the present quarrel was resolved, which they prayed might be done without bloodshed, by the making of a just peace. The letter was signed: Bleddyn and Rhiwallon ap Cynan ap Gwerstan.

"O Gruffyd," said Harold. "O Gruffyd, my Welsh incubus. This time you are lost." He opened and closed the fist of his right hand in a slow squeezing motion. "This time, indeed, I shall have you."

8 ✻ The Cauldron Boils

The first day of the Eisteddfod, the Bardic Contest, was given over to the Welsh musicians, but on this the second day, the visitors from other lands were to have their trial. To judge them fairly, famous minstrels had been invited from abroad and they sat with Lord Berddig, chief judge and organiser, on the slate ledges that made natural seats along one side of this green mountain valley. The winners would perform before Gruffyd himself, later. Once, it had been hoped to hold the contest itself in front of him, but now, with the muttered rumours of a huge English offensive in preparation, and secretive whispers against Gruffyd sneaking underground like peat-fire all through Wales, and Gruffyd's own muster of men in progress, the Prince of the Welsh had no time for such amusements.

The slate ledges had been given the air of thrones by casting coloured cloths and rich pelts over them. Berddig sat on crimson velvet and his friend Brian O'Seamus, the lean and dark Celtic bard from Ireland, on sableskins. A Scandinavian and a Scot flanked them. On the grass in front of the slate ledges, the audience was gathering.

The audience—men and women from hamlets for many miles round, in colourful holiday clothes—made a wide semi-circle, leaving a space for the performers. The vale hadn't been so populated since the vanished pagan days when, so legend said, the Druids had held conclave there.

Yesterday, the Princes Rhiwallon and Bleddyn had shared the judges' ledges and Berddig experienced a twinge of disappointment at their absence today. They lent the contest status. But there were other things to be thankful for. The weather was good. Round the valley the peaks of the Snowdonian mountains, still white from the winter, were crystalline in an enamelled blue sky. There would be no rain or mist to dampen the instruments. Also, the gathering so far had been remarkably peaceful: a triumph, when one considered that three of yesterday's competitors had recently been in fights of a patriotic nature and had injuries to prove it.

Reportedly, the fights had had a broad similarity. Each man, in tavern or market or mead-hall, had sprung to the defence of Gruffyd on hearing him slandered. One had heard him called a trouble-bringer, one had objected to the epithet "slave-dealer," and the third had heard him described as "half off his throne, and he's asked for it." But these ardent spirits had confined themselves to talking about their experiences and refrained from singing about them. Their lays had dealt with long-departed and non-inflammatory heroes. If today went as smoothly, Berddig thought, there would be much to be grateful for.

Three Scottish pipers opened the proceedings, walking out in single file to the greensward. A single piper, an Irish Celt, came next with an instrument tuned to a higher register, and then a competitor from the Western Isles. Beside Berddig, the Irish bard moved restlessly. Berddig frowned. "The man is competent, if not inspired," he murmured reprovingly.

"It isn't that," said Brian. "But what is going on in the crowd down there? Who are all these people streaming into the valley now? What have they come for, Berddig?"

Berddig looked over the heads of the crowd and blinked. Where there had been people in dots and clumps was now a massing, predominantly if not totally male, and growing steadily as more trickled in through the valley entrance. The gathering was quiet and well-mannered, but unaccountable. Berddig poked in front of him with a foot, and his chief assistant, sitting on the ledge below, turned as a toe prodded his shoulder blades. "Owen, find out what's afoot over there. Who those people are, pouring in, look you."

Owen was gone some time. Other performers came and went. The last pipe entry started with a solo lament from the Hebrides—a poor attempt, for the piper was not skilled at keeping his air supply even and the drone notes wavered discordantly. Owen's reappearance was a welcome distraction. "Word got round the villages," he whispered, "that something special was to be heard today, but no one knows what. And it's a queer thing, seeing half these folk can't understand one word of the strangers' songs they'll hear today."

Berddig shrugged. "If they behave, they're welcome." He nodded towards the lamenting piper. "With a little luck, most of what they hear will be more worth listening to than that."

After the pipers had been judged, the lyre minstrels took the arena, a very international group indeed, with entries from France and Normandy as well as the north. And then it was the harpers' turn.

This event was somewhat like the Welsh competition of the day before, but with wider subject matter and more elastic musical rules. Competitors were not bound by the strict laws of Welsh metre, and used their own languages. An Irish singer opened with a haunting lay of Tir-n-an-Og, the Isle of the Immortals, and then came a Norwegian skald with bright eyes and a warrior stance, who proceeded to recount the loves and wars of Harald Hardraada of Norway, who had wooed the Empress of Byzantium and fought her battles for her and then fled to Russia to escape her and married the Russian king's daughter instead.

"He shall have the prize if the choice to me is left," muttered the Scandinavian judge enthusiastically.

"The next contestant claims to be Welsh-born, though he comes from Ireland," Berddig said. "The harp is his ancestral instrument. Hear him before you decide."

The Welshman, announcing himself as Dafid the Homeless One, and stating that he was qualified for the international contest by virtue of many years spent across the Irish Sea, was a short, unsmiling man at sight of whom Berddig scratched his head. "It's been worrying at me since he entered himself for the competition yesterday," he whispered to Brian O'Seamus. "I've seen him before and he was not called by that name then. But what name he had and when and where it was, I am damned if I can call to mind."

"His voice may call it for you, if you ever heard him sing," said Brian.

"I will commence," declared the Welshman, "with a traditional song in accordance with the rules of this contest. I give you the Lament for Cynddylan."

At Aldith's wedding, Berddig had stopped the Lament for Cynddylan from being played, but in this context it was acceptable enough, dealing with the death of a Welsh leader and the destruction of his property at English hands more than a hundred, indeed nearer to two hundred, years before. Berddig sat back to listen. The minstrel's voice did not after all stir his memory. It said nothing to him except that as a singer this man was in no way remarkable. But within a few verses, he realised that the performance did have something exceptional about it and that was the intensity with which the song was sung.

Other minstrels today and yesterday had sung with power, had given themselves to the music and to the audience. But when a man had a personal link with a song, one always knew; there was a dimension of passion that only belonged to such a link. Once, Berddig had heard a man whose wife had died a week before sing a love song, and that man's melody had seared like a branding iron. This man, despite his grating voice and his uninspired harping, grieved for Cynddylan and his abandoned hall as if for a leader and a hearthside of his own.

> "*The hall of Cynddylan is dark tonight, without fire, without bed;*
> *I shall weep awhile, I shall be silent after.*
> "*The hall of Cynddylan is dark tonight, without fire, without candle;*
> *but for God, who will give me sanity?*
> "*The hall of Cynddylan is dark tonight, without fire, without light;*
> *longing for you comes over me . . .*"

The audience had picked up the subtle difference between this and the preceding songs. They were hushed, unmoving. The lay continued, growing harsher and more bitter. Eagle and kite rejoiced in the blood of the slain and with their talons attacked the beloved flesh of the dead.

> "*I had brothers who were not vicious, who grew up like hazel saplings;*
> *one by one they have all passed away.*
> "*I had brothers whom God has taken from me, it was my ill luck that caused it; they did not earn fame by fraud . . .*"

"It's terrible singing but it's grand singing too," O'Seamus muttered. "What do you think, Berddig?"

"I've a pricking down my spine and a flock of black ravens croaking ill-omen in my head. I don't like it," said Berddig.

Five minutes later he was liking it still less. Dafid the Homeless One finished his traditional lay and took his applause and declared that he now humbly offered his hearers, as the laws of the contest required—with a bow towards the judges—a lay of his own, the tale of the death of Iago ap Idwal, lord of North Wales, father of exiled Cynan; Iago ap Idwal, who died by treachery . . . "For not only by English hands have the leaders of Wales perished. Listen to my song!"

"He's not a minstrel at all," said Berddig viciously, after half a stanza of it. "He's here on a mission. Oh God, can't anyone stop him?"

He half rose to do so himself, but the mood of the audience was not with him. In the crowd one or two other protestors had been silenced by their neighbors, and faces were turned studiously away from Berddig's single abortive interruption. The crowd wanted to hear. Iago had been a good Welsh hero, hadn't he? And if the treachery that slew him had been brewed by that controversial figure of today, Gruffyd ap Llewellyn, what of it? Berddig sat down again, fermenting.

It was propaganda. This was no minstrel. The lay itself was neatly turned but not inspired, and it showed more plainly even than the Lament for Cynddylan had done the limitations of this man's harping and his voice. But once again the ring of personal involvement was there and the words of the lay were evidence that this displeasing choice of subject was no tactless accident. Dafid the Homeless One had come to blacken Gruffyd's name, and his methods were skilful, and poisonous, and insidious.

For Gruffyd's name was never spoken. It was Iago that the song was ostensibly about. Iago the heroic, the magnanimous, the wronged, and the murdered. His enemy was called only "the rival," "the foe," and "the kinsman from an unlawful bed." Later on, he became "the usurper."

Only, of course, there was no need to utter Gruffyd's name. The audience knew who was meant, quite as well as the minstrel did.

Berddig placed his hands over a stomach queasy with rage. It was for this that word had been put round that there was something at the contest today worth hearing. It was possible even that Prince Rhiwallon and Prince Bleddyn had been warned to stay away from today's meeting to safeguard both their sensibilities and their neutrality. This monstrous exhibition had been very well planned.

As the lay was ending, small pockets of disturbance once more broke out in the crowd. But they died away again, quickly, sparks on stony ground. Only a handful, it seemed, felt angry enough to protest in the first place, and they were being silenced. And now a young man, noble judging by his jewellery, was haranguing his neighbours at the back of the crowd, talking against Gruffyd. Some trick of the valley's acoustics carried his phrases back to Berddig. And somewhere else a claque had started a low chant, like a drone pipe accompaniment to the harangue. It grew louder and he heard the words.

"Down . . . with . . . Gruffyd. Usurper, usurper! Down . . . with . . Gruffyd. Usurper, usurper! Down . . . with . . . Gruffyd . . ."

The lay was ended, its closing lines lost in the growing uproar. "This will the festival ruin!" exclaimed the Scandinavian, half indignant and half with natural and instinctive pleasure in a fight. A woman's voice in the crowd, shrill, carrying, cried: "The English'll kill us all! Down with Gruffyd!" And then the harper in the midst of the green grass raised both hands for quiet, and got it, and faced his audience.

"Men of Wales! Men of the north! I call on you to be my support against the usurper, Gruffyd ap Llewellyn. He will bring you to ruin! I will give you peace and good fortune! I am no minstrel, as you may have guessed from my rough voice! Nor am I called Dafid the Homeless One, though God knows I am homeless enough and have been these many years. I am Cynan ap Iago, son of the man whom Gruffyd betrayed, and if you give me your swords I will give you your future. I will bring you a thousand men from the King of Dublin, sent to help you lay Gruffyd in his grave! And it's in his grave he should be, or you will all be in yours! English forces have crossed the border into Wales, coming from Chester, and ships with the insignia of Wessex are harrying our coasts already! Who is with me?"

"Cynan!" muttered Berddig. "I should have known him at once.

Cynan!" In a short, hard undertone he spoke to his assistant. "Owen, get down there and have my horse saddled, by the valley mouth in that hazel clump, in ten minutes. Quick!"

The speech went on. Cynan's short, tough figure was outlined in cruciform, legs astride and arms stretched up and apart as if in invocation, against the seething crowd. A dozen men near the front, arms round each other's shoulders, had begun to sing, of all things, a mangling of Gruffyd's favourite hunting song, the one he so often sang to his daughter:

> *"And when we see them come to our land,*
> *Spear on shoulder, club in hand . . ."*

He had wondered, once, who would sing that song at this festival. "Someone always sings it," he had remarked. God, what a piece of twisted prophecy. He saw that some of the Welsh minstrels, including those who had stood up for Gruffyd before the festival, were standing up for him again and getting the worst of it, and he longed to join them; but he had a task of greater importance even than that. He began to edge his way out.

He knew where Gruffyd was. Gruffyd was at his mountain hall on the flanks of Snowdon, not so far off in a straight line, though far enough by the mountain trails. Berddig, however, allowed himself a grim smile. There was one way to contact Gruffyd that he would bet any money, or his life, that Cynan didn't know about—or Harold of Wessex, either.

His horse was ready for him among the hazels, out of sight of the crowd. As he took the reins, he realised that his friend O'Seamus had also left his seat and was with him. "Berddig, I shall set my own guards to lead them off your track," said the Irish bard softly, coming to the horse's head. "They will tell lies if I order it. You are going to Gruffyd, I take it."

Berddig, with his usual overweight grunt, hoisted himself up. "What else?" he demanded. He reached down and prodded Brian in the chest with a thick forefinger. "If you get a chance to do any more prize-giving—which I doubt—I recommend the harper who sang of the Immortals, with the lay of Hardraada as runner-up. But don't . . ." He kept his face bland, letting out his anger in a jest to make his enemy small. ". . . give a prize to Cynan. That surly brute—for that's the reputation he has in Ireland—could no more put a tune together or turn a line of verse than he could catch the moon in a fishing net. Someone else wrote his lay for him, and by the rules, he's disqualified."

"What do you take me for?" said O'Seamus, shocked. "I know all that as well as you do. And him with a voice on him like a laryngitic corncrake, at that! Godspeed, Berddig!"

9 ❈ The Drinking of the Cup

"Witchcraft!" said Harold. "Well, what else is it?" On his wrist, the sparrow hawk sensed his rage and clutched his sleeve with her talons in sympathy. His horse arched its neck and danced.

"It's a likely land for sorcery," Tostig remarked. He turned in his own saddle to wave a hand at the vista before the grassy slopes of Snowdon, where they were riding. Range on range, the lesser mountains rolled away, cloud veiled here and there, some peaks standing stark and others like changeable grey ghosts in the mist. At the mountain's foot lay a quiet lake, turquoise under the sun. A cloud shadow passed over it as they watched and its deep colour turned to indigo, as secretive and menacing as the wild hills themselves and the withdrawn, unfriendly folk who lived among them.

To some extent their plans had gone well. The agents Harold had sent among the Welsh to create fear and darken Gruffyd's name had sown a vigorous seed. From it Cynan ap Iago, coming from Ireland at precisely the right moment, had reaped a fine harvest. Yet if the Welsh were learning to hate Gruffyd for bringing the English down on them, they had not learned love for the English as a corollary. The two armies, Tostig's Northumbrians marching from Chester and Harold's Wessex squadrons plunging in three spearheads from the coast, had met a warlike reception. So had Cynan's Irish reinforcements a little later. Gruffyd had even won back a certain amount of support and among his supporters there appeared to be a useful sprinkling of warlocks. Or how else did he know his enemy's movements almost before his enemy did?

"The last two strikes we planned," said Harold, "only you and I and two thanes were at the council, and the thanes were different men on the two occasions. We decide to swoop on the area where we think Gruffyd is . . . If only we knew exactly where he was, it would help, perhaps! But, anyway, we ride headlong for where we hope he is. And we find that we've missed him, that he was there, but is now gone, just ahead of us, warned of our coming—again. But it makes no sense unless he's reading our minds in a magic mirror or the entrails of a goat!"

Tostig said coolly: "His luck can't last for ever. He has foes among his own that he doesn't know the names of. His time will come."

"It would come faster if they ever knew precisely where to find him, either! They might reach him disguised as friends, but . . ."

"Your hawk's seen something," said Tostig.

The sparrow hawk was never off-duty when she was out. Her head turned constantly, scanning the world for prey. When she saw a likely victim, her fierce eyes would blaze and her talons clench on her master's arm. "I can't see what she sees," said Harold, "but . . ." He loosed the jesses and tossed her up. "Away you go then, little killer!" He sat still, head thrown back, and with narrowed eyes watched her purposeful ascent.

She soared strongly and now they saw it, the little dot in the patchwork sky which her keener vision had glimpsed already. She rose above it, drifting eastwards, and they shook their horses into a canter to follow. The quarry, whose species they could not yet tell, took fright as the sun came out and the hawk's shadow touched it. It lost height, seeking safety near the ground where the hawk dare not stoop at speed. They saw that it had pale plumage.

But it had been too high to start with. It had no time. The hawk plummeted. The quarry veered, dived, dodged, escaped the first stoop but failed to outfly the assassin a second time. The sparrow hawk rose from her second dive bearing double weight and hung in the air at leisure, a bundle of bloodstained feathers in her grip. Harold rode up as she finally descended. She had caught a plump pigeon, a delightful table morsel. It was as big as she was but it was quite dead.

He slipped from the saddle, drawing his knife, and sheared the pigeon's head off for his hawk's reward. "Pigeon pie, if we can get some more," he said as Tostig trotted up.

Tostig leant down to look and then looked closer. "That's a most unusual pigeon," he said. "Look at its left leg."

Osric of Hereford, with his idiomatic Welsh and his local knowledge and his passionate longing for revenge on Gruffyd, was ideal material for the provocateur operation, but they had had to disguise him. The fair-haired Welsh had distinctive features and their own shades of blond; there was no pretending that Osric's bones and Osric's version of flaxen were the same. But . . .

"Dye me dark with walnut juice," Osric said, "and I'll dye Gruffyd's reputation a hundred times darker. Let me try!"

So they stained his skin and hair black and if his blue eyes were still something of a shock, such eyes did look out of such brown faces in many border villages where the races were mixed. Osric, thus adorned, would do.

He was among those, therefore, who went out into Wales primed with a dozen nasty stories about Gruffyd. He returned content, when the paleness was beginning to show at the roots of his hair. He sat now in Harold's tent and looked at the little roll of vellum, two inches by three, which had been tied with silk to the pigeon's leg. On it was writing, traced with a fine quill, spidering over the scroll. It was in Welsh.

"You said you knew your letters," Harold said. "Can you read Welsh?"

Osric, breathing heavily, was following the letters with a blunt brown forefinger. "Just about. There's words left out because there's no room, but . . ." He muttered to himself, converting shapes into noises. "They don't use letters the same," he complained. "But I think it says: 'The English' . . . that's us . . . 'coming from east. On Snowdon. Northwards clear. Leave now.' Yes, I think that's right. 'Leave now.' "

Harold took the tiny piece of vellum from Osric and laid it on his palm. "So that's how it was done. Messages flying through the air, from wherever we go to wherever he is—or might be. He's probably got information going to all his hideouts and bases. I've heard of this trick pigeons have of flying home. He'll be using priests, I expect, to send the messages, since priests can write. Collecting batches of pigeons from Gruffyd's bases and sending them off with news and then collecting them again . . . Priests move about their parishes anyway. Who'd take notice of a priest riding piously along on his mare, with a coop full of pigeons slung from his saddle, the makings of a dinner when he gets home? We must have passed them ourselves and not molested them! God, so simple. Tostig, where's that map? Does Gruffyd have a base west of here?"

"Caer St. Mary's," said Osric. "That must be the place. He must be there. It's directly west." Tostig opened the chart and found the place, tapping it with a forefinger. "And if he is there, my lord," said Osric, eyes sparkling, "he thinks he's sitting safe and pretty. And he's just waiting for us to take him!"

"There'd be more than one pigeon, for a message like this," said Harold dampingly, "and from more than one messenger, most probably. There are wild hawks too, as well as my little darling. He'll have thought of that. He'll get his warning. But if we can't catch him there . . . The message says that northwards is clear. So it is. Clear of us, I mean. It almost tells him to leave in that direction. So where would he go?"

"Llanberis way, I think," said Osric. "He's got a lodge there, high up." He came to the table and stared at the chart. He had begun to learn how to read one now. He found what he wanted and pointed. "Gives me a queer feeling, this does," he observed. "Like being a giant, seeing all the land from high above. If the message gets to him, he'll be there by tomorrow . . . Here, I mean." His forefinger pressed down hard. "This is Llanberis."

"Then," said Tostig, "we can move in at once and surround him the moment he's there, before anyone has time to send him any pigeons."

Osric shook his head. "It's like an eyrie, sir. He'd roll boulders down the mountain on our heads. Or slip away in mist or dark. He knows the mountains the way you know your own face."

Harold put his weight on his hands, studying the map as if it were the magic mirror he had suspected Gruffyd of consulting. "So we can't surround him there . . . But we think he must make for Llanberis? How sure are you, Osric?"

"I can't think of anywhere else he'd be likely to go, sir. He's slippery and I may be wrong, but I can't think of another place."

"He'll get there then and stay there presumably, if we don't frighten him away. He is in our hand. We have only to close the fist without letting him see . . ."

"The secret allies," said Tostig, stepping back from the map. "The ones Osric named for us. They'll know where to find him, this time."

"Cynan ap Iago," said Harold. He drew the map from under Osric's hand and rolled it up. "Not known to Gruffyd by sight. Dafid of Conwy, sitting in his valley and brooding over his kinswoman's wrongs. Both within easy reach. And you, Osric, would you like to smear some more walnut juice on your face and be there at the kill? While you and I, Tostig, ride to Rhuddlan and await events, looking harmless as far as clever priests with pigeon lofts are concerned. Rhuddlan was his chief seat. I shall hold my triumph there."

The Llanberis lodge was forlorn and dusty, its servants demoralised, and half its guards unaccountably vanished. Stumbling from her saddle at the door, Aldith thought that every refuge they reached looked more desperate than the last. Her knees gave way as she descended and Wulfhild hurried to help her. Aldith was not yet strong after the miscarriage brought on by journeying from place to place in haste and dread, since the English invasion had begun and her husband's name had been slandered and so many Welsh had turned on Gruffyd. This was the sixth move in seven weeks, and every stronghold they came to was emptier than it ought to be. That emptiness had become, in the end, a paradoxical thing of cold substance in Aldith's stomach, thrusting out the child she carried. In the crisis she had hardly had time to cry for it, this child that was the gift of Gruffyd's love. But as if to make up for the lack of tears, the bleeding had gone on and on. It had barely ceased when at Caer St. Mary's a pigeon flew in at dawn, warning them away, and Gruffyd had carried her in his arms on the ride north, hoping that his body would absorb the horse's jolting. Nest and Myfanwy they had sent to a nunnery, but Aldith did not want to part from Gruffyd and he in turn feared to trust her to the roads with only the small escort that he could spare. She would be a prize, if the English captured her. So she and Gruffyd would live or die together instead.

He dismounted after her and Wulfhild left her to him, going

ahead of them into the hall. They heard her voice penetratingly raised to ask why the fire was out and where all the servants were. ". . . Rake out those ashes and start another . . . My lady's sick . . . Meat broth and eggs . . . Do as you're told! Yes, my lord Gruffyd's with her! Fire out at this hour in the morning, indeed!" The efficient storm of orders died away into some remoter region and Aldith uttered a slightly hysterical laugh.

Gruffyd said: "Softly, now. We're safe here." He led her into the hall. "I've feelers out," he said, "to bring what loyal men are left, to join me. Berddig's scouring Wales for them and so are my sons. Trouble is, *they* can't find *me*, half the time, the way I've hidden our trail. But they'll come in the end. Here we are. By the Face, your Wulfhild is stirring up the place like a badger in a wasps' nest. You'll soon be comfortable."

The steward, shrunken with worry, came to meet them. "My lord, I'm glad to see you safe. The place is disordered, but we can manage. The sow's farrowed; there's sucking pig for tonight if it pleases you, sir."

"It pleases me very well," said Gruffyd, too cheerfully. His face was bloodless under its natural brown and his eyes had sunk too far into their sockets for health. "I've ten men with me and we thought to commandeer some sheep on the way. So we can have mutton as well. Here's a settle, Aldith, and here's Wulfhild with water to get the dust off you."

"And it's cold water," said Wulfhild disgustedly. "But the fire'll soon be going again. The day's warm, Saints be praised."

Some hours later, fed and a little calmer, Aldith lay on the couch in her bower. A light coverlet was over her but she was dressed except for her overtunic. Her sense of security was not yet great enough to let her take off her clothes to sleep. Wulfhild sat by her, repairing a mantle torn by brambles on one of the wild mountain paths. Outside, the day had descended towards a long and tranquil evening, and the scents of honeysuckle and warm grass and thyme drifted from the hillsides into the room.

"It isn't like the middle of a war," Aldith said wonderingly.

"Even wars have pauses for breath," Wulfhild remarked.

"What will be the end of it, Wulfhild? And when?"

"Your husband will gather his men again and drive the enemy out, of course," said Wulfhild briskly, her ears strained for the sound of incoming wings at the dovecot. She prayed that the enemy would not drive Gruffyd and his family out from here before Aldith had had time to rest.

Aldith made herself smile. "Dear Wulfhild, may you be blessed with the power of prophecy." She sat up abruptly. "That's a horn!"

She was off the couch and into her overdress in time to go to the bower door and see the horsemen dismounting in the courtyard. They were laughing and one was embracing Gruffyd, who had hastened from the hall. Gruffyd was laughing with him, his face easing into lines of relief. The steward was on the steps, bowing. Gruffyd pushed his guests towards the hall and himself swung towards the bower, where Aldith's questioning eyes searched his.

"All's well, *merched*! That's Dafid of Conwy, did you see him? Fence-perching Conwy, but he knows whose side he's on now. The English have done a little too much ravaging for his taste, on our good Welsh soil. And he says my brothers are feeling less neutral and more brotherly these days. They're on their way here! Twenty of Dafid's own men are behind him; they'll be here tonight. He left them scrounging up supplies to bring with them. Listen, love, we'll be talking strategy in the hall half the night. You stay here. I'll send food to you. Later I'll be with you. Rest till I come."

"Wake me," said Aldith. Thankfulness warm as sunshine half melted them to coalescence as they stood in each other's arms, but it was the wrong time. They unwillingly drew apart.

"Later," said Gruffyd with a smile and he went away to the hall. He looked taller than he had in the morning.

The promised score of men arrived at dusk, just as the blue shadows were gathering and the cooling air had begun to distil the dew. When they had gone in and the courtyard was once more still, Aldith went to her bower door again. The tall arched windows of the hall showed wavering red-gold from the torchlight inside, and a muffled burst of male laughter suggested that the strategic conference was under way to the accompaniment of rejoicing and imbibement. She smiled.

The laughter stopped.

In the sudden quiet, Aldith's body stiffened. For the string that sang, like a lyre-string, between herself and Gruffyd was suddenly taut. He was at the other end, dragging on it, filled with some passion that pulsed through walls and air to reach her. Then the silence ended in a hoarse, harsh uproar: shouts, the scrape and clash of weaponry, and a man's scream, and the tension broke, releasing her. She ran.

Wulfhild followed, but hopelessly in the rear. Aldith sprang up the hall steps, three to a stride, and plunged in. She already knew what she would find. She had seen it before, that other time, when she took another man's body for Gruffyd. It had been a natural error, for this scene was her destiny, had been ever since her thread was first spun from the tangle of unborn lives, and she had known it, and been waiting.

There had been dead and wounded on the hall floor that other time, at Rhuddlan. There were dead and wounded here. The steward was among the dead; she thought he was the one who had screamed. A group of living men stood together near the dais, their backs towards her, their attention on something at their feet. She knew what it was, and dashed towards it.

As she ran, she pulled her own small meat dagger from its sheath. She had it in her hand as she knocked aside the man who blocked her path. She gripped it tight as she looked.

This time it was Gruffyd and no resembling cousin. A great red stain oozed over his chest and another was soaking through on his left side. He had taken off his armour to greet his so-called friends. Hardly anyone in the hall, indeed, was in mail. His outflung left hand was red as if he had tried to stop the flow with it, and his sword was fallen aside. But his eyes were open and aware. Oblivious of the men around her, she knelt beside him.

He spoke, weakly, but with perfect clarity. "The Cwmanog was a mistake. We should have had nothing to do with the Immortal Ones. They drive such impossible bargains, *merched* . . ."

The recognition went out of his eyes and if he had more to say it was lost in bubbling blood. She was alone with their enemies. She stood up. She was face to face with a short-legged man whose eyes were the dull blue-grey of slate. He held a reddened blade.

"Did you kill him?" she asked.

"I did. Why not? I am Cynan ap Iago and he destroyed my father."

Aldith put a hand on his arm and he glanced from it to her, expecting some appeal for pity. Her hold hardened. She lifted his arm and plunged the dagger in below it.

Her last view of the hall as they dragged her from it was of
Cynan sitting on the steps of Gruffyd's dais, beside his victim's
body, his hand clutched to his side and blood welling through his
fingers, while men crowded round him, and Dafid of Conwy, who
had betrayed his lord, swiftly padded a napkin for a dressing. A
black-haired young man knelt by Cynan, cutting off his tunic. She
knew him too. Despite his oddly darkened face and hair, she knew
by his blue eyes and the expression in them that he was the Saxon
thrall-boy, Osric, whom she had freed.

She and Wulfhild were not molested that night, but spent it guarded
in the bower. Dafid of Conwy gave the orders. He seemed to regard
them as some form of booty, to be safely delivered to some more exalted recipient. The sleepless darkness passed at length and morning
came, just as if the world were going on as usual. A guard brought
food which Aldith would not eat. Presently they were taken out and
told to mount the horses waiting there.

"Where are we going?" demanded Wulfhild.

"Rhuddlan," said the guard.

"To Earl Harold," said a man already mounted. His voice,
thick with satisfaction, was familiar and hateful. Aldith had heard it
confess to killing Gruffyd. Cynan ap Iago was not dead. He was riding with them, a padding bound under his tunic on the left side. She
would have his company all the way to Rhuddlan. She looked round
her for Gruffyd and then became afraid that her mind was breaking.
For Gruffyd could not ride with them. He was dead.

Then she saw him.

She was not the only prize they were taking to Harold. What
she had at first vaguely supposed was some sort of carved standard
borne by the man who rode beside Cynan, was at closer range Gruffyd's head, on a pole.

She rode through the morning, misty grey brightening slowly
into sunlight, in an unbelieving trance. This could not be happening,
therefore it was not happening. Gruffyd could not be dead, therefore
he was not dead. The stiff, dark streaks on the clothes she had worn
all night could not be his dried blood, nor could Gruffyd's head possibly be a filthy, red-smeared, matted-haired thing on a pole. She
rode in sight of it all the way and stared at it all the way and continued not to believe it. Wulfhild spoke concernedly to her several

times and she did not answer. No one else took any notice of them at all except for the guard, one of Dafid's men, who brought bread and cold pork and mead to them at the halts, and urged her, not unkindly, to take them. She tried to comply once, but was immediately sick.

There was a night on the road, spent at a fort which had once been Gruffyd's but was now in English hands. Wulfhild slept exhaustedly on the straw pallet they were given to share, and even Aldith dozed restlessly. The next day, towards evening, they reached Rhuddlan.

Rhuddlan was ready for them. At the sound of the horn, the gates of the camp palisade were flung back and beyond them Aldith saw the walls that had ringed her one-time home. But within those walls, she knew, that home was burned. She had seen the smoke from the ship as they fled down the Clwyd. She turned to say: "Do you remember . . . ?" to Gruffyd and was surprised that he was not there.

She and Wulfhild waited, mute and weary, while Cynan and Dafid conferred with a group of men who had come out to meet them. Then soldiers, armed and helmeted and respectful in a disquieting, slyly amused manner, came and told them to dismount, that a tent was ready, and that they were to come this way.

In the tent they found towels and a silver basin, a couch with rugs, a stool and candles. A young boy, probably someone's page, brought water in a steaming earthenware jug. Wulfhild persuaded her mistress to lay aside her mantle and wash her dusty face and let her hair be freshly braided. The page came back with hot capons in a covered dish, and wine. Aldith once more shook her head at the food. Her throat closed at the sight of it.

Wulfhild, who did not consider a fast the best means of meeting a crisis, took some of the chicken and gratefully swallowed a good deal of the wine, which was red and rough and very potent. She felt stronger afterwards, if muzzy-headed. When the page came to take away the dish, she drew a deep breath and asked him what was to happen to them, but he said he did not know. They were left to wait.

Dusk deepened. Flints had been provided and they lit candles. They needed the light. It was a comfort, a symbolic armour, to people beleaguered in the midst of foes.

Aldith presently sank into a withdrawn speechlessness, sitting rigidly on the one wide stool, hands folded in her lap, back propped against one of the tent posts. Wulfhild curled up on the end of the couch, out of the candlelight. Soon she would sleep, whatever Aldith did. Exhaustion was flooding Wulfhild's mind again, and the wine had numbed her power to feel fear.

Presently, noises broke out from a neighbouring tent, bursts of merriment and the sound of lyre music. Wulfhild roused herself and tiptoed to the door to peep out. She saw bright torchlight shining through the chinks in the hide walls of a huge tent fifty yards off. A feast of triumph, no doubt. She and Aldith might be grateful that they hadn't been invited as exhibits. Going back to her shadowed couch, she said: "They've treated us well so far." Aldith did not answer.

Wulfhild began to doze, nuzzling into the rugs, knees drawn into stomach. Images of the long road from Snowdonia spun through her drowsing mind. When the tent flap was flung back, it entered her dreams at first as the tossing of her horse's head. Even when she opened her eyes she was still confused and did not at first recognise the man on the threshhold, until Aldith named him.

"Earl Harold of Wessex," said Aldith flatly, not in greeting, but as if she were branding him.

Wulfhild struggled fully awake. Aldith was right. But this was not the Earl Harold she recalled from Saxmundham long ago. Dazedly, she saw that this was a stranger, to whom she could not speak, a frightening, triumphing apparition, who smelt of menace.

He had been drinking and the wine had tinged his cheekbones red and lit a fire in his eyes. But if wine had lit the fire, the fuel was in his own nature. He was a descendant of Vikings. He had reverted once before, when he slaughtered his own people like a berserker in Porlock, years ago, fighting to get back from exile. Tonight he had reverted again. His thick, springy fair hair, the very antithesis of Gruffyd's blackness, glinted as if sprinkled with gold dust. His narrowed eyes were those of a warrior preparing to make a final end of his foe. His shape, outlined in a great shadow cast by a thick candle, looked enormous. There was no doubt why he had come. He had set up his tent to carouse where his enemy had once caroused. He had taken his enemy's head for a trophy. One thing only remained to complete the erasure of Gruffyd, and that was to claim his wife as a trophy as well.

"Harold of Wessex," he agreed, with a formality beneath which was mockery. "And I present myself, do I not, to Aldith of Mercia?"

He had not, Wulfhild thought, registered her own presence at all. Mind and body alike were directed towards Aldith only.

"Aldith of Wales," Aldith corrected him. She sat quite still, feet together, hands still clasped on her dreadful skirts. Only her wide eyes revealed that emotion lived in her.

"Not now," said Harold. "Not Wales any longer, my dear," and striding forward he seized both her wrists in one broad left hand and dragged her to her feet. His other hand grasped one of the thick red-brown plaits and tugged roughly at the thin silk cord that held the plait secure.

Wulfhild, fully conscious now, alert and furious and hot with the wine she had taken, moved. Straight off the couch, to the table where the silver basin stood, still half full of water. She snatched it up and flung the water over Harold and hit him as hard as she could on the back of the head with the basin.

As she struck she heard her own voice screaming: "Leave her alone, you devil, leave her alone! I'm ashamed of you, to do such a thing, *my own father!*"

For the space of two deep-drawn breaths, everything stopped. The trio were motionless: Aldith, released from Harold's grip and half leaning on the couch; Harold frozen in mid-lurch, against the tent post, a hand to the thick hair at the back of his head; Wulfhild still with the basin upraised in an attitude of threat. Then the wet basin, an inconvenient weapon with neither gripping point nor fulcrum, slipped through her grasp and crashed to the floor, and the still-struck figures sprang back to violent life, Harold and Wulfhild confronting one another, Aldith shaking uncontrollably, her hands to her slackened mouth.

Harold's expression was dazed, but more from mental than physical shock; the basin had been too awkward to do him much damage. "What are you talking about?" he shouted at Wulfhild, "and who the devil are you?"

The fury in front of him shook clenched fists in his face. "I'm Wulfhild, don't you remember? Wulfhild from Saxmundham. And you're my father, my father, my *father!* I've always known it and I used to be proud of it and now this, *this!* She's the Lady of Wales and the Lady of Mercia and you're a bloodstained barbarian and I have to call you my *father*! What if the Lady Eadgyth saw you now? If I ever get a chance to tell her, I will, I will! Is this how you got me? You're my father and I hate you and if I could kill you I would!" And the small, thick-browed bundle of vindictiveness thrust its raging face close to his and spat. Harold swore and sprang forward, knocking her hands away before she could claw him. Silent, panting, venomous, they glared into each other's eyes.

"Who," demanded Harold at length, in a voice savagely soft, "told you I was your father? Yes, I remember who you are. But who told you *that*?"

He was still looming with anger, but the curious light that had been in his eyes when he came in was fading. His normal personality was reappearing. Angry or not, this was the Earl Harold of long ago, the godlike creature whose anger was only the other face of his frequent laughter, whose recognition as a daughter she had longed for in vain and dared not request. Wulfhild found that she was crying.

"No one told me . . . but I knew. My mother never said who my father was, but I was brought into the hall when she died. And why, unless I belonged there?"

There was a moan and a sigh and Wulfhild, spinning round, was just in time to break Aldith's fall. "Oh, help me lay her on the couch," she said with impatience, Aldith's unconscious weight sagging in her arms. Harold speechlessly took Aldith's feet. "Oh dear Christ, the bleeding's started again!" Wulfhild pulled off Aldith's veiling and began to wad it into a hasty dressing. "She miscarried not three weeks ago, but did you ever think of anything like that? Is there any wine left? It'll help her . . . yes, thank you. She's coming round."

So here was the extraordinary climax of his triumph. He had come to take Aldith as a conqueror's prize and ended by offering her wine to sip, and bathing her face in water from the ewer, while Wulfhild bound the torn-up veiling into place. He heard himself assuring his intended victim that he meant no harm to her. Across her, he said to Wulfhild: "If you bang on that gong behind you, hanging on the tent post, the page will come. He'll fetch my physician."

The physician was a priest. He enquired what had happened, eyed his lord with wordless disapproval when told, and sat down beside the couch to offer reassurance and the consolations of prayer while the page, on his instructions, went to fetch the ingredients for a soothing draught. Harold gripped Wulfhild's elbow and drew her towards the door.

"Listen, Wulfhild. Listen to me. Your mistress is in good hands now and safe from me. Get the hate out of your eyes. There is something I must say to you."

"Yes?" Wulfhild waited, sullen, her tears dried and her strength drained off by too many crises too quickly. She stared at the ground.

"I'm not your father."

She looked up, disbelief in her face. "Lady Alveva thought you were. She used to hint at it. She said once I had eyes like yours."

"You have eyes like your mother. I wish you *were* mine. I'd have my daughters act as you did tonight. I'd be proud of you." He considered the defiant young creature who had half stunned him and threatened to kill him, and grinned appreciatively, the broad, entirely masculine grin which made men follow him and would have brought him women by the score had he wished it. "You were taken into my hall," he said, "because when she was dying, your mother told Lady Eadgyth your father's name. But it was not my name. Or my lady would have been more likely to drop you down the well, believe me!" He grinned again. "Did Lady Alveva think she'd take you in, supposing you were mine? She doesn't know my wife! No. Your father was once a friend of mine, and there were other reasons why we should feel responsible for you. I'll tell you those reasons presently. But for now I'll tell you two things. One is that you were not the product of rape. The other is your father's name. You may need time to grow used to that. But believe me, you need not be ashamed of that name. He was—and I am sure still is—a brave and honest man. You've heard, haven't you, of Brand Woodcutter?"

Strangely, in the morning it was Aldith who seemed to be recovering, her physical ills subsiding and her manner stricken but rational. It was Wulfhild who gave way, racked with headache and too dizzy to cross the tent without help. Through the waves of vertigo in which her world lurched like a ship on a wild sea, she told an anxious Aldith that she did not want anything but to lie still, that she was not lonely for Maredudd, that she would soon be well.

Earl Harold came to the tent presently, and renewed his promise of safety to both of them, and looked down at her with concern.

"I am having Lady Aldith and yourself moved to a convent until you are both quite well. It isn't far and you can go by litter." He sat down and dropped his voice. "Wulfhild, does it hurt you very much that you are the Woodcutter's daughter? It need not."

"No, no, it isn't that. You and Lady Eadgyth, especially Lady Eadgyth, always spoke well of him. It isn't that." It was beyond her to tell him what it really was: the piled-up fear and stress of the last perilous months and then at the end of it the death of a dream, the loss of Harold as the golden image of her father—to be replaced by a man whose name was all she knew of him. "I wish I could meet him," she said. "Does he know about me?"

"No. But if a chance comes to change that, I'll see to it. You're very much his daughter. Brand used to go sick when he was in distress, too. He courted Lady Eadgyth once . . ."

"Yes." Everyone at Saxmundham had known that.

". . . and when he lost hope, he promptly went down with smallpox. You're very like him. You even have his eyebrows."

In the king's hall at Gloucester, the reception was to be formal. The king sat on his dais, on the western side of the hall. Leofwin and Gyrth Godwinson flanked him, and the thanes of six earldoms stood grouped about the dais' foot. Standing on it, close to the king, were Waltheof Siwardson, who had been at the court since his father's death and was now in his teens, and eleven-year-old Edgar, son of the dead Edward Edmundson. Both were dressed for the occasion: russet brown under a tawny mantle for Waltheof's amber fairness, orange under blue for Edgar's mousier colouring. Both were motionless, conscious of the occasion, dignified. When the trumpets rang at the door of the hall, they did not stir.

Harold and Tostig walked up the hall together, pacing steadily to the centre and wheeling to face the dais. Harold's standard-bearer walked at his lord's shoulder, one pace behind. But he was not carrying a banner. On the top of the pole he bore was Gruffyd's head.

"My lord!" Harold halted at the dais' foot, with the admiring semi-circle of thanes to either side. "I bring you the head of your enemy Gruffyd ap Llewellyn, once self-styled Prince of All Wales, and now a trouble to you no longer."

Edward looked at Gruffyd's head, stained with corruption, dwindled in death, its black hair straggling and its closed eyes still showing slits of deathlight where the lids had not quite met. He inclined his own head fractionally, and his ceremonial crown glinted as he moved.

"We are pleased with your service, my lord Harold, my lord Tostig."

Waltheof said: "So would my father have served his enemies and yours, my lord Edward."

Edgar Edwardson surveyed the thing with a face that crinkled with horror, and turned away and was sick.

"I'm disappointed in Edgar," said King Edward. The ceremony was over and he and Harold and Tostig were together at dinner, formality at an end, and something like private conversation now possible between them, since the other thanes at the table would not presume to interrupt, or attempt to listen. "He falls off his pony more times," said Edward disapprovingly, "than one would think possible, and today's exhibition. . . !" He left it eloquently undescribed. "As a Christian I shall pray for Gruffyd's soul," he said. "But as a king, it is not my business, nor would it be Edgar's if he succeeded me, to sicken when a foe is defeated. What alarms me with Edgar is that he shows no sign of changing."

"He's still very young," said Harold mildly.

"My lord," Tostig enquired, "have you made any declaration concerning your nephew Edgar?"

"No, Tostig, I haven't. Now I am seriously thinking that I should not." Edward looked down at his thin hands. "I'm less strong than I was," he said suddenly. "I hunt, but not for the hours I once did, and I cannot keep all-night vigils easily any more. Cold and damp reach my bones as they never used to do. It's a nuisance for me to be anxious for the future of my kingdom after I leave it. I want to be free to make my soul. I should also like to be free . . . quite free . . . to make my choice. Of an heir, I mean. Edgar or another, depending on what seems the wisest course as time goes on."

The two Godwinsons were silent. A shadow passed across them and Edith leaned over them with a dish of fruits. "Strawberries from Wilton Abbey, my old convent," she said. "They cultivate fine fat ones there. May I offer them to you?" She smiled at the king as she held the dish towards him. "I heard a little of what you were saying," she observed.

"Your advice is always valued, Edith," Edward said. "Tell us what you think."

"If I may suggest, my lord," said Edith gracefully, "I and my brothers . . . have a brother and a nephew in the hands of William of Normandy. You were referring to that, I imagine?"

"I was."

"If you desire freedom of action, my lord, you should take steps to bring them home. As long as they are there, William has means to influence you."

"He didn't use that means when I brought the Atheling over," said Edward.

Edith passed the dish to her brothers and seated herself beside her husband. "No," she said. "But where is the Atheling now? Can you trust William never to use that means? Can you be sure?"

Edward sighed. "I had one other nephew," he said, "though not one likely to be of help to me. A brother of poor Ralph of Hereford. You recall his name, Harold? Walter of Mantes. He always lived on the Continent and had his own career and titles there and was content with them. I never considered him as heir, for I had heard he did not wish it, any more than Ralph did."

"*Had* a career and titles?" asked Harold shrewdly.

"Had. While you were in Wales, news came. He was in dispute with William over the overlordship of the province of Maine. They each claimed it. Walter is dead. He died of a sudden, mysterious stomach ailment and his wife died with him. That is not to say," said Edward, glancing from one face to the next, "that William is responsible. Such things can happen by the will of God. But I cannot be sure. I cannot be sure what killed Edward Atheling either. I can only wonder. It was once my wish that William should succeed me. It isn't my wish now. It isn't even an acceptable possibility. Yes, Edith, your kinsmen should be fetched out of Normandy. They're not in trustworthy hands."

"I'll carry a letter to Normandy . . ." Tostig began eagerly.

"Oh, no, Tostig, not you!" Edith looked horrified.

Harold smiled. "Edith, there's no danger even for your favourite brother in acting as King Edward's ambassador to Normandy. An ambassador is privileged. William could only say no and send him home empty-handed. But I should prefer to go myself. If you will permit me, my lord Edward. As it happens, I have . . . business in Normandy."

"You must miss your daughters, Sir Brand," said the abbess of the convent in which Brand Woodcutter had placed the two girl-children Hild had given him. "Have you any family at all in Normandy now?"

"Only a nephew," said Brand. His French was still heavily accented and ungrammatical even after twelve years. "No one else. I make do with Hakon."

Part

IV

THE RETURN
OF THE
WOODCUTTER
1064–1065 A.D.

1 ✼ *Capture*

Along the rutted tracks through the green summer fields and woods of Ponthieu province, near the northwest border of Normandy, the cavalcade wound like a snake with a brightly patterned skin. The hides of the powerful, religiously groomed horses were red-bay, blue-roan, golden-sorrel, black and white, and strawberry. Their saddlery was a riot of dyed leather and colourful caparisons, with silver buckles and gem-studded brow-bands. The men of the escort were mailed, but the principals were glorious in all the hues known to man. The only exception was Count Guy of Ponthieu himself, who wore sober brown and was mounted incongruously and apologetically on a mule. He was taking his—guests was a misnomer but he persisted in using it—to meet Duke William, and it was likely to be an embarrassing encounter.

The meeting was to take place on the road between the Castle of Eu and the Norman border, not in the castle itself. Wulfhild knew she was not alone in being thankful for this. None of them wanted to spend a moment more than necessary inside any of Count Guy's castles. She had heard Earl Harold say as much only this morning. And his feelings, she thought, were understandably stronger than anyone else's.

"I've spent a week in the dungeons of your castle of Beauvais," he said acidly to Guy. "Your hospitality leaves much to be desired. I prefer the open air. We ride to meet William."

It had taken King Edward many months to decide finally that Earl Harold should go to Normandy to fetch his brother and nephew home, or at least to attempt it. By then the autumn of 1063 had come, with gales in the channel. "We must wait now, anyway. It will give you more time to think," Edward said. But the spring of 1064 found Harold of the same mind, and the royal permission was at last granted. A week later a messenger, a man called Odi, who said he had once known her father, Brand, came to Wulfhild in Mercia, where she and Aldith had gone when they were strong enough to travel.

Odi brought word from Earl Harold. He was sailing soon for Normandy with some of his thanes, two of whom were taking their wives. If Wulfhild wished to meet her father, Odi would escort her to Bosham on the south coast, from which the ships would leave. She should attend one of the ladies, whose regular maid was prey to seasickness and had asked to be left behind. In Normandy, if he could, Harold would arrange for her to meet her father.

"If I go . . ." said Wulfhild.

"You may stay with your father, or your new mistress. You cannot promise to come back to me," said Aldith. "You have the right to know your father and I would not keep you from him. I shall be sad to part from you but I am not the child who depended on you so much in Thetford. Much has happened since then."

"Yes," said Wulfhild. "You have had a husband, and you still, thank God, have your daughter. Thank you. With your consent, I will go "

So she sailed from Bosham and if she felt nervous of what lay ahead, Earl Harold was reassuring. He himself was interested at the prospect of meeting the famous and intriguing Duke of Normandy face-to-face, and full of eagerness to see his kin again. They set out hopefully, in beautiful weather. One of the sailors muttered as they waded to the ships that the morning was a bit too bright in his opinion, but no one took any notice.

The clouds raced up from the west on a strengthening wind, before they were two hours from the coast. They ran before the storm, making for the nearest land. Borne on the backs of perambulating grey water-mountains, they arrived with the sound of grinding and splintering, on the shingle of an unknown shore.

All three ships were damaged, two beyond repair. Fisherfolk from huts close by came running through the rain. They were more interested in booty than rescue; their faces were visibly regretful when they learned that no one was dead. But they were helpful in their way, taking the castaways to the biggest of their huts, offering broth and the drying warmth of a fire, and producing a mixture of garments and wrappings for the shipwrecked ones to wear while their own clothes steamed. Harold, sitting on a bench by the fire, in this hut festooned with netting and redolent of fish and seaweed, wrapped shroudlike in coarse sailcloth, with just one hand out to hold his earthenware cup of broth, thanked their hosts politely. But his face was sombre, and presently Wulfhild, herself in a voluminous gown belonging to a large fishwife, saw why. Their hosts had also retrieved most of the voyagers' goods and made a neat pile of them, along with the weapons discarded when the wet clothes were shed. But the pile was on the far side of the hut and three young fishermen were sitting on top of it.

After a while, one of the men spoke to Harold, in the thick local patois which Wulfhild could not follow and with which Harold, fluent though he was in French, clearly had to struggle. Then Harold turned to his companions. "This is Ponthieu, he says. They've sent the count a message. I don't know if that's good or bad. I don't know much about him. We must wait." His eyes turned again, anxiously, to their sequestered belongings. "I never felt more kindly towards poor Robert Champart," he remarked. "This is exactly what happened to him."

"But the fisherfolk did him no harm," said one of the thanes encouragingly.

"We're not archbishops," said Harold with foreboding. "Once he'd convinced them that he was, he was safe. But . . ."

His pessimism was justified. The Count of Ponthieu had ransom in mind and the fisherfolk had their percentage in mind. Guy of Ponthieu was courteous after a fashion, when the escort he sent for them had brought them to him at his castle of Beauvais. He even, at first, handed back the weapons which the fisherfolk had given to his men separately. But what he said in his polite manner, this squat small man with the face that looked as if someone had placed a powerful palm on top of his head and another under his chin and attempted to clap hands, was that he meant to keep them until King Edward paid a heavy fine for their return.

Harold, plainly, could hardly believe his ears. You expected such treatment if you were captured in battle, but they were not at war with Ponthieu. The Earl of Wessex, the smell of herrings still adhering to him, and his newly dried garments shrunken and stained with sea water, remarked glacially that the Count might have been misled by their shabby appearance. "Do you understand who I am?" he demanded.

"But of course! Harold, Earl of Wessex and the first man in England next to the king," said Guy with a happy chuckle. "Above all since you wiped out Gruffyd ap Llewellyn. The king relies on you now, *n'est-ce pas*? He'll pay high to get you back."

"I am also," said Harold warningly, "an ambassador from King Edward to the court of Duke William of Normandy."

Guy shrugged, a Gallic gesture with elbows in and palms upturned. "Ah well, ambassadors. He can send another."

Harold told Guy what he thought of this attitude, carefully translating some choice Anglo-Saxon phrases into idiomatic French so that his views should be perfectly clear. Ten minutes later, they were shackling him to the wall in one of the dungeons. One of the drier dungeons, Guy informed him. There were wetter ones, if he felt like sampling them. It could be arranged, on receipt of a few more profane remarks like the previous ones. Harold shut his mouth hard. He was not, he remembered, in Ponthieu alone.

Describing their leader's new quarters to Harold's shocked companions, Guy said that the same would befall any of them who insulted him. As it was, their weapons and valuables would be taken from them again and they would stay under strict guard. The ladies need fear no insult, of course. Provided that they behaved.

It was Wulfhild's temporary mistress, Lady Winefred, wife of one of Harold's Wessex thanes, who whispered to her husband: "They haven't taken everything, not quite. I've a chain of pure silver links inside my girdle, if we can find an itchy palm."

"Who do we send to?" muttered Thane Alfmaer, not a quick-witted man.

"Normandy, of course!" replied his wife in a fierce undertone.

The itchy palm was easily found; one of the housecarles looked about for disgruntled faces in the household, dropped a wary hint or two, and produced a cook who said he had lately been unjustly beaten. He was a free man, he said, and about to seek new employment. Winefred's girdle was ripped open and the chain wrenched into lengths ("Keep some back in case we need to try again," Alfmaer advised), and the cook took one of them and went. The reply was back in four days. Two knights, each with two men-at-arms, arrived with a formal request for Guy of Ponthieu to yield his captives to his suzerain, Duke William.

Guy firmly refused to comply. His captives, he said, were potentially far too valuable to him.

The second message arrived in three days, God and the saints alone knew how. This time the delegation consisted of two very senior knights, with escorts of twenty-five men each. They thundered into Beauvais, a foam-flecked mini-invasion, and marched into the castle without ceremony, nailed boots ringing on the stones.

If Earl Harold and his suite were not handed over to Duke William instantly, said the spokesman, slamming a heavy palm down on the table in front of Guy's nose, then Count Guy of Ponthieu would experience the full weight of William's wrath, of which, said the knight significantly, he had some past knowledge, had he not?

He had. Guy had been a rebel against William once, and been seized on the battlefield, and spent two years in William's custody. Everyone knew that tale. To the delight of Harold's eagerly listening companions, most of whom were in the hall breaking their morning fast, Guy turned unmistakeably green.

He made no verbal reply to the delegation. He looked at the mailed figures before him, shoulder and calf muscles bulging disconcertingly under their close-fitting armour, and William's devices on their shields and authority in every tone and gesture, and waited for what came next. Their next words were milder. It was of course customary in Guy's district for wealthy castaways to buy their way to freedom. The tone suggested that Guy's district was peopled by barbarous and ignorant savages, but Guy did not protest. In view of this, continued the spokesman, William, always prepared to observe local practices, was willing to pay a ransom himself. Certain lands of value would be given to Guy of Ponthieu. He advised the count to close with this generous and merciful proposal at once. A serious view would be taken of further defiance, or of any attempt to haggle. As it was, Duke William would not forget this impertinence. Should any similar insult be offered to him in the future . . .

The worth of the lands being offered was considerably less than the value of the ransom Guy had intended to demand from King Edward, but Harold was out of his dungeon and preparing for his journey to Normandy before the delegation had left.

And now, at last, they were near the Norman borders. The track had brought them to a low ridge, looking across a shallow vale to another ridge opposite. The track and its verges made a parting in the trees on that crest, and in that parting something glittered.

"Horsemen," said Harold. His voice was loud enough to carry forward to Guy. "Helms and spear points, surely. How far is the border?"

Guy looked over his shoulder. "A mile beyond that ridge. That will be William." He sounded morose.

They rode slowly on, a light wind shaking the Wessex dragons and Harold's personal standard of the Fighting Man, both of which were being borne prominently, close to Harold. Then, more quickly than anyone expected, the cavalcades had met.

The man heading the Norman procession was tall and magnificent and rode a black horse with a white blaze. He drew up a few feet from Guy's mule and raised a hand to halt the riders at his back. He sat still to appraise what he saw, before he spurred past Guy, acknowledging the count with a cold and barely civil nod. He came straight to Harold. He stopped his horse with its head alongside that of the earl's horse. "You are Harold of Wessex?"

"I am. Whom have I the honour of addressing?"

"Normandy," the tall man said with brevity.

They studied each other while the others watched. This, then, was the famous duke, "invincible" and "omniscient," in the words of his friends, "arrogant as Lucifer" and "sharp enough to cut his own throat one day," in the hopeful opinion of his foes. They saw his dark, hard eyes compare Harold's pallor with the tone of his companions' faces, and then drop to the earl's hands, one resting on his knee and the other grasping the reins, both bearing red gyve marks on the wrists. "I heard you had been kept in a dungeon," said the duke. "It was a dark one, was it not? My apologies for your appalling introduction to the Gallic lands. I was told what you looked like, my lord, by someone in my court who knew you once. Between his description and your banners, you were easy to recognise. Welcome to Normandy, where I hope you will find your treatment more fitting than in Ponthieu." His voice was deep and a little harsh, like the lines which were scored too strongly on his face for a man of only thirty-six.

He touched his horse with the spur and drew nearer to Harold. For a moment they all thought he was about to offer the embrace of an equal. But he did not lean forward and Harold, obliged to speak at last, said: "My lord, I have to thank you for bringing us out of Ponthieu. We are happy to be here."

"As I said," repeated William with a faint smile, "welcome." He held out a hand, fingers straight and together, and knuckles uppermost, and Harold perforce kissed it.

He was a grateful beneficiary now, in debt to the Duke of Normandy, and the duke knew it. The duke had seized on this chance to bring it about, like an expert chess player exploiting an unexpected opening. This was Duke William of Normandy, who had ruled his duchy since he was in his early teens, in the face of his own illegitimacy and the concerted opposition of men far older than himself. Harold's long duel with Gruffyd ap Llewellyn had been only an apprenticeship. So had King Edward's with Earl Godwin. Harold would never meet, and King Edward would never meet, a greater adversary than William.

"There are horses enough for all your suite," William said. "I wouldn't deprive Guy of his own animals. Besides," he added with his smile gleaming in his clean-shaven, weather-brown face, "mine are better. I've a fine stud of Barbs which will interest you, Earl Harold. I believe you have horse-breeding experiments in progress in England at present?"

"I shall be delighted to see your stud," said Harold, with sincerity.

The exchange of mounts was made, accompanied by introductions. William paid a little brief attention to Guy, to preserve the appearance of decorum and also the family proprieties. They were related, after a fashion. Once, many years ago, Guy's brother and William's sister had been man and wife. The relationship ended abruptly and acrimoniously when Guy's brother perished while assisting at a rebellion against Duke William. But there were children of the marriage and its existence could not quite be forgotten. Guy,

however, did not seem disposed to presume on it. He appeared relieved, if anything, when the duke moved away and Harold began to
present his own suite to the Norman.

Throughout the introductions, Wulfhild was acutely aware that
William and Harold were silently assessing each other, each listening
keenly to the timbre of the other's voice, each watching the movements of the other's face and body. During her years at Gruffyd's
court, watching the stratagems of Welsh politics, she had learned a
good deal about reading faces. She knew that Harold, within one
minute of meeting the duke, was estimating his strength as a potential foe. She knew that William had recognised in Harold a warrior
of stature, like himself, and was drawn to him. Friends or foes:
which would they become?

The introduction reached Lady Winefred and now touched on
herself as Winefred's companion. Also, surprisingly, as a ward of
Earl Harold. William's gaze paused on her; he was evidently wondering what the relationship was. But he did not ask, and passed on
to the next member of the entourage. She tried to take in who,
among the Normans, was who.

The slim dark man was William Malet, she realised with interest—Lady Aldith's Norman uncle of whom they had heard so
much in Mercia. An older man who had removed his helmet in the
warmth, to reveal short, greying hair, was the duke's seneschal.
"Another namesake of mine, William FitzOsbern. His father was my
guardian and died in my service," said the duke. A somewhat obese
prelate was the duke's half brother, Bishop Odo. "And this is Count
Eustace of Boulogne . . . But you and Earl Harold have met, I
believe, Eustace?"

Since Eustace had been the leader of the Frenchmen who
caused the Dover riot which had precipitated the Godwins into
exile, this was a tactful way to put it. The large, dark, florid count
exchanged uneasy civilities with Harold.

"And now," said William, adroitly separating them, "you know
you're among friends, Earl Harold. But I must tell you you're also
among relatives. We couldn't bring your brother Wulfnoth. He's in a
monastery and studying for the priesthood. But let me introduce you
to your nephew Hakon Sweynson. Hakon, this is your uncle
Harold. He may have grown a little since you saw him last, Earl
Harold."

And there he was, an undeniable Godwin with his vivid ginger head and lightly tanned skin. Only his brown eyes were not those of the Godwin clan. Harold, his face opening suddenly into a great gladness, leant from his saddle to embrace his nephew and they were both laughing and thumping each other's backs.

Then Harold detached himself, straightening in the saddle, and turned to Wulfhild. "Wulfhild, bring your pony over here. You must meet your cousin, Hakon."

Hakon blinked. "My . . . ?"

"This," said Harold to Wulfhild, "is the son of my brother Sweyn and one Edgiva, sister to Brand Woodcutter. And this lady, Hakon, is Wulfhild daughter of Brand. Tell me, Hakon, where *is* Brand?"

In Rouen, William had built himself a ducal palace. It had fortifications, but it was not a castle. It was of light-coloured stone, with a red tiled roof, and its watchtowers had been designed by an architect who had visited Byzantium. They were shaped like minarets.

Within, the palace was comfortable, even luxurious. William himself was not a luxurious man, but the Duchess Matilda liked warmth and elegance and she had supervised the furnishing. Thick, richly embroidered hangings and well-fitted doors kept out draughts and there were good furs to upholster the carved, ornate stools and settles. The great hall with its double line of stout supporting pillars still had something castlelike about it. But the rooms given to Harold and his suite offered both graciousness and a measure of privacy. He had no fault to find with them.

There was one room of fair size, with lively hunting murals round the window and two braziers on silver stands. Here Harold and his immediate companions could sleep. The three smaller rooms adjoining could house the married thanes and the rest of the party, more or less. Some of the housecarles would sleep in the hall and Wulfhild and the other maid could share the nearby chamber which housed Duchess Matilda's ladies.

For the moment, Wulfhild was needed by Lady Winefred, to plait her hair neatly and put away her clothes. Travel on pack-mule did nothing for good fabrics, which usually came out of their hampers looking like colourful dusters. Wulfhild brushed and braided, shook and pressed, assiduously. She was glad to be occupied. It steadied her hands and kept her mind off the cold quivering in the pit of her stomach.

Earl Harold had asked her cousin—her debonair, flamboyant, foreign, and improbable cousin Hakon—to fetch his uncle Brand to these apartments.

In a short time she would be face to face with her father. She herself had asked to meet him. She ought to be glad. But he would be a stranger and till today he had not known that she existed. What if he were angry, or embarrassed? She folded gowns away in a chest and thought: What have I done? And arranged sandals in a row beneath the chest, with extreme care. If there was nothing alive between herself and her father, she would still have this other self, Wulfhild, the experienced attendant, to retreat to. Winefred liked her. Perhaps she might stay with Winefred.

In the adjoining room, Harold was almost equally nervous. His unease was twofold. He too was wondering if it was wise to introduce Wulfhild to her father. In England, he thought, Wulfhild had been foremost in his mind; time had made Brand Woodcutter unreal. But Brand Woodcutter would be flesh and blood in the same room as himself within the next few minutes, and if he had made a mistake, Wulfhild might pay for it. And there was the old quarrel between Brand and himself. That was his second cause of uncertainty. Even now, he realised, he did not know what the sight of Brand's face would do to him. He had understood, long ago, the reasons for the Woodcutter's betrayal. But it remained, for ever, a betrayal.

Brand probably felt the same, he supposed. He had not come with the welcoming party to the border, though Hakon said he had been invited. So Harold sat on a wide, expensively covered stool, with polished oak arms at each side, and looked through a narrow, angled window at the roofs of Rouen, and worried.

He had said to Hakon: "Send your uncle to me, if he'll come. But don't come with him. I must meet him alone." And Hakon, obviously disappointed of an intriguing meeting, had looked petulant. What sort of job had Brand made of being Hakon's guardian? The boy was handsome and a fine horseman, but he had showed off all the way back to Rouen, making his horse dance and rear. The sort of thing Sweyn used to do. Oh well, the boy was probably Sweyn's son all through and Brand had no doubt done his best. But where *was* Brand? Had he refused to come?

"Sir Brand," said a page in the open doorway, and Brand was there.

Thirteen years, Harold found, could make differences in unexpected ways.

The unexpectedness this time was the sense of unfamiliarity. He had expected to see someone he knew, a one-time friend and later betrayer, the focus for the powerful and incompatible emotions of affection and hate. He had expected, and partly feared, to see conciliation in that man's face. What he actually saw was a dark, stocky stranger with heavy eyebrows and watchful brown eyes, with hair cut short and chin shaven in the Norman fashion, clothes of Norman cut, and a stiffness in his bearing which suggested that from cervical vertebrae to coccyx bone he was rigid with reluctance to be here at all and had not the slightest desire to conciliate anybody.

The page went out, shutting the heavy door after him. The two men were in privacy, nothing but a stretch of flag-stoned floor, thirteen years, and a quarrel between them. "Sir Brand . . . you are a knight now, Hakon tells me . . ." Harold said, and immediately thought it sounded sarcastic. The dark man said: "I hear you are the Earl of Wessex now, my lord," and then fell silent, awaiting whatever came next. Harold was forced to start again.

"There's a seat here and a jug of wine. Will you sit down?"

The dark man did so. "I congratulate you," he said, "on your rescue from Guy of Ponthieu, and on your escape from shipwreck. I imagine you have come to take your kinsmen home? I shall miss them but it is probably best for them to return to England." He spoke in English, and it still had a faint trace of the country accent he had brought from his home in Worcestershire to Godwin's hall long ago.

"Brand," said Harold, reaching for the jug and abandoning caution in favour of plain speaking, "will you stop talking like a conversation in a Latin primer and unbend? You've made your life in Normandy. I'm glad of it. You're right that I hope to discuss the return of my kinsmen, but it will all take time. The duke doesn't know about it yet, by the way, so please don't mention it. I'm relieved that you think it a good idea too. Only, since I was in the Norman court at all, did you think I wouldn't ask for you? You've only been the guardian of my nephew for thirteen years! And what do you mean," said Harold, pointing at Brand with a forefinger spared from the hand that grasped a goblet, "by refusing to join the welcoming party at the frontier? Now, just tell me that. Here's your wine."

Brand took it and their fingers met and they checked. Harold's other arm shot out and gripped Brand's shoulder. "*Brand.* I'm glad to see you, will you believe it? Did you refuse to come to the border because you got us exiled once? Did you think I'd pull a blade on you when we came face-to-face? It's all right, man. It's all over. Forget it."

"I didn't know what you'd think or say," said Brand, as Harold released him. "I didn't know what I'd think or say myself. How . . . how is everyone at home? Tostig? Your other brothers? Lady Eadgyth?"

Awkwardness dissolved, of itself. The simple business of exchanging news was the solvent. It supplied absorbing topics which were not fraught. Harold said he was sad to hear of the death of Brand's wife, and asked after the daughters.

"In a convent," Brand said. "Though not to take the veil, I hope. I saw enough of that with my sister. In fact, the elder girl is betrothed. But a convent can teach them the things girls need to know, better than I can. I have some land, of course—my knight's fee—and my friend Peter who came to Normandy with me manages it for me. But the girls couldn't stay out there without Hild. The younger one, Edgiva, does talk of taking up the religious life, but I hope it comes to nothing. Is there any news of my own relatives in Worcestershire?"

He had a mother and a married brother with a family, all still living on the old farm. "They escaped trouble in the Welsh raids," Harold told him. "As far as I know, they're well. Did you get the news about Wales, over here?" He launched into an account of the war against Gruffyd and the perfidious behaviour of Earl Alfgar.

Brand had heard some of it. "A minstrel, a man called Ivon Taillefer, went from here to a bards' festival in Wales last year. He told us that a campaign had begun. But we didn't hear about the trick with the pigeons. I call that clever. But your own family? You didn't say . . ."

"Tostig has trouble at times in Northumbria. I think he mishandles his thanes and I'm sorry to say he quarrels with his bishops as well. Countess Gytha is well, and Eadgyth and I have five children now." Brand flushed and Harold smiled. Then he put down his goblet and reverted to the thing on the surface of both their minds.

"Thirteen years is a long time. At the time, I'd have put a sword in you with pleasure and trodden you flat with my foot on your body, pulling it out. God knows I've a temper. But you saw my mother afterwards, and she put it to me differently. She said that in your place she'd have done the same, because that grim old woman, the king's mother, was wrongly accused and there was no other way to clear her, and she was entitled to be cleared. Besides, we did get home again. If we hadn't, I might feel savage still. As things are . . . I surprise myself. It's true, I'm glad to see you, and I thank you for your care of Hakon."

"Did your father ever forgive me? I saw him last in Flanders and he walked by me as if I didn't exist."

"He never spoke of you."

"Then he didn't forgive me. I couldn't expect it."

"He's dead," said Harold. "You can't call him back now. He would have recalled some, if he could. Every man that died at Gildenford, I think. You can still see the mounds on that hillside, where those men are buried. These hard choices come to all men and maybe to women too. I wouldn't know about women. But you just have to learn to carry the pack so that it doesn't gall your skin. Tell me the Norman news."

Brand thought. "What news do you mean? The duke will have an audience with you later on and arrange for you to see Wulfnoth in his monastery. He'll tell you all about that himself. He's with an emissary from Maine now." He grinned. "There is a man who wants to transfer his allegiance. He owes it to Brittany and would rather owe it to the duke. The Count of Maine died suddenly after falling out with William, and now Count Conan of Brittany is squabbling with William too and a number of men are nervously rushing to make it clear they're on William's side."

"You admire William?"

"I owe him a great deal."

"I see," said Harold, and looked as if he did.

"He's generous, at least sometimes." Brand was not good at analysing people. "He's a good law-giver and he wins his wars."

"You prefer Normandy to England?"

"No," said Brand.

It was an unconsidered answer, Harold saw. And Brand, under the blue, waiting gaze of the man in front of him, wished he had considered it longer. He knew that Harold was waiting for him to say more. For the first time since they had met again, he became conscious of the Godwin aura, the overwhelming glamour of all members of that astonishing family. Once again, as so often since he first met the Godwins in his boyhood, he felt clumsy and inferior and obliged to do as he was bid.

"I'm English," he said, defensively. "So I suppose it's natural. I don't mean I want to come back. I've made a life here, as you said. I didn't want to be reminded of the past." Harold continued to wait and Brand took a deep lungful of air and in turn referred to the unmentionable. "What I did, that day when I talked about Gildenford to King Edward, I'd do again. You'd better know. But for all that, I honoured your father very much. I'd sooner have stayed in England to serve Godwins than come to Normandy to serve the duke. But now, as things have turned out, I have a future here that's worth having. I'm English, yes. But it doesn't matter."

"The man you left with my father in Flanders reached me safely," Harold said. "And without being marked by William's spies. If you got us exiled, you helped us out of it again." He laughed. "Your man took his time, God knows. It would be Odi Pathfinder, the man with the worst sense of direction in Europe! He went to the wrong end of Ireland first . . . But he arrived in the end and I kept my father's rendezvous. We were grateful for Odi. So!" He sat up straighter, uncrossed his legs and recrossed them the other way, with the air of one about to introduce a difficult subject. "One way and another, Brand, what with looking after Hakon and lending us Odi, you've paid your debts. Now it's my turn to do something for you . . ."

"I don't need . . ."

"I'm sure you don't, but you're going to get this, all the same. Be quiet while I tell you what it is, can't you?" He tilted his head back and raised his voice. "Wulfhild! Come here!" To Brand he said: "I'm about to give you a shock. But it may be a pleasant one."

A young woman entered from the adjoining apartment. Brand glanced questioningly at Harold, and then at the new arrival. She was about twenty, he thought, a brown-haired, sturdy girl with very blue eyes. Her features were strong, her jaw too square and her brows too heavy for beauty, yet the face was perfectly female and even attractive. Her voice, in which she answered Harold's greeting, was touched with an East Anglian accent.

"This is Wulfhild," said Harold, rising. "She's the daughter of one of Eadgyth's thrall women, but Eadgyth educated her when her mother died. Since then she's had a very interesting life as attendant to Lady Aldith of Mercia. In fact, she defended her mistress valiantly at Rhuddlan when a rude fellow, I'm sorry to say, offered Gruffyd's widow some insult. You should be proud of Wulfhild."

"*I* should?" said Brand.

He and Wulfhild stared at each other. Wulfhild thought: Yes, he is just a stranger. I don't know him. It makes no difference that he sired me. *I don't know him.* Then she remembered that she did know something, that Brand Woodcutter had not done what Harold had tried to do at Rhuddlan, that she had been born, after an unlikely fashion, of love. Harold had told her the circumstances. And she had asked to meet her father. She must try. She said: "I should be happy if you approved of me. I hope that you will."

"Yes, Brand, you should be proud." Harold led Wulfhild forward. "I told you I had a shock for you. No, stay sitting down. You'll wish you had, if you don't. It's time you got to know your eldest daughter. Wulfhild, my dear, give your father some more wine. I rather think he needs it."

2 ⚓ Courtship

"You ought to have told me," Brand said to Earl Harold. "You say you found out who Wulfhild's father was before I—you—before any of us left England. You could have told me. Why didn't you?"

"You had married Hild by then and we thought it might cause trouble in your life. Especially considering the circumstances . . ." The circumstances. Brand thought about that and admitted that the circumstances were disturbing. "The girl was safe with us," Harold said, "and we had a sense of . . . responsibility for her."

"Yes, I see . . ." said Brand.

His mind had slipped back through time, to a fenland hall, on a spring evening, with mist on the marshes . . . and Eadgyth . . .

When Harold had spoken her name at their meeting in Rouen, the sound of it had struck into him like an arrow, embarrassing and startling him. He had thought himself free of her long ago, even before his marriage. Hild, indeed, had grown in his mind for years before they married, slowly thrusting others out, and during their union she had kept him content. His and Hild's had not been a passionate kind of marriage. But it had been relieving and satisfying, like fresh water to a thirst. Only now, Hild was gone and his first grief was past and his body was growing hungry again and his mind was restless. And then Harold came, and uttered Eadgyth's name . . .

At the time of that fenland evening she had been young and unwed, slender and flamelike. At twenty-three he was desperately in love with her, not knowing that she had eyes only for Harold and that she was in anguish from Harold's holding-off. He remembered the evening meal in the hall that day and Eadgyth pausing by him on her way out, making a tryst with him, leaning over him so that he could smell the herbs her hair was washed in, speaking in a voice that only he and those near him could hear.

Harold had been near him.

Then the long, long wait in the moonlit courtyard for a girl who did not come, while yearning turned to despair and despair to agony. His retreat from the footsteps of a strange thrall girl, and his opening of a door into a hay store. And what he had seen there: Harold resting his back on a hay bale, and Eadgyth in his arms.

He had left the barn silently, his anger like hard-fired steel inside him. The thrall girl was by the well, drawing water. Brusquely he asked her for some. She gave it to him and with it a candid invitation. He accepted the invitation.

He passed the night with that nameless thrall, taking her in anger which she mistook for virility, knowing no better. After that he took no more notice of her, and forgot her entirely when he left the hall a few days later. But his seed had been planted without his knowledge and now it had grown and flowered and here was Wulfhild of whom he ought to be proud because she had valiantly defended her mistress in Rhuddlan and . . . "I gather," Harold had said, "that it was Wulfhild and one of Gruffyd's sons who invented between them the communication system with pigeons. Your enterprising daughter nearly lost me a war. She believed she was *my* daughter at one time. Well, I wish she was!"

Brand was still thinking it over, still on terms of cautious politeness towards this unheralded disturbance in his life—the caution was essentially the same as that with which one would greet the first warnings of an earthquake—when Duke William began a vigorous programme of entertainments for Earl Harold. There were hunting and hawking parties, visits to studs and farms and fortresses, and something new: tournaments.

For years, William had encouraged competitions in the knightly arts, in the form of mock battles between teams, with blunted weapons and a rough points system. But this time, as well as these mêlées there were to be competitions in which men could ride as individuals, throwing javelins or putting spears through a mark, or engaging in mock duels. The prizes offered were valuable. Harold

watched and was noticeably impressed, while William watched
Harold and seemed grimly and inexplicably amused. During the second of these tournaments Brand, who was taking part, was thrown
and sustained a broken collarbone. A real campaign in Brittany was
coming soon and for that he must be sound. He was not only out of
the rest of the programme, but Wulfhild was seconded to look after
him.

"Of course, let the child take care of her father. I've more ladies
than I can find occupation for, chérie, so let my Sybille maid you,"
Duchess Matilda said to Lady Winefred.

So for the next fortnight Wulfhild competently tied Brand's
sling every day and for the first few days helped him in and out of
shirts and tunics. The physical contact and the exchange of need and
service broke down constraint between them faster than any of
Harold's diplomacy could do. By the time they were seated side by
side to watch the prize-winners parade after the last mock combat, at
Lillebonne, they had become, after a fashion, friends.

To such a degree that he would miss her if Harold went home
soon and took Wulfhild with him. But there was no sign of Harold's
leaving yet. At the moment, indeed, embedded in the midst of William's family higher up in the stands, with the duke's eight-year-old
daughter, Agatha, holding his hand and telling him the names of the
winners, he looked established in Normandy for life.

The prize winners included Brand's and Harold's mutual
nephew, Hakon, and the young minstrel knight Ivon Taillefer,
whose dual gifts of music and warrior skills had made him one of the
leaders of the younger set at William's court. He and Hakon were
somewhat alike, both fashion-setters in dress and similar in possess-
ing the unusual combination of light hair and brown eyes. Both,
now, as they cantered round the arena on the sun-browned grass,
with the towers of Lillebonne in the background, were light-
heartedly showing off. Hakon was making his horse perform difficult manoeuvres as he had on the way to Rouen the day Harold
had arrived, and Ivon was throwing a naked sword up in the air and
catching it again, without injuring himself.

"I wish," said Wulfhild, "that Hakon wouldn't make a display
of himself like that."

Her father turned to her. "Why? It's natural. He won the prize
for throwing a javelin into a target. He's pleased."

Down in the arena, Hakon overreached himself, and his horse, fretted by the constant use of bit and spurs, wrenched its head free and bucked. Hakon kept his seat only by an undignified grab at the pommel. He at once, angrily, took it out on his horse with the spurs.

"That's why," said Wulfhild shortly. She added: "When Ivon Taillefer makes his horse dance, or throws up his sword, you *know* he'll do it successfully. But with Hakon . . . !"

Brand considered her, surprised. She had expressed something which he had felt for a long time but not been able to tease out into words. He felt, for the first time, something more than friendship for her. It was a sense of kinship, a knowledge that they were indeed of the same blood, father and daughter, with minds that could reach one another. But if they were to accept that relationship fully, things still remained to be said, and cleared away. Things that might well undo the link altogether. Without giving himself time to think, he said: "Wulfhild, I never asked your mother her name. What was it?"

He had dreaded asking that. How on earth did you ask your daughter her own mother's name and not offend her? But Wulfhild knew the circumstances of her extraordinary begetting, and he must know what they meant to her. This was a way to find out.

"She was called Berta," said Wulfhild calmly. "No, I know she didn't tell you. She never told me yours, either. She didn't think it mattered till she was dying. Then she told Lady Eadgyth."

"Did you mind? That I didn't ask her?" he said abruptly.

"No," said Wulfhild, mildly surprised. "Why should you? These things happen."

Her attention went back to the field, where Ivon Taillefer, who was the overall champion, having unhorsed more opponents during the mock battle than anyone else, was receiving a gift from Duchess Matilda. Brand studied his daughter's face. The definite, completed contours of it told their own story. "These things happen . . ." They had almost certainly happened to Wulfhild. She was not worldly in the sense that the nuns who were educating Hild's daughters used the word. They meant by it someone who had exchanged innocence for experience. Wulfhild had never really been innocent. She had been bred where no one was sheltered from life: in a thrall's hut, where mating followed maturity as naturally as it did among the cattle. He had let that happen, because it had never occurred to him that his single night with . . . He must think of her as Berta now

. . . could have an aftermath. It was his fault. He must be relieved that at least she hadn't condemned him for it.

"You have your mother's eyes," he told her, making amends. "If I didn't ask her name, I remembered her eyes. They were beautiful. The same blue as yours."

Wulfhild glanced round and smiled, accepting what was tacitly an apology. "Yes, Earl Harold said they came from my mother."

Duchess Matilda, having given Taillefer a small purse, was putting an amethyst brooch, silken-looped, on the end of his spear. "Give this to the lady of your choice . . . now! Let us see who you honour."

Taillefer grinned and lowered his spear. He wheeled his horse and began to canter round the arena, scanning the audience, the spear held at an angle to retain its ornament safely.

"I wish," said Brand, "that you would let me take you to see your sisters. I have told them about you. They want to meet you."

"I might embarrass them. Didn't you tell me that one of them is betrothed? What if her prospective family disapprove? I'm a very irregular member of your kinfolk."

"So is Hakon. His mother was a lapsed abbess. Your sisters were almost brought up with him. They're sensible girls, and in any case—this is Normandy. The duke's parents weren't married either. If you're afraid they'll be hurt on their mother's behalf . . . well, you were born long before I married their mother. You won't upset them, Wulfhild, and you won't upset Elfhild's marriage, either."

"Are you sure of that?" She turned and gravely examined his face and he saw, touched, how much she longed for that assurance.

"I'm sure," he said.

Taillefer had circled the field away from them and was coming to their part of the crowd last of all. He reined in as he reached them. His eyes and Wulfhild's met and she smiled. He extended the spear. Wulfhild, rising to acknowledge him, gently drew off the brooch. There was cheering, and a few indignant mutters from damsels of higher birth, who did not consider Wulfhild qualified to be their rival. Taillefer wheeled his horse for a final, solitary triumph canter round the field.

Brand blinked at his daughter. Was she considering a life as the wife of a Norman knight? Not that he objected to Taillefer; the

knight's name meant iron-cleaver in English and he was a noted warrior. But Wulfhild was so very English . . .

She had placed the brooch in her mantle and was studying the
effect with pleasure. "I miss England," she said. "Couldn't you come
home? When Earl Harold does?"

The evening feast was merry. The day had been successful. The
prize-winners were worthy of their prizes; the mêlée had been exciting. Too exciting, perhaps. There were some empty seats at the
table. Ivon Taillefer sang of the day's exploits, eulogistically of some
and hilariously of others, and was applauded as hard for his songs as
for his warrior's prowess earlier. Tumblers performed and a juggler,
and a man with a dancing bear came to show off its abilities. After
that, William's fool, Gollet, took the floor and inspired laughter at
the expense of all the most solemn people present. They were sitting
back to enjoy it when a small disturbance eddied at the door and a
man who looked like an English thane, with an escort of housecarles
in armour of the type favoured in Wessex, was brought in.

An usher hastened to William's side and whispered to him.
William looked along the table to Earl Harold. "It's Thane Ethelric
of Aldham, a place in your earldom of Wessex, apparently. He's asking for you."

"Times change," said the fool sorrowfully, shaking his head.
"Visitors to the court of Normandy ask first for Earl Harold these
days." He turned a couple of somersaults and popped up grinning in
front of Harold. He adopted a beggar's whine. "Will you employ me
when you're in the duke's seat, my lord?"

"Not if you make jokes like that," said Harold dispassionately.
William frowned. Years ago, Gollet the Fool had discovered an assassination plot against his master and run a grave risk to warn him,
and Gollet had a licensed tongue which was virtually never rebuked.
But it looked as if William was on the verge of rebuking it now. He
was opening his mouth to speak to Gollet, but Harold said quickly:
"My lord duke, may Thane Ethelric join us at the table? There's
room for his men lower down."

"So *that's* what the mêlée was really for!" exclaimed Gollet,
unimpressed by William's expression.

"Gollet," said the duke, "come here and stop annoying Earl

Harold. Some matters aren't for jesting. Let him hear his news from home in peace." The usher was now leading Thane Ethelric through the hall towards them, and William's sharp gaze flicked knowledgeably over the man's face. "We don't know that it's all good news," said the duke.

Watching from lower down, Brand thought, as Harold and the stranger sat side by side in talk after a brief personal introduction to the duke, that the news was far from good. Harold's face was grave and growing graver. Intent on the earl, Brand himself did not notice anyone approaching him. Then a hand pressed down on his shoulder and a voice he knew, though he could not at once identify it, said in his ear: "Sir Brand?"

He looked up. A flaxen, thick-set man with an amiable face was regarding him with comical hopefulness. Memory strove for a name and found it at last. "Odi!" said Brand. "Odi Pathfinder!"

It felt as if everything he had left behind in England had come to Normandy to find him. He left the table with Odi, to talk in a corner. They tumbled out news and greetings, in joyful undertones. "I heard you got to Ireland safely, Odi. Thank you for that. But what brings you here?"

"I came with him." Odi jerked his head towards Thane Ethelric. "Countess Gytha and Lady Eadgyth sent him. They're sending word that they've heard of Earl Harold's safety after the wreck and his capture in Ponthieu, and they're glad, but they want him to come home. There's trouble in Northumbria."

He was the same Odi, good-natured, cheerful, with a total inability to recognise news of momentous importance when he heard it. "Trouble over taxes and Wessex laws against feuding," he said unconcernedly. "Earl Tostig's own thanes wouldn't cooperate with him, so he took a few friends up from Wessex to help him and now the northern thanes have threatened to revolt. Some of the bishops went to protest to Earl Tostig and he confiscated their lands and now the Church is angry with him as well . . . Can we get any food here? We've been riding all day."

"Yes, of course," said Brand, his mind elsewhere.

In the Norman court, English affairs were known and the guardian of Hakon Sweynson could keep himself informed of major events there. If Tostig were in that kind of trouble, Earl Harold would be bound for home as fast as he could get his hands on a ship.

But since Harold and William had met, their meetings and conversations, many of which had taken place in public, had had interesting nuances. Repeatedly Harold had tried to discuss the purpose of his visit—the return home of the Godwin hostages—and repeatedly, smoothly, William had changed the subject or deferred it. And there was something else too, a species of undeclared rivalry, in their exchanges. Gollet, this evening, had lit it up in his too shrewd jesting.

Silently, Brand qualified his thoughts. Earl Harold would be bound for home as fast as he could . . . if William, Duke of Normandy, would let him.

Except on great feast days, William's court ended dinner well before bedtime. Afterwards, people scattered about their own business, to tend horses or play dice or meet their sweethearts or simply foregather with friends. It was the duke's habit to retire with Matilda to their private chamber, where they would sit with any favoured guests until William, an early riser, withdrew. Matilda, who was of the breed which sleeps late and rises reluctantly, generally sat on for a while, chatting with her ladies and continuing to talk to the guests. Of late, the guest in the case was usually Harold. It was becoming a habit.

After closing his talk with Thane Ethelric, Harold went to the ducal apartment later than usual, but with more purpose. His footsteps rang on the stone steps up to the door. The ducal couple were waiting, attended only by a page and Matilda's favourite lady. Matilda herself was stitching by the window, sitting on a pile of cushions because she was so small that without them she couldn't get the best of the light which the window still let in on this summer evening. William sat, body relaxed, in a chair of carved elm wood. The single cup of wine he commonly took after dinner waited politely untouched on a table beside him. A third chair was invitingly set for the tardy guest, and wine stood beside that too.

"We thought you'd forgotten us," William said lightly. With a motion of an upturned palm, he signed Harold to sit down.

"Earl Harold had his Englishmen to look after," Matilda said, studying the effect of her last few stitches, her head on one side. "They are well housed, I hope?"

"Thank you, yes," said Harold.

He sat down, knowing that they were watching him. Among the amusements which William had lately provided for him had been an exhibition of animals from far-off lands. An intrepid keeper had gone into the cage with a pair of lions to demonstrate their tameness. He felt, now, very much as the keeper must have felt. How long would the great cats go on purring? he wondered.

"You had news of Northumbria, I believe?" said William. "I overheard a little of it."

Naturally. And if he hadn't, someone would have overheard on his behalf. Nothing was secret from William, in William's court.

"It was very serious news." Harold sipped his wine. "Tostig is in danger of a revolt. I have much appreciated your hospitality, my lord, and I can't be sufficiently grateful for your intervention in Ponthieu. But it's time I concluded my business and went home."

"Oh, surely not!" exclaimed Matilda. Disappointment informed her voice and her heart-shaped face. "You've been here so little time and you may never come again. You never came before. So we must make the most of you."

Matilda was most decidedly feline. Neat and economical in build and movement even after seven children, she was paler in colouring than her sister, Tostig's honey-haired wife, and Harold thought she was colder emotionally. She was sensual without warmth, like a cat, and with a cat's savage streak. Her passion for William was founded in violence, if the rumours were correct. He had seen her appear in the morning with a face simultaneously bruised and smug. It was true that she had great charm. She was using it now. But one could be conscious of charm and not succumb to it.

He kept the dislike out of his voice as he said: "Your sister is Tostig's lady, madam. Are you not anxious for her?"

"I have every confidence in Tostig. I've met him," said Matilda serenely. Her light eyes met his limpidly. "I'm quite, quite sure he can master his earldom successfully. He struck me as a most resourceful young man."

"Brothers may mean well, rushing to each other's help," said William. "But a man can be the better for settling his own affairs. Besides, he has two more brothers in England, has he not? You need not hasten back on his account, Harold, I feel sure of it. Sleep on it and you'll realise that." He yawned. "I shall go to bed, I think. I was up before dawn this morning and I will be tomorrow too. I have a campaign to plan."

"Brittany?" said Harold civilly.

"Brittany," William agreed. "And the matter is now urgent. Count Conan of Brittany is besieging that former vassal of his who transferred his allegiance to me. The man has sent to me for help; a messenger came this morning . . . Well, he came over to me because he thought I was the stronger lord. I had better prove it. That reminds me. Only this afternoon I heard you regret that you were not taking part in the exercises. Tell me, Harold, what do you say to a real battle instead? Stay here with us long enough to bring Conan to heel, at least. Then we'll talk of concluding your business. Wulfnoth won't leave his monastery, of course, as you know. But we might discuss Hakon. But only after Brittany. I won't have time before that, alas . . . Don't keep our guest up too late, Matilda. Goodnight."

"You really must not leave us so soon," said Matilda as the door shut after her husband. She gave Harold her most enchanting smile, small teeth bright and pearled between pink lips. "You are such a good influence on my sons. They imitate you. And little Agatha would break her heart to part with you. The child adores you, did you know?"

Count Conan of Brittany's defecting liegeman was entrenched in the Castle of Dol, near the Breton coast. The way there led by a seaboard route across the mouth of the River Couesnon, which divided Normandy from Brittany. As they neared the river, the land grew increasingly wild, and in the grey, windy weather that descended at the outset of the campaign, it looked far from friendly. A sullen sea gnawed at the shores and ahead, overlooking the estuary, was a tall rock mass, dark and portentous. It was the kind of land that moulded men instead of being moulded by them. It was different from Normandy proper, the same difference that distinguished green Devon from Celtic Cornwall, at home. Harold, riding at William's side, commented on it.

"Celts?" said William. "The Bretons are Celts, yes. They have their own language and they're an obstinate, independent people. Only half Christian. They go in for polygamy and the priests can't stop them."

"I feel I'm coming among infidels!"

"Oh, not as bad as that. Come. Your own wasn't a priestly marriage, or so I've been told."

"No, it wasn't. But I've only one wife, all the same."

"Some of the Breton men," said William, unheeding, "have eight or nine wives, and one is said to have fifty sons. They've a fine population of warriors."

"Yet you are quite confident of the outcome of this war?"

William, for answer, looked over his shoulder.

Harold looked too. The Norman force was following in good order, half of it mounted and riding four abreast. Helmets and mail gleamed like a river of steel under the grey sky. Each mounted man had a tall horse up to his weight in full armour, trained not to shy at bloodshed, and replaceable from the excellent studs of Rouen. After the mounted men streamed the long, well-accoutred column of foot soldiers, moving steadily in close formation.

"The Bretons," said William, "tend to be disorganised. It offsets the advantage of numbers."

"If I were Conan, I should tremble," Harold said.

"I hope he is," said William.

A trumpet spoke and the column halted. William reined in and Harold stopped beside him. The river estuary lay before them, wide, but calm and shallow with sand banks breaking the surface in places. "Why have we stopped?" Harold asked. "We can ford that, surely?"

William smiled. "If you rode into that nice shallow water without a guide to help you, you and your horse would sink out of sight within minutes. God have mercy on any boatman who runs aground here. The local men use that great black rock of Mont St. Michel as a warning landmark and keep well clear. Most of that sand is quicksand. Ah! Here come our guides."

It seemed that there were safe routes across the sand, if you knew them. The guides were three foot-soldiers who had been bred in this locality. They led the way, and the armoured serpent which was William's army began a cautious advance across an invisible bridge. The serpent's licking tongue was the lead man's pole, constantly testing the ground ahead of him. William, riding on the heels of the guide, led the first company over, with Hakon Sweynson bringing up the rear. Harold, at William's request, remained to lead the second.

"I don't like this," said Odi Pathfinder grimly to Sir Brand Woodcutter, surveying the estuary before them. The sky was darkening, and under it the sand and sea had a desolate air.

"You could have stayed in Rouen with Thane Ethelric. You asked to come with me," Brand pointed out, amiably.

"I did. To a siege. No one said anything about quicksands."

"Get formed up," said Harold, riding past them. "I want to move off as soon as Hakon's away. The duke timed the journey to get us here at the ebb tide and we've got to take advantage of it. We can't cross the estuary fast, but we can at least start promptly."

They set out, imitating the company ahead, two abreast. "If I suddenly vanish," said Harold over his shoulder to Brand, "you'll know I took the wrong path."

"We ought to have Odi leading us!" Brand answered. Odi, who was used to jokes of this sort at his expense, merely snorted.

But though they made jokes and laughed at them all the way across, they were relieved when the long, tiring journey was done and they were pressing their mounts up the blessedly firm bank on the far side. Reaching flat ground, they turned their horses round to see how the rear of the column was faring.

It was still coming, the tail of it only in the middle of the estuary. A cold rain had begun, and where the sand cleared the surface of the water the spattering drops made pockmarks in it. Its greyish-yellow face looked evil and diseased. "I'll be thankful," said Harold quietly, "when they're all across it safely."

The men in the estuary agreed with him, Brand thought, judging by the way they were pressing on, afraid to lag even by a foot in case they failed to follow the man in front correctly.

"The horsemen shouldn't ride as close as that," said Harold sharply. "They were ordered to watch their distances." He rode forward, cupping his hand to his mouth, about to shout a warning command in the hope that it would reach at least some of the approaching knights. He was precisely three seconds too late.

A few yards from safety, one over-eager horseman had pressed too close to the rider ahead, and the horse in front kicked. They saw the horse which had received the kick toss up its head and leap sideways, and behind it another startled animal plunged as well. In an instant, it seemed, two horses and three men were in the sands, all screaming on a note of shimmering terror that set the whole line shuddering.

One of the horses was close enough to safety to get a purchase on firm ground under the sand, and someone had got to its head and was dragging it out. But the other horse, and the men, were sinking.

"Brand! Odi!" snapped Harold, dropping out of his saddle, "bring your shields and come!"

Long ago in Godwin's hall, Brand had learned how men fighting in a group must fight as one, blending their minds and moving their bodies in unison. And side by side with Harold in a shield wall against the Welsh, years before, he had found that this rapport varied, that it was easier between some men than others, and that between himself and Harold it was strong. It was still there.

He knew without further explanation what was wanted, and his shield was held out to the earl as Harold flung his own down on the sand. Brand's and Odi's shields followed it, the three together making a raft on which a man might safely lie flat on the breast of the quicksand and reach out his hands to a victim trapped within it.

"Hold my feet!" Harold ordered, and threw himself down on the raft.

Behind them, there was shouting. Out of the corner of his eye as he knelt by Harold's feet, Brand observed William, motionless on his horse, watching, more interested in Harold's performance, apparently, then in the lives of three of his own men. All over again, Brand, sliding wormlike after Harold with the earl's footsoles an inch from his nose, discovered that he loved the house of Godwin.

Ahead of him, Harold's voice boomed above the frantic cries of the men and the horse. "Keep still. You'll sink faster if you fight it. . . . I'll get you out, but *keep still!*" The promise was only for the men. There was no hope for the horse. Its heavy body was already sunk above the withers. Only its neck and head, with terrified eyes and distended nostrils, remained clear of the sand. Harold was within an arm's length of it. He reached to his belt and pulled out his dagger. The horse's screaming was swallowed into a gurgle and ceased. The head dropped on the suddenly crimsoned sand. Harold rested an arm on it and dragged himself forward another precious few inches to get the nearest man under the armpits. Over his shoulder he yelled: "*Pull!*"

Brand, kneeling up, gripped the earl's feet hard and dragged. The shield under him pressed down into the sucking sand but held. Harold's shoulders flexed, massively. The man came clear with a squelching plop and Harold almost threw him to safety where, behind Brand, Odi had collected other shields and made a wider raft. Choking and retching, the rescued man crawled the last few feet to firm ground. Harold had almost reached the second man.

The third had sunk furthest and was in despair, stretching out desperate hands. "I'll get you both out, *don't move*, I tell you!" Sweat poured off Harold's face, mixed with rain. He had grasped the second man and his muscles cracked as he strained. *"Brand! Pull!"* The words came in gasps, between huge, deliberate breaths. "Stop struggling, damn you! Leave it to me . . . *I'll save you* . . . Don't want a rupture for my pains!" He managed to laugh and the man in his grip clutched at that sound of sanity as if it were a rope and was still a moment. Odi joined himself to the human chain. The second man came free of the sand, which had had him to the thighs, and collapsed on top of them. Between them they dragged him clear of danger.

Two were free. One to go.

The sand was creeping towards the belt of the third victim and he was crying. Harold seized hold of him and dragged, uselessly. He dropped his head, to ease his breathing. He could support the man but no more. The mineral enemy was too powerful. Harold raised his head again. *"Rope!"* he bawled.

Through the swish of the rain, which had become a downpour, they lip-read as much as heard him. Mercifully, someone had already thought of rope and was bringing it. It sailed out, uncoiling. Harold looped it under the trapped man's armpits and bellowed for another. It came, and he fixed it round the captive's waist. A dozen pairs of hands, and a horse, were already on the shoreward ends. "Haul away!" roared the earl.

The quicksand surrendered, inch by inch. The rescuers could not use the full strength at their disposal for fear of injuring the man they wished to save, so fierce was the hold of the morass. But it was done in the end, and he collapsed into semi-conscious repose on the shore, and the rain pelting on his prone body washed the clinging grains from his limbs. Harold slithered backwards off the shields and knelt to see if the man was hurt. Nearby, the second man rescued was being violently sick and the first was gulping wine from some-one's leather flask, which shook in his hand.

William rode slowly towards them. He dismounted, as Harold straightened up. "I shall be glad to have you at my side in any battle, Harold Earl of Wessex," said the duke.

3 ❋ *Ravishment*

Count Conan had heard of their approach and he retreated. They pursued him zestfully to the town of Rennes and on again to Dinan, where he took refuge in a stout stone castle. But if the castle was stone, the surrounding town was not and neither was its timber palisade. William encircled the town, fired the palisade, and loosed a hail of fire-arrows over the top of it. Presently the gate opened and the town's chief citizens marched out to make a formal surrender. Without their support, Conan had no access to their supplies and every chance of treachery from their numerous kinsfolk inside the castle. He too emerged, a small, sharp-featured man, carrying the keys of the castle on the end of a spear. He solemnly presented them to William. Majestic and ceremonious, mantled in crimson velvet, statuesquely seated on his muscular black charger, William received them and invited Conan to his tent that night to dine.

The tent was as big as a young hall and was doing duty as one. The banquet was as populated and formal as any Rouen feast. When stomachs were agreeably full (mainly with beef and mutton commandeered from Conan) and the excellent wine (presented by Conan as an approximately voluntary gesture of goodwill) was coursing warmly round everyone's veins, Ivon Taillefer rose to sing. He sang the exploits of Harold of Wessex, the mighty English earl who lifted men from quicksands as a giant would lift children from their beds.

"Earl Harold is the hero of this campaign," William said to his guest of honour.

"He looks sad for a hero," said Conan glumly. Conan thought that the earl's expression was as bleak as he knew his own to be.

"I shall amend that," William assured him. "I have a great honour to confer on him."

"Is *he* to put his hands between yours as well?" asked Conan dryly.

"He is. I shall make him a knight of Normandy today."

"And he will swear fealty to you. I see," said Conan, and did.

The oath-swearing followed the feast, before the serious drinking set in. Conan went first, after a speech by William explaining that from henceforth he and Conan would be pledged to each other's support and could never again quarrel over their vassals, since to follow one was to follow the other. Conan dutifully knelt and promised to make William's enemies his, and never to take up arms against him. William in turn promised Conan aid in all lawful quarrels and to refrain for ever from unprovoked aggression. The duke swore with a conviction that pointed Conan's lack of it. But with or without conviction, the oath was binding and Conan knew it. It was a witnessed contract. Only an oath sworn on a holy relic would be more sacred.

"And now," said William as Conan went back to his place, "for our second ceremony. There is no more joyous business than to reward great deeds fittingly. Here at my side sits Earl Harold of England, of whom my minstrel knight Ivon Taillefer has sung to you. He is an earl in his own land. But here in Normandy he still lacks a title that a warrior such as he should possess. He is not yet a knight." Harold's face was blank. "Some of the ceremonies of a peacetime knighting must be omitted," said William, addressing him. "But on the battlefield, mettle is tested without vigils and mere games of war. Yours was tested and not found wanting. Harold of Wessex, kneel for your reward."

Harold did as he was bidden. He made the oath of fealty which all knights made to their overlords. His voice did not utter the words much more easily than Conan's, and his thanes looked on unsmiling.

Hakon Sweynson said under his breath to Brand Woodcutter: "What's wrong, Uncle? Earl Harold has been honoured today and he looks as dismal as if he'd just buried his best friend. Why?"

"It would take too long to explain," said Brand. "And you ought to be able to work it out, anyway."

In the morning, to seal the new, perfect, and trusting amity between Conan and William a hunting party was arranged. Within an hour of setting out, Harold found that he and the duke had become separated from Conan's party and indeed from their own companions. He scanned the duke's countenance thoughtfully and commented on the poor scent-holding qualities of stony ground.

"It's all one to me. I am not hunting stags today, Sir Harold." The duke's smile was candid and friendly. "I think we should talk."

Harold pulled up and sat still, watching the lean hounds quest among the granite pebbles and the heather. "Yes, I think that too. I'm concerned for my brother Tostig and I have other responsibilities at home. I also have a mission to complete. It's time I talked of the date when I set sail to England, and who is to accompany me. You have honoured me with arms and shown me hospitality I can never forget. I hope one day to repay it. But for now, it's time I left Normandy."

"Quite. I understand." William was calm. "As to the matter that brought you here, we can settle that at once. Your brother Wulfnoth has told you personally, I believe, that he wishes to remain in his monastery?"

"Yes."

"I have great respect for the houses of God," said William. "Wulfnoth's value as a hostage has been nil since he entered one. As for Hakon, he may return home with you. But before you go, there is something that must be discussed openly. We are both thinking about it, so let us have it out in speech."

"Yes?"

"Your King Edward is aging. I am his designated heir since he has no sons, and I hear that the Atheling's boy Edgar shows little promise of growing into a king for England."

"He's young yet."

"At his age I was running Normandy. And at his age you, Sir Harold, were in your father's confidence and assisting him in his . . . duties. You were with him at Gildenford, I know."

A hound whimpered and the horses pricked their ears. Their riders held them back. Harold waited silently. "England," said William, "needs a strong, experienced ruler, from all I can learn. She's beset with potential foes on the Welsh and Scottish borders and over the sea in Norway, and divided by power struggles within. Am I right?"

"If you mean Tostig . . ."

"Am I right?"

"There are always problems in Northumbria. And there are always those outside England who cast covetous glances at it."

William smiled. "Do you mean me? But I was named heir."

"I was not there when . . ."

"No, but I was. And so was King Edward. I make no unjust claims. His Witan of the day confirmed the nomination. Did they not?"

"Yes," said Harold bleakly.

"Last night," said the duke, "you put your hands between mine, when you became a knight. You owe me support in all my lawful causes now."

"Yes, I know."

"We understand each other. Well, we both have Northmen for forebears; we are cousins in a way. I hardly need to ask more of you than you gave last night. But this matter is heavy and perhaps merits separate treatment. From what I have seen of you, Sir Harold, I could ask no better support when I come to England than yours. You could turn the scale for me between a peaceful accession and one with bloodshed. I am not seeking bloodshed. I want the English leaders with me, upholding my rule in their earldoms and on their manors. Those who do uphold me I shall treat well . . ."

"And those who don't?"

William shrugged. "What use is a disloyal man to me, and can he expect to hold land in my kingdom? I should dispossess the men who defy me and replace them with trustworthy ones. But not gladly. It would be better if I could avoid war and confiscations. Your support could make the difference between peace and war—for the English, not just for me. Give me that support. Pledge it. When I am king in England I will refuse you nothing of power or wealth that you ask for, short of the crown itself. Help me to inherit in peace."

"The final disposition of the throne lies with the Witan Council at the time of the king's death," said Harold slowly. "Even the king only recommends a successor. The Witan can countermand his deathbed wishes, if they feel it right."

"But generally speaking, they respect those wishes," said William.

Harold stared straight ahead between his mount's ears. Here in

Normandy, in William's power, was no place to repeat Edward's latest remarks on the subject of William as a candidate.

The hounds seemed to have given up. One had sat down to scratch. "What if I refuse?" Harold said.

"But, my dear Sir Harold, why should you?"

"I might have reasons. I ask you again: What if I refuse?"

Huntsmen were coming to collect the hounds and try for a new scent somewhere else. "Naturally you want to think it over," said William pleasantly. "It's a serious matter. But I know that when you have considered, you'll agree. Indeed, my duchess has some inducements to offer which I know you'll find irresistible. I have no doubt of your consent at all."

"Am I to understand," said Harold, "that I shall be kept here, a prisoner, till I swear?"

"A prisoner? Certainly not. You are my honoured guest as long as you remain in Normandy."

"Which could be the rest of my life?"

"The rest of your life?" William turned his horse to follow the retreating hounds. "If you chose to make your future here instead of in England, rest assured you would be welcome. You would have every chance of a glorious career unless King Edward sent an army to get you back. Do you think he would?"

"I should like to know one thing."

"And that is?" Side by side, the horses broke into a lope.

"What did Walter of Maine and his wife die of?"

The dark hawk face turned to him. "I didn't poison them, Harold, though I know that has been rumoured. Nor did I order their deaths. Believe me." A few minutes later, as if he had been following a secret train of thought, the duke added: "A good wife is a wonderful thing, Earl Harold."

"So you sail for England soon. You will be missed," said Ivon Taillefer to Wulfhild.

They stood on the walls of Rouen Palace, to which the triumphant army had returned two days before. They rested their elbows on adjacent crenellations and a soft summer wind blew in their faces. A smell of cut corn came up to them and a little drowsy birdsong. It was late afternoon.

"Is your father going?" he asked when she remained quiet.

"He hasn't said so. Hakon, my cousin, is to come." During her time in Alveva's household, Wulfhild had learned a serviceable amount of French and it had improved in Normandy.

"And you? Wulfhild, if your father stays, will you stay with him?"

"No. I want to be with him, but not in Normandy." Wulfhild nodded to the view of fields and forest. "It's too different from England. It even smells different. It isn't home."

"What if Normandy offered you a real home of your own? A manor, an estate, to go to as its mistress? Would you stay then?"

Wulfhild turned to look at him. Taillefer in maturity had a fair-skinned face with a strong aquiline nose that had been less apparent a few years before. His shoulders had broadened as he entered his twenties and his hands, dusted on the backs with light gold hairs, were shapely and strong. She read a question in his brown eyes. The dovecot boy had asked it at Thetford; and later on, in Wales, so had Maredudd. To them she had said yes. But this was different.

"Say plainly what you mean," she said.

"I'm inviting you to marry me."

"I thought perhaps you were," said Wulfhild, and left it there. He waited. At length she said: "Your father wouldn't have liked it."

"My father's dead."

"I've no dower. I'm the natural daughter of Sir Brand by a serf."

"My lord duke is the natural son of Duke Robert by a tanner's daughter. He's the greatest man I know. And I've enough without your dower."

"But why *me?*" Wulfhild said almost exasperatedly. "What can I offer you? We're not alike. I can't sing. I don't know one string from the next on the lyre. You live in a world of . . . heroic deeds and music and words and I don't understand your world. I live with practical things, like worrying about Lady Winefred's seasickness. So, why me?"

"I met the minstrel Lord Berddig in Wales. And later, he visited Normandy. Minstrels have each other to talk music with, you know. We travel and meet each other and exchange news. He told me of Wulfhild, the attendant on Lady Aldith, who fought to save her mistress from assault at Rhuddan. I knew that tale before the rest of the court heard it. You belong more to the world of heroic deeds than you think. Who was the man at Rhuddlan, by the way?"

"Some drunken soldier," said Wulfhild with inward amusement. "But I did nothing much. Lady Aldith was the brave one. She stabbed the man who killed her husband. He died of it six weeks later, so he never got a share of Wales. Prince Gruffyd's brothers and the southerner, Caradoc, divided it between them in the end."

"Mistress and maid were well suited, I think. Valour and faith are knightly virtues and you possess them. We are well suited too. Wulfhild, will you say yes?"

His voice was urgent and so was the hand he now laid on her arm, but in that warm, demanding grip she stood still. He shook her gently. "Wulfhild!"

"I was thinking of home. Trying to imagine . . . not saying *yes* to you, but *no* to going home. I can't. Ivon, places mean more to me than people. People . . . don't stay put. They die or wander away or turn out to be not what you thought. Places stay where they are and don't change much. I must go back to England. I can't live out of my own land. I was homesick in Wales. I want to be where my own tongue is spoken and the land has the shape and colour and smell of home. I miss the fenland most, but anywhere will do, as long as it's England. I'm homesick here and now. I think of England all the time." Her eyes met his gravely, sorry for his disappointment, apologising because for her the pain was so small and easily borne. "I'm the wrong wife for you anyway," she said firmly. "I'm not the well-born maiden you should marry. I'm not even a maiden."

"Nor am I. You'll want no man after me, I promise. I'll make all the rest seem wraiths beside me."

"I suppose," said Wulfhild, "you couldn't do that in England?"

It was Taillefer who now stood silent. Then he said: "Live there, you mean? But I've no lands or lord there, Wulfhild. My estates are here and William is my duke. I can only come when he does."

"And will he come?"

"He thinks so. But not yet. So for the moment I must say no to you, as you are saying no to me. You are saying that, I think."

"I'm sorry. But if I said yes . . . I *can't* say yes, if it means not going home!" For the first time there was conflict and distress in her voice and she drew her arm away from his grasp as if she feared him. She did fear him. It struck her suddenly that he might ask to show her his concept of love now, without marriage, and that he might indeed make all men wraiths beside him and then the choice between Ivon and England might cease to be easy but would become hard, intolerable, dragging her apart.

"Perhaps," he said, searching for hope, "it won't be so long. King Edward isn't young."

"I can't imagine William king in England."

Ivon raised surprised brows. "Why not? He would be better than that other one . . . Edward Edmundson, the Exile, the one who died. I met the Exile, you know. He wasn't a strong enough man for kingship, in my opinion."

"Met him?" Wulfhild was willing to encourage the conversation in a new direction. "When?"

"I was a travelling minstrel in his cavalcade from Cologne. In fact, my father had been looking for me and snatched me away on the very evening that Edward Edmundson fell ill. But on the journey from Cologne I had seen a good deal of him. I wasn't impressed. Now, William is a king born. No one will ever manage to poison him."

"Do you think Edward was poisoned, then?" said Wulfhild, who in Harold's train had heard a different story: that two different enemies had tried to dispose of Edward without success, and that Fate, ironically, had stepped in and done it for them.

"Wasn't he? I have always supposed he was, because I saw something odd myself that evening. I actually saw a man—he was a merchant thane and I think I heard someone address him as Thane Rolf—put his wine down beside Edward's wine, and then pick the Atheling's cup up. Leaving his own in its place. Oh, we've all done that by accident . . . But when I heard afterwards that Edward Edmundson had collapsed only a little later, it made me wonder. Only, by the time I did hear, I was far away and it was long after."

"There were attempts on him," said Wulfhild. "I even know who arranged one of them. Earl Alfgar of Mercia."

"Earl Alfgar . . . ? But how do you know?"

"Lady Aldith let it out, after her father was dead."

"Earl *Alfgar*! I'm glad," said Ivon sincerely. "I've always wondered if it was Duke William. And I didn't want to believe that. Thank you for telling me, Wulfhild."

Wulfhild, who knew that if Alfgar had been the source of one attempt, Normandy had almost certainly launched the other, smiled, and gently drew away from him. "I must go. Lady Winefred will need me." She hesitated. "Ivon . . ."

"Yes?"

"Ivon, I'm sorry I couldn't give you a happier answer. I'm sorry if I hurt you. I didn't want to. Goodbye."

She did not touch him in parting, and pretended not to see the hand he stretched towards her. Had they touched again, she might have stayed.

Brand came awake on the instant, springing alert from the depths of sleep, as he had been trained to do by Godwin. Godwin had held surprise exercises, waking his men to imaginary emergencies with a shout and a horn blast and if you weren't outside, armed and wide awake, before he had counted sixty, heaven help you. Now he was in mid-floor in seconds, shedding dreams like bed-rugs and face-to-face with the man who had called his name. Harold, clad only in shirt and hose, held up a flaring torch to light the room and they stared at each other. The guards past whom the earl had just brushed were bristling in the doorway and Hakon, who shared Brand's quarters, had rolled from his own bed, grabbing for a dagger and shouting.

"Go back to sleep, Hakon. I'm sorry I woke you," Harold said sharply. "Brand, come with me."

Bemusedly, wrapped in a snatched-up robe, Brand followed the earl. Harold's own chamber was lit with half a dozen torches and a weak, waning moonlight and was empty, though snores came from the adjoining chamber. The earl barred the door and sat on the settle. He passed a hand over his forehead. A wobbly mixture of flambeaux and moonbeams was enough to do odd things to anyone's face but the distraught expression on Harold's wasn't due to that. Brand stood opposite him and waited, still bewildered and now with a dawning annoyance at being dragged from his bed as if the castle were on fire, which it patently was not. Harold had companions of his own, hadn't he, if he wanted someone with him? Brand contemplated the earl's desperate expression with little sympathy.

As he had on the occasion of their first, awkward meeting in Normandy, Harold offered hospitality, wine and a seat. He pushed a jug at Brand. "Sit down. Pour yourself some of that."

"I think I'd rather know what . . ."

One thing had changed since that first meeting. Brand had grown used to Harold again. At the first meeting, he had spoken in English. Now habit had reasserted itself and he used French. Irritation suddenly possessed the earl's face, and blazed into anger. "It wasn't an order, you . . . you half-Gallicised wantwit! I'm a human being in need of another human being and I've also got to make you an apology, so naturally you're the human being I want! Sit down on this stool . . . Yes, this big wide one, *here* . . ." He shot out a foot and hooked it into the light. ". . . and drink!"

Blinking, Brand obeyed the order Harold said he was not giving, sat down, and took the jug. "An apology?" he said.

"An apology. No, two. One for dragging you here from your bed as if you had no right to your sleep. Still the same old Brand, aren't you? You come with me just as you always did when I called you to drop whatever you were doing and ride with me because your old pony steadied my wild Stormcock. Why do you put up with us Godwins, Brand? We debauch your sister and steal your girl and still you come when we whistle."

He had already had a good deal of wine himself. His voice was slightly slurred and the jug in Brand's hands was only a quarter full. There was another on the window seat in arm's reach of the earl. He grabbed it and splashed the contents impatiently into his goblet.

"I didn't always put up with you," Brand said with some acerbity. "I laid Sweyn on his back at swordpoint once and I broke the oath I swore to your father."

Harold's eyebrows jerked upwards. "I was wrong, you're not the same. No more you should be, after thirteen years. Brand, I want to ask you to come back to England with me, but before you answer you must listen to my second apology because it might make a difference to your answer. Because you might, if you don't hear me out, hesitate on account of that broken oath."

"I should," said Brand.

Harold shivered, though the room was not cold. He gulped wine. "I came here tonight," he said, "when I left the duke's rooms. I sent all my people away. I walked the floor for an hour. Now that I know it all . . . the final thing . . . all that William and his dear duchess are planning, I had to talk to someone or run berserk, bang out my brains on the wall or kill someone! Of all men, you should understand, Brand. If you don't, no one ever will. This is why I must apologise to you. When I first met you here, I wasn't sure what I should say to you. I harboured bitterness, anger, in spite of all my mother and my wife have said in your defence and all that I myself could see . . ."

"That was natural."

"Don't sound so prim, damn you! It's that that I'm sorry for! I swallowed it when it came to the point. I greeted you as a friend. But my face hid my heart and now I'm sorry for what was in my heart. I had no right to be bitter. We were guilty. We sold Alfred Exile and six hundred men to an ugly death at Gildenford. What right had we to demand your silence, or to sacrifice an innocent woman, an aging woman, to save ourselves?"

"Still, I swore to be silent. Oaths are sacred."

"Are they? That's the point, Brand. If a broken oath ever lay between us, it's wiped out now. I," said Harold in a voice as hard as the stone walls of Rouen Castle itself, "am about to become a bigger and more thoroughgoing oath-breaker than you ever were. There's a ceremony tomorrow. Do you know what it's about?"

"Your leave-taking from Normandy, I understood."

"Leave-taking! It's an oath-taking! I am to pledge myself to support William's claim to the throne when King Edward dies!"

"I see." Brand nodded. He had in fact wondered about the nature of that ceremony. William would not be William, he thought, if he failed to wring some kind of pledge of support from Harold on the grounds of that oath of fealty in Brittany. All the same, Brand had a question. "Aren't you pledged already to support King Edward's wishes, or at least the Witan's?"

"Of course I am. And King Edward's wishes now aren't what William imagines, either, let me tell you! But frankly I don't feel inclined to tell William that. I've gone as far as hints . . . But the fate that overtakes so many people who get in William's way is discouraging. William prefers to think of himself as still the designated heir and that's that. But that isn't all! By God, that isn't all! There's a betrothal ceremony as well. A *double* betrothal ceremony." Harold put his goblet down and folded his arms as if trying to hold his own anger in. "I'm to promise my sister Elfgiva to a Norman to ratify my support of William . . . Do you remember Elfgiva?"

"Your youngest sister? I never saw much of her. She was often ill, as far as I remember."

"She's still ill and I don't think she could stand the journey to Normandy, but William won't listen when I tell him. And on top of that I'm to . . . to . . ." He stumbled for words, so great was the outrage. Brand prompted: "Yes? You're to . . . ?"

Harold said at last in strangled tones: "It was the final thing that they sprang on me tonight. I am to pledge myself to . . . to . . . Brand, I don't know how to say it to you, to you of all men . . . To set aside Lady Eadgyth—yes, *Eadgyth!*—because I didn't marry her before a priest, and take to wife William's daughter Agatha. She's eight years old," said Harold bitterly, "and I'm forty-two. But she'll be marriageable in five or six years, says Duchess Matilda, which will give me ample time to 'arrange my affairs and provide for my existing family'—as if they were old horses or retired servants! The child Agatha adores me, so the age gap need not alarm me, apparently! Matilda even cited that Norwegian savage Harald Hardraada at me! He has two wives, she said. They live in friendship, sharing him! For rulers, the left-handed union and the state marriage, run together, are sometimes necessary, she said! William's father had a left-handed bond with William's mother, as well as an official marriage; and King Cnut had a church marriage and a concubine too. There are precedents, she cooed—the pretty, beguiling little monster!—and wise, mature people accept these things . . . She is sure that Eadgyth wouldn't stand in my way. What does she know of Eadgyth . . . ?

"She's hinted at this before; William keeps going to bed early and leaving her to entertain me. I suppose he thinks I'm more easily persuaded by an attractive woman! But till tonight it was only hints. Then she came out with it as settled. 'Of course, we'll announce both betrothals together!' It's all prepared for tomorrow: the oath of support in England and the two bethrothals, and all on the same basis. And do you know what that basis is?" Harold unfolded his arms and wagged a finger at Brand. "If I refuse I shall never go home. I'll be kept here, a tame bird in a luxurious cage, till I give in. I don't believe Matilda's human," said Harold murderously. "The marriage to Agatha is her idea, I'm sure of it! Her special contribution to the great scheme of getting a grip on me and a foothold in England. All of a piece with rescuing me from Ponthieu and making me a knight with my hands between William's. He and Matilda never miss an opportunity . . . ! Eadgyth and our children don't matter. What would Matilda do, I wonder, if William set up a second love nest?"

He paused to draw breath, got up with an angry movement, and started to walk about the room. Halfway across it his fury seized hold of him anew and he whirled round, shaking his hands in the air with fingers crooked as if he were throttling Matilda, against whom his rage seemed chiefly directed. "She's a changeling, Brand! The original Matilda was stolen from her cradle and this . . . this bloodless goblin put there instead. She isn't even human *size*! I understand," said the Earl of Wessex savagely, "that William beats her regularly. I'm not surprised. I'd like a turn at it myself. Now do you see my position?" He flung himself into his seat again. "I may have to break my oath of support to William . . . It's almost sure, in fact. It's for the king and the Witan to say, and they'll never consider him now. As for the betrothals, I *intend* to break them and that's the end of it. Elfgiva has constant sore throats and fevers. Even if she made the journey and went through with the marriage ceremony, I think childbearing would be the end of her. And I will not abandon Eadgyth, I *will not*! Agatha may adore me all she likes. She's a delightful child, but I shall never go through a marriage with her or anyone else. I'm a faithful husband. Give me credit for that, Brand . . . But I have to take the oaths, or I shall never get home—and I must get home because Tostig is in trouble and I have a life and a family there. So I'm perjured before I begin. But what else can I do?"

Brand shook his head, slowly.

"No. Exactly." Harold dropped his head into his hands. "There's no way out. So we're two of a kind now, aren't we?" He looked up. "Well, Brand? What about you? Will you come with me? It's not a question of me forgiving you. There's nothing to forgive. I can offer you a future in accordance with your status here. You're a knight here and Hakon's guardian. I can make you a thane, with appropriate landholdings. You can get that betrothed daughter of yours married before we leave. I hear from the young husband-to-be that she'd be very willing. Wulfhild and the other girl can come with you."

Brand shook his head. "My life is here, now."

"Are you so sure?"

"Yes. Look . . ." Brand was not good at discussing abstractions. He ran a hand through his short black hair, searching for words. "I changed my allegiance once, when I left your father and became Duke William's man. I've . . . You don't think I *wanted* to tell King Edward about Gildenford, do you? But since I did, the best I can do is not change sides again. I'm Duke William's man now."

"You were his man when you lent my father Odi Pathfinder, to bring a message to me. Did you ever really change your allegiance? Do you like Duke William?"

"I don't see what that . . ."

"Like him so much that you'll follow him to war against England? Think, Brand! If William considers himself the legal heir to England, what happens when King Edward dies and William isn't summoned? Brand, if William lands with an army do you want to be in that army? To fight your own folk? Come face-to-face with me, or Odi Pathfinder, or your own brother, on the field?"

Brand looked appalled. In the uncertain light he tried to read Harold's degree of earnestness. "Could it happen? Could it come to that?"

"I hope it won't, but it could, yes."

Brand leant forward, elbows on knees. It was his turn to put his face in his hands. He gave his consent without words. It took three days to find the words.

The following morning, on the other side of the Channel, King Edward and Lady Edith prepared to be shown round the section of the new West Minster which had just been finished. They waited in sunshine, escort ranged behind them, on a path of wooden boards laid over what was still raw building site and leading to the completed doorway. The master mason had rushed away, having apparently glimpsed beyond the door some small imperfection.

Hand on her husband's arm, Edith said: "Tostig was sorry not to be here. The man Gospatric—that uncle of Thane Ulf, the Gospatric who turned out to be the worst troublemaker of all in the north—wanted audience with him. To make more impossible demands and threats, no doubt. Do you know he has threatened to call out his followers and march on York? It's pure rebellion. You should hang Gospatric."

"As I grow older," said Edward calmly, "I see how little these things matter in the end. After all, we're here to nurture and save our souls. You're kind to care so much for your brother, but his troubles are very small in the eyes of God. This minster, which will stand as a place of prayer as long as men can speak the words of prayer, is infinitely more important."

"Here comes the mason," said Edith, recognising the mental wall between herself and Edward, the wall she could not scale. Edward could give his heart to an edifice of stone, she thought, because he felt a kinship with stone. She gave her heart to Tostig because he was in trouble and he was her brother and she had no one better. Edward was no husband and she had no child.

In Normany, standing bareheaded in a crowded chamber, Harold swore his oaths of fealty and betrothal. He spoke the lying words clearly since there was no way out and the least trace of falsehood might yet keep him from England. His hand was on a cruciform swordhilt, lying on a white-draped table; and Bishop Odo, half brother to the duke, received the oath. With his plump hand he raised the white cloth and beneath it Harold saw the relics, the holy bones of saints and martyrs on which, unknowing, he had sworn. They would turn his oath-breaking from a simple crime to a mortal sin. He knew that Brand was watching him in shock and pity and that William was watching him in triumph. He also knew that, mortal sin or not, it would make no difference.

4 ※ Escape

Oars splashed in a moving herringbone pattern with the three slim vessels as spinal columns. In single file, forging steadily through the usual scattering of fishing boats and traders and triremes, they were entering the Thames estuary.

For some of the travellers it had been a journey so sudden and unlooked for that it possessed the quality of a dream. It seemed so to Brand Woodcutter. And when he glanced towards Harold, standing motionless by the figurehead, he thought that the earl was lost in an unhappy vision and had forgotten the human world.

Throughout the voyage Harold had been very silent. The ship was called *Gerfalcon* and its figurehead was a brooding falcon's head, atop a fantastically elongated neck. In Harold's face, all the time, had been an expression as far-seeing and sombre as the falcon's. Scanning it sidelong, Brand found a startling new thought in his mind. Harold's face might have been that of a king.

It discouraged any attempt to break his loneliness with conversation. Brand turned to Wulfhild. "I never thought to see the Thames again. I shall wake up in Rouen soon, I think."

"I always meant to come back to England one day," said Hakon, sprawled amidships with his ginger head pillowed on a bundle of spare clothes. "It's a good thing you made us learn English, Uncle Brand."

Brand's youngest daughter, Edgiva, sitting wrapped in a dark hooded mantle that concealed her from inquisitive eyes, as became an intending nun, said: "Are we nearly there?"

"No," Brand told her. "At least, we're in English waters. But we have twenty miles to go before the Thames looks like a river and then there's a long haul upstream to London. This stretch always makes people impatient."

"What shall we do when we get there?" Edgiva asked.

"Stay in Earl Harold's hall. Visit your Uncle Rolf if he's in London. Then go to our own hall. Earl Harold has promised me some lands. We'll make a real home then. Shan't we, Wulfhild?"

Wulfhild smiled at her sister. Edgiva responded. The long-dreaded meeting between Wulfhild and her sisters had taken place without calamity. Elfhild had been too excited about her forthcoming marriage to feel anything but goodwill towards everyone, and if Edgiva had begun by being dutifully forbearing towards this product of her father's ungodly past, a more genuine friendship had put out shy leaves during the voyage.

But the smile faded. Edgiva drew her mantle closer. "A home? But, Father, you promised . . ." Brand sighed.

In making arrangements in Normandy for the other people in his life, he had met no difficulties. Elfhild was happy to marry, and his old friend Peter Longshanks, steward of his knight's fee, had married a Norman girl and chosen to stay where he was. They had parted with regret but no grief.

But Edgiva was another matter. Edgiva, on learning that she must leave the convent and go to England, wept, pleaded, and refused to eat. "As her father you have the right to insist," the abbess said concernedly to Brand. "But I must tell you that I have had two hundred novices through my hands and I know a vocation when I see one. You think this is only a child's fancy, because she bears the name of a nun who lapsed. But I think God was guiding you when you named her Edgiva. Take her to England if you must, but find a convent for her there. It is her rightful place."

"Yes, I promised," he said heavily. "If you really wish it. Your abbess gave me the names of several good houses in this country. But I want you to see your new home first, before you enter one. You should be able to recognise your own father's hall before you leave it for good. That's all."

They tied up for the night alongside a muddy islet and slept on board. The dawn tide carried them into the river proper and the evening one pushed them on the final miles upstream. As shadows were lengthening, they came to the landing stage and the steps of Harold's south-bank hall at London.

Word of their approach had preceded them. A crowd came out to the landing stage as they slid towards it. Brand, sparing a moment from the business of fending off as the current swung them nearly into a barge already moored there, felt his pulse lurch in recognition. The tall woman with the unveiled head was Countess Gytha, whom he had loved like his own mother, who had spoken for him. The woman beside her, with the red plaits escaping from her green-scarved head was Eadgyth, wife of Harold and once . . . Oh, forget that. He had forgotten it before; let it stay lost. In front of Eadgyth another figure had now moved, powerfully built, yellow-haired, male, its hands on its jewel-belted hips. Surely that was . . .

"Tostig!" Harold cried, and sprang neatly, without unbalancing the boat, out of it to the landing stage. "Tostig! I didn't know you were . . ."

Tostig ran down the steps to meet him. "We heard you were coming," he shouted. "The news left Normandy before you did." The words might have belonged to a fraternal greeting but something was seriously wrong with the tone. "So," said Tostig as he came within arm's length of his brother, "you've sworn away England to the Normans, have you?" And his fist swung up as he spoke.

Harold had spent much of his time in Ponthieu and Normandy restraining his temper in the face of provocation. Months of frustrated fury now released themselves. His left hand knocked Tostig's arm up and his right shot out and seized the front of Tostig's tunic. There was a short, savage scrimmage. Then somebody's feet slipped on the wet planks of the landing stage and they both fell into the river.

Brand and Odi, who were nearest, scrambled on to the stage to help. The adversaries surfaced, gasping and cursing, shaking wet hair out of their eyes. Harold accepted Brand's extended hand and Tostig, snarling, lunged for Harold's legs to drag him back. He was foiled by a thrust from an oar in the hands of the Countess Gytha, who had hurried down the steps to intervene.

"Welcome home, Harold," she said in her most dignified and arctic tones, laying the oar down in a handy position, and herself offering her eldest son a hand. Harold got a knee on the landing stage and Brand and Gytha pulled him upright. "How very clumsy of you to fall in just as you come ashore," said Gytha. "But you had no need to jump in after him, Tostig . . . That's right, Pathfinder, help Earl Tostig out . . . Harold can swim."

Tostig scrambled ashore and stood beside his brother. Both were dripping, ominous, and purple with anger. Their mother moved adroitly between them and stared them both down in turn. "Harold, here is Eadgyth," she said, and Eadgyth came eagerly down to dilute the emotional hell-brew further still, with a wifely embrace for Harold, regardless of the wet. Tostig, scowling, was left with recourse only to verbal attack.

His angry gaze wandered over the rest of Harold's companions. "So you've brought back the Woodcutter. I see. Well, one of you's as treacherous as the other. You make a handsome couple!"

He had been captured by Guy of Ponthieu, tricked by William of Normandy, and attacked by Tostig for the means of escape which his very care for Tostig had forced on him. Furthermore, this fraternal quarrel remained unhealed. Word came, the day after Harold's return, that a rising had started in Northumbria, emanating from one of Thane Gospatric's estates. Gospatric himself was at court but no one doubted that he had started the trouble by remote control, like someone shooting a fire-arrow into thatch. It would be the worse for him later, said Tostig menacingly, as he rounded up two hundred helpers from friends in Wessex, and prepared to gallop north to extinguish the flames. He refused aid from Harold. He could do without Brother Harold, he said ungratefully. He, Tostig, was grown-up now.

King Edward was pleased to see Harold safely home, distressed about Tostig's quarrelsome behaviour and Tostig's earldom, sympathetic about Harold's predicament over the oath-taking—but piously ineffective about all of them. They were but earthly concerns, he said, and drifted away to his chapel to meditate. Harold, rebuilding his self-respect, must seek for help elsewhere.

This being so, to become a benefactor, a giver of rank and riches, and a forgiver of ancient wrongs was balm to Earl Harold's abraded spirit. On the fourth day of August, 1064, the document was signed that made Brand Woodcutter one of Harold's thanes, and a landholder of Sussex.

They sat in Harold's hall—the earl, Brand, and Brand's two daughters—while Harold expounded on the details of the holding, a slate in front of him so that he could draw sketch maps on it. His hearers were attentive. It was a momentous day for Brand, who had never held a yard of English land in his life before, and he had impressed the importance of the day upon his daughters.

"The name of your chief holding," Harold said instructively, "is Fallowdene. It means the Golden Brown Valley. Something in the soil turns the leaves a superb colour in autumn; that's how the place got its name. It's about four miles long . . ." His hand swept over the slate. ". . . and contains a high proportion of woodland. Timber is part of your Lady Day dues. You have hunting rights: no one kills deer in the valley without your consent or mine. Now, as to its position. It's in the West Sussex downs about eight miles inland." A coastline appeared on the slate. "Andred Forest lies to the north, here. There aren't many rivers in the downland, but you've got one. You have a water-mill. You also have a steward and two thralls, as well as the usual free villagers. At the western end of the valley there's a separate village with its own farmlands, sublet to a tenant and called Westwater. In addition, there's another subletting over the hill to the south, in a bowl-shaped valley called Little Dene. The dues have been short from all three since the old lord died—not enough grain, and bull calves and lambs in lieu of honey. But you're farm-bred; you'll soon see to all that. Your fields are on the slopes above the woodland and it's good, well-drained land. This holding may be a little run-down, but it's essentially productive and valuable and it needs a good lord. Now, conditions of tenure . . ."

He listed them. Brand nodded. They were ordinary enough: grain and timber, honey and wool. "And ten able-bodied men if I go to war," Harold concluded, "of whom five must be professional housecarles."

Brand, who had risen to lean interestedly over the slate, straightened sharply. "I only have Odi. I brought none of my men from Normandy. I forbade them to come because of your warning that Normandy and England might one day fight . . . and I tried to persuade Peter Longshanks to come back with me because of that. But he chose to chance it. Only now, I've no followers!"

"I know. That's taken care of. The old lord had housecarles and some may still be there. Meanwhile, I've put it about among my thanes, and so has Gyrth among his, that you're looking for young men. You'll get volunteers fast enough. One or two have come forward already. There's one called Osric of Hereford, for instance. I recommend him. He was a Welsh prisoner once and he helped me defeat them by giving useful information . . . But about these tenure terms: I hadn't finished. There's Heathwood."

"Heathwood?"

"The old lord held Heathwood as well as Fallowdene and he never sublet it. It's under a steward. But he didn't hold direct of me. His immediate landlord was Heathwood Abbey. The abbey and the manor are both on the coast near Pevensey. The manor's small, but valuable because it has a salt pan and a local fishing community who pay rent in fresh fish. But the abbey attaches certain conditions to the tenancy, which may not appeal to you. Fallowdene can support you very well if you don't want Heathwood. You're lucky." Harold grinned. "Fallowdene was held by the abbey too at one time, but they failed to send any men to my father when he called out his army in 1051, after the Dover Riots. So when we got back from exile, my father took Fallowdene away from them. Fallowdene is clear of complications."

"What are the conditions with Heathwood?"

"That a member of the tenant's family, within two degrees of cousinship, should be in the Church. As priest, monk, or nun doesn't matter. But that's the condition and the abbey won't waive it."

Whereupon, and he had known that she would, even before Harold finished speaking, Edgiva volunteered. In her sweet voice with its underlying forcefulness, like honey on an iron spoon, she asked to be the member of the family who entitled Brand to Heathwood.

"There's a religious house for women near Fallowdene," Harold said, watching Brand's face. "A good one. May I ask why you're so against it? Your daughter wishes it, and I can tell you that my sister Gunhild has taken the veil and is very happy."

"*My* sister . . ." began Brand, but Harold cut him short.

"Your sister was forced into a nunnery. Your daughter wants to enter one. It's not the same. She'll be a novice to begin with, you know. She could change her mind. There'll be time . . ."

"I shan't change my mind," said Edgiva calmly.

". . . and Heathwood is worth having, in my opinion."

"Father," said Edgiva patiently, "you *promised*. Would you break your word?"

Brand flinched. He had lived with that reproach for thirteen years. "No," he said. "I would not."

Moving into the position of prospective mistress of Fallowdene by means of a single, natural sentence, Wulfhild said: "We brought few goods from Normandy and we don't know what we'll find at Fallowdene. Should we not buy some household goods to take with us?"

Brand turned to Edgiva. Edgiva, eyes on her lap, made it mutely plain that to her the household goods of Fallowdene were matters of no concern. "I suppose we ought to visit Rolf," Brand said. "He's a merchant, after all."

He and Wulfhild made the visit next day. It was not their first. Brand had paid his respects to Rolf shortly after arriving, and Rolf had amiably made his kinsfolk from Normandy welcome. Furthermore, when Wulfhild was sprung on him, he took her in his stride. Rolf's own life, in both the business and the private sectors, had had its chequered moments and he was not a censorious man.

They went, therefore, to call on him without formality. They were directed from his hall to the riverside berth where his ship the *Bridegift* lay. The sight of her recalled memories to Brand. "I helped build that ship," he said to Wulfhild as they went towards her. "For Rolf's father. In fact, I paid for her, to overcome old Eric's annoyance when I married Hild."

Just now, the ship was lying with a gangplank and guard rails leading to the bank, and a herd of somewhat scruffy cattle was being driven aboard her. Rolf was directing the operation, his fur-trimmed thane's mantle tossed aside and his middle-aged stomach looking very visible under his working tunic, which was too tight. He was getting to look remarkably like his father.

"Going into the cattle export business?" Brand asked as they joined him. "I thought you never touched livestock?"

"One must be ready to make changes as necessary. The market is good."

"For those?" Brand pointed at the cattle, whose tufty hides and thin flanks were evidence of their poor condition.

"Oh, I'm not selling these. I borrowed them for a trial loading to see how the ship needs adapting. Terrible, aren't they? God in Heaven, I'd never find buyers! We'll need a bit of work on the ship, that's obvious. We need pens that fix to the timbers inside. But I know now how many she can carry. All right!" He raised his voice to address the drovers. "That'll do. Unload them and take them back. I've seen all I need." He picked up his mantle from where it was flung over a post. "Well, what brings you here, Brand?"

"I've acquired land in Sussex. I may need some goods. Wulfhild thinks so. We'd like to look round your warehouse. Fair prices, of course."

"What sort of goods? I've got a few embroidered hangings from Italy and things of that kind. But pots and knives and furniture . . ."

"I've bought some pottery," said Wulfhild. "But we'd like to take some new tapestries and some silver and glass. Have you . . . ?"

There was no doubt, thought Brand, as he watched Wulfhild unroll the Italian hangings and unwrap protective fleeces from the green Cologne glass that now formed a regular part of Rolf's stock (despite its unfortunate associations, it sold well), that Wulfhild was better fitted to care for his hall than Edgiva. She possessed, in equal quantities, household expertise, judgement of quality, and instincts of economy.

"These hangings and this glass are just what we should put in a thane's hall, Father, but they're costly."

"I'm not a pauper," said Brand, amused. If he hadn't brought men or goods from Normandy, he had brought a treasure chest. His steady workmanlike method of fighting had inspired Sweyn Godwinson's nickname of Woodcutter, but it had also brought him some worthwhile contest prizes. "I like this green glass beaker," he said, picking one of Rolf's samples up and holding it to the light. "I've never seen one like it before."

"It's from Cologne," Rolf said. "They get the colour by means of the wood ash they use in the forests there. But just how it's done is secret. I've had some experiments carried out in England, but they didn't even produce good glass, let alone glass like that. So I've had to go on importing it. I discovered it when I was over there the year Edward Atheling came to England. It's brought me a good many new customers."

"Did you meet the Atheling?" Wulfhild asked idly, rolling hangings up again.

"Yes. I travelled with his train on the way back to England. You'd like some of that glass?"

"Yes. These pieces, if Father agrees." Wulfhild pointed to several items which she had set aside. Rolf considered them and his relatives and visibly struggled with himself. Family feeling won. "I'll reduce the price for you," he said generously.

5 ✳ Homecoming

Earl Harold, having business at one of his coastal estates, chose to bring Thane Brand to Fallowdene in person.

They did not take the quickest route from London, which would have been by the Chichester Road, which ran to the west of the downland. They wanted to visit Heathwood Manor first, which lay to the east. "You should come to Fallowdene last of all," Harold said. "It's your chief hall and you're not home till you get there. And once one is home after a journey, it's natural to want to stay there."

"Home," said Brand. "Yes, I shall want to stay there. Very well. Heathwood first."

Heathwood proved to be in excellent order and Harold, with Tostig's bitterness aching in him like an enflamed wound, was glad to watch Brand's enjoyment. The news from the north was of fierce repressive measures on Tostig's part and grumbling wrath on the part of the Northumbrians. He was angry with his brother and afraid for him, and grateful for this happier distraction.

Now they were nearing Fallowdene at last, riding westward under the northern edge of the downs, where Andred Forest swept up to the hills like a green sea. The chalk path meandered to and fro between downs and forest. Its latest turn was bringing it gently uphill again as it entered a fold in the chalk escarpments. The woods straggled after it; Andred was as insinuating as any ocean of water. But they were losing their grip now. One tree that grew above the path had struck solid chalk only just under the surface and only the fine root tips had been able to bury themselves. The rest made a tangled latticework on the ground all round the trunk. "The soil looks thin," said Brand doubtfully.

"Your soil is better than this," Harold reassured him. "It grows wheat and rye very successfully. You'll see."

They fell into single file as the path narrowed, awkwardly carved by the rains of centuries. Harold, Brand, and Brand's daughters were in front. The escort was behind, a mixture of Harold's men and six volunteers including the young man Osric. The six were Brand's future housecarles and were gradually being welded into a unit by Odi Pathfinder. Hakon had remained at court.

The path tipped itself over a narrow saddleback. They were high up now. The downs were a subtle, late-summer colour, not green, or golden or brown, but a blend of them all. "There's Fallowdene," said Harold.

Before and below them, wide and gracious, lay a long downland valley running east to west. They were looking across its width to a further side, far enough away to be dim with summer haze. The valley was almost filled with green woodland, but on the hillside to their left, and on the misty slopes opposite, a few great fields lay draped: rye and wheat as Harold had said, and what had been hay, harvested now. In the field nearest to them, the light wind blowing over the rye made swift footprints on its surface, like the fleeting paws of invisible hounds.

"Look! Rye dogs!" Wulfhild said delightedly. "My mother used to say they were Woden's hounds, the same that ran with him in the Wild Hunt. I missed them in Normandy."

"There's rye in Normandy," Harold said, amused. "And wind."

"Yes, but in Normandy wind is all it is," Wulfhild said seriously.

Across the valley, harvesters were at work, small figures strung across a wide field, working bent-backed with scythes. Brand shaded his eyes to see better. "There's a strip of that field not being cut," he said. "Why?"

Harold frowned. "That's your strip, I think . . . Yes, the villagers are cutting their own first. Well, I said you might have a few things to set to rights. Come on."

His brow creased again as he led the way on and down. The beehives were the next feature of Fallowdene to appear. They were empty monuments to weather and neglect. There had been no honey for the dues. No wonder. There had been no honey at all.

"There are hives at Heathwood. I shall get advice," said Wulfhild cheerfully, as her father and his overlord halted before this dispiriting sight. "Is it far to the hall now?"

Harold shook his horse up. "I'm glad Heathwood was as it should be, at least. No, it's not far. In fifty yards you'll see it."

An undulation of the land had hidden it before. But now they crossed another smooth crest of ground with short, sheep-nibbled grass on either side and larks twittering invisibly overhead, and they saw that beyond the river which flowed through the valley, a place had been cleared in the trees and habitations stood there. The hall stood upwards of its satellite houses, commanding a view over most of the trees. It was sturdy and gabled and its thick thatch swept low, the eaves almost touching the ground so that the building resembled a stout, shaggy pony with a long mane. A little above the hall stood what must be a church, squat and small, identifiable by the little square tower at one end. When they had plunged into the woodland and over a ford and emerged from the woodland again, into the clearing, they could see that where the thatched roof of the church didn't hide its walls, a vigorous growth of ivy mostly did, but in one place the wall was bare, and it was stone, and there were slender windows with small round lights at their tops.

Wulfhild had seen such little circular windows before and knew that at close quarters they would be vividly coloured, little precious discs of stained glass, blue and green and amber, which would throw jewelled roundels on to the floor of the church. "That's beautiful!" she exclaimed, pointing.

The hall had a palisade with a gate, now standing wide. Through it they saw outhouses and a couple of round bondmen's huts. The village houses made a double line outside the palisade, leading to the river. Hearth smoke rose from some of them and geese and hens pecked on the ground nearby. Some women in bright-coloured clothes, who were laying washed garments to dry in the sunshine, stopped work to stare curiously at the strangers. The scene was homely and welcoming and Harold drew a breath of relief as they approached the gate.

"Abandoned hives and careless harvesting are ills soon cured," he said lightly.

They were inside the fence before they saw the huge torn patch in the hall's thatched roof, and its rough mending with cattle hides. The gable had hidden it till then. Just as the palisade had hidden its own broken places on the far side, and the plot, now rank with thistle and nettle and dandelion, which had once been a vegetable garden. A few thin onion shoots and strangled cabbages still remained to prove it. An old hound lying on his side in the sun opened an eye at them and lifted a lethargic tail but did not seem to think his home worth barking about.

"Oh, *God!*" said Harold violently, and snatching his horn from his saddle bow, he winded it, as if announcing an invasion.

Within the hall, Wulfhild and Brand stood listening while the steward, who was very elderly and walked with a stoop, and who was among the people the peremptory horn had brought scurrying, offered a confused mixture of greetings and hangdog apologies. Other villagers—the women who had been washing clothes, the reapers from the wheatfield, two men who had been out setting coney traps, and a swineherd and a cattleman—stood uneasily about. A priest too, also old, had come from the church. They made a semi-circle round the newcomers and the apologetic steward. Wulfhild voicelessly condemned the cobwebby rafters and the draught board scratched with a knifepoint on the seat of a settle. Her father, with equal disapproval, surveyed a worm-riddled wooden pillar, the hooks on the walls where well-kept weapons and fire-brooms should have hung and didn't, and somebody's bedroll still on the floor in mid-afternoon.

". . . The old lord's been dead this twelvemonth past . . ." the steward was saying tremulously.

"So I heard," said Brand.

". . . and he was so sick these last few seasons, we didn't like pestering him with every little thing . . . Alfred Thatcher hurt his ankle falling off the mill-house roof when he repaired it and he's still lame. My wife Editha and my daughter Eve that's married to Britt Blacksmith, they'll be glad to serve the ladies . . ."

"What happened to the housecarles?" Harold demanded. "There were housecarles here once."

"Yes, my lord, oh yes, but they got bored and wandered off to find a new lord and we were glad to see the back of them, the idle big-heads . . . lounging about and bullying us. And Gerda Millers-daughter is with child by one of them and didn't want to be . . . she's a good girl and she clawed his face for him, but he was too strong for her. They lived in the hall and acted as if they owned it . . ."

"I see," said Brand. He examined the hall and its human attachments without saying anything more for a few moments. Harold, watching him, waited to hear what he would say when he did speak. He was himself appalled. He had meant Fallowdene to be a rich present, gold given in an open hand. This was an insult, not an honour. Waiting for Brand to speak, the earl was stony-faced with embarrassment. But there was no one here to lose his temper with but thralls and churls of no standing. The Earl of Wessex could hardly draw a sword on an aged, timid steward, or knock down a swineherd.

"I shall want to see everyone in the hall tomorrow morning," Brand said at length, quite calmly. "I shall ask who everyone is and what work they owe and I shall set in hand the repairs that are needed. My man Odi Pathfinder—this is Odi—will train the younger men in arms. My daughters will give the orders for the hall management. For now, I want beds made up for tonight for all of us and food got ready. Is there an ox you can kill?"

"Er . . . no," said the steward miserably. "Those house-carles . . ."

". . . are going to be the reason for every shortcoming I find, I imagine," said Brand. Harold's eyes expressed appreciation. "Well, there's plenty of poultry. They didn't eat that. And I saw sheep on the downs. Kill a sheep. As for vegetables, your own plots must provide for us, since the one outside hasn't seen a hoe since Candlemas, by the look of it. We shall drink mead or ale, whatever you have. As quick as you can, please. We're hungry and we've ridden far. I'm glad the fire's alight, at least!"

The steward began to shoo the other folk away, instructing and admonishing. Brand removed his cloak and sat down on the scratched settle, as one who takes possession. He threw the cloak across a small table. Edgiva sat quietly down on a stool, untroubled by her surroundings, which for her were only temporary. Wulfhild walked over to the hangings which adorned the north wall, and fingered pulled threads with pursed mouth and clicking tongue. Harold cleared his throat.

"Oh come!" said Brand, for once on top in his relations with the Godwins. "No regrets!"

"I brought you here. If I'd known what it was like, I'd have found somewhere much better. If you wish, I will even now. It wasn't deliberate, Brand, I promise!" Harold's big shoulders were slumped, his self-respect failing. "Brand, when I took you from your career in Normandy, I swore I would see that you had a comparable future in England. I meant that!"

"There's nothing seriously wrong here." Wulfhild came back to them. "It wants cleaning and repairing, that's all. We've hangings with us for half the hall, at least, and I can make others. I can run a hall and my father understands farming. We shall do very well."

"Brand," said Harold firmly, "tell me: are you willing to take on this estate? You need not." He pushed Brand's cloak aside and perched on the edge of the table. "Believe me, Brand, I never, never meant . . . *God's Teeth!*"

Woodworm was not, apparently, confined to the pillar. It was also in the furniture. The table cracked and gave way under the earl's weight and deposited him, with a splintering sound and a thud, on his back in the midst of its debris. "Oh, Brand," said the Earl of Wessex helplessly, amid the shards and the wood dust, "what have the blasted Godwins done to you now?"

"We haven't made ourselves clear," said Wulfhild. She helped him up and he saw, first with anger and then with astonishment, that she was laughing. She caught her father's eye and knew that she was right, that with the deep-level certainty that near-relations sometimes have about each other, she had divined his thoughts. She and Brand were experiencing the same stirring under the breastbone, as if they knew this place, as if it was already part of them.

It was their land, their place, as the Norman knight's fee, as even the fenlands, never could be. Fallowdene might be tired and neglected, but it was the more endearing for it, like an unkempt child in need of loving and care.

"Please don't be so upset," said Wulfhild, kindly, to Harold. "Don't you see? We like Fallowdene."

6 ❈ A Time of Quiet

The faggot end of the year was not the best time to begin reha-
bilitating a run-down manor. But matters could have been worse.
The rot had not passed the point of no return and Fallowdene was
essentially fertile. It already had a good stack of seasoned timber
which could be used to repair palisades and the worm-eaten pillars;
Wulfhild hoped for a door between the partitioned-off kitchen at one
end of the hall and the hall proper, as well. The leather curtain
which did duty at present blew about in bad weather and was a
nuisance to anyone cooking.

Brand called his new dependents to the hall on his first full day
and discovered thereby what needed doing and what manpower he
had to do it. At first, most difficulties were explained to the accompaniment of a sentence beginning: "Those housecarles . . ." Until
Brand, in the dangerously quiet tones of battened-down exasperation, said he would demand double labour dues from the next man
to mention the housecarles. After that they got on faster.

He visited Heathwood again, thankful that the abbey had kept
the manor in good fettle. He collected some useful supplies there:
flour and salted fish and bags of salt for Wulfhild's kitchen. She
would need the salt to preserve meat through the winter, after the
November slaughtering.

Returning, he found that Wulfhild had not wasted her time.
She had visited Alfred Thatcher, found his ankle mended, and insisted that he begin work again. When Brand rode in, the thatcher
was on his ladder, stomach-down on the hall's roof, binding reed

bundles into place where the cattlehides had been. And Wulfhild, satisfied, was deep in talk with the cattleman, the shepherd, and the swineherd over the choice of animals to be kept for next year's breeding.

These things were entirely Wulfhild's province. Edgiva was gone. Brand had delivered her to her nunnery before he went to Heathwood. The nunnery was called Withysham Abbey and was only five miles from Fallowdene. Countess Gytha sponsored the girl and gave a present of silver ingots to augment the dowry that Brand provided. It was a valuable gesture, which would give Edgiva status in her new life. He was glad of it, for he hated her going. He still had ugly memories of the day he had seen his sister enter Leominster Abbey. His sister Edgiva had wept every yard of the way and been handed over like a calf to the butcher. His last view of her was of a twisted mouth and tormented eyes, which still haunted him. But his daughter Edgiva went serenely, greeting the abbess with gentle calm, kissing her kinsfolk farewell with cool lips that had already taken leave of the warm and carnal world, and stepping away into the cloisters with the air of one going home. The only grief was Brand's, departing without her. Of his three daughters only Wulfhild, the near-stranger, now remained.

But, blessedly, he had Wulfhild. He thought about her a good deal as the autumn darkened into winter and the shortening days closed them in. The woods turned to the gold-brown of a fallow deer's hide and glowed through the blue October dusks until the gales and rain came vaulting over the downs from the sea and roared among the branches and tore the leaves away. The first frosts began, and Wulfhild providently set the thralls to cut kindling and herself went gathering dead sticks under the trees. It was she who thought to order the main meal earlier, so that they could eat by daylight, in comfort, and without wasting tallow.

He was learning to rely on Wulfhild.

After the meal, the household usually stayed together for a while in the hall enjoying the hearth fire, augmenting its light with torch and candle, enough to illuminate the space immediately round it, while the new thatch settled above them and cattle stamped and snorted in the byre that adjoined the hall. Odi and the men, and Alric Steward and his weather-beaten, whiskery, capable wife, Editha, would sit with them while the two thralls squatted by the fire. They told tales or sang or played games with draughts or pebbles, or did such tasks as the poor light allowed. Fine needlework was impossible, but one could mend a torn tunic or clean horse tackle. Sometimes Wulfhild and her father, thus employed, sat side by side and talked while the others followed their own occupations. At these times they were almost private together.

Brand wondered at his easy acceptance of her. Only a little while ago she had not existed for him, and he had formerly been part of a different family. Now Hild was dead and her daughters, respectively, married and immured, and instead he had . . . Wulfhild. Once, he said: "When you heard who your father was, was it a shock to you? You must have heard my history."

"Lady Eadgyth used to defend you," said Wulfhild. "I knew both sides of the tale. No, I didn't mind that. But it was hard to accept that Earl Harold *wasn't* my father. I thought he was, you see."

"Hard to exchange Harold for me? Yes . . ." said Brand with feeling. "That would be difficult. But why did you think he was your father?"

"It explained why I was taken into the hall as I was. And I have blue eyes like his and I like animals and birds. He is a great horseman and hawkmaster."

"He's half Danish. Your mother, whose eyes you have, may have had Danish blood as well. There's plenty of it on the east coast. Did she ever tell you anything about herself, her own parents and kin?"

"No, but I was so young when she died."

"Yes, I forgot." He rasped rust from a stirrup. He had never known Wulfhild as a small child. Her infancy did not exist for him. Only her womanhood. "Wulfhild . . ."

"Yes?" Her head was bent over the seam she was closing. Candlelight made her beechnut brown hair look soft, and found new planes and modellings in her face. Wulfhild was not beautiful except as any young animal, healthy and normally shaped according to its kind, was beautiful. But one day she would make a good wife and she would have children and he knew that more than one man had been drawn to her already.

". . . one day," he said, "you'll marry."

"I suppose so," said Wulfhild. She brushed a daddy longlegs away from the candle and went on plying her needle, undisturbed. "But I shall hate to leave Fallowdene. It's home."

"When you marry you'll have another home. Wulfhild, did Ivon

Taillefer speak to you before we left Normandy? He told me he meant to. Asked my permission, in fact, although as I hardly knew you, I hardly felt I had the right to give or withhold it."

"He approached me, yes. But I had to come back to England. I was sorry for him and I liked him, but I *had* to come back. Normandy was too alien. Like Wales. He said one day he might . . ." She stopped.

"Go on."

In a lowered tone, glancing at the story-telling huddle on the other side of the hearth, Wulfhild said: ". . . He told me he might come to England with Duke William one day."

"I see." Brand burnished the stirrup mechanically. "If that happens," he said at length, "it will mean he comes across a battlefield. Wulfhild, when you want to marry, tell me. I'll find you someone. I might even arrange for Fallowdene to be yours. I can live at Heathwood. It's no use to wait for Ivon Taillefer. He'll come as an enemy if he comes with Duke William."

"Yes, I know," said Wulfhild, and her stitching did not falter.

"That young man there, Osric," said Brand, also in an undertone, indicating the flaxen-haired housecarle who sat beyond the hearth, lovingly cleaning the sword which was his emblem of freedom, "how do you like him?"

"I like him," said Wulfhild unemotionally, "but he complains too much about having been a thrall. It isn't so bad, if you're fed properly. My lady Aldith, in Wales, freed a thrall and he had to go to war when he was free. He was killed."

"He died with a sword in his hand," said her father. "Thralls get killed in war as well, with no chance to defend themselves. The Church is against the practice of thralldom. I've heard Archbishop Aldred preach against it here. And in Normandy it's forbidden."

"Forbidden? They have serfs in Normandy."

"Yes, serfs who can't leave their land. But they can't be sold off it, either. There's no export trade in them. I don't like to think that you were once in bondage yourself. I've thought it over . . . given the whole thing more of my mind than I ever did before . . . since I heard where you were born. The archbishop is right and so is Osric. But Osric irritates you?"

"At times."

Brand nodded, and let the subject drop.

By Christmas, something resembling a spirit of unity had been engendered in Fallowdene. There was a feast for Christmas Day, with the head of a boar which Brand and his men had gone out and hunted for the occasion. Everyone in Fallowdene came to the feast, and there were guests from Little Dene and Westwater too. Their tenants were prosperous freemen very much as Brand's father had been, in his old Worcestershire home. He felt at ease with them, and they praised Fallowdene's hospitality. Life had begun to stir in the manor's clogged veins, after long inertia. In the new year, Hakon came to visit them.

He arrived accompanied by swirling snow and stood in the hall, glorious in blue-jay finery, tugging off his gauntlets, shouting for mead, and eyeing the young female thrall simultaneously. Brand remembered Sweyn Godwinson and thought, as he led his guest to the fire, that Hakon was just like him. Astonishing, this miraculous process by which a man's careless sowing could bring forth the harvest of a complete human being filled with new promise and yet hauntingly marked with the lineaments of dead forebears.

"Well!" said Hakon, appraising his surroundings, "Uncle Harold said the place was falling down, but it looks sound and warm to me." In a few months he had picked up the elegant accent of Edward's court. "Do I smell venison?"

"From our own woodlands," said Wulfhild. "Do you like life at court, Hakon?"

"There are surprises." Hakon seated himself, stretching his feet to the blaze. "More Normans than I expected and more French spoken. And yet a powerful anti-Norman faction as well. It's an odd arrangement. Uncle Brand, I have a summons for you. You're wanted for your annual court service. That's what comes of being a thane. You'll have to put up with Uncle Tostig's scowls. He's back in the south." He grinned. "But you needn't come till May. You'll miss the Welsh campaign, which is good news, I expect. It'll be a tedious business in wild country . . ."

"What Welsh campaign?" demanded Brand and Wulfhild together.

"Oh, I suppose the news takes time to get down here. There's been trouble over merchants' tolls." Hakon waved a hand in a never-mind-the-details gesture. "There were new trade agreements made with the Welsh when the Princes Bleddyn and Rhiwallon, and that man Caradoc, took over Wales between them, and now the agreements are being broken."

What had happened, Hakon explained when they demanded the details after all, was that although the Welsh princes had been willing to cooperate over a system of tolls on various goods passing out of Wales, their people had been less so. The Welsh didn't mind charging tolls to English traders but vigorously evaded paying their own. "And I believe Uncle Harold thinks insubordination from tne Welsh is a personal insult," Hakon said. "So an expedition's going to Wales this spring. And Uncle Harold is going to build a fort on the north bank of the Severn Estuary—it's at a place called Portskewet; he's got a manor near there himself—to make a safe shelter for our ships coming up the Severn and needing to lie up overnight. There's been a lot of piracy too. But all this is small news. There have been much more exciting events at court this season. Guess!"

"How can we?" said Wulfhild. "You'll have to tell us. What?"

"Well," said Hakon with enjoyment, "I told you that Uncle Tostig had come to the south again . . ."

The news, assuredly, was worth a pause for effect. Tostig, Earl of Northumbria, had settled his earldom's rebellion and come back to court. Thane Gospatric, who had fomented the rebellion in the first place, had promptly returned to Northumbria, avoiding any meeting with Tostig. Having got there, he had proceeded to fan the embers of rebellion back to life. He had inspired his nephew Ulf and the bleached, sarcastic Gamel Ormson to take to arms and resist both Tostig's tax gatherers and Tostig's banishment of some of the original rebels. He had then come zestfully and unwisely back to London to fill his stomach at the king's Christmas court. King Edward, it seemed, had rebuked him but done nothing more, and Gospatric, unimpressed, had gone on enjoying the feasts and the admiration of his own men and his friends.

On the seventh of the twelve days' feasting, Gospatric had left the royal hall, a little merry, and unarmed. He had parted from his cronies in the courtyard. He had walked, humming a tune and not quite steady, to the door of his guesthouse, and stepped over the threshold into a wall of scissoring steel.

Tostig, said rumour expectably at first. *Tostig.* And that was scandal enough. But then the song changed key. A few days later a man who was among the humbler housecarles at the London court grew boastful in an alehouse and declared that he had helped to cut Gospatric down, and named his employer, and his employer wasn't Tostig.

It was Edith, Lady Edith, Edward's pious queen.

7 ✠ The Family Way

In May, Brand reluctantly said goodbye to Wulfhild and Fallowdene, and with half his force of housecarles behind him set out for the court at Winchester. At least he could look forward to meeting Harold there. The Welsh campaign had been successfully concluded and the earl was back at court.

News of the campaign had reached Fallowdene. But no news had come of the queen's banishment to a nunnery or any similar event. Yet something of the sort must have happened, Brand thought. The Christmastide drama as reported by Hakon could not have gone unremarked. When one of the king's chief guests is discovered lying on the floor of his guesthouse in a lake of his own blood, sword-hacked almost out of recognition, some comment must surely be addressed to his slayer.

But Edward and Edith were together at Winchester: calm, smiling, a little withdrawn, but otherwise seemingly on the best of terms with each other and everyone else, attending Mass and engaging in works of charity. In Winchester, it appeared, the weeping of Gospatric's widow went unheard. Other things too were surprising.

"Does the king often dine apart like this?" Brand asked as he and Harold walked towards the royal apartments, in the late afternoon, a week after Brand's arrival.

Harold had commanded his company at a private dinner in the king's rooms. Nor was it the first time the king had eaten away from the hall that week. He had been absent on three occasions already. Brand, indeed, had hardly seen the royal pair. Even on the days when they came to the hall, his seat was at some distance from the dais, and there had been no council meetings. He was not eager to encounter them. He had not met either Edward or Edith face-to-face since his return home, and since Edward had personally ejected him from England in the first place, he dreaded the hour of such a meeting. It was Harold who had insisted that the time must come and would be better over. But even Brand's uneasiness could not quite mask his sheer surprise at this strange new innovation, the private dinner. Brand remembered the royal hall in Godwin's day, when no main meal was ever consumed by the king anywhere but in the midst of his household. He raised questioning brows at Harold.

"He tires quickly these days," Harold said, "and his memory is failing. If he hasn't seen people for a while, he's apt to forget who they are and that worries him. So he dines apart when he can, and when he can't, Edith jogs his memory for him as tactfully as possible. The chances are he won't remember you at all. Your name means nothing to him. Don't worry so, Brand. This is just a good chance to introduce you as a new thane and get it done. There'll be no one there but Edward and Edith, and you and me and Tostig . . ."

"Tostig!" Brand stopped short, in front of the royal doorway. The king's rooms stood apart from the main hall. They occupied a well-thatched building with oaken door posts on which convoluted serpents and hounds and boars were carved in a tangle of curves and wedges. "You didn't tell me Tostig would be here," said Brand, scowling at the door posts. "And both he and Lady Edith will remember me, if the king doesn't! Ever since I got here, Tostig . . ."

Tostig had been consistently offensive whenever Brand encountered him. Some of the thanes, hurtfully, had followed his example, the worst offenders being a clique in the Royal Bodyguard. Others were courteous, and Brand knew it, only to please Harold. There was a noticeable tendency these days for men to court Earl Harold's favour.

"I've told Tostig and Edith that I don't wish your past discussed today," said Harold sharply. "As for Tostig's disapproval . . . can't you see that he has simply got to get used to you? He'll do it all the sooner if you take a normal part in court activities. All the thanes dine with the king at times. I'll share Tostig's dirty looks with you. Come on! In we go!"

The king's apartment was comfortable and shadowy, smelling of incense from a little altar, and beeswax from the polished settles. Tostig was there already, a page behind his chair and his feet on the bulk of a sleeping deerhound. Edward sat on a thronelike seat with Edith by him on a lower one, as her custom had always been. A fool was doing acrobatics to amuse them and the table was set. Brand made his greetings and took his seat and tried not to stare.

Since his return to England, this was the first time he had been close to Edward and Edith. His memories of them before he left the country were still undimmed. Now, the contrast of those memories and the present reality struck him between the eyes.

Edward he recalled as a pale lean man, thin-bearded but with a straight back and a vital step. This round-shouldered figure with sad wisps of white hair trailing from the back of a balding scalp was a difficult replacement. And as for Edith . . .

He recalled her as a dignified young woman, exquisitely dressed, with thick flaxen hair in fashionable ringlets. Despite her pious interests, that hair had actually drawn ecclesiastical criticism. A married woman's hair was for her husband only to see, said the prelates, and Edith was setting a worldly example. They wouldn't be saying that now.

No one would call this woman worldly, in her clothes of white and grey, with her hair hidden in white linen. Its concealment left her face naked. It was a calm, pale face, unlined despite her forty-one years, its features clearly marked. They were Gytha's features, Gytha's generous width from temple to temple, her high cheekbones, her engraved mouth. But it was Gytha in parody: Gytha, the very symbol of fecundity, looking out of the face of a nun. Edith turned to welcome Harold and the girdle she wore low on her hips suddenly accentuated them, showing their breadth, their perfect shape for childbearing. Then she looked at Brand and spoke to him, and her hazel eyes, Godwin's legacy, were empty and hungry. When he answered her, he stammered. He had seen eyes like that before. In the face of his sister Edgiva, the day they took her to the convent.

He glanced again at the bloodless Edward. Dear God, what a fate for the passionate little girl he had seen on his first day in Godwin's hall, fighting with her brothers. She was drawing Edward's attention to Brand now, carefully, describing him as Thane Brand of Fallowdene, who had lived for some years in Normandy. Edward obviously recollected nothing. "Welcome to my hall, Thane Brand. Did you live many years in Normandy? Perhaps you knew . . . ?" said Edward graciously, and Brand pulled himself together to make a conventional reply and regret that he had not met the man after whom Edward was enquiring. Edward's memories of his early youth were clearly better than those of his middle years. Edith had had Gospatric killed, of course. Those eyes would be capable of anything to further the cause of anyone, anyone at all, who would let her love him, would love her back, would feed even a crumb to the starving animal inside her. Tostig had given her affection; he was known to be her favourite brother. And she had rewarded him with her partisanship. As for Edward, he would not condemn her because he needed her, though not as a wife. He should have been a monk, thought Brand crossly. It would have saved Edith a wretched marriage and probably saved Gospatric's life.

Tostig greeted them offhandedly, barely acknowledging Brand at all. Brand wondered grimly how far Harold's request not to discuss the past would weigh with the truculent Earl of Northumbria. "You're late, Harold," Tostig said, presenting Brand with his shoulder. "Did you forget the time out hawking?"

"There are worse reasons for forgetfulness," said Edward pacifically. Tostig's voice had had an edge to it. "I've been late for a Witan Council before now, when the hunting was good. I hope to hunt tomorrow, Harold, if my rheumatism permits. And if you'll invite me to that manor of yours near Portskewet in August as you promised, I'll bring my hounds and show you some lively sport. Is the merchants' burgh at Portskewet finished yet, by the way?"

"It progresses slowly. There were delays over getting seasoned timber and properly dressed stone, and we had some local resentment too. I think some of the locals have a vested interest in piracy. Brand, you should join us in August. My manor there, just on the English side of the border, has the fattest deer you've ever seen." Harold courteously included his brother in the invitation. "I hope you'll be with us, Tostig."

"Not if Thane Brand's in the party, thank you," said Tostig pugnaciously. "I shouldn't be here now if you'd warned me earlier that you were bringing him." Brand sat still, his face rigid. "In any case I shall probably have to go north; Northumbria needs attention these days. Wessex is easy to look after."

"I spend a good deal of time there," Harold snapped. "Absentee landlords rarely flourish."

"Tostig," said Edith appealingly, "and Harold. Please don't . . ."

"It depends where they spend their absence," said Tostig. "You can do quite well for yourself, going abroad to the right place. You can come back loaded with presents and honours . . . plural. Perhaps with a little less honour, singular, but one can't have everything."

The page giggled and the first of the servers, coming in with the food, schooled his face to a careful blank. "Shame on you!" said the fool, "for stealing a poor man's livelihood!"

"Tostig," said Edward plaintively, "please!"

The meal, frugal by court standards, began. Brand, who had stayed coldly silent through Tostig's gibes, avoided Harold's apologetic eye and tried to eat.

"Bring Wulfhild in August," Harold said to Brand, giving up the attempt to further brotherly relations with Tostig. "Edith, did you know that Brand has a charming daughter in England? Could he bring her to court?"

"Of course. She would be most welcome."

"Would she?" asked Tostig. "She isn't his wife's daughter, you know. She's the result of some early indiscretion."

As an attempt to bring royal disapproval on Brand's head, it failed. Edward murmured: "Few men have a blameless youth."

Edith asked: "Is Wulfhild pretty?"

"I think so," said Brand. "I would have brought her with me this time, but she didn't wish to leave Fallowdene."

"It might have embarrassed her," said Tostig sympathetically. He nodded knowingly at Edward. "She's the daughter of a thrall, though I believe that for years she was under the impression that she had Harold for a father. It must have been a saddening surprise when she found out her father was the exiled oath-breaker Brand Woodcutter. Enough to make anyone feel shy. A thrall for one parent and Woodcutter for the other . . . That's who Thane Brand is, my lord Edward. Did you not realise?"

Brand stood up. "My lord," he said to Edward, "I don't want to cause a violent scene in your presence. May I withdraw?"

Edward was considering him with renewed interest. "Brand Woodcutter . . . yes, I do recall . . . But it was so long ago. You told me the truth about Gildenford, did you not? But I wanted to know it, if my memory serves me. It isn't what it was, I'm afraid. There is no need for you to leave. Tostig, we do not allow guests to be driven from our presence. Mind your manners or leave our presence yourself. Fool, tell us a riddle and distract us!"

Tostig fell silent and Brand sat down again, attending with forced interest to the fool. The entertainer sank cross-legged on to the floor. "A royal dinner is no place for quarrels. There are other ways to bring tears to your eyes," he said and forthwith embarked on a thoroughly salacious description of some unknown object. "Guess what it is?" he invited them, springing up and capering, watching them with bright, knowing eyes. "Guess!"

Brand made an obvious answer, more as a contribution to the effort at distraction than because he believed it was correct. Harold laughed at him. "Don't be a wantwit, Brand, that's what we're meant to think. Though I admit I can't do better. Well, fool, let's have the answer."

"I've heard this riddle before," said Tostig, brushing honey cake crumbs fastidiously off his red tunic. "It's an onion."

"An onion?" said Edward. Edith laughed, the appreciative merriment that Gytha would have uttered. "He said it would bring tears to our eyes . . . Of course! An onion!"

Harold guffawed, the page tittered, and the fool murmured some of the lines again. Edward suddenly beamed. For all his piety he had never been prim about humour. The lascivious accuracy of the onion's description came home to him and he threw back his head and joined in the laughter. "Stands in a bed!" he gasped. "And it's only a vegetable bed!" He turned crimson and started to cough. Fragments of honey cake flew from his lips. Harold sprang up in alarm.

Edith was patting her husband's back vigorously and urging him to drink something. Harold pushed his own mead horn into the king's hand. "Take some of this, quickly." He watched with relief as Edward gulped the mead and the spasm passed. The king's eyes were streaming and he wiped them with the back of his hand.

"Thank you, Harold, I can always depend on you. My right hand, as usual. God bless you. I'll bless you myself, one day, wait and see."

"I've been waiting for that!" shouted Tostig.

They swung round to look at him. He had shot to his feet and the fury in his face had turned it the colour of his scarlet tunic. He pounced towards Harold, still standing at Edward's side with the mead horn, and grabbed his brother's hair, yanking him backwards, away from the king. "Waiting for it!" bellowed Tostig. "God damn you, Harold, you and your worming ways!"

Harold roared and tore his hair from Tostig's grasp. He once more whirled to face the infuriated Earl of Northumbria. "What the devil do you think you're doing?"

"By the Face of God, that's enough! You make me puke!" Tostig shouted. "You and your fawning. *Fawning*! Can't the king see through you?" He rounded on Edward. "Well, can't you? He licks your boots and holds a mead horn for you, and for what? Because he wants your throne! That's all it is! Like a cat purring round your feet for cream! Him—the man who swore away England to the Normans just so that he could get back to it and seize it for himself!"

"Are you jealous, Tostig?" asked the king. The royal lion might be old, but he still had some teeth left, Brand rejoiced to observe.

Tostig looked the violence he dared not offer. "You swore away England," he said to Harold, "and now you'll perjure yourself, piling sin on sin, to get the throne yourself. Did you murder Edward Atheling as well, to better your own chances? I've never been certain. Did you? Tell me!"

"No," said Harold with surprising calm. "And if I had intended to I should have avoided the responsibility for his safety. I may not be an angel, Tostig, but I really am not a village idiot, either." His control faltered and his own face suffused. "My lord Edward, did you hear what he accused me of? Do *you* accept my innocence?"

"Yes, Harold, I do," said Edward. "Tostig, sit down at once or else leave. This is disgraceful in our presence."

Tostig showed his teeth. "Leave? Who'd want to stay under the same roof with these two? Brand Oath-Breaker and my beloved perjured brother? I'll be overjoyed to get back into the clean open air!"

A moment later, leaving a door that swung and banged, and

banged again behind him, he had gone. Edward said: "He gets more like his brother Sweyn every day."

Edith said: "I'm sorry, Harold. It's because of Northumbria. He is angry and bitter because his reforms were not accepted there. He feels he has earned a reward that hasn't been given him, and that you . . . have had rewards you haven't earned. Please don't mind too much."

Harold said: "I wonder where he'll go?"

8 ✖ The Casting-Out

But in the very considerable relief of Tostig's absence, they didn't concern themselves too much with his whereabouts. Other matters supervened. The court moved to London, where Edward began detailed plans to consecrate his West Minster at the year's end. He spoke serenely of his intention that one day it should house his tomb. It seemed that his interest in the life to come had almost ousted his interest in his present realm. Young Earl Edwin of Mercia was heard to say, indeed, that the sooner old King Edward took himself off to Heaven the better, since he would plainly be happier there and his Witan Council would be happier with a less other-worldly head. There were sidelong smiles at Edwin's expense. Edwin, with his Norman connections, was known still to hope for William's accession. But those in the king's deeper councils looked in a different direction nowadays for the heir.

July came and Brand's release from court. He paid a short visit to his home village in Worcestershire. His mother was very frail now, and between the travelled, landowning Brand and the farmer who was his brother and who rarely left his lands near Worcester, the conversational gap had grown impossibly wide. Brand asked after his brother's family and heard that the two younger boys were serving in arms with local thanes. The eldest was to inherit the farm and was living there with his parents, and had a wife and son of his own. The two daughters were married and gone. Brand gave gifts to everyone and rode unregretfully away to Fallowdene.

He found peace and order. The hay was in. The midsummer

shearing had been done. The hives were reinstated. Rolf Ericson had paid a short visit and Wulfhild had bought more glassware. The leather curtain still flapped across the kitchen doorway but they couldn't manage everything at once, Wulfhild explained.

"Though it's a nuisance," she said. "Some monks on a journey spent a night here last month. While Eve and the thrall girl got the food ready, they talked about Eve's last miscarriage all the time, and with only the curtain there the poor monks had to listen to every word. They tried to talk about King Edward's new cathedral and shut it out, but you know how Eve's voice penetrates."

Brand, chuckling, asked her if she would like to come to the court hunting party at Portskewet, but she shook her head. "There's so much to do here, and I don't want to leave Fallowdene anyway. I'm happy here."

Seeing her deep content in the life of the manor, and sympathising with it, he did not persist. He would have preferred to stay there himself, drawing his home and its trivial, satisfying events round him like a comfortable old tunic. But he had promised to go to Portskewet. "I shall be back for the harvest," he said, and once more took to the road.

They came to Portskewet on the north bank of the Severn, on a warm August afternoon, a noisy, song-singing party on holiday. Harold and his thanes were a day ahead of Edward and the court proper, to see that all was in order at the manor. They could move quickly, a group of men unhampered by litters, mules, children, old folk, expectant ladies, or any of the other impedimenta that slowed the court down whenever it went on pleasure trips. Nearing the place with time in hand, Harold suggested an excursion to look at the new merchants' burgh, now near completion. "If we bypass my hall on the south side, we can be there and back before sunset."

They jogged on, in and out of shaded forest, over heathland thick with broom and brambles and patched with heather in bloom, until the horizon ahead showed a glitter of sea. "We shall see the watchtower in a moment," Harold said to Brand. "I had a wooden tower put on a mound, as a landmark for sailors and a lookout combined. There's a palisade right down to the sea on both sides of the harbour, moorings and jetties and a guard house, and some resthouses and storage huts. And a chain to go across the harbour mouth if necessary. If we bring goods to Wales, the Welsh can damn well pay for their purchases." He called over his shoulder: "We can see the burgh from the top of the next rise," and the party spurred its horses. "There it is," said Harold presently, pulling up.

"Where?" enquired Brand. "That's smoke."

Harold's breath went out of him with a hiss. A swift gallop downhill and up the next rise, and they could see better. The mound was there but on it was only a blackened ring and a tall, thin column of smoke, weakening now. Bits and pieces of the palisade remained but many of the buildings within were flattened and smouldering. Harold cursed and in his wake they thundered forward to the site.

They went in close formation, weapons ready, but no one challenged them. Within the fallen fence they halted. Two of the horses shied. There were dead men scattered on the ground, their blood congealing. The air smelt of burning and violence. The raiders had gone, but not long ago.

"You two," said Harold, pointing to two housecarles at random, "guard the horses. The rest, follow me." He slid his feet out of the stirrups.

They advanced warily, on foot. The dead were workmen, disturbed at their tasks. Their implements lay beside them: shovel, hammer, saw. Near a ransacked storehouse, still there because it was stone and wouldn't burn like the timber buildings, they found a body worse than the rest. They were all war-hardened, but this curdled the saliva in their mouths. The dead man's back had been slashed open and his ribs wrenched up to make a travesty of some winged thing.

"A bloody eagle," said Harold. "It's a Viking trick. Viking pirates, maybe. Odd. I've heard no reports of any recently."

"The Welsh and the Vikings have run in the same pack at times," said one of the other thanes. "The Welsh have used Viking tricks before now. It's the Welsh who have made trouble at this burgh before."

Brand went to the storehouse door and peered in. Some barrels, empty, lay overturned and scattered about. Drag marks showed where others had been hauled away over the earthen floor. A few had been left apparently untouched at the back, but there were signs of disturbance round them. The floor was scuffed and stained, and some miscellaneous objects were strewn over it. The back of the building was in shadow, and it was hard to see what these objects were.

At one side of the storehouse was a pile of surplus building stone. Brand's gaze, travelling round the place, reached it and stopped. He stood still, listening.

Harold came to his side. "It can't have been a general raid on the district. The last hamlet we passed was quite near and it was peaceful. This was aimed at the burgh alone, I fancy."

"I heard something," said Brand.

They both stood motionless. It came again, a tiny scraping from behind the stones. Sword out, Harold stepped towards them. Then he lunged, reaching out to seize something with his left hand.

The man he dragged from hiding collapsed, sobbing and shuddering, at his feet. He was a workman, in such a condition of terror that it was some time before they could convince him that they were not raiders. He did not seem to be hurt, only frantic with fear. Not until Harold exclaimed: "You're Eadred Foreman, we met when I came to the site in the spring," did the shaking and mumbling lessen and the frightened eyes at last focus properly on the earl's face. When he finally recognised Harold he began to sob again, this time from relief.

Fortified by someone's mead flask, Eadred mastered himself and sat on the pile of stones and said, as Harold's men crowded in: "It was Prince Caradoc, Prince of South Wales. Him and his men. I knew him . . . saw him once before, on a progress round these parts. They slaughtered all the rest, but I was in here looking these stones over and I hid before they saw me. I didn't dare come out even when it was quiet. I thought maybe they'd left someone behind, cat at a mouse hole. Oh Christ, I was so afraid!"

"How many were there?" demanded Harold.

"I dunno. Looked like thousands. Must have been fifty, anyway. They . " He made a gesture towards the barrels that still stood upright at the rear of the building. He shivered again and edged away along the stones. "In there," he said in a whisper. "Look in the barrels. But don't ask me to look as well."

Harold nodded at the three nearest housecarles. They went towards the barrels. Now that they were inside the storehouse, it could be seen that the things on the floor were mostly discarded clothing, including sandals and garter thongs. Those waiting with Eadred exchanged glances. The three men came back from the investigation with faces hard and pale.

"Bodies," said one shortly. "Can't tell how many. Stripped, dismembered, salted down." He had looked at Eadred with scorn a few minutes before. Now his face was kindlier. "Reckon I feel near as bad as he does," the housecarle said, jerking a thumb at the foreman.

"They laughed," said Eadred, "Caradoc's men, I mean. Then Caradoc—he was here himself—he said . . ." He stopped and seemed to be terrified again. His eyes sought Harold's. "I daren't tell you," he said simply. "You'll have my head for it."

"Don't be a fool. What did Caradoc say? I'll have your head if you *don't* tell me!"

Eadred stared at the floor. "Reckon you ought to know, at that. But . . ." He licked his lips and then blurted it. "He said he must make sure that if you . . . he named you, sir . . . were entertaining the king soon, you didn't run short of salted meat. Then he said he must tell . . . tell Earl Tostig the joke because . . . because he . . . I mean . . ."

"Yes, go on, it's all right. *Go on*, Eadred!"

". . . because Earl Tostig'd wish he'd thought of it himself," said Eadred miserably. "I'm sorry, my lord, but that's what he said. What Caradoc said. I heard him."

The workmen were mostly local. Word was sent to the villages nearby so that kinsfolk might collect their dead, and as far as possible Harold's men made the bodies decent. The dreadful contents of the barrels, and the mutilated man, they buried at once with the help of a few workmen's shovels that were lying about. A priest would be asked to bless the graves, and Eadred, by a process of elimination, had worked out which of his men must be in them, although some of their individual identities were in doubt.

After that they rode back to intercept the king's party and cancel the hunt. Harold did not speak Tostig's name till he was face-to-face with Edward, when he repeated as if by rote the words that Eadred had repeated to him.

"So," Edward said, "Tostig set Caradoc to this? Where is he himself, I wonder?" Tentatively he added: "He may not have meant Caradoc to go so far."

"I hope not," said Harold, without conviction.

No one had much sense of surprise when the next news of Tostig only piled outrage on outrage. He had gone to the north, it transpired, and there he had found waiting for him Thane Ulf Dolfin-son, nephew of the murdered Gospatric, and with him Thane Gamel. They demanded to see him and he granted it. They demanded a safe conduct and he granted that as well. The full details did not reach the court at Gloucester at once, but the gist was enough. The thanes had come, they had met Tostig, they had sought weregild for Gospatric and been refused, they had quarrelled with the earl. They went fuming back to their guesthouse. In the morning they and their servants and followers were dead. By violence, and no one doubted who had given the orders this time.

And now, said the deputation of lesser Northumbrian thanes who had halted north of Oxford, and sent, with prudence and propriety, a monk to Edward as messenger, Northumbria would stomach Earl Tostig no more. He had imposed foreign laws on them, contrary to their customs. He had condemned men harshly for small sins and stolen their lands. He had even snatched land from the Church, on small excuses. He had taxed the people of the north till they could scarcely feed their own children. He had brought in bullies from the south to enforce his odious rule. And now, he had taken to murder.

The old earl Siward had a son, said the messenger, but Waltheof was fitted out now with an earldom in Mid-Anglia and they heard that he might not care to come to Northumbria. Failing him, Earl Edwin had a brother who was without an earldom and of whom they knew no ill except that he was young. They had therefore agreed among themselves that he should be invited to replace Tostig, and the young man had consented. He and his brother were already in arms and had gone to Northumbria. It required only the royal signature to make the arrangement legal. Tostig was believed to be fleeing south and making for the court. The insurgents hoped that his banishment would be upheld by the king and Tostig sent out of the land . . .

Edith wept uncontrollably on the day that Tostig left the court to go raging and impotent to Flanders, an exile, with only a handful of men at his side. His family had foreseen the banishment and were in Flanders already.

"Why wouldn't you reinstate him, *why*?" Edith demanded of her husband.

"Because the Northumbrians wouldn't have him and frankly I

agree with them," said Edward. "He'll come to no harm in Flanders." He looked intently at her. "I didn't have him killed, as anyone would suppose from all these tears. He's quite safe. He may even come home one day."

"It isn't fair. He only tried to give them peace and order. But he's so upright and they're such savages. All he got from them was ingratitude. It made him ill, don't you understand, ill with grief. They made him bitter and wild. Is it any wonder?"

"No," said Edward. "With his family background, probably not. You passionate Godwins. It'll be your undoing one day."

"He needed me," said Edith. "I could help him. No one else ever brought their troubles to me as he did. Now he's gone and no one else will turn to me."

"There's me," said Edward mildly, offering her a napkin for her damp face. "I turn to you. Without you I'd never be in the right place at the right time wearing the right clothes. Without you my cares would have weighed me down into my grave long ago. I need you, Edith. Didn't you know that?"

Her tears continued to fall, though less violently now. "Oh Edith, don't. You *passionate* Godwins," Edward repeated. "Edith, this napkin is all wet. I shall have to fetch a sheet from the bed in a moment. Please stop . . . Edith! What's the matter?"

She had drawn back and was pressing the palm of her hand against his neck. Her face was frightened. "You're so hot!" she exclaimed.

THE COMING OF THE COMET

1066 A.D.

1 ✖ New Sun Rising

The light in the upper room of the London palace was pale and cold, cast from the reflected whiteness of snow. It made a chill background for the figures in the room, who, in their coloured clothes and their immobility, and in the emotions which spoke only in the attitudes of their rigid bodies, were like figures in a window of stained glass. But had it been a window, the artist would have put in Azrael. Edward of England had received the last rites and the end was only hours away.

A king does not die alone. But the physician and Queen Edith would not let too many crowd round the narrow bed. Only six people were present: the physician himself, watchful, with cups and brazier and packets of herbs; the archbishops, Aldred of York and Stigand of Canterbury; Edith the queen and her brother Earl Harold; and one Norman courtier for whom Edward had asked, as a friend. Gyrth and Leofwin had been sent for, but had not yet come.

Others waited in an anteroom: Agatha the widow of Edward Atheling, and her children, and the two young earls, Edwin of Mercia and Morcar of Northumbria. The door between these people and the royal chamber, however, was shut.

"They'll tell us when anything happens," Edwin said.

"I hope so," muttered Morcar. "And I hope it's the truth."

Agatha said: "We should pray for the king, not wrangle over his will." She carefully did not glance at her son, Edgar, nervously pacing the anteroom, but he answered anyway.

"I don't want to be named, not with William as a rival, thanks.

But we all want to *know*, Mother. Someone's got to inherit. And I shouldn't think the king needs our prayers. He's almost a saint already."

"Perhaps," said Agatha. "But we are not. Perhaps we should try harder."

In the bedchamber, Edith crouched near the foot of the bed. Edward had kicked his feet free in a fit of restlessness and she had caught hold of them, resting them against her breast, trying to rub them warm again. "He's so cold now," she said repeatedly. "The fever's gone and now he feels frozen." She caressed the feet hungrily, as if trying to crowd into this last day all the caresses her husband had rejected during the years.

"He's uneasy again," said Stigand. "Should we rouse him?"

His earlier restlessness had culminated violently. Edward had suddenly flung himself upright in the bed and burst into alarming, incoherent speech, pointing at Harold and the archbishops and hurling accusations at them. He had dreamed of long-dead friends, he said, who told him that all his great men were Satan's servants and that the realm would be cursed for their sins. *Fire and sword*, within a year of his death! he'd cried. Harold and Aldred exchanged agonised glances. Only the worldly, robust Stigand remained unperturbed. "It's delirium. Dying men often turn against their friends. Physician, have you no soothing draughts?"

Edward had begun rambling then, reverting to his boyhood French, and in such slurred tones that only the Norman courtier, whose ear was finely attuned to the tongue, could make it out, and even he made little sense of it.

"He's talking about a tree," he said helplessly, "cut in half . . . and the curse will be lifted when the two halves join and bear fruit. I don't know what it means."

"Nothing," said Stigand, firmly and compassionately, and took the draught from the physician's hands, administering it himself.

After that Edward had fallen back into coma, for which they were thankful. But now the restless, jerky movements had begun again.

"Wake him if you can," said the physician, "but gently."

"We must try to reach him before it's too late, anyway," said Stigand, looking down at the king with sorrow, but also with anxiety of a more temporal sort. He shook Edward's shoulder, carefully but with persistence. "My lord," he said in a quiet, conversational voice, "my lord Edward . . . will you name your successor for us? Your Witan needs to know."

The cool, everyday pitch of the voice seemed to penetrate Edward's mind. His eyes opened. They gradually focussed. "What . . . what day is it?" he asked.

Everyone let out a small, relieved breath. He was rational again "January the fifth, 1066," said Stigand. "You've been ill for some days. My lord, can you tell us . . . ?"

Edward mumbled and groped with his right hand in the direction of Harold, who offered his own hand. Edward pushed it, weakly but insistently, towards Edith. She too reached out and the king awkwardly put their hands together. "Take care of her . . . been a good wife to me. Don't cry, Edith, I may get well. If not . . . care for her, Harold." The voice was weak, but it held as he went on. "Care for her and the realm. Bury me . . . West Minster. Don't conceal my death. Pray for me." He gulped breath, exhausted by the effort. He dropped their hands and turned his head into the pillow as if he sought sleep.

"Don't rouse him again," said the physician.

"There's no need. What he said was clear enough," Stigand replied.

Ten minutes later, the physician held a silver mirror before the white, calm face, and laid his ear to the unmoving chest and said: "My lady Edith, and my lords, King Edward no longer rules in England."

The archbishops crossed themselves. The Norman courtier gave a sob and then choked it back as he saw Edith's hands go to her face. Aldred murmured a blessing and drew up the linen sheet. His eyes met Stigand's across the bed and Stigand turned to Harold. "Earl Harold of Wessex, he commended his realm to you at the end. I ask you now, formally, will you take this burden upon you? Will you, if the Witan consents, accept the crown of England?"

His own wishes, Harold thought, had little to do with it, which might be as well. He had guessed for a long time that Edward might name him at the last, but he had been shocked, as the moment drew near, at the fierce surge of desire that rose up in him. He was glad it was not his hand on the steering oar, that the Witan would finally decide. Not that they were likely to quarrel with his nomination.

The alternatives were the predatory Norman stranger with his trick-
eries and forced oaths, and Edgar Edwardson, a scared youth aged
fourteen. At least such unsuitable rivals gave him some semblance of
a right to rule. "If it is the will of the Witan," he said carefully, "I
accept."

He wished Godwin had lived to see today. Godwin had died
too soon, hounded out of the world by Edward's implacable dislike,
all through one honest error. As they took leave of Edward's body,
the others wept but Harold could not weep with them. His grief was
leavened with a triumph he could not help. The house of Godwin
had fought the king's unforgiveness for twenty-three years and the
Godwins had won. Never mind Edward's prophecies; dying men
often talked wildly. And never mind the voided oath of Rouen:
down with William of Normandy.

There were few men in Normandy who did not fear their duke, but
William FitzOsbern, his seneschal, was one of them. He had been
the young duke's companion and sometimes instructor. And his father had died for William. The latter, he thought sometimes, with a
touch of wryness, was probably the stronger influence.

His father, Osbern, had been the young duke's guardian, when
William's own father was absent on pilgrimage and the boy only
seven years old. There had been men enough who thought an absentee duke represented only by a child provided a magnificent opportunity to seize power—if only they could dispose of the child and leave
his obstructive and obstinate supporters with nothing to support.

William rarely spoke of, but would never forget, a certain night
in his childhood, at the island castle of Vaudreuil, when Osbern, for
the boy's comfort and protection, had shared his charge's bed. Till
he himself died, William would carry the memory of wakening in a
grey daybreak, from an uneasy sleep, and moving nearer to the
friendly bulk of his guardian, only to find Osbern's body alien,
stone-heavy, and cold. He had sat up in the pale light and seen the
bed rugs black with blood and torn with stab marks. Someone, striking at the vague heap under the rugs and thinking it to be William,
had killed Osbern in his sleep. William, giving way then to terror as
he would never give way in all the rest of his life, roused the castle
with his screams. An uncle sleeping nearby had come running, seen
the slain man and the torn bed, and rushed the boy headlong out of

the castle to safety in a woodsman's hut. Just in time, they learned later, before the assassins had had a chance to realise their mistake and repair it. It was because of that, FitzOsbern had slowly come to realise, that no blow had been struck at the infant Edgar in England, though someone had certainly been sent from the Norman court to attend to Edgar's father.

It was also because of that that FitzOsbern was at the moment the one to whom all eyes turned, as the only man who could dare approach the duke just now. No one else was going to do it. Yet it must be done.

The hall at Rouen Palace was as silent as a sepulchre and as perilous as a precipice. It was full of people who neither spoke nor moved. The duke, sitting with his cloak huddled round him and his back hunched, on a bench by a thick stone pillar, did not speak or move either and it was his stillness which enforced theirs. The air was breathless with his anger.

No one quite knew what had caused it. There had been a messenger, just as William was getting ready to hunt. The man had spoken to him, low, so that only the duke and FitzOsbern at his side could hear. Then the duke abandoned the hunt and came back to the hall, and men stepped aside from the sight of his face. That was all. Now and then someone hurried unknowingly into the hall and stopped short as if he had plunged unexpectedly into cold water. A few started to ask questions but were hastily shushed. To speak aloud here might draw the duke's wrath like a lone tree drawing lightning.

FitzOsbern had stayed to see the hunting party disperse. He stepped into the hall, and interpreted the scene before him, with disapproval. Quite apart from his own friendship with the duke, it was his business as seneschal to see that the duke's household ran smoothly, and the duke's household was now virtually frozen where it stood. People were here who had come to conduct business and could not get on with it. Petitioners were here, people seeking work, messengers, merchants. One of the merchants, whom he vaguely recognised as a man called Lyfing Thorkellson—one of those, come to think of it, whom gossip named in connection with Edward Edmundson's death—pulled his sleeve as he stood considering.

"Do *you* know what's happening, Messer FitzOsbern?" Lyfing murmured.

"You'll hear in good time," said FitzOsbern. The interruption annoyed him, but he saw how to turn it to account. He pitched his voice to carry. "I've no doubt the duke will release his news when he thinks fit!" Out of the corner of his eye he saw William turn towards him. Pulling his sleeve free, he strode to his suzerain's side. "My lord," he said softly, when he was near enough to speak for William's ear alone. "This will not do."

The anger in William's eyes was enough to make the bravest quail. FitzOsbern did not quail because, though he was not quite ten years older than William, he had tutored the youthful duke in arms and he trusted in the strength of the old relationship. As well as in his early-greying hair and his father's sacrifice. He gave back stare for stare.

"What do you suggest I do instead?" William enquired. "You have heard the news. My cousin Edward is dead. Harold has seized power. He was crowned on the day of Edward's burial, so eager he was to get his title ratified." William's teeth showed, unpleasantly. "Harold, who swore to help me to that crown, whom I betrothed to my own daughter. Shall I hold a banquet and drink his health?"

"Of course not. But brooding won't help either. The news will get out anyway, if that's on your mind. All England knows it by now and the first ship across the channel will bring it, even if the messenger didn't talk—and who knows if he did or not? Slighted you may have been, but you can't hide it or undo it." The duke's hand dropped to his sword hilt but FitzOsbern ignored it and the angry fingers relaxed. "What you should do," said the seneschal, speaking with deliberate roughness, as he had spoken long ago when ten-year-old William flagged under the armour he must learn to carry even in stark exhaustion, "is send an official protest and then be ready to wrest back your rights by force if need be. You have a secretariat full of clerks and a duchy full of strong men at your disposal. You know all this as well as I do. This is a time for action!"

William, harsh-spoken himself, responded unresentfully to the brusqueness. He unwound his tightly clutched mantle. Round them the atmosphere slackened, as if people had let out long-held breaths. "Look at them," said FitzOsbern. "The whole hall's been afraid to speak, in case you went for them with a blade. Save your edge for Harold."

"Very well, FitzOsbern, that's enough. There'll be no audiences today. Send these people away. But summon my clerks." William stood up. "I trusted him," he said. "I trusted Harold. I liked him. I thought an oath as heavy as that would hold him." The dark, slanting eagle brows drew together. Unexpectedly, he answered the question that even FitzOsbern dared not ask, talking, FitzOsbern thought, to himself. "There'll be no short cuts. This is not a matter of an atheling, or a rebellious count. Harold is anointed now and that is a sacred thing. He has betrayed an oath to God and God is an injured party. Only God can judge between us. The case will have to be tried. Ordeal by battle, if necessary."

"However unbecoming it may be to say so, Mother, I think you must be out of your mind," said Edwin of Mercia to Alveva. His blue eyes were as round as coins. He waved his hands to reinforce his words, and Alveva saw with irritation that they were red and clumsy on the end of long wrists, and that the wrists were shooting out of the fur-trimmed cuffs of his best tunic.

The Earl of Mercia was still growing and he was far as yet from completing the process. And when he did complete it, what sort of man would he be? Why were none of her children really hers? Aldith was the closest to her in looks, and even Aldith was like a stranger in her character. All that exaggerated grief over her husband. Men were always getting hacked to bits on battlefields; it showed how little sense they had and proved that loving them was a waste of good nervous force. As for the others, they were all undeniably Alfgar's offspring, right down to little Lucia. Only in her, the golden curls and the big pale blue eyes were assets. On Edwin and Morcar they looked plain effeminate. In any case, boys needed force of personality more than good looks, and her boys did not possess it.

"I'm not in the least out of my mind," she said with dignity. "I know exactly what I'm doing and I'm doing it for your sake."

"For our sake!" Edwin almost shrieked. "Sending letters to an enemy . . . well, that's what Duke William is, now that Harold is king! King Edward banished his own mother from the court once, and took all her treasure away, for that."

"And returned it all later," said Alveva. "Besides, I took care the king shouldn't know. You ought to trust me. Edwin, stop staring at me as if I had two heads, and sit down. You too, Morcar. You may as well rest while you can; you've a long journey ahead."

"Where to?" demanded Morcar. He and Edwin sat down, obediently.

"Back to your earldoms. Away from London till things settle down and William's messengers have come and gone. He's bound to send some. You've taken your oaths to Harold and no one will question it if you go quietly home now, and it will look better."

"I don't understand," said Edwin fretfully. "Are we going to be arrested for treachery if we stay? Well, and whose fault is that? You sent that messenger to Normandy, Mother. We didn't."

"Exactly," said Alveva immovably. She shivered as the cold wind blew through the shutters behind her. Their town house was usually used only in summer. It was built on an airy plan with a balcony and larger-than-average windows. In January, it was frightful. Shutters had to close at midday and candles burned in quantity at all hours. She huddled her black fur cloak round her shoulders into a more draught-proof arrangement and folded her mittened hands again on her lap, black-skirted in mourning for Edward. "Exactly," she repeated. "I did it on *my* responsibility. I have a brother at William's court. Why should I not write to Normandy? Someone would send the news sooner or later. By doing so myself, I leave the impression that this house—which means Mercia and Northumbria, and that's a good deal of England, let me remind you—contains possible allies for William if he gains power. At the same time I leave your accord with Harold untouched. You're in no danger of arrest. I want you to go home for quite another reason. If there is a struggle between William and Harold—and I think there will be—we shan't lose, whoever wins."

"Harold will win," said Morcar gloomily. "The man in possession has an advantage. There doesn't seem to be any reasonable doubt that King Edward did name him. Even that Norman who was in the room says so. Harold will win and we'll have to make the best of it, and we've made a very bad start."

"Nonsense," said Alveva. "We've made an excellent start, by securing ourselves against all eventualities. You don't let me finish. The north, especially Northumbria but not excluding Mercia, is notoriously wilful. Morcar, Edwin, if there is actual war, how many of your thanes can you count on to rally to Harold? How many really care who rules in London as long as they are allowed to run their own affairs their own way? I know they lent their support to the Witan in electing him, but that's a matter of shouting yea. How many would back words with swords, on the battlefield?"

Morcar shrugged. "They'd need inducements."

"They would indeed. Harold knows that. He watched his own brother struggle with the Northumbrians for years, for one thing. The Northumbrian and Mercian thanes could be bought . . . by Harold, but on terms very advantageous to us. If we're wrong about William and he conquers after all, of course we shall claim that Harold gave us no choice. Whereas really"—Alveva smiled—"we shan't give him one. If William conquers, I doubt if Harold will still be alive to argue about it. How dense you are, the pair of you. Do you still not see?"

"No," said Edwin plaintively, "we don't. We haven't the faintest idea what you're talking about."

Their mother, with a touch of impatience, told them.

"And you are certain that this is the message you want carried back?" said William Malet, gravely, to King Harold, whom he still thought of as Earl Harold, the great warrior, the preserver of men from the quicksand, whom he was proud to call his friend. If Harold was bent on quarrelling with the duke, he, Malet, must take the duke's side. But he would rather not choose.

"Quite sure," said Harold.

The letter lay on the table between them. A clerk, Norman by birth, English by adoption, and extremely embarrassed, had been reading it aloud. "Don't look so unhappy, man," said Malet, addressing him. "It isn't your fault."

"I'll read it through again if you wish," Harold said. Malet nodded. The exercise might encourage second thoughts. The king picked the letter up and read it aloud, in his vibrant baritone. "To William, Duke of Normandy, from Harold, King of England. Greeting . . ."

Malet's stomach muscles flinched. The very salutation was an insult, a king condescending to a duke.

". . . We have received your representations that the crown of England is rightfully yours and not ours, because of the oath we took in Normandy.

"We must insist that the oath was not valid. The inheritance of England is not in the gift of anyone but the Witan Council of England. They would never agree to the election of a foreigner. The oath we took in Rouen was as void as a promise of betrothal made by a lovesick girl without her father's knowledge, while living in her father's house.

"You raise, indeed, the matter of betrothals. You speak of a promise of marriage made between ourselves and your daughter Agatha, and between a Norman baron, unnamed, and our sister Elfgiva . . ."

"I wish you would reconsider!" Malet burst out. "My lord, what of the prophecy King Edward made when he was dying? I have heard witnesses speak of it. Something about a danger being averted when two halves of a cut tree come together and bear fruit. Could it not mean that the throne of England has been split between England and Normandy and that they should unite to avert war? If you marry Agatha . . . The duke would sooner call you son than enemy, I know it!"

"King Edward was delirious. His visions meant nothing. And if I did marry Agatha, that wouldn't necessarily stop me from quarrelling with William. Close relatives quarrel frequently." He wondered where Tostig was these days. "I don't believe the duke would ever waive his claim, Malet, if I married all his daughters. He wants England, and I won't surrender it, and I want that understood clearly." He went on reading.

"The Witan's consent would also be needed for us to take a foreign wife and in this case they would not agree. As for my sister Elfgiva, to our grief, she died in November. We cannot suppose that the baron you intended for her husband would want in his bed the kind of body she is now."

Malet groaned. "Too bitter?" Harold asked.

"Much too bitter! Please, my lord, don't say that!"

"I am bitter," said the King of England. "Bitter at being held to ransom over an oath that was forced from me. Bitter that King Edward ever offered the crown to Duke William at all. He did it from spite against my father, did you realise that? I repeat, I will not cede the crown to Duke William, nor will I marry his daughter. I have a wife already and I am not a man to marry little girls."

"He'll be angry," said Malet.

"With you?"

"No, I think he expects an answer of this sort." Malet's brown eyes sought Harold's uncompromising blue ones seriously. "I could even say you're sending the answer he wants. He's holding his temper in readiness for it. It won't be the first time I've seen him turn provocation into a stream to turn a mill. And he grinds his enemies small."

"I once employed the same technique against Gruffyd ap Llewellyn," said Harold coolly, holding out his hand for the seal that the clerk had in readiness. "And I carried it through. *I* ground *him* small. Will you drink with me before you leave, Malet? It may be a long time before we meet again as friends."

2 ❋ Thunderbolt

Aldith of Mercia and Wales was in the herb garden at her brother Edwin's Chester hall, tracing with a stick the line of a new path she wished to place between the mint and the colewort. It was cold, but she was snug in furred cloak and boots and she loved the garden.

This, the dead time of year, was the time to plan improvements. She might bring bright primrose plants from the woods later and see if they would take, she thought. They'd make a pretty border. She stooped, collecting stones to mark the edge of her new path, humming as she worked. A distant commotion of horses and horns a few minutes since had informed her of someone's arrival from somewhere, but she would wait to be summoned. There was no one for whose coming she looked with eagerness now. The newcomers were probably no concern of hers. To Aldith, the garden mattered more.

But the unseen arrivals were going to disturb her. She raised her head in irritation, as a figure came through the gate. This, no doubt, was a request for her presence in the hall. Then she saw that the cloaked and hooded figure was her mother, Alveva.

Alveva must have been one of the arrivals, then. She and the boys, Edwin and Morcar, had been at York, where the new king was holding a conference with the northern thanes. Aldith had not expected them back so soon. "Are my brothers back too?" she asked as Alveva came within talking distance. "What was the journey like?"

"Cold," said Alveva. "How you can moon about here in such frosty weather, I do *not* know. I was thankful to see a fire in the hall and surprised not to see you sitting by it. Yes, your brothers are here. We want most particularly to talk to you. You look well, I must say. Which is all to the good. Come back to the hall with me now."

"Why is it all to the good if I look well?" asked Aldith as they passed under the gate arch. "Does my state of health matter?"

Alveva gave her a sharp glance. "Very much. Well, you'll hear in five minutes' time, so you may as well be prepared now. And listen, Aldith, there's no room for argument in this. It's a matter of political necessity. You must do as you are told. Edwin will explain what I mean by necessity . . ."

"*What* is a matter of necessity, please?" said Aldith. It wasn't going to be anything she would welcome. She sensed it and her back stiffened.

Alveva, feeling the cold despite her cloak, set a brisker pace and spoke over her shoulder. "Your next marriage, my dear," she said.

"No!" said Aldith. "No and no and *no*! I will not! You don't understand, any of you. You can drag me to the altar if you like. I'll repudiate the marriage at the rail, when the priest asks if I am willing. I'll knife the man, as I did Cynan. I mean it. *No*!"

The three countenances facing her, Alveva's and Edwin's and Morcar's, did not change. They had expected this. Alveva, who was seated on a wide fur-covered stool, with her well-kept hands folded, said without moving them: "Naturally you feel like that at first, but you haven't considered. We understand that you need a little time to get used to the idea. But surely you are not indifferent to the thought of becoming Queen of England?"

"I prefer to remain the Lady of Wales," said Aldith stiffly. "And the King of England happens to be Harold, who took my husband's head as a trophy. I would prefer to enter a nunnery, please."

"Had God not decreed otherwise," said Alveva calmly, "Gruffyd might well have cut off Harold's head instead and put it on a pike outside the hall at Rhuddlan. He would have asked you to admire it. And you would have admired it, and you'd have called him your hero. These things are part of war. There's going to be another war. Did you realise that?"

Even a widow living in retreat couldn't be entirely deaf to the talk of the dinner table and hearthside. "I know," said Aldith impatiently. "William may invade. What of it?"

"Tell your sister about it again, Edwin," said Alveva. "I don't think she followed you the first time."

Edwin, thumbs in his belt, striking an attitude meant to express strength of personality, spoke. "We're the sworn earls of King Harold and must go to war for him if he calls us. But frankly, Aldith, our thanes have minds of their own. They would rather wait to see who wins before they declare for either. To get them to back us, we need to involve their interest."

"How difficult for you," said Aldith. "I do sympathise."

"If our sister were to be Harold's queen," said Morcar, "I think they might feel more interest in his fortunes. They would feel they had a voice, a supporter, in his near-circle."

"And if William wins?"

"If that happens . . . we have connections at his court and we've shown his cause some sympathy," said Alveva. "We could make our peace successfully, even profitably. But while Harold is king and if he remains king . . ."

"What an awkward dilemma for you," said Aldith, with irony. She stared angrily at her mother. She had left Mercia a girl, who could be bullied if recalcitrant. She had returned a woman, whose fire-forged character could at times intimidate even Alveva. She was not afraid of her family now. "Perhaps you could consult soothsayers and find out in advance which of them to support," she suggested acidly. "Then the thanes would know, as well."

"Soothsayers have a trick of contradicting each other," said Morcar, and Edwin laughed.

"You two are boys, only boys!" Aldith said violently. "What do you know of marriage or bereavement or what it is to be treated as nothing but a backgammon counter, moved here and there, married to this man or that, to suit someone else's convenience?"

"A woman of your position, Aldith, never is much more than a counter," Morcar said brutally. "It's what you're fed and protected for. Do you expect to wear silk and sleep on a down mattress and give nothing in return? We are asking you to make your return now, to build all our fortunes for us by marriage with a king. For God's sake, girl, he's a king and a great warrior and a damned handsome man as well! What are you complaining about? Half the women in the kingdom would cut off their right hands for such a chance!"

"Would they? They're welcome. What about my sister Lucia?

She's as much a child of Mercia and a sister of Northumbria as I am."

"She's a child. One purpose of this marriage is to get a son to bind north and south together in the body of an heir who represents both."

"Who thought of this?" Aldith asked bitterly. She was beginning to be frightened, after all. She felt like a mouse surrounded by three cats. They looked so certain of themselves.

"The king came north seeking support in Mercia and Northumbria," Edwin said. "There was deadlock between him and some of our chief thanes, however. I made the offer as a means of reconciliation."

"I had suggested it earlier," said Alveva. "It could raise our families to the skies! Your son could inherit England, you stupid girl. Pull yourself together, Aldith. No one's asking you to love the man. Take his hand at the wedding and then lie on your back with your eyes shut if you like. Once you have a son, he'll leave you alone, I expect. He has a concubine himself."

Aldith was trembling. She felt giddy and spots danced in front of her eyes. "Sit down," Edwin said, "here's a stool. Of course it's a surprise, but you'll soon get over that."

She sat down and at once felt even more frightened. The three bland, contented cats were standing over her. They had made up their minds to eat the mouse and were only waiting till it stopped squeaking and scuttling, before they sank home their claws. But she wasn't a mouse. She was Aldith, Gruffyd's lady. She must act with courage and cunning, as he would expect.

"I must pray for guidance," she said. "May I go to the chapel?"

"By all means," said Morcar. "But don't pray too long. And don't attempt to take sanctuary there. We shouldn't drag you out, of course. But we could starve you out."

"We wouldn't need to do that, even," said Edwin. He seemed pleased with himself. "Aldith, do be sensible. Go to your bower, have a little cry, get over your distress, and then get out your needle box and start making a veil for your marriage. You'll have the finest wedding a woman could dream of. You may as well give in. You'll have to in the end." He gave Morcar a reassuring grin.

"What do you mean?" Aldith asked sharply.

"You'll be expecting to find Nest and her nurse in your bower. I didn't have time to mention this before Aldith came in, Morcar. I'd only just given the order to remove the child and her nurse to a house in Chester. They'll have gone while we've been talking. Unless you consent to marry the king, Aldith, you'll never see your daughter again . . . so don't you think you'd better agree to be reasonable?"

Harold thought, when he first entered Chester hall, coming there to learn whether he was to be Aldith's husband or not, that the expressions on the young earls' faces meant the end of the nightmare. Decidedly, neither Edwin nor Morcar had "Congratulations on Your Forthcoming Marriage" written on their countenances. Aldith had refused, then. Relief raced through his veins. Then his mind began to race also, on beyond the present, into the distant future, to show him an ugly vision of that future. Himself with only half a fyrd-army, facing the might of Normandy under that puissant commander Duke William. A Duke William, at that, with a possible Papal Blessing. Report said he was suing for one. Unless the north of England could be bonded to the south, that vision could become reality. He would have to fight William handicapped, and lose. And England would lie exposed to the Norman with his strange tongue and his harsh foreign laws. All because Aldith had said no. If she had, it wasn't the end of the nightmare. Only a change to a different one.

He knew now that he had dreamed of the crown for years, not realising it. Now that it was his, he saw that it was a treasure guarded by a dragon whose name was William. Unluckily, he would need help to kill the dragon and it seemed that he must buy it, and the price was his manhood, and his beloved Eadgyth.

The proposal to marry him to Aldith had come so suddenly that he still felt stunned by it. He hadn't believed his ears at first, and when he found that his hearing was still functional he hadn't believed they meant it. Everyone knew he was handfasted to Eadgyth and had five children with her, and had refused William's daughter for her sake. But the two young, fair faces, Edwin's and Morcar's, had been perfectly serious. He saw that they did mean it. He'd studied them with exasperation. A pair of lightweights. But they could be dangerous by default, if they failed to help him on the battlefield.

And it might not be altogether their fault: Tostig, a much stronger personality, had failed with the Northumbrian thanes. He had had a taste of the latter's pigheadedness himself, at that very conference. His sympathy for Tostig had increased since it began. He wished he could get his brother home again. But only the promise of his earldom would get Tostig back, he knew, and the north would never stand for it. So Tostig would remain an enemy . . . perhaps another dragon.

Meanwhile, Harold wondered grimly whether the present northern intransigence was entirely spontaneous, or whether Edwin and Morcar had encouraged it as a way of levering their sister on to the throne. He suspected that they had. Perhaps he ought to have stuck to writing books on falconry. It hardly seemed worthwhile to be a king.

And meanwhile they had talked, at and around him, while in his mind he stared at the ghastly choice. To betray England, or Eadgyth. ". . . We do recognise," Morcar was saying, "that you may feel some personal reluctance." He was being pompous, bolstering himself up in the presence of the king. "You have a private union, we know. Also, Aldith is the widow of a former enemy, Gruffyd ap Llewellyn. But these things can be arranged. We should expect proper respect to our sister . . ." Morcar dropped his voice so that no one else in the crowded hall at York could hear. "And certainly everyone would expect the marriage to produce an heir. But discreet visits to . . . previous acquaintances . . . I'm sure Aldith would not object."

So he could have Eadgyth and England both, if he were careful. A few empty words at an altar, a simple animal act . . . that was all it amounted to. And she was beautiful. He had been willing enough to sleep with her at Rhuddlan. But what, after that, would she think of him?

"I will agree if your sister agrees," he said. "Ask her."

"She will agree," they promised him, and he said: "I will come to Chester myself, one week behind you, and you shall tell me then. I shall hold conference with the thanes of Mercia, and while I am there, if the Lady Aldith has consented, I will speak with her." And now he was here and their faces were solemn. He didn't blame her if she had refused. But if the marriage did not take place . . .

The earls were formally seated on the dais. The place of honour was vacant and he took it unwillingly. "Is the Lady Aldith ready to receive me?"

Edwin cleared his throat. "We . . . we could arrange the ceremony for a week today, if that pleases you. In York, as you wished, of course."

"You haven't answered my question. Will Aldith receive me?"

They looked uncomfortable. "Naturally, she was against the idea at first," said Morcar, "but . . ."

"She's a sensible girl," said Edwin. "I'm sure she will . . ."

"She's refused?" Harold cut in.

"No, no, no!" Morcar shook his head in energetic refutation. "Not at all, my lord. The wedding will go forward. Her mother has been reasoning with her . . ."

"She wants to refuse and you're using coercion?"

"My lord, the importance of this matter . . ."

Harold's fist crashed on to the arm of his chair. "What kind of reasoning? What kind of coercion? I *demand* to be told! What did the Lady Aldith say to the proposal?"

"She's confined to her bower," rasped Morcar, abandoning prevarication. "This is a matter of the safety of the realm, is it not? One girl's whim can't be allowed to upset it. Surely, my lord, you see that . . ."

"Where is her bower? I insist on seeing her. Since I am the man she is to marry, I think I should reason with her myself. I might even be more convincing than her mother. At least, it's my proper task to try. Conduct me to her, if you please. Now!"

"A prisoner," said Aldith coldly when they told her that Harold was coming, "has no choice in the company she keeps. I have no knife, even. So by all means bring him in."

She sat waiting, hands tightly clasped. At least she knew that Nest was safe and well. Myfanwy had managed to elude surveillance and walk beyond the palisade, close to Aldith's bower. As she went by, she sang loudly in Welsh the news that the child was in good health and being properly cared for. Other parents parted with their children, Aldith knew. Little girls were sent to convents to be educated, little boys to learn the arts of war in other households less indulgent, it was thought, than their own. As long as Nest was safe,

Aldith could endure their separation. The child would grieve for a while but she would grow used to it. Aldith could not consent to marry Harold. She prayed that they would not think of actually harming Nest, but with her uncles great princes in Wales, it was unlikely. She put her trust in that.

Harold came in escorted by the two earls. But at the threshold he said: "Leave us," and to the waiting woman who sat in the bower with tapestry work on her knee: "Go into the other room." Left with his prospective bride at last, he stood quietly and waited for her to speak first.

They had robbed her of all but bare comforts. She wore a thick mantle but she needed it, for there was no brazier. The boarded floor was bare of rushes. The remains of a meal on the table consisted of an uneaten crust and some stew at the bottom of a bowl; there had been no other dishes. Aldith did not rise at the king's entrance. She met his eyes and, as once before, hers widened a little, but she did not speak. They surveyed each other.

His view of her at Rhuddlan had been brief and she had been less a person then than a symbol of Gruffyd's defeat. But he had brought away an impression of charm: warm brown eyes and a fine skin with little freckles strewn across the nose had stayed printed in his memory. Yes, she was beautiful. And she hated him.

He kept the silence, determinedly, and at last she was forced to speak. This was a duel, so let the other side make the first move. By the nature of the move, he might get a clue to the nature of the mover.

"You need not tell me why you're here," said Aldith. "I already know."

"I'm here to propose marriage, and to offer you a crown," he said, recognising an attempt to raise a stone wall, and swiftly moving to knock it down.

"The last time we met," said Aldith expressionlessly, "you came to violate me, as though you were conquering an enemy."

No feinting, no faltering. A direct attack. Take that and let's see what you do with it. The unfriendliness in the brown eyes was disconcerting. He wasn't used to being looked at like that by women. But she wasn't just a woman. She was a bitterly angry opponent. He would have to begin from there, because Aldith was clearly not going to begin from anywhere else. Very well.

"On that day," he said, and sat down uninvited, "you were an enemy."

"Then you should have driven your sword through me. I wouldn't have cared. Gruffyd's blood was still on my clothes and his head was still on a spear in the middle of your camp. The sword would have been decent, and I could have followed him. But no, you came with nothing so clean in mind. You came reeking of wine . . ."

"You are talking," said Harold, and knew it for a base defence, even as he spoke, "to the king."

Aldith, silent and dead white, rose to her feet and swept him a magnificent curtsey which was more aggressive than a blow. She was far beyond personal fear. "Was it kingly," she asked contemptuously, resuming her seat, "to come to me in drink and half crazed? Though I could excuse the drinking. You had been celebrating a victory . . ."

He had been prepared to conciliate, but the mirror she held up to him showed such an extremely unflattering image. He almost forgot his mission. "How magnanimous of you! Would you expect me to celebrate by drinking milk?"

"No. I said, I could excuse the drinking. But what I cannot excuse is that you came to commit, in the name of conquest, the same act that you and *your wife* presumably call the act of love. What you came to do was to dishonour all three of us. What would she have said if she had seen you then?"

"I told her," said Harold unexpectedly. He had thought that Wulfhild might one day carry out her threat and inform Eadgyth. He preferred to confess and let Eadgyth throw something at him. He had got her to forgive him, after a few stormy days. "She was angry at first, but after a while she understood."

"Did she?" Aldith asked scornfully. "Women often pretend to accept what they can't change, especially when they love the man. I wonder what she *really* thought? Women don't understand such behaviour, King Harold. They never have and they never will and why should they?"

"Women . . ." Harold began, but she saw the dismissal of her argument appear in a half-smile on his face and her temper blazed.

"Don't smile! Why do men always think that when women have a different opinion from theirs, that it's always they who are right and we who are wrong? In this I tell you in the name of God Himself that we are right and you are wrong! Don't talk to me about the customs of the battlefield. They're an offence to God and all his angels!"

"All right." Long ago, learning swordsmanship from his father, Harold had been taught the technique of yielding at an unexpected moment. "All right, they are. But they won't change, Lady Aldith, even though they're abominable." There was a silence. Harold took a deep, calming breath. "We have not yet discussed the subject I came to discuss. We must. It is important."

"It's unthinkable," said Aldith, and turned away her head. "You had my husband killed and mutilated. Do you really expect me, ever, to marry *you*?"

"Oddly enough," said Harold, "I think Gruffyd of all people would understand it. His first wife was stolen from a vanquished foe, I believe."

"Not stolen. Rescued."

"Forgive me, but we have only Gruffyd's word for that." He let the idea penetrate. Then he said: "It may be true. But suppose it isn't. Suppose she loved her husband and clawed at Gruffyd's eyes. Would that have stopped him from taking her? Are you sure it would, Aldith?"

"No," said Aldith, contemptuous again. "He was a man and, as you say, the customs of the battlefield don't change. Perhaps he too mutilated his foes and gloated over their deaths. You were going to say that too, I expect."

"I wasn't, but it's probably true, yes."

"It makes no difference. Perhaps he did, at some time, do what you did. But he and no other man was my husband. I loved him and no other man. And it was you who destroyed him and for you that his head was made a trophy, and for no other man. I will not marry you!"

"Not even," said Harold gently, "to keep England from Duke William?"

"What's that to me? I'm half Norman."

"You are not," said Harold, "the only person in England."

Aldith did not follow this. For the first time, her eyes were doubtful, inviting communication. He pursued his advantage.

"Most of the folk of England don't want William," he explained.

"For good reasons. They're used to their own speech and laws. Why should they want a stranger from Normandy, bringing Norman barons who would take English lands and force their foreign ways on the folk and turn England into a second Normandy? What do you really know of Normandy? Did you know that there a man can't hunt freely in any forest for food, that the king owns all the deer? And did you know that the Duke of Normandy can sit on his horse and watch men drown in a quicksand and do nothing? I saw that happen. Except that the men didn't drown because I pulled them out myself. William didn't even dismount. *You* may not mind if William comes to be king, but others would mind. Why should England have William forced on her against her will, to suit Aldith? The English Witan elected me as king, with the consent of their folk behind them . . ."

"And your own consent."

"Your family are fairly ambitious as well, my lady! It's not necessarily a crime. My will, in fact, had little to do with the matter. They chose me and would have pressed me, if necessary. I had little say in that and I have little say in this marriage that we're arguing about. I, the king of England, haven't even the freedom to be faithful to Eadgyth. God in heaven . . ." Harold leapt to his feet and strode about the room. "Do you think," he threw at her, "that I want to marry you any more than you want to marry me? I'm telling you that we can neither of us choose. We're not a man and a woman; we're the north and the south. Unless we unite, William will seize his advantage. He'll come, he'll win on the battlefield, and then he'll burn and ravage to make the country accept him—because they won't unless they're forced, not the English folk. He'll take the lands from the men who resist him and give them to his followers. Do you care or not? Answer me! Do you? Would Gruffyd have cared? Suppose it had been Wales?"

Aldith dropped her dazed head in her hands. Gruffyd. Approachable by anyone. Settling an inheritance argument across a horse's back in a forge, giving a comprehending judgement through clouds of smoke and the smell of scorching horn. Listening to a dispute while he ground a blade on a whetstone. Gruffyd. Caring.

"You want a son," she said in a muffled voice.

"I need one, which isn't quite the same thing. I need one from you, a future king for the north and the south together. No, it can't be a marriage in name only. I come to this as much a sacrifice as you do. I shall hurt Eadgyth. Do you think that . . . pleases me?"

A break in his voice made her look up. To her astonishment, there were tears in his eyes.

"Did you know," she said, "that they took my daughter from me? To make me consent. But I wouldn't. I thought I might hold out until you gave up the idea. I had decided to take the veil as soon as I could. Did you order them to take her away from me? Edwin said it was his idea, but was it really yours?"

"By God, it was not!"

The denial sounded genuine to her. "She was lodged in the town at first," she said. "But she's back in the hall now, somewhere. I heard her crying for me one day. I think they meant me to hear." To her annoyance, her voice quivered.

Harold stood still. His expression was withdrawn. He looked like a chess player considering a dangerous move. Then he went to the door and bellowed.

His bodyguard and several Mercian housecarles came at a run. "Somewhere in this house," said Harold, "is my lady Aldith's little daughter. Bring her here. Don't frighten her."

One of the Mercians said: "It was Earl Edwin's order that she was to be kept away from the bower, sir."

"And it is the king's order that she should be brought to it! Before I have time to count a hundred!" barked Harold, and stepped back, dismissing them.

"If you refuse me," he said to Aldith, "I will send you and your child under safe conduct to whatever refuge you name. If you do marry me, I shall see that both of you are cared for and honoured as long as I live. I can do no more. I don't ask love from you. I don't pretend to give it. But the folk of England ask that we . . . perform a rite. Will you help me?"

Somewhere outside, a child's voice was upraised in excited questions, coming nearer.

Aldith said faintly: "I will answer you tomorrow. Will that do?"

He nodded, knowing already, just as she did, what the answer would be. He had gambled and thrown away an advantage, just as a chess player might sacrifice a valuable piece for strategy's sake; and he had won. They were opponents no longer.

"I shall go now," he said, "and leave you to your reunion with your daughter."

He wanted to be alone himself, to bury his head in his arms, and pray for Eadgyth's forgiveness.

3 ✺ *Comet*

In Lillebonne, to which the Norman court had now repaired in accordance with its custom of moving from castle to castle throughout the duchy, an uproar was in progress.

William had that morning presented to his barons the news that the Pope had authorised him to invade England, had excommunicated Harold for perjury, and was sending a papally blessed banner for the Norman leader to carry into battle. He had then retired to let his barons talk—or bellow—the matter over among themselves. Now they had recalled him and he sat on the dais while his nobles stood in a crowd on the floor of the hall. His seneschal and friend William FitzOsbern stood on the steps of the dais halfway between William's level and theirs.

FitzOsbern was flushed and grim-mouthed, and the barons were furious. He had been their spokesman, but . . .

"What the hell's he talking about? We never told him to say that!"

"You're mad, FitzOsbern, *none* of us said we'd give four knights where we only owe two, to attack England!"

"I'm not even giving one; the whole venture's crazy!"

Confused agreement rising from a score of outraged throats drowned individual protests out. Fists, some of them mailed, were shaken towards FitzOsbern, who was saying something no one could hear. William waited to see if the din would subside, but it did not. He raised a hand and bawled: "*Quiet!*" After the fourth repetition, the racket dwindled. He pointed at one man who stood out because he was taller than most others, the Bishop of Evreux, thin, long-legged and articulate. "You! Speak for the rest."

"My lord," said Evreux angrily, "we never asked the seneschal to say to you that we should back you to twice our lawful amounts. He invented it. Perhaps he thought we wouldn't dare deny it in your presence, but we do dare. We'll serve you in your own lands because that's our duty, but the terms of our fealty don't compel us to follow you abroad. Many of us feel that England is a foreign land where you have no claim, Pope or no Pope. And we know that the English sailors are gifted seamen who could challenge us before we ever reached their shores. The risks are enormous and the justification is not enough."

William's face darkened—not a flush, but an actual charcoal tint on the skin. His fists clenched on his knee. It was a personal attack.

It was an attack, to start with, on his private dreams of a kingdom. Not to be lord only of a small duchy hemmed in by bigger neighbours and bound in fealty to France, but king of a realm with sea as a rampart on two sides and weaker nations on the other two. A king owing fealty to none, but ruling in his own way. Ruling was his vocation and he knew it, and God did not give men talents to waste.

But it was more even than that; it attacked his very command of Normandy, let alone England. He had won control of his duchy and his barons the hard way, by strength, not merely by inheritance. The barons had revolted in the past. They had tried to kill him when he was a child of seven and they had tried again when he was eighteen. That was the attempt from which his jester, Gollet, had saved him. Gollet's professional idiocy was so well maintained that men tended to discount him and talk too freely in his presence; Gollet had eavesdropped, at first casually and then with purpose, and the same night William was roused from sleep by a Gollet in whose face no trace of foolishness could be seen. "There's a squad on its way to murder you and this area is full of their supporters. Bolt!" said the jester succinctly, and there was nothing else to do, so he had bolted. But during that headlong ride through the light of a half-grown moon, not reaching friendly territory until dawn, he had seethed at the shame of fleeing and resolved within himself that one day, and soon, he would show these arrogant noblemen who ruled in Normandy.

Well, he had showed them. He had got the French king's aid and put the rebellion down, hard. But now it seemed that they were rebelling again. And if he could not control his duchy, how could he control a kingdom?

To do either, he must first control himself. The anger faded out of his face. Evreux, who had stopped, dry-mouthed, took new courage. Behind him someone said: "Go on, Crane-Legs, we're all with you."

The bishop took another breath. "We also think that if we follow you overseas, it will become a custom and a burden on our descendants and successors. We are sorry, my lord. No doubt FitzOsbern meant well. But we are not offering four knights for two in this adventure. We are not offering any knights at all. We're not bound to do so and we're all agreed on that!"

He finished amid cheering. William shouted for silence again and this time failed to get it. He looked at FitzOsbern, who put his fists on his hips and scowled at the turbulent assembly. "I did my best, my lord. Shove a physic far enough down a dog's throat and he'll have to swallow it, I thought. I tried to shove England down theirs."

William's hands were clenched hard over the chair arms. He pushed down on them and stood up. "It's not your fault, FitzOsbern. I shall leave the hall now. But no one is to leave Lillebonne. The conference will resume tomorrow."

He went, with a heavy, angry stride and a whisk of his cloak. But FitzOsbern saw him pause at an arrow slit as he started up the steps from the hall, and when he went on again it was slowly, and more thoughtfully. FitzOsbern fiddled with his cloak clasp, to hide his hopeful expression. His master, he knew, had thought of something.

"Now, Evreux," said William reasonably, gesturing the long-legged bishop into a seat in the little stone room, "let us talk this over sensibly, just you and I. We were all excited in the hall yesterday. I think we may have misunderstood each other."

"I can't speak for the assembly without referring to it, my lord. Do you want me to carry a further message to them?"

"No, Evreux. I want to talk to you, personally." The duke had had himself carefully shaved today and was dressed in his most impressive best, with gold edging to his red tunic, and a violet velvet cloak. His black hair was sleeked flat. He looked like a newly minted coin and he was in a newly minted mood with a set of arguments fresh from the coinmaker's dies. Evreux considered himself a man of the world but William was making him feel as gawky as the crane after which his friends had nicknamed him. He waited nervously. One could defy this man in a hall full of supporters. To be shut up here tête-à-tête with him was another matter.

"What I don't think you understood," said William calmly, "is that I don't demand anyone's services in England as a right. Of course it's outside the usual terms of fealty. And it will stay outside them as far as all of you and your heirs are concerned. I ask it as . . . a favour. To me as a friend. If the expedition succeeds, it should be fruitful. England is rich and all those who follow me will share in the profits. But one can't get profit without risk, Evreux. Even as a churchman, you should know that. How many of the gracious saints would have won to sanctity without hazarding their bodies? And on a more earthly plane, I know you speculate with your considerable wealth. Last year you and Lyfing Thorkellson bought up three thousand head of sheep from the estates of a banished baron, at a time when there was no market for wool, and held on to all the fleeces until two months ago, when the price soared . . ."

"It was a foregone conclusion. Those slumps never last."

"So is England a foregone conclusion, if I get enough investment. You had to invest capital in those sheep. Now I'm asking you to do the same for me. The more support I have, the better the odds for us all. What about it, Evreux? My brother Odo is backing me. He promised me a hundred ships this morning. My other half-brother, Robert of Mortain, is giving me a hundred and twenty. You need only speak for yourself. I don't ask you to mortgage anyone else's goodwill. Nor will I ever ask such a favour again, and you can have that in writing. Well? How many ships will *you* wager on my English enterprise?"

"I . . . suppose it is a wager, in a way," said Evreux weakly.

"A hundred, like Odo?" asked William interestedly. "You have timber, and serfs enough to cut it, I think? You certainly have enough men to man the vessels."

"Fifty," said Evreux, attempting firmness. "I couldn't guarantee more, if you want them this year."

"I want them this summer. Perhaps a hundred is a little high. Eighty-five? Oh come, Evreux, I know what your resources are. I know the details of every holding of my barons, by heart, and most of their chief tenants' holdings as well."

"Sixty-five," said Evreux and then thought: Oh God, I've agreed already. I may as well do it properly and with luck he'll win the day and remember me afterwards. "Well . . . eighty."

"Done!" said William, clapping him on the shoulder with a powerful palm. "The clerk's waiting outside to record it. You won't regret it, Evreux."

He was already regretting it as he made his way down to the courtyard, but there was comfort to be found there. A baron whom he knew, Roger of Beaumont, was in the courtyard gloomily watching a groom prise a pebble out of a horse's hoof. He turned at Evreux's footsteps. "Have you just come from William? I saw you go up. How much did he get from you?"

"Is he doing it to all of us?" Evreux asked. "Just taking us one by one and . . . wringing us out?"

"Apparently. Well?"

"Eighty ships," said Evreux exasperatedly.

"Ah well. Take that horse back to the stable, lad, he's too lame to hunt today. I'm glad that some people are worse off than I am. I only promised him sixty."

Towards dusk, William, his long day of interviews concluded, found Matilda sitting in their chamber, not stitching for once, but feeding a small caged bird with seed. He stopped in front of her.

"I have succeeded," he said. "There will be an army. We shall sail to England this year."

She turned her face up to him and saw how rigid he was, how tired with the long effort of ingenuity and argument, and held out a hand to him. He took it and then with an extraordinary, uncharacteristic movement, dropped to his knees by her chair and briefly pressed his face against her. Drawing back, he said: "I have to succeed. I had to win in Normandy today and I must win in England this year, or lose them both. I shall die on that battlefield or conquer, Mald. But I cannot live on as a failure. May Harold be damned for his perjury. He has brought this on us."

"Yes, damn Harold indeed," Matilda echoed softly. She shook

her head sadly and caressed his with a small, gentle hand. "If only there had been some other way. I wish . . ."

"No," said William, and his native strength was back in his voice. He rose and stepped away, the weak moment over. "Not that, Mald. Not for Harold, who was once my friend, and not to settle an insult to God . . . God can do His own judging. And above all," William said, "not for an anointed king. A king may be slain on the battlefield, but never by stealth. He's God's appointee while he wears the crown. Do remember, Mald, I hope to be a king myself. This year."

So here she was again, unbelievably, going through the bridal ritual, surrounded by women who brushed her hair and sponged her skin with rosewater and pushed back the cuticles of her nails. But this time the man wouldn't be Gruffyd, not Gruffyd with his dark, compact, black-pelted body, his warm Welsh voice, and his bright brown eyes. It would be Harold, his enemy and his opposite: gold-haired, blond-bearded, blue-eyed . . . and strange.

There was no happy giggling this time. Alveva, however triumphant, had known better than to congratulate or lecture her daughter tonight. Aldith, cold and unfriendly, had announced that she would marry Harold for the realm's sake. She did not mention her family. She had worn blue velvet over a tawny, tight-sleeved underdress, and she had stood by an altar and said: "I will," and Nest, with eleven other little girls, had stood behind her to hold up her long white stoatskin cloak. She had sat by Harold at a wedding feast packed with smug Northumbrians and Mercians, the thanes who had forced them into this, with or without encouragement from Edwin and Morcar. She had overheard comments and pretended to ignore them.

"It's hard on her, maybe. He took her first man's head."

"Bah! That's war. The woman ends up with the better man that way. Most have sense enough to see it in time. He'll make her forget Gruffyd in a year, you'll see."

She kept her face still while her thoughts hurtled. Forget Gruffyd? O Gruffyd! Gruffyd of the roaring falls of Cwmanog, where we tossed in pebbles for each other's love, how can I forget you? Is this part of the price? Wasn't it enough to watch you die, but the Immortal Ones must ask this too? Gruffyd of the winter beechwood, how can this man replace you? *Forget* you . . . ? But she must not think about him now, she *must not*, or she would cry. And she mustn't cry. She had held up her head and replied to the small talk of the big blond man beside her and, later, would go to bed with him.

She now put up stonily with the traditional foolery, as she was taken to his chamber. The bridegroom came and there were more jokes and her brothers insisted on helping Harold to climb into the bed beside her. Edwin addressed her as "Queen Aldith" and Morcar wished her joy and told her to see that she got a fine morning-gift the next day. "He's the king; he can afford it." She didn't answer.

When they had gone, Harold turned to her, propping himself on his elbow. He put a hand on her shoulder, the only time throughout all this weird courtship that he had touched her except for taking her hand at the wedding. "It's only a rite," he said reassuringly. "A spell, if you like, for the safeguarding of the land. Our heathen ancestors did it, with strangers, to make the corn grow. We must both endure it." He made a face, which Aldith recognised as self-disparagement. "I sound discourteous. Aldith, if I were a freeman I should want your love because you are beautiful and brave. I admire you for killing Cynan. Your love would be worth having. But Eadgyth is alone tonight. For us both, then, this can only be a ritual."

Some time later, he drew away from the passive form which neither resisted nor responded, and turned his back. Then he said: "God help me, I can't. I can't take you, Aldith. My body's a traitor to the land I swore to defend. I'm a pretty king, aren't I?"

Aldith felt for the flints at the bedside, and lit a candle. "There's wine here, my lord. You had better drink some."

He let her fill a cup. "Call me Harold, if you can bear to." He sat up to drink and the sheet fell away from him. The candlelight showed her his vigorous torso, the rounded spring of the rib cage, the smooth padding of muscle on the broad shoulders, the line between tanned skin and white at the base of his neck. On Gruffyd that line had been barely discernible, even in hot weather. But Harold was not Gruffyd. His beauty was of an utterly different kind.

Yet, it was still beauty, and Aldith saw it. She had seen it before, both at Rhuddlan and at Chester, when it had momentarily ambushed her senses, jolting her pulse and widening her pupils, until her anger rose and threw it back. But tonight it was better that she shouldn't reject it.

He felt her scrutiny and looked at her, his own eyes more black than blue in the dimness. "Aldith," he said, "Lady of England now, as I am its lord, will you help me?"

And because she had been married before, and that to the imaginative, uninhibited Gruffyd, she understood him and did what he wished, performing with lips and hands, for Harold's salvation, what she had once done for Gruffyd's pleasure.

Presently Harold said: "I believe you're laughing. Why?"

"It's so absurd," said Aldith. "I came to sacrifice myself, like a victim to a Norse priest's pagan knife. And then I had to help the priest, and I was afraid, in case I failed. What could be more ridiculous?"

"Not ridiculous," said Harold. "It was kind."

Brand Woodcutter, Thane of Fallowdene, formerly Sir Brand of the court of Duke William, lay in a patch of mud with one arm plunged inside a labouring ewe, and gave some philosophical thought to life's curious twists. He had been a warrior in the greatest houses of England and Normandy. He had called such a man as Earl Harold, who was now King Harold, his friend. Yet at heart he had never ceased to be a farmer's son and here, in this undignified, uncomfortable attitude, he was at home. So much so that it could assuage his sadness that, with his smudged reputation, he could never be one of the Royal Bodyguard, that chosen band of thanes and their best followers, who would guard King Harold's person on the field. He had hoped for a little while, after Harold's crowning. But the clique in the bodyguard who would not speak to him was still there and still powerful. The hope faded. In Fallowdene, he could forget that.

He peered up, panting a little, over the heaving fleecy back to where Wulfhild, bucket and cloths beside her, sat sponging the ewe's face. She too was at home here. It was in their blood.

"I think I hear someone calling," she said.

"Whoever it is must wait. Ah! I've found two forelegs and I think . . . I think they both belong to the same lamb. Gently now . . ."

"Brand! Your steward said you were here. Whatever are you doing?"

"Sorting out tangled twins and you're standing in the light," said Brand without looking round. His arm had vanished above the elbow. The ewe bleated.

"Hush, sweetheart," murmured Wulfhild. "Father, it's Earl Gyrth."

"In person," Gyrth Godwinson agreed, moving so that his shadow no longer fell across the sheep. He squatted down, the better to talk. "I'm making for London to join the king. I've six of my thanes and their men with me—getting dry round your hall fire just now; the whole world seems to be made of mud—and I've a message for you. I've already delivered one to Leofwin. Do you have to do these jobs yourself, Brand? Haven't you got a shepherd?"

"He was old," said Wulfhild. "He died. No one had thought of training a successor and he hadn't any children. But my father knows the work."

"Sweyn called me a country boy sometimes," Brand said. "And he was right. I'm a plain churl more than a thane . . . Here it comes! Here's the first one. The forelegs were doubled back, Wulfhild. They're straight now and I've pushed the other lamb back for the moment . . . There!"

He slowly withdrew his arm and a wet, limp object followed it, sliding headfirst on to the damp April earth. Gyrth, without speaking, picked it up and handed it to Wulfhild, who rubbed it briskly with a cloth. She presented it to the ewe to lick. It bleated feebly and struggled to stand. The ewe heaved again and another pair of forefeet appeared. Brand took hold of them. "I used to do this at home as a boy. Funny how it comes back." The second bundle of damp wool slid into the world and the relieved ewe tried to rise, bleating for her babies. The first one, looking like an animated toy, began a wobbly progress towards the teat, found it and drank, its tail a joyful whirligig. Brand went to sluice his arms in the bucket. "So," he said, watching the ewe set to work on the other lamb, "what's your message, Gyrth? What brings you to Sussex?"

"Recruitment," said Gyrth. "I've been making personal visits to my estates in the southeast. I have two in Kent and one in Sussex. While I was at it, I undertook to visit my brother Leofwin and yourself, with word from the king. King Harold expects a Norman invasion before the end of the summer. He wanted Earl Leofwin to start recruiting in his own territory, and he wants you in London, Brand. William will have mounted knights. We need a cavalry of some sort to put in the field against him. We have a nucleus, but no more, since the training lapsed after Hereford, though we kept the horse-breeding programme going. You heard about Hereford?"

"I'm afraid I did. It was a good story and it travelled well." Brand dried his arms. "Let's go back to the hall."

They set off along the winding chalky path towards the house. Above them the clouds showed signs of lifting for the first time in a week, and a gleam of setting sun appeared at the western edge of the sky.

"The point is," said Gyrth, "we have something to work on but we badly need men who know the art to train the rest. Hakon's been co-opted, but I can't say he's a skilled instructor. Just between us," said Hakon's paternal to Hakon's maternal uncle, "he likes to show off his own knowledge, but he can't transmit it. Harold can, but Harold has a thousand other things on hand. We want you, Brand. You were a knight in Normandy. Harold told me to say that his need for you in London is urgent."

Brand sighed. He was in his mid-forties and beginning to feel it. He had had enough of courts and campaigns and more than enough of Godwin power struggles. He wanted to stay at home and farm Fallowdene. "Are there enough horses?" he asked.

"No, though there are more than there were. We shan't risk using ponies this time. We have two or three hundred horses of the right type and another fifty or so that will do, and that's enough to be valuable if properly trained. How soon can you be ready?"

"Tomorrow, if I must," said Brand.

"Most of the lambs are born now," said Wulfhild, "and sowing's well over. I can manage." She spoke cheerfully, though he had seen her brace herself to do it. He looked at the furrows dusted green with the first shoots of corn and at the hearth smokes of his villagers rising from their roofs, and secretly cursed the Godwin importunity. But he would go. Harold could not help the invasion peril, after all.

The hall was full of bustle, with the steward's wife, Editha, and their daughter, Eve, busy with preparations to feed twenty extra mouths. Fortunately they had had two sheep, ewes which had died lambing, on the spit when Gyrth rode in.

They dined, while the green April twilight settled on the world under a quickly clearing sky, and Brand, dragging his mind with difficulty away from the lambing, and the approaching summer tasks of shearing and haymaking, which Wulfhild would have to supervise without him, talked to Gyrth about tackle for warhorses and intermittently tossed reminders to his daughter about things she should pack for him to take. Darkness fell and the torches were lit, and the bones were flung to the dogs, who settled contentedly down by the fire to gnaw them. Eve went round the tables with a basket, collecting leftovers for the stockpot, and then again to gather useless scraps for the midden. She went out to deposit the midden pieces, and the open door of the hall showed a clear patch of sky with stars in it. "We shall have a drier ride tomorrow," said Gyrth.

Outside in the starlit courtyard, Eve screamed.

A shrill note of pure terror was in that scream, which brought them all out of the hall headlong. Brand seized his sword from the wall as he ran. Odi snatched down his axe. Osric, also reaching for an axe, cried to Editha and the steward to wait, as they were unarmed, but they were Eve's parents and brushed him aside. They were first through the door. In the yard, Eve was kneeling on the muddy ground, her face upturned, and she was pointing. Her mother followed that upward-stretching finger with her eyes and she too screamed and crouched beside her daughter. Then some of the men cried out and Brand heard a sound of horror in his own throat. His sword drooped, useless. It could not fight this enemy.

There was more in the April sky than the simple stars. How many nights it had been there, no one knew. The sky had been cloudy for six days and nights. But it was revealed now. It shone overhead, a dazzling star with a triple, luminous tail that streamed away southwards. It dominated the sky. It was a thing against nature, a harbinger of the unknown, an omen.

"Oh, what is it?" wailed Editha.

Osric said shakily: "It points south. Towards Normandy."

"They're coming!" sobbed Editha.

But Tostig, as it happened, came first.

4 ❊ Hailstorm

Tostig came from nowhere like a May hailstorm, hurling his spears against the south and southeast coasts and then, having left a trail of wreckage behind him, he proceeded to sit down in Sandwich and dismantle it. He was in a rage, said the frantic reports borne inland by refugees, because so few upheld him. Most men, already tensed to receive William, had scant time to spare for Tostig and his irrelevant quarrels, and in the south, in any case, he was now a stranger, a wild man from Northumbria, with a murderous reputation. Harold remembered how he and his father had been rejected by their own folk once, in the days when they had made their first bid to return from exile. He understood Tostig's frustrated anger. But . . .

But one could understand a foe and still fight him, said Aldith, on whom, to her and his surprise, had come the nature of a queen. She felt the burden of England as he felt it, and when they talked of it they drew close whether they wished it or not. "The folk of the coasts look to you for help," she said, "and also, you must be ready for the Norman onslaught. Tostig is your brother, yes. But brothers are not always one's best friends."

"No," he said quietly. "You have no reason to love yours, I realise."

But whatever bitterness she still felt in this forced union, her advice was wise. No one knew what William was doing. Agents had gone into Normandy, French-speaking men under cover of trade or pilgrimages, but none had yet returned. It was safest to assume that invasion was imminent and, if so, then the pest in Sandwich must go. Harold put it to Gyrth and Leofwin and they, with evident relief, concurred.

To deal with William, he must raise the fyrd, that ultimate army made up from all the able-bodied men in the land. It might as well be raised now. The word went out by relays of hard-riding messengers, who started eight or ten messengers more from every town they went to, spreading the summons wider . . . "The king is in London, rally to him, to fight the rebel Tostig . . . Bring your sword if you have one; if not, a stave or a bow or a homemade spear will do . . . But hurry, hurry, hurry . . . !"

The men came. The warships sailed down the Thames, and Tostig, finding outnumbered even the fifty ships he had by now rounded up to help him, fled from Sandwich and went north.

But the message had sped north before him and Earls Edwin and Morcar, obedient to the marriage bargain, were ready with local fyrds of their own. On the coasts of Yorkshire, a discouraging reception awaited him.

"So he's gone," Harold said to Eadgyth. He lay face down on the deerskins of the restful couch that awaited him wherever Eadgyth was. This time, as so often, it was at Saxmundham, where he had broken his journey for one precious day before going back to London to resume preparations for William. "But he'll be back," he said. "He may make for Scotland or Norway or the Orkneys, we don't know. Some of his ships were from the Orkneys. We picked up survivors from one we sank and got that much out of them before we dumped them overboard. He's had Viking help, in other words, and he may try for it again. Eadgyth, I want you on one of my estates nearer London. I want you away from the coasts and nearer to me."

"And what," said Eadgyth, "will Aldith say to that?"

He rolled on his back, fists balled against a tired, corrugated forehead. "She's pregnant," he said.

Eadgyth, who had been kneeling by the couch, rose abruptly. Her face was stiff. He put out a hand. "Don't go, Eadgyth. Sit on the couch. That was one of the objects of the marriage: to make a king for the future, in whom the north would have a stake. You ought to pity the poor baby, conceived to order to a dynastic specification, instead of made from love, because its parents couldn't help themselves. You should pity Aldith too. How would you feel about a man who'd taken away my head as a trophy, on a spear?"

"I should stab him," said Eadgyth.

"Well, she did stab Cynan. Are you sorry she failed to kill me too?"

"Yes!" said Eadgyth defiantly. They stared at each other. "It might be easier to mourn your death than to think of you . . . Yes, I mean it!" she said.

"I believe she threatened something of the sort when the idea was first put to her. But would even you have killed the king, leaving England open to the Norman? She agreed, and I agreed, to keep William off. Aldith won't care if you come to London. And neither she nor her child will ever have the part of me that you and our children have."

"I wish *I* felt so sure of it," said Eadgyth bitterly.

News of his marriage had come to her ahead of rumour, for he had written. His letter assured her that the marriage was only a political convenience, that his love for her endured and that he would return. She cut the parchment to pieces, wept and cursed and stamped on the shreds. She went to the kitchen and took all the clay pots from the shelf and smashed them in fury, one by one. She went to the couch where she had so often slept with Harold and tore its rugs apart, scattering them over the floor. Her waiting women quietly swept up slashed parchment and broken potsherds, and reassembled the rugs, but wisely did not try to stop her from rampaging.

When Harold finally came, her rage was long blown out. She had planned in her imagination a dozen ways to greet him. She would be cold and formal like a stranger and have him politely shown to a separate guest chamber. She would leave the house at his approach and not meet him at all. She would spring at him and scratch his face, hurl plates and knives and anathemas. She would . . .

In the event, she ran to greet him as usual, and at close sight of his weary face and anxious eyes she was thankful. She saw that he had dreaded just the greetings she had plotted. "It makes no difference!" she cried to him, holding him hard. "I know you had to do it and it makes no difference!"

But it did.

"You've changed," she said now, as he sat up, jerked fully awake by the edge on her voice. "You're . . . remote."

"I have William and Tostig to think about. How to prepare. How to use the cavalry Hakon and Brand Woodcutter are shaping for me. How to keep the fyrd happy and fed if we have to wait all summer for William. Isn't that enough to make a man absent-minded?"

"Yes. And I know that sort of absent-mindedness. I didn't mean that. I mean that your face alters when you speak of her and I can't tell what you're thinking. Except that I believe you're thinking of her. She isn't . . . just nothing to you, is she, Harold?"

"She's carrying my baby and she was forced into marrying me." He did not add: "And she's brave and kind," because Eadgyth couldn't be expected to understand that. It puzzled him too, at times, that there was room in his soul for an Eadgyth and an Aldith too. "She can hardly be 'nothing,' as you put it, under the circumstances. But she isn't you. Your place, no one can usurp. You were and are and always will be, my Eadgyth. She is the queen and she lives in my palaces with my sister Edith and Agatha, Edward Edmundson's widow, for her companions, and Agatha's children play with Nest. Young Edgar makes a pet of the child, and she tries to teach him Welsh. Aldith, in fact, shares my throne and my court. You share my life."

"What does your mother think of her?"

"She likes her, in a polite way. She's sorry for her, I think. And she worries about you. She'd be glad if you were nearer London." His hand reached for her again. "Eadgyth, don't abandon me now. I've foes all round me, armies mustering against me and what seems like ten thousand leagues of coastline to defend. And I'm so tired. You were always the place I came to for rest. Don't shut me out when I need you so much. With you, I can forget William and Tostig for an hour. No one else can do that for me, *no one*, do you hear, Eadgyth?"

Eadgyth sighed and kicked off her sandals and stretched herself at his side. He smiled and said as she snuggled close to him: "You'll come to be near London then?"

"I'll come," said Eadgyth.

They dozed. Presently she woke to find his chest and belly hot and receptive, pressed against her, and desire stirred in her. But in the midst of their lovemaking she suddenly saw in her mind a picture of Aldith in his arms like this, and she sank her teeth into him where his neck joined his shoulder, in a passion compounded equally of love and rage.

June came, and the summer seas stayed innocent of war fleets. Tostig had vanished into the far north and William made no visible move in the south. Yet the air was tense with expectation and the tension did not slacken.

In Fallowdene, Wulfhild, after much careful thought, worked out that if the Normans landed and took to ravaging, it might be possible to hide the Fallowdene folk and some at least of their stores and cattle in Andred Forest. The forest was near enough. They might, of course, come back later to find the hall burned down. She stayed awake all one night over that one, and then ordered two men off the haymaking to fell trees instead. To avoid causing alarm, she spoke mendaciously of a change in the annual dues and the inclusion of more timber henceforth. But when enough trees had been felled and lopped, she had them stored in a rough thatched shelter in a glade in the Fallowdene woods. The men looked at her oddly and clearly guessed at some unnamed purpose, but they asked no questions. She was pleased when the work was finished. At least they had the means now to raise a new hall quickly.

The fyrd remained ready. Harold moved here and there overseeing channel patrols, drilling, organising. Food must be found for the army. Supply lines must be set up, livestock and ale and flour kept where they were needed. One slept each night in the knowledge of unresolved questions which must be answered next day without fail. In London, Brand, with help from Hakon, forged two hundred and thirty horsemen into something resembling a cavalry unit and damned the lack of good horses. Gyrth's estimate at Fallowdene had been too optimistic. In July, Harold went to the Isle of Wight to keep watch there in person. It was there, as the month wore on, that his agents returned to him.

Their news was ominous. The duke was assembling a great fleet at the port of Dives, they said, and had already declared that in his absence his wife should be Regent of Normandy on behalf of his twelve-year-old son, Robert. The men mustering at Dives were very orderly, said the spies uneasily. William had told them that this was a holy war and so they must behave like men of God and respect all honest folk and their property and treat even the humblest bond-women as sisters.

"It's unnatural, that's what it is," said one of the agents, resentfully. "All those soldiers, and the local serfs take no notice of them. Behaving like an army of bloody angels, they are! When they get here we'll see the other side of the coin. They'll turn into devils when they set foot on our shores, mark my words."

"You may be right," said Harold, "but repeat it outside this tent and I'll have you skinned for a wall hanging. William's a raider like any other pirate, as far we're concerned. We want no talk of angels or devils or holy wars. We've had trouble enough with signs in the sky."

"Talk about holy wars is going round already," said the agent glumly. "But it makes some folk ready to fight harder. They don't like being pushed about, whether it's by the Duke of Normandy, or the Pope, or things in the sky."

"That," said Harold, "is an idea you can spread about, and welcome!"

Last of all the agents to return was a monk, a man whom Aldred of York had personally chosen. He had been on a visit to a Norman monastery, ostensibly to offer to sell valuable relics from his own small religious house. "There's a link between the two monasteries," Aldred had said. "The English one was founded by the Norman house, in the early days of Edward's reign. It will seem a very natural visit. The man is simple and unworldly in his manner, though extremely intelligent. I don't think he'll be suspected."

"I'm very sorry," he said ruefully when he was brought into Harold's presence, "but I was caught."

"Were you indeed?" Harold's voice was taut. "But you got away?"

"I was sent away, sir. With a personal message for you."

"Well, tell me, then."

"I asked a question or two too many, in a hostelry," said the monk, "and then someone overheard me talking English to my horse. The next I knew, I'd been arrested and taken to a camp, like this one, and there was the duke himself, and I stood there and listened to him being told how I'd asked about the number of ships—

all this happened at Dives, sir—and how many men they'd carry and so on. I was accused of spying. The duke was sitting in a great chair with knights all round him and a sword across his knees. I was too afraid to speak. I thought in five minutes I should be dead. And then the duke laughed, sir. He laughed and told them to bring me something to eat and drink, and he said I was to bring you a message and that he would see I got a safe passage home. I must have looked a fool," said the monk wryly, "with my eyes popping out of my head. He said to me: 'I cannot understand why King Harold'—except that he didn't say 'king,' sir—'spends his money on sending spies to Normandy. He'll know everything he needs to know very soon, when I come in person to tell him.' " The monk swallowed. "Then he went on: 'Go home and tell him that he'll have nothing to fear, and can live unmolested all his life, if before the year is out he hasn't seen me in his chief citadel.' "

"I shan't see him in my chief citadel under any circumstances," said Harold. He went to the tent flap and held it back, looking at the blue and empty sea. "Before he enters London, either I shall be dead or he will. In your opinion, when will that fleet be ready to sail? Did you gather that much?"

"I'd estimate next month, sir."

"August," said Harold thoughtfully.

But August came and brought no William. Instead, the weather changed and rain and gales swept from the north and west. With the wild weather, a restlessness began to grow in the fyrd. William couldn't sail in this, said camp gossip, and if the spies' reports were right, he would depend on sail. His ships would be heavy-laden with men and arms and horses, with no room for rowing gear. The corn was ripening at home; must it be left for the women and the young ones to scythe as best they could between the downpours? Half of it would rot standing, if so. William's men would be fretting after their own harvests, too. The word sped through the fyrd, wishful thinking expressed as rumour and then as fact. "William won't come this year."

In September, Harold returned to London and called a number of his southern thanes to him. "I'm disbanding the fyrd," he said.

They were in the small council chamber which had once housed a passionate argument on the pros and cons of mounted warfare. Harold scanned his fifteen selected men. "I shall keep a professional core with me," he said, "and the cavalry, under Hakon Sweynson. My thanks to you for your work on them, Thane Brand. But I have other work for you now. I want all of you to go back to your homes in Kent and Sussex and Hampshire." He embraced them all with his voice. "You are to be my watchdogs. Every one of you has coastal lands . . . I picked you out for that. I want a day and night watch kept from beach and cliff for enemy shipping. I also order a chain of beacons to be built, to carry the warning from the coast to London when and if the time comes. If I have to leave London, a beacon chain will be set up behind me. You all understand? You are going home, but not off duty . . ."

Before he left London, Brand visited the new West Minster and lit a candle on the altar. It was a private prayer that William might come soon, and the war be quickly over, and that he, Brand, might then go home to Fallowdene and till the soil in peace.

5 ✲ *Shooting Star*

Countess Gytha was a pious woman. Had anyone told her as she sat at her spinning wheel, with her long white hair in hanging braids and her thin fingers plying the thread, and her eyes still so bright in her old, strong face, that she resembled a wyrd-wife spinning the lives of men, she would have been annoyed. But it was true and the sybil look was the plainer by contrast with Agatha. Edward Atheling's widow sat with her own spinning on the other side of the fire that they badly needed in this cold September. Agatha was pious too, but her piety was to pattern: high calm brow, light calm eyes, and an immobility strengthened by the Magyar bone structure. The overall effect was nunlike. She and Gytha were too different to be close friends, but when the king and his family were in London, Agatha joined them out of courtesy.

Harold, glancing to where Aldith sat idly regarding the river outside, was grateful for Agatha's presence. It diluted an uneasy atmosphere.

It was expected, by that bodiless but potent entity called public opinion, which considered that it owned the king and could dictate his behaviour, that if he fell ill, his wife should care for him. It also expected that if his mother were in the same palace, she should join them. What the conventions failed to specify was what the three of them were to talk about: when Harold wished for someone else's ministrations, when Aldith was six months pregnant with a child she didn't want, and when Gytha was sorry for them both and sorrier still for Eadgyth, domiciled only three miles off but unable to come to Harold. Agatha's small talk of her children, and of church affairs and bower gossip, at least kept conversation going. Edith, the late king's widow, might have helped had she been there, but Edith had retired to Winchester since her widowhood. They needed Agatha, he thought.

He fidgeted, even so. Gytha spun with vigour and said: "If you don't keep that foot up, Harold, your gout will never mend."

"If William or Tostig comes tomorrow I'll have to fight, gout or no gout," he said. "Gyrth and Leofwin are doing my work for me now, and it's wrong. Gyrth is downriver inspecting refits and Leofwin is in the city dealing with complaints about bad provisions. I ought to be there."

"Aldith," said Gytha, "put another cushion under his foot."

Aldith had been watching swans on the river, as if these were of the most absorbing importance. She brought the cushion, her hands kind and impersonal. He thanked her. Since her pregnancy became definite, they hadn't had to share a bedchamber; the physician gave it out that this was for the queen's health. Harold, in any case, had been much away. Their relationship, mercifully not strained by too much proximity, had settled on to foundations of ordinary good manners. It worked, almost too well. As the child grew within her, Aldith had ripened to match the harvest season of glossy, rounded fruits. It was a shocking trick on the part of Fate that her beauty was now of an order to stop his breath, had not Eadgyth and Gruffyd stood between. She disturbed him and he wished her away. "I think," he said, hoping that she did not know he had recommended London to Eadgyth on grounds of safety, "that London may not be the best place for you, Aldith. It'll be a first objective with William. Could you stand a slow journey north to Chester?"

"If you wish," said Aldith. "I'm perfectly well."

Gytha pursed her lips. "By litter only and well wrapped up, Harold. She's carrying the heir, we hope. And she's very big already. Travelling won't be comfortable."

"Mother," said Harold, shaking his head at her, "*I'll* decide. I'm the child's father and Aldith's husband. And it's no good twirling that spinning wheel *at* me like that. I can remember you pummelling dough and needling embroidery at my father in just the same way, but . . ."

"Your mother's advice should be valuable," said Agatha mildly. "Countess Gytha has had a large family, my lord."

"I do know something about having children!" said Harold irritably. His foot throbbed. "I . . . ." Gytha's gaze became fixed and Aldith turned back to contemplation of the swans. "I had seven younger brothers and sisters," he finished.

"And five children of your own," Aldith said with her back to him. "As a child myself, I played with them. Please don't pretend. There's no need." She turned round at last. "If I weren't here, you could see Eadgyth. Yes, I shall go to Chester." She thought but did not add: And in that way I may escape the inexorable process of Gruffyd's image being overlaid by yours. Aloud, she said: "Something's happening. A boat has drawn up, and men are springing out of it."

A horn sounded somewhere and a gate slammed. Harold sat up at the sound of feet running and distant shouts, and brought his gouty foot warily to the floor. The door was unceremoniously flung back and Edgar Edwardson stood on the threshhold, pale and out of breath and full of momentous news. "My lord!"

Harold was up, leaning on his stick. "What is it?" It was lucky that the boy bore him no malice for taking the crown. If anything, Edgar seemed thankful to be rid of it, and he made himself helpful when he could.

"It's a courier from the north, from Earl Morcar! Tostig has landed."

"Tostig!"

"He's got that Norwegian, Harald Hardraada, with him! They've taken Scarborough and they're marching on York!"

They were all on their feet. "Have you sent for my brothers?" Harold demanded. Edgar nodded. "Good. Thank you. With my other brother," said Harold with venom, "we shall deal, and quicker than he expects. I take it that Morcar and Edwin need support? They shall have it. I shall call out the fyrd again. To bring Hardraada down on us *now* . . . I'll dig their bodies into the fields they come to ravage, by the Wild Hunt and One-Eyed Woden, I will. Don't worry about my gout, Mother. Rage may be a better cure than all the sawbones' potions!"

"Harold!" said Gytha. He paused. "Yes?"

"If there is any chance to make peace with Tostig . . . I've always thought, when Cain killed Abel, that Eve must have suffered most. You are both my sons."

"I have not forgotten," said Harold harshly.

The north wind had dropped. In St. Valéry on the estuary of the River Somme, the Norman fleet lay resting after a desperate, storm-racked attempt to sail. William, who had prayed in the abbey of St. Valéry and overwhelmed the abbey itself with gifts, in vain, stood on a low cliff and with a wetted finger tested the direction of the wind, and wondered if this new calm did indeed herald a change. His head hammered with the force of the frustrated yearning inside him. His fleet was ready. His supplies were piled, his men trained. The Pope was his sponsor. Yet for nearly two weeks the wind had blown against him, and before that men had drowned in the storm when they sailed out of Dives; he had had the bodies buried after dark, when they were washed ashore. He had even had the whole army kneeling before the coffin of St. Waléric, the abbey's canonised founder. When he woke the morning after that and found the north wind still blowing, he had wept, the first tears he had shed since boyhood. But now the air was quiet and it was warm. Was God turning His face to His servant at last? The Duke of Normandy knelt on the rough grass of the cliff top and shut his eyes in silent, passionate petition, for once at the mercy of a power greater than his own.

"O God," he said within himself, "why did You give me the brain and the soul of a king if I am not to have a kingdom? O God, let me have the England I was promised!"

In the north of that same England, about eight miles from the satisfactorily captured city of York, Harald Hardraada, despite the objections of the more cautious Tostig Godwinson, stretched out his big-boned, powerful frame on the turf of a hillside under a blessedly warm sun, pillowed his head on his stripped-off mail-coat, and waved an amiable arm at those of the men who were doing likewise. It was already the twenty-fifth of September, and such weather was welcome. It would be churlish not to enjoy it and foolish to be dissuaded by a few men who had had bad dreams on the voyage from the north. Omens were for women and priests. He was a warrior.

Part of the time, anyway. He was not at war today. "This is business," he said in his deep voice to the disapproving Tostig. "It isn't war or I should have brought the full force with me, not left a third behind. We come to receive hostages from the thanes, as you call them, not to fight anyone. We showed them who the master was, in York. They won't challenge us after that."

"We ought to have looted York as we did Scarborough," said Tostig restively. "That would have convinced them even more thoroughly."

"You might prefer it not looted, if we become kings there. It will be our capital. No, my bloodthirsty friend," said Hardraada, whose own name meant "ruthless" in his own tongue and whose bloodthirstiness was a byword from the Mediterranean to Russia, "York was best left alone. The thanes will be the more willing to trust their sons to us." He linked large, hilt-calloused hands behind the mane of hair where the grey now jostled the flaxen. He laughed. "That was a good fight, Tostig, outside York, when we filled the ditch with the dead and walked across and never wet our feet . . . And I thought my fighting days were done till you came to my hall at home. You've made an old hound into a young dog again, Tostig Godwinson."

"There's plenty of fighting to come," Tostig said ominously. "Sooner or later we have to confront my brothers and show them how to treat their kinsmen. They'll shed tears of repentance for their usage of me, before I kill them."

"And then we conquer the Norman, eh?" said Hardraada. "We'll be the heroes of sagas to last a thousand years, you and I."

They fell silent, Hardraada still extended at ease, while Tostig sat up and scanned the countryside for the first signs of the local dignitaries and the hostages who were to meet them here. He could see nothing of them yet, though he glanced from one to another of the five tracks that met at this ancient crossroads of Stamford.

The track immediately in front went down to Derwent river and crossed it on a stout wooden bridge. In the valley the Derwent flowed slow and wide between green meadows and some of Hardraada's men, attracted to it in the warmth, had shed their boots in order to paddle. Others had wandered over the bridge and were idly exploring, or amusing themselves with mock combats. Still others, instead of going down to the river, had remounted their ponies and were rounding up cattle from a nearby pasture, by way of commandeering some useful provisions. Lowing and whooping and yodelling drifted from their direction.

Harald yawned and Tostig felt his own jaws ache sympathetically. "It's warm," he remarked. "Look at that heat haze over the hill crest beyond the river. There are stones up there, glittering in the sun, too. You don't often see that effect in England at this season."

Hardraada shaded his eyes, stiffened, and came to his feet in one smooth movement. "And you're not seeing it now!" he snapped. "Glittering stones? Are you blind, Tostig Godwinson? Those are the points of spears and what you call haze is dust. Over the crest of that hill, there is an army!"

Tostig sprang to his feet beside the Norwegian. They both glanced swiftly round, at the unprepared men and the grazing ponies, at the cheerful, unsuspecting cattle herders, and the arms and mail left piled on the grass. And on the far side of the valley, a line of horsemen now topped the rise and two great banners were blowing in a gusty breeze. It grew stronger and the banners rode out on it. One was Harold's insignia of the Fighting Man. The other was the Golden Dragon of Wessex. Days before anyone had dreamed it possible, the southern fyrd had come to Stamford Bridge.

There was nowhere to retreat. Horns sounded and men dashed for their discarded weapons. Tostig ordered three of the cattle herders, who galloped up on their ponies, to ride to base for reinforcements. The English, still mounted, were racing down to the river's west bank, cutting down the men they met on the way, making for the bridge. Most of the other cattle herders, however, had seen the danger and spurred for the bridge as well, springing from their saddles as they reached it to fight on foot as they were used to doing. Hardraada, with one eye on the bridge and appeals for supernatural support rumbling out through his beard, addressed to Thor and Odin without a trace of Christian pretence, was on his own black horse and marshalling the shield-wall that was hastily forming up on the slope. It was a great circle, with goods and horses inside and an inner ring of bowmen behind the shield-bearers. As it took shape, Tostig mounted also and sat on his horse in front of it, staring at the river. "The bridge is holding," he said. "It's narrow . . . Oh, sweet Christ!"

Beside him, Hardraada swore. A savage charge from the English, wielding spears from the saddle, had almost broken the resistance at the bridge. Only one man remained on it, a tall and lonely figure who was taking oncomers one at a time. His sword rose and fell almost with rhythm, and black objects, men and horses, tumbled into the water to drift away downstream. But he was only one and the English now filled the opposite bank. Tostig opened his mouth to order a squad to his support.

But Hardraada, fatalistically, had seen that it was too late. "There's a boat slipping downstream," he said, and Tostig saw that the boat, carrying an English soldier judging by his helmet, was gliding into the shadow of the bridge. The occupant shipped his oar and drew his sword. The blade darted upwards. The lone defender, stricken from below, sank from sight among the blades and helms of his adversaries.

"So. The battle will be fought up here," said Hardraada.

"They're sending an embassy," said Tostig.

A knot of riders had detached itself from the English, who were now pouring over the bridge. The riders were cantering up the slope, obviously not with warlike intent. They slowed to a trot. Tostig looked at the man who led them and then kicked a bow out of the hands of a Norseman next to him. "They want a parley! What the hell do you mean by trying to shoot? Their swords are sheathed!"

The riders halted within hail and the foremost put his hands round his mouth to make a trumpet. "Is Earl Tostig among you?"

"He wants you?" said Hardraada, who could not follow southern English speech well but had heard Tostig's name. Tostig nodded. "Well, go on then. They're your people. You talk to them."

"Do you trust me? My brother commands that army."

"We're brothers in arms. That's a closer kinship. Go forward."

Tostig pushed his horse slowly out of the Norse ranks. He halted a yard or two short of the other leader. Across the quirking ears and blowing manes of their two gently champing mounts, Tostig and Harold Godwinson considered each other.

It was a silent meeting at first, for both were simultaneously assailed by the same sense of seeing double. There is my brother . . . We shared a bed as children, played and studied together, told lies for each other against the adult world, sparred and feasted and hawked together as men. *There is your enemy, who betrayed you.*

But Harold had moved first to call the parley and it was for him to open it. He saw tiredness and defiance in his younger brother's face and something else, a ravaged look, as if Tostig were sick. Edith had been saying, with emphasis, that he was sick when he left England. Perhaps he was. Perhaps sorrow and failure had mated in him to breed maggotty imaginings that all men were his foes. If he, Harold, did not give Tostig one last chance, their mother would not forgive him, and that sick look moved him. "We took some prisoners over the river," he said. "I heard from them that Hardraada has had bad omens. They think his luck's running out. Tostig, I want to offer peace."

"Our strength impresses you?" Tostig asked. "We routed the fyrd of Mercia and Northumbria together at York. Edwin and Morcar ran away. Are you afraid we shall make you do the same?"

"No," said Harold, holding himself in. "You're outnumbered and unready. I saw men scrambling into their armour just now. But we are brothers."

"What difference does that make, Oath-Breaker? Can I trust your word after the oath you took in Normandy—my God, what an oath!—and then retracted?" There was in Tostig's voice no hint of any response to the conciliation in Harold's. "Can I trust you," asked Tostig, "after you brought home that other oath-breaker, Brand Woodcutter, and made him a thane, to insult all honest men?"

"I may be an oath-breaker," Harold retorted, "but I never sent a pack of Welsh barbarians to slaughter unarmed men and salt their flesh like pork!"

"Nor did I "

"No? Oh, perhaps not." Harold too was weary. His gout had eased a great deal, pushed aside apparently by his sheer need for health. But it was not quite gone and now his left foot pulsed with pain against the pressure of his stirrup. He must make one more attempt, for Gytha's sake, he thought. "I can believe that Caradoc betrayed you. Such things can be. King Harefoot betrayed my father . . . our father . . . at Gildenford, when he killed men we thought would be ransomed. Tostig, I took that oath in Normandy only because I was forced, and it was void from the beginning because of my duty to King Edward. Brand was forced to break his word too . . . if Brand has anything to do with this and I don't see that he has. You're inventing grievances."

"I was thrown out of Northumbria and you did nothing to prevent it. Did I invent that?"

"I'm prepared," said Harold steadily, "to offer you your earldom back and to make you joint ruler with me over one third of the realm. If, that is, you will leave your foreign allies and resume your proper loyalty to England and its king. What more can I offer? Do you think I want to fight you, Tostig?"

He knew as he spoke that his words were empty. The Northumbrians would never take Tostig back, not if fifty kings commanded it. Nor could he cast his brother-in-law Morcar out. He knew he would not have made the offer had there been the slightest chance of it becoming reality; and despite the hunger in Tostig's eyes, Tostig knew that too. And besides . . .

"What do you offer my friend and ally Harald Hardraada?" Tostig enquired. "I brought him here. I can hardly desert him now."

"Hardraada is a stranger here. He has no business in England. Moreover, he came with an army and slaughtered fyrd-men on their own land. I came to make peace but not to surrender England. If he insists on staying, he may have six feet of England for his own, to be buried in. Or perhaps," said Harold, since it was clear now that no peace would be made and offending Tostig no longer mattered much, "I might make it seven. He looks tall."

They exchanged another long, silent stare. "You've a low opinion of me," said Tostig. His snub-nosed face was sullen. "But I don't betray my friends, and lately Hardraada's been the only friend I have. We'll meet in the battle, Harold." He backed his horse, turned it, and rode away. Harold wheeled, and cantered back to the river.

His brother Gyrth was waiting, his face strained with hope. "Well?"

"It isn't well. We fight. Tostig won't desert his allies."

"Do we use the cavalry or hold them back for William?"

Harold leant on his pommel, to take the weight off his stirrups. "I was trying to decide that, all the way up England. We covered forty miles yesterday and all the men are tired, and so are the horses. But that only means we must strike hard from the start to shorten the engagement. Or we'll lose, even now. They've sent for more men, I think. I saw riders going off. We use the cavalry, Gyrth. With javelins, from a distance. We must break that shield wall."

On top of the rise Hardraada asked Tostig: "Who was their spokesman?"

"My brother Harold. He came in person."

"Ah. I wondered. You should have told me," said Hardraada.

"In spite of your finger-wagging at my bowman, we might have won the battle with a well-aimed spear, and maybe we'd have been wise. Still . . . he is your brother, as you said. He's not a big man," said the Norwegian, from the majesty of six feet eight inches, "but he sits his horse like a commander."

"He is," Tostig said.

In the evening, Harold went to his pallet and lay on his back and no one disturbed him, for his face rejected comfort.

He had won. He had flung his horsemen against the wall of shields and broken it. The infuriated Norsemen had rushed out, yelling war cries, Hardraada leading them, two-handed sword raised above his helmet. He had run straight into a whistling shaft. A Norseman they seized some time later said that, as he died, Hardraada had shouted to Tostig to make peace with his brother. But if that were true, Tostig had preferred to answer his dead comrade's good faith with good faith of his own. Tostig the Upright, honest after his own twisted fashion, had made peace with no one. He fought on and the Norsemen fought on with him. Ten minutes later Tostig too was dead and the reinforcements from York, arriving shortly after, rode weary and sweating on to a leaderless battlefield where the existing forces were already demoralised. Before long, what remained of Hardraada's and Tostig's army was driven back and the last remnants fled for their lives.

"Yes," said Harold to a spluttering oil lamp. "The Battle of Stamford Bridge is mine. I purchased it. I hope it's worth the price."

For he had spent almost all he had on it. The fyrds of the northern earldoms no longer existed; Hardraada had seen to that at Scarborough and York. Half the forces he had brought with him from Mid-Anglia and the northern home counties had been wiped out today. And he had lost his precious, tiny cavalry. He had led them against the shield wall and they had broken it, yes. But they had been destroyed themselves, in the storm of arrows shot from behind the shields. His own horse had fallen under him. Nearly all the fine big horses were dead and could not be replaced this year or next year or even the year after.

Worst of all, he must go home and tell his mother, Gytha, that he had killed Tostig. God alone knew what would have happened if Tostig had tried to accept his terms. He couldn't give Northumbria away to anyone, and he and Tostig would have quarrelled again. Perhaps he would have had to kill his brother in the end, even so. But Gytha might find it hard to see that.

He was a victorious commander. He should be out there with Gyrth and Waltheof, Earl of Mid-Anglia, and their thanes and housecarles, feasting, but he could not bring himself to go to them.

He wished that he were dead.

6 ❊ Storm Gathering

Wulfhild was actually beside the beacon when the moment came to fire it.

She had climbed the down between Fallowdene and Little Dene, in order to sit on the grass of the hill crest and savour the quiet. The waiting woodpile, placed conveniently near the path, was only a yard or two away. She turned her back on it at first. It was an emblem of a responsibility that might soon fall heavily upon her, and it was from responsibility, for an hour, that she wished to rest.

The men had come back from the fyrd to cut the corn, but with a late start and bad weather that constantly interrupted the work, every hand that could hold a scythe had been needed if the task were to be done before the weather broke altogether. Wulfhild had taken her turn. She had also fed the harvesters every day and organised the great thanksgiving feast when it was all over and everyone who had worked in the fields came to the hall to eat and drink and rejoice. She had slept only five hours a night, if that, for two weeks. The burden of seeing that the work was completed had been hers. Her father could not be there.

He had come back with the fyrdmen, but after giving orders for the beacon to be built, he rode straight on to Heathwood. Heathwood was a coastal manor and a watch had to be set up there to look out for William. It must be Brand's base until summer ended. He had reappeared for the harvest thanksgiving, but once more it was a very brief visit. And, departing, he had given her his instructions for the care of Fallowdene if the Normans landed.

"You are safer here than at Heathwood," he said, standing at his pony's shoulder in the grey morning. "You'll see the beacons long before the Normans can reach Fallowdene . . . Wulfhild, I have been thinking. If it happens, I may have little chance to send you advice, even—let alone come myself. Do you know what to do?"

"The able-bodied men must go to the muster in London."

"Yes. All of them, this time. Some stayed behind when we were called out to fight Tostig. Odi will see to that. I'm leaving him here. For the rest of you, if the Normans come this way, drive what stock you can and take what goods you can into Andred. You've made sensible preparations. Use them. But remember that the forest is no place to be in winter, so don't go till you must. Don't go the minute you see the beacons kindle. Post watchers to warn you of an enemy approach. There's a chance that they won't come this way. Be wary, but don't panic."

He had paused, unhappily. He adjusted a stirrup leather and stroked the pony's mane. "Wulfhild, listen carefully. This is important. We shall give battle, somehow, somewhere, if William comes. You'll hear the outcome fast enough. That sort of news travels quickly. If the king wins, all is well. If you're in hiding, come out and come home. If I live, I shall soon join you. If not, Fallowdene is yours. King Harold has made me an owner now, not just a tenant, and I have willed it to you. The will is with your sister Edgiva in Withysham Abbey. Edgiva and Elfhild have had their portions and Heathwood goes back to its abbey, but you are to have Fallowdene. You'll need to marry, but the king or Countess Gytha will help you there. You can't look after a manor alone . . ."

"And if William wins?"

He wanted to say that that was unthinkable, but it had to be thought about. "Then I am afraid . . . we shall lose Fallowdene. The duke told Harold once that he would confiscate the lands of Englishmen who defied him. Go to your sister's abbey for shelter. You need not take any vows. Again, if I live, I'll come for you. If not— and if we are defeated I probably won't survive, nor do I want to— then God keep you. You'll be safe in the abbey until the country settles, and then the future is with God. What else is there to say?"

"Only, God keep you, too, since you are going to war," said Wulfhild, and with the formality which in both of them was instinctive in times of crisis, she had buckled on his sword.

But William might not come this year, she now thought hopefully, sitting with hands clasped round her knees, looking affectionately out over the woods and the shaggy-roofed hall and the shining curve of river. Soon the autumn gales would harass the channel and frighten shipping off. They'd have a season's grace and perhaps by next year Norman passions would have cooled. Could William keep an edge on his army so long? She hoped not. She did not like to think of Norman feet trampling here, of Norman bridles jingling through the quiet woods of her home, where the first of the acorns and the sweet beech mast had begun to drop and Higg Swineherd was already foraging with his pigs. What business had the Normans here?

Her father was right about marriage, she supposed, whatever the result of the war. She herself was beginning to feel the need of it. But she wanted to stay at Fallowdene. She would like to have her children here. She pictured herself teaching them the daily tasks of hall and farm, showing them the paths, telling them the words for sheep and pig and acorn and wheat. Fallowdene must not be lost, she thought, and felt panic leap in her. It *must not*. King Harold, it was said, had gone north to drive off Tostig. He must succeed. And then he must drive off William too. But he would, of course. He was . . . Harold.

She shifted her position on the hard ground to look the other way, over Little Dene and southwards.

Southeast of her, on a distant line of hills, standing into the sky and breaking away at the top to stream out on a southeast wind, was a thread of smoke.

"No," said Wulfhild aloud. "No, *please!*"

But the thread was thickening, becoming a column. She knew it was a beacon; Brand had shown her exactly where it was. And down in Little Dene, they had seen it. Tiny figures were running from field and byre, and some purposeful ones were striding towards the down. She would save them a climb. With hands that she steadied by an act of will, she found the flat, marked stone under which kindling materials were hidden in a hole, drew out tallow and torch, steel and flints, and struck the flints. It took three tries to get a spark that would catch the tallow; starting a fire from nothing was always a nuisance. But she got the torch to light and coaxed the flame from uncertainty to vigour, holding it downwards and guarding it from the wind. She lit the beacon in seven places and threw the torch on to the pile as well, and then sped downhill into Fallowdene.

The villagers were congregating outside the hall. The steward was telling them to stay calm, in a voice that shook with fright. The miller had snatched up a scythe and was holding it as if he expected the Normans to ride over the hill at any moment. His daughter Gerda stood beside him with her child on her arm and her spare hand grasping a kitchen knife. The handful of housecarles that Brand had left in Odi's charge had been out foraging. They appeared just as Wulfhild came up. One carried a sack through which spines jutted. Hedgepigs for dinner, Wulfhild thought distractedly. That would have been tasty, with beans and cabbage. Now what sort of dinner shall we get? She stopped in front of the crowd. "Is everyone here?"

She repeated, concisely, her father's orders. The able-bodied men to London, with Odi. The rest to make ready to flee to the forest if the Normans were reported to be approaching. Herself to see them to safety there. "Goods to be packed and shelters to be got ready in the forest," she said. "No stock left in outlying pastures. I myself will . . ."

The priest, arriving belatedly from the chapel, where he had been offering a hurried paternoster for King Harold, demurred. "My lady, I think you should go immediately to Withysham Abbey."

"If the Normans win the battle," said Wulfhild, ignoring horrified gasps at the suggestion, "I may have to. But not before."

"Have you ever seen a ravaging army?" persisted the priest.

"I've been captured by one," said Wulfhild shortly. Half her mind was elsewhere. "Odi, the men of Little Dene and Westwater understand they are to gather here?"

"Yes, ma'am. They'll be here before dusk. If they aren't, we'll fetch them," Odi said, and behind him Osric nodded.

"Good." She ran her eye over the assembly. "Alric Steward had best stay here, and Esgar Oxherd and Ulf Potter. They're none of them young enough for battle. Ufi Lame-leg can't go either, with his pegfoot." She raised her hand at protests from the steward and the oxherd. "Alric, I shall need your years of experience to help me. The other three must act as lookouts, in turn, on the north edge of the down. The Normans will come that way if they come at all. I hear the track out of Little Dene, leading south, has been waterlogged since we had all that rain. Ham Hayward can stay here too and help keep the firewood stacked." She smiled encouragingly at Ham, who was simple. The priest opened his mouth again and she rounded on him.

"We'll talk of the abbey later! The enemy isn't even in sight yet. I advise you to pack the church treasures ready for the evacuation, if we have to make it. That altar cloth in there is worth something and so is the silver chalice." Through the open door of the hall, she glimpsed part of its interior, and other things that were also worth something, though in a different way . . . the hangings they had bought at reduced prices from Rolf Ericson, others that she had embroidered herself with large-stitch designs in coloured wools, a stool her father had made, the hearth basket she filled each day with sticks from the woods. A fierce and trembling desire took hold of her, to keep Fallowdene and to protect its folk, who were part of it, to abandon neither place nor people, whatever happened on the battlefield. "If necessary," she said, "even if the Normans do come, we might treat with them."

Odi's mouth dropped open. *"Treat* with them? With *them?"*

"Lacking swords as arguments, we may need to, to survive," Wulfhild said briskly. "We can't spend all winter in the forest. It will be up to you warriors, Odi, to chase them off quickly, won't it?"

They had made remarkable speed on the first three days of their journey south from York, but it had cost them something.

Too much, maybe. Harold, his own face seamed with the dirt of hard travelling, looked back at the trailing line of men, some afoot and some mounted but all desperately weary and many of them walking wounded. He had lost some who had set out from York with him. Already exhausted, already injured, they had simply dropped out of the line. Every time a halt was called, a few were missing from the roll and rarely was desertion a likely cause. Those who had fallen away near habitations might find someone to care for them; others had certainly been rewarded by death at the wayside for their gallant support of him, riding north and in the battle of Stamford Bridge. He faced forward again and said to the haggard-faced horseman with the lathered mount: "William has landed?" It was a question, but only just. The news was in Brand Woodcutter's face, and a burned-out beacon on a hill to the east was a message which had preceded him.

Gyrth Godwinson and Waltheof of Mid-Anglia came cantering down the line to join them. Brand waited until they were at Harold's side before he spoke. Then he said: "You saw the beacons?"

"I did. I set out instantly. But I hoped . . . it was a false alarm. When and where?"

"Pevensey, four days ago. They've dug themselves in there and they're ravaging the area. There isn't a homestead standing from Brede River to Pevensey Bay. I saw them land. I was on watch near the shore, near Hastings village."

"How many men?" Gyrth asked.

"Impossible to say. But a powerful army. The fleet came in to the west of me and I tried to get along the coast further and count. But there were hundreds of ships, all sizes. All overloaded by the look of them and carrying horses and wooden fort sections as well as men. I sent word off to warn local folk and get the beacons lit. Some of the folk left their homes in time to save the things they could take with them, but their houses are burned. Those who didn't flee in time were killed if they resisted. Otherwise they were let go, empty-handed. They kept their lives, but nothing else." Brand was carefully keeping all emotion out of his voice, but his eyes were hot and angry. "The Normans are well defended," he said grimly. "It's a good defensive position they've taken, water inlets all round it. I waited a day to see what they'd do. Then I left men on watch on the other side of Brede River to send word if they started to move again, and rode to meet you myself. My lord . . . what happened in the north?"

"Hardraada is dead," said Waltheof.

"And so is our brother Tostig," Gyrth said, sombrely. "And hardly anything is left of the fyrds of Mercia and Northumbria, beyond the younger sons and older men who were left behind this time to care for the farms." Like Harold, he glanced over his shoulder, at the stoically waiting forces at his back. Some had sat down at the roadside; a few of the riders had slipped from their saddles to rest the ponies, and the ponies' heads drooped thankfully. "The forces we have," said Gyrth expressionlessly, "are what you see."

"My brother may have been with the Mercian fyrd," Brand said.

"We share a similar grief, then," Harold commented. He was silent a moment. Then he asked: "Has my brother Leofwin sent for the rest of the southern fyrd? I left some areas not called on when I went north."

"Yes. I found that out on the way," Brand said. "And men are coming in of their own accord since the beacons went up."

"I'll have an army of some sort, then. What I have here is only half of the force that went north with me. If it hadn't been for Tostig, I'd be at William's throat *now*. With men enough to overwhelm him. Oh, God!" Harold's gauntleted fist thudded on his pommel. "Tostig! I've wept for him and cursed him."

"Cursed him, mainly," observed Gyrth.

"Not quite, Gyrth." Harold shook his head. "I'm sorry for him in a way, the valiant fool that he was. I think he hardly knew what he was doing at the end. He clung to whatever he had left, I think: his dreams of Northumbria, and the friendship of Hardraada, whom he'd brought here and couldn't desert. I respected that . . ."

"Personally, I could have wrung his daft neck for it," interrupted Gyrth. "Harold, we're wasting time. We need to . . ."

"It's my mother I'm sorriest for," Harold said to Brand, and then shrugged. "Why do I so often bare my soul to you, Brand? I'd hardly say as much to my confessor as I sometimes say to you, and I've ridden miles out of my way to talk to him, at times. Gyrth is right. We must push forward. Can your horse manage a few more miles today? He looks shaky."

"He can manage." Brand tried to say something encouraging. "At least we only have one foe to fight now."

"Yes, but what with?" Brand had never heard open despair in Harold's voice before, and stared at him, shocked. "My cavalry's gone, did you know that?" said the king. "Your cavalry and Hakon's. I led them to conquest and disaster at the same time. It would have broken your heart to see it. I can only meet William with a shield-wall now, as Hardraada met me."

"A shield-wall," said Waltheof, "is a strong formation."

"Hardraada lost," retorted King Harold.

7 ✖ Tempest

It was the longest night of his life. He cursed his sleeplessness, knowing the toll it would take next day. But oblivion would not come. Gyrth and Leofwin snorted and grunted in slumber nearby and the housecarles who lay rolled in their rugs outside the tent muttered uneasily in their dreams. None slept soundly. But Harold was unable to sleep at all.

His senses were too sharp tonight. Distant sounds were as clear as if they were in the tent with him. A far-off challenge . . . a spy? a late arrival? A whinny from the pony lines, an owl, a fox. Now a cockerel. He propped himself on an elbow. Dawn must be near.

For the hundredth time his brain trudged the hot, cindery track it had worn for itself in the night. Had anything been forgotten? Left undone? Aldith was safe in Chester by now, he hoped. He had sent her off the moment he returned to London. She would do what she could to stir the remnants of the Mercians to follow him south. But he knew that the chance of either Edwin or Morcar arriving with even a few reinforcements was slim, and growing less by the hour. Well, they'd been loyal in the emergency in the north. Defeated but loyal. His marital sacrifice hadn't been wholly in vain. But probably they had no more to give.

His mother and Eadgyth were less well protected than Aldith, since they had insisted on coming to the coast with him. They were lodged now in a farm a mile behind his lines. He had allowed himself Eadgyth's company for one night on the road.

He must not think of her now. Dreams of home and domestic peace unmanned you. His young sons were with her, sulky but obedient; he had forbidden them to fight. If he were killed, the future might be vested in them. It was bad enough that Gyrth and Leofwin and Hakon were all here. Gyrth had even urged that he, Harold, should stay behind in London while his brothers led the army without him! A fine way for a king to behave. And when they came in sight of the occupied territory and saw the smoke of William's ravaging, like dust in the sky, he knew he had been right to refuse, and right to march to the battle. His duty waited here. He had rounded on Gyrth, he remembered, for that protective suggestion. Yet he honoured the loyalty behind it. After Tostig, he could be thankful for Gyrth.

It would be best not to think about Tostig now. Gytha had forgiven his death, for which Harold was grateful. "What will be, will be," she said resignedly. She added: "He was so like Sweyn. His own most savage enemy."

The army, think about the army. He had nearly eight thousand men now. He had left London with only four thousand but others had come in on the way, from all over the south, and they, blessedly, were uninjured and fresh. If only he had the northern fyrds. If only he had his cavalry. Then he could sweep the Normans into the sea as if he were brushing crumbs off a table. Had he enough to hold the ridge that was William's gateway to England? Eight thousand was better than he had hoped. Could he trap William in his neck of occupied land, with water on all sides but one, until the Norman gave up and sailed for home? If he could sail at all: the wind was lying south. If it held, William wouldn't be able to retreat even if he wanted to. He must surrender, or be massacred . . . or win.

It was getting light. He rose impatiently and went to the tent entrance, stirring up the sleeping housecarles with his foot as he passed. The air outside was cold and damp, smelling of mist. A hazy, waning moon hung low. The camp was moving sluggishly in the greyness. Crouched forms, half draped still in the rugs and cloaks that had kept off the dew all night, were coaxing embers back to flame, and someone was watering the horses. Somewhere close by, an irritable voice complained that its mead flask had been filched. "I need the warmth. God's Teeth, this cold ground's enough to give you the rheumatics for life!"

God send the poor devil wasn't sleeping in that same cold ground for ever, by this day's end.

A figure moving in the gloom turned into Brand Woodcutter and stopped at his side. "Brand? You're awake early."

"I didn't sleep much."

"Nor did I. I was mourning my northerners and my horsemen. Your horsemen, too."

"I know. So was I."

"Cavalry would be useful," said Harold angrily, "if nothing else, to chase the Normans with when they run away. A shield-wall can't do much chasing, that's its weakness. Even if it's a full shield-wall, with fit men, well rested. Oh God, should I have sat it out in London and waited for him, after all? Is that a horn you're carrying?"

"Yes."

"Then sound it and let's get this lot on their feet, or William may wake up first and join us for breakfast." The sun was coming up in earnest now and suddenly the enchantment of full dawn was on them: grass touched with frost began to sparkle, and colour, green and gold, was instantaneously painted on the gorse. Harold brightened. He clapped a hand on Brand's shoulder and laughed. "Cheer up, Brand. You look so worried. It's only another war!"

Standing outside his tent in the sunrise, freshly shriven and freshly shaved, William of Normandy said to his friend and namesake, William Malet: "The day has come. And Harold with it."

"From what the scouts tell us," Malet remarked, "he's picked a good place for his stand. I still wish we had pressed straight on to London."

"We might have found it hard to capture. His men could have recuperated behind its walls, waiting for us. No, it was best to tempt him down here, in a hurry, with his forces tired. The best defensive position on earth avails you nothing if you're too tired to fight."

"In his place," said Malet thoughtfully, "I think I should have withstood the temptation."

"So would I. But . . ." The duke turned his head slightly and, following his gaze, Malet saw in the distance the burned ruins of what had been a small farming hamlet; a faint ashen odour still drifted from it. ". . . Harold is the man who risked his life to rescue three total strangers from a quicksand. He came full-pelt from the north to protect his people here from my ravaging, Malet. I knew he would."

The wait, in formation, before the start of a battle, was the hardest part of all. Brand hated it. You had nothing to do and nothing to think about. You tested your blade and resettled your shield straps and made bad jokes with your neighbours and tried resolutely not to notice how green the grass was. It probably wouldn't stay green for long, anyway. It would be reddened and torn up before the day was old.

This part of a battle was also the tidiest. Harold's shield-wall on the crest of the long, broad slope was beautifully designed, a rampart made of men and armour, built (one hoped) to withstand the most murderous of onslaughts. The far-off line of the enemy at the hill's foot, between the rising ground and the pool that lay further back, was orderly too. Spearpoints glittered in a long, narrow crest like the edge of a breaker. Banners waved at equidistant intervals, marking the divisions under the various leaders. From his sojourn in Normandy, Brand could read the constituents of the line from the standards. The Bretons were on the west flank . . . a restless division, that one, with horses constantly tossing their heads and fidgeting. William's Norman leopards were in the middle and another banner was with them which must be the papal banner the spies said William had received from Rome. Silently and blasphemously, Brand cursed the Pope. William FitzOsbern, Bishop Odo, Eustace of Boulogne were all in William's central division. The French fleur-de-lys waved on the east flank: William had rounded up some French auxiliaries, evidently.

Brand wondered, with a sick feeling, if his old friend Peter Longshanks was there, or if Elfhild's young husband was. But he must forget about them now. This was England and he was with Harold, where he belonged. He would never change allegiances again. He withdrew his eyes from the enemy and glanced instead at his friends.

He stood, with his followers, among the thanes of Wessex, and the only place he would have preferred was higher up the hill, among the Royal Housecarles who surrounded King Harold, the gilding on their helms a golden patch in the midst of the formation.

Hakon was near Brand, among the Wessex men. To the left stood Leofwin with his followers; Gyrth stood to the right with his. Rolf Ericson was somewhere among Leofwin's men; Brand had seen him briefly the previous night. The wings were held by thanes from all over the land, including the remains of the Mid-Anglian forces, under Waltheof. The standard of weaponry was extremely uneven. The professional housecarles and some of the fyrdmen were well armed enough. After Stamford Bridge, someone had had the forethought to collect weapons from the field and send them south. But there hadn't been enough to go round. Beside their more fortunate companions, the have-nots in the peasant contingent presented a sorry and makeshift contrast. Harold had ordered them to be placed at the back of their respective leaders' divisions, for their own safety. He was trying hard to keep up morale, forcing good cheer and vigour into his voice and mien, but every now and then weariness and grief showed through. If you knew him, you could see it.

He had made a great effort to encourage the nervous peasant soldiers. "You're the last gate to England," he had told them, "the last defence. With luck he'll never reach you, and if he does he'll not have much left to attack you with. Face him boldly and stand fast. William's in a trap and while you stand he can't break out to terrorise the rest of the land. He's done more harm than I like to think of on this little bit of it, so in God's name don't let him get at any more. Be stout gateposts and don't fall!"

And the gateposts had grinned and shuffled their feet and taken a firmer grip of the clubs and pitchforks and bill-hooks and other agricultural and domestic ironmongery which represented their armaments, and tried to look equal to the occasion. And Brand had watched Harold turn away, quickly, before they could see the hopelessness in his face.

Was it as hopeless as that? And would nothing ever happen this morning; would they never get on with it? Yes, something was happening now. Men on foot had walked out from between the gaily coloured line of Norman horsemen with their painted shields and harness and their gaudy banners, and were advancing in a thin single line. Bowmen. Arranged neatly, with breaks in the line. And the horsemen were moving forward after them. The great size of the cavalry forces could now be clearly and unnervingly seen.

Behind Brand, one of the Fallowdene men spoke suddenly,

from the heart, and no one refuted him. "From the fury of the Normans," said Alfred Thatcher, grimly amending the prayer for protection against Duke William's Nordic ancestors, "may the Good Lord deliver us!"

Trumpets sounded at the foot of the hill. A few riders galloped up and down in front of the cavalry. One swung his horse to face up the slope. Another trumpet rang out with a fierce note that stiffened the muscles of the waiting shield-men. The lone Norman, a knight in full armour, spurred his horse through one of the breaks in the ranks of the archers, and up the long green hillside, straight towards the defenders at the top.

A herald? No, he bore no flag of truce. On the contrary, he was brandishing a sword, tossing it up and catching it by the blade, with a careless juggler's grace. Odi said enviously: "I wish I could do that." Brand said: "I know whose trick that is. That's Ivon Taillefer."

He watched, in sorrow and admiration. He would have been so glad, once, to call this man son-in-law, to know Wulfhild safe in the company of a man like Taillefer. Ivon was singing, they could hear him now, a song about a bygone hero. Brand had heard him perform it in Normandy. He sang as he rode alone against the whole English army.

He must have asked to strike the first blow. And he would strike well. Few had Taillefer's gift of controlling a horse with the knees alone, of casually tossing and catching that lethal blade. None had his strong mellow voice that still found breath for the Song of Roland even at full charge. As they watched, Taillefer, still melodiously praising Roland, sheathed the sword and took the reins and pulled a javelin from its holder. His horse was near enough now for them to see the white-ringed eyes and the foam flying from the bit. The drumming hooves could be felt in the ground. Taillefer reined the horse on to its hocks and hurled the javelin. It sailed over the shields and in the second rank, someone screamed.

As it always did, that first cry sent cold shock knifing into one's vitals. Later, the world would be filled with that sound. But as yet it was still able to horrify.

The javelin was answered. Osric of Hereford had a bow as well as his freeman's sword. The arrow missed Taillefer but furrowed his stallion's flank. The horse reared. Taillefer fought for control but his mount, shaking its head to be free of the rein, pawing and plunging, bucketed straight towards their line. The shield-wall parted obligingly to let it in and half a dozen swords struck. Horse and man went down and six red blades were raised amid triumphant war cries.

Someone shouted: " 'Ware arrows! "

And below, where the Norman archers stood, the first flight of shafts, like a flock of sharp-beaked birds, sprang into the air.

Shafts whistling. Feet pounding. Blades clashing. Whoops, screams, trumpet calls, oaths. Dry mouths, hot feet, short breath. An acrid smell of ordure and blood from a dead horse which kept getting in their way. The wide-nostrilled, monstrous heads of William's cavalry appearing dinosaurlike over the heads of the shield-men as the Norman knights took their turn, charging after the bowmen had shot and the foot soldiers had attacked to soften the line in readiness for them. William had held his cavalry back for some time, but he had sent them into the field now. The English line was shrinking. Men died inconsequently under the repeated rain of arrows, and their comrades drew together to close the gaps. It was in all their minds that there were not enough of them, and that many were worn or hurt already. Yet the shield-wall, if shorter, still stood, and the sun said it was past midday, and the numbers of the Norman dead were heartening to see. If they held fast long enough, Harold cried to them, then William would spend his strength and ebb like the tide. If they held fast.

A lull. It was deceptively like an interval during a tournament.

The whole battle so far had been comparatively orderly, like a large, tough, mêlée event. Curious that so much hung on its outcome. Better not brood on that, Brand thought. And when would the outcome be known? At this rate, they would still be standing fast when the sun went down, and what then?

"Now what's William hatching?" muttered Odi sourly.

William of Normandy, on a black horse, could be seen in the distance, haranguing the Bretons. "I hope it's addled, whatever it is," Brand growled.

Another charge. But this time the Breton division broke away from the rest and came in at a new angle, apparently trying to reach round the westward extremity of the shield-wall. Harold's trumpets spoke, the command to the west wing to prepare. Brand, at the westward end of the centre formation, saw them brace themselves, saw them draw bows and swing javelin arms back and freeze, poised, a heartbeat from loosing their weapons. Then the rapidly magnifying Breton leaders somersaulted, plumed tails vaulting over maned necks, men and horses crashing to the earth and apparently into it, out of sight. The horsemen in the ranks behind yelled and dragged at their reins. Horses reared and whinnied, plunged, bolted, fell, strewing knights on the field like seeds in sowing time. A whoop of joy went up from the English right wing.

"Who didn't do his homework then?" enquired a happy voice somewhere close to Brand. "Didn't know about that ditch there in the long grass, did he? Useful things, ditches. Drain a lot of useless muck off a hillside, they do."

From the gleeful right wing, a mass of men broke suddenly from behind the shields. It was against orders. Brand felt in himself the desire to give chase to the thrown knights, but he held himself back. The Norman and French divisions were still coming on, in any case. William—yes, that mace-bearing knight in the forefront was the duke himself—was leading. Brand snatched up a spent javelin and threw it. It took the duke's horse in the chest and the horse went down. An anguished outcry rose from the attacking forces.

Cheering, more men broke from the sheltering shield-wall. Brand saw Gyrth and Leofwin pelt after them, sounding their horns to bring their errant followers back, in vain. The axe-flourishing English darted among the confused Norman horse, striking for hamstrings and cleaving the skulls of thrown knights. Someone had raised a cry that the Norman duke was dead.

The urge to rush out and join the destruction was now almost past bearing. Brand risked a glance backwards. Harold was visible; he had climbed on someone's back the better to direct the battle. He too was sounding the recall, again and again, as if in desperation. But this was victory. Wasn't it? Renewed noise from the opposite direction made Brand's eyes turn swiftly to the front again. William was not dead. He had been unhorsed. He had got another horse, he was mounting it, he was riding among his men, helmet off to show his face, rounding his knights up. The English who had left their formation began to retreat towards safety.

Not soon enough. William had got his knights together, welded into a charge again, and he was flinging them forward.

"I wish I had cavalry to chase the Normans with," Harold had said. Because of Tostig, he had lost his cavalry. Instead, his men were the pursued and the weariness of the battle in the north and the long march down England was telling. The charge overtook them and, when it receded, their bodies lay like driftwood on a beach. Behind him, Brand heard a groaning murmur, the names of Gyrth and Leofwin. They were out there among the dead. Harold's brothers were gone.

Another lull. The sun had gone in, but a dull luminosity showed its westering position. One trusted, though more as an article of dogma than with real conviction, that eventually it would set. One's bodily processes had mostly ceased. No hunger, even after long hours without food. No weariness. No need to relieve oneself. Thirst was there, yes. During the pauses, waterskins were passed forward from non-combatants, the usual odd mixture of monks and camp followers behind the lines. The water was the only sustenance given or sought.

A fresh attack. A dangerous one this time. The shield-wall gave way in one place, fell back and broke, and a wedge of confusion speared into the ranks. Men fought to live, that and nothing else. Osric died in that attack, fighting three Normans at once, dying a free man at least, Brand thought. He had tried to come to Osric's aid but was himself too much beset. In the chaos he caught brief glimpses of others whom he knew, swirling out of their places, leaves in a whirl-pool. He saw Earl Waltheof Siwardson, who had some of his father's inches, springing at a Norman knight and hauling him out of the saddle. A moment later he glimpsed his own brother-in-law, Rolf, hand to hand in a struggle with a burly soldier who, while Brand struggled to reach his kinsman's side, succeeded in throwing Rolf to the ground. But Rolf, desperately thrusting with a dagger, found his mark somehow—very typical of Rolf, that; he always did manage somehow—and the big man doubled and clawed at his belly and went flaccid. Then a horn call summoned them to form a ring and stand, and they did it, and by some means, as much through the power of their wills as the strength of their arms, the shield-wall was mended and the defence stood solid again. For a time.

For a time. Again and again the knights thundered up the slope and again and again the shield-wall staggered under the shock. Yet the gate to England remained shut. Surely, surely, the chargers were tiring now, and they were fewer. Many knights had had to join the foot soldiers. Surely it must be over soon. One way or the other.

But here came the knights again; brace yourself for it. Harold's voice sounded, remote, hoarse, shouting orders. He must leave grieving for his brothers till tomorrow. Plant your feet firmly and press your shoulders hard against your neighbours'. The thunder of hoofbeats is growing. Be ready to stand fast once again . . .

No. Something untoward. A new note in the Norman trumpets. The charge slowing down, halting . . . retreating, by God and Old Grim, they were *retreating!* All round rose a screech of delighted war cries and though Harold's horn and Harold's voice forbade it, the shield-wall broke again. A few resisted the temptation, repressing their hunting instincts in obedience to the imperious restraint of the trumpet. But the majority, weary of their long stand in one place, tore after the vanishing foe. The housecarles went first and after them the peasantry, bawling, bellowing, waving their weapons. Brand elbowed Odi back as he was going with them, and yelled: "*Stand!*" over his shoulder at the rest of his men. Alfred Thatcher and Higg Swineherd got away, brushed past him and pounded off, roaring like madmen, down the hill. But the Norman trumpets cried again and the thing that Harold had feared, as Brand had guessed, was happening. The Normans wheeled. It was a ruse. They were charging. Not a chance for the men caught in the open, and this time it was half of Harold's force. They vanished, overwhelmed, and still the charge came on and there was no solid phalanx to meet it. The knights were through the breached shield-wall and the world dislimned into butcherly chaos: Normans and English, foot and horse, mixed up and struggling hand-to-hand.

"To me!" Brand cried to his remaining followers. "To me!"

His place in this collapsing universe was with Harold. He was part of the Royal Bodyguard in spirit, whatever his official status. The Fighting Man banner still waved up there among the gilded helms. If they could get there and help to make another, smaller shield-wall round that banner . . .

They fought as they went, guarding each other as best they could. A charge of three knights cut Brand and Odi off from the rest, but the two lived and struggled on together, Odi walking backwards, guarding their rear. Harold was still alive, just. Still on his feet amidst his tight-packed knot of Royal Housecarles. But his face was a glistening mass of scarlet, and one eye had been destroyed. A bunch of knights with Boulogne's insignia on their shields went past, ignoring the two isolated men, intent on the Fighting Man. They crashed into the Royal Housecarles. Limbs and heads flew like hail. A severed hand with a dagger still in it fell at Brand's feet. An unhorsed Norman appeared in front of him and they engaged. He could not get to Harold. By the time he had killed his man, the Normans had done their work and retreated. Nothing was left but a heap of stained bodies on the hilltop. Even to die with Harold, he was too late.

8 ❧ Nightfall

Leaning his back on the hollow tree which had sheltered him all night, Brand surveyed a world whose continued existence came to his exhausted senses as surprising. Harold and his brothers were dead, alongside half the freemen of England, and the Norman duke reigned alive over the field where they had fought. Yet the sun had come up as usual this morning, and a robin, perched on a stone nearby, sang as unconcernedly as if October 15th, 1066, were a day like any other.

The sun was quite high. He must have lain half-conscious for a long time. He could remember stumbling away from that place of carnage, downhill, searching in a blurred, disconnected way for water. He'd found the pool at the bottom . . . and then found that the water was of no use. He put his hands to his face, wishing he didn't remember that. In the gleam of starlight he had seen the flaccid shapes of the men who lay half in and half out of the water, who had crawled there for its benison in their last moments, and whose blood had entered it. He could not drink that.

He had wandered on. He had heard spring water tinkling somewhere and followed the sound. He had laved his dirty, trembling hands under the spring and cupped them to ease his thirst. He knew he should try to get further from the battlefield, but the need for sleep was too strong. His legs were heavy and his head swam. He found the hollow tree and crept in, thankful to be protected a little from the chill night wind. When he woke, stiff and weak, it was day. After a long time spent in an inert semi-awareness he forced himself to move, but so far he had only managed to get just outside the tree and prop his back against it. He was still within sight of the battlefield.

It was directly in front of him, indeed, and raising his eyes, he could see William's triumphal tent. It was a shocking sight.

The duke had camped in the midst of the carnage. Under the cool, silvery October sun, the morning hillside was littered with death, and the bodies of Harold and his guard lay where they had made their last defence. William's great white tent with the Norman leopards waving proudly above it was only yards from that horrible heaping. It was an obscene jest, a crown placed in mockery on the head of a dead king. Brand stared at it with hatred.

His eye, travelling downwards, rested on a small group of people descending the hill from the direction of the tent. He watched them idly and saw that they were likely soon to pass near him. He did not move. If they were Normans they might kill him, but what of it? Harold was dead and defeated. Brand Woodcutter had no right to survive. He let himself slide to a sitting position at the foot of the tree and waited unemotionally for what the future brought.

But the approaching party was not Norman. It consisted mainly of monks walking together in a sad, cowled group except for four who between them carried an empty litter. Behind the monks were two women riding mules. They were almost past him, lost in their own world of grief, when one of the women pulled up and pointed and they all turned towards him. Then the other woman rode forward and in a moment was out of the saddle and kneeling beside him.

"Brand!" said Countess Gytha. "You're alive!"

"I'm alive . . ." said Brand, and once more thought of Harold and Harold's brothers, and Osric, who were all dead, and found that he was weeping. "I don't know why I'm alive," he said. "I didn't want to be. I'm sorry. I shouldn't be alive."

"But you are," said Gytha and her voice held no reproach, only gladness. "And there's work still for the living to do. A battle isn't a whole war! Eadgyth! You've bread and meat in your saddlebag. Bring it here!"

He found himself eating, and drinking wine brought by a monk whom he recognised as Harold's confessor, Father Wulfstan. He had not known he was hungry or cold, but the sustenance warmed him.

He could take in their faces: Wulfstan's grave, withdrawn; Gytha's stricken beyond tears, her eyes looking resolutely to the future because she dared not look at the past; Eadgyth's white and desperate and stained with crying. He realised, belatedly, where they must have been this morning.

"Did you go . . . up *there?*" he asked.

"We had to go," Gytha said. "Father Wulfstan and his monks went at dawn and asked permission to search for King Harold's body, and Duke William granted it but . . ."

"We could not find it," said Wulfstan quietly. "At least . . . not to know it."

"When he told us that," Eadgyth said, "I said I would look for it myself. I would know it. Gountess Gytha wouldn't let me go alone. So we both went up the hill. Yes, we found him."

She glanced upwards with a shiver. A sickening picture sped through Brand's mind, of Eadgyth, the beautiful, fastidious Eadgyth, known to the bards of all the land as Eadgyth of the Swan Neck, toiling among the dead, handling stiff limbs and meeting the stare of glazed eyes, and finally discovering . . .

"There were marks on his breast, where a hawk savaged him once with its talons," Eadgyth said. "It left white marks on the skin." Her voice trembled. She had tried to pretend to herself, looking at that mutilated shape, that many men kept hawks and acquired such scars. Then she saw that where the neck joined the shoulder, there were the marks of teeth, the imprint she herself had made, in love and anger, when he told her that Aldith was pregnant by him. And then there was no more pretending.

Aldith had seen her husband mutilated too. She pitied Aldith now, as Harold had asked her to do.

"No one could have known his face, and his armour was all torn off," said Gytha, unnaturally calm. "But Eadgyth was sure. So we went to William's tent for permission to bury him. He refused."

The robin was still twittering, poised on its stone. Eadgyth snatched up a pebble and flung it at the bird. The robin fluttered away, barely in time. Eadgyth turned back to Brand with eyes full of tears and agate-hard behind the tears. "He wouldn't let me bury him," she said, and the words were a curse on William.

"I cannot," William of Normandy had said, when the guard led them to his tent. He considered them with interest and what might have been compassion, had compassion not been an insult. There was something else too in his eyes, that might have been respect. They were respect-worthy, these two, the straight-backed, aging woman with the face of a sybil, who had lost four strong sons in a month and who yet faced him coolly and with the strength of an equal; and the younger woman, whose braided hair escaping her dark hood was still red, whose every movement was utterly graceful even within the muffling mantle, and whose face was stark with her loss. She was not Harold's lawful widow. He had been going to ask her what she meant by it, to behave as if she were. But he dismissed that intention now. If any had the right to call Harold husband, she had, for this quality of grief, and the devotion of her search, could belong only to Harold's wife. But he still had to say it. "I cannot give you his body. You would bury it in hallowed ground."

"Where else?" demanded Gytha harshly.

"He died perjured. He was excommunicated. He once swore to support me, swore on the bones of the strongest saints in Christendom. He broke that oath. It would be sin to bury him in consecrated soil."

"*You* talk of sin?" said Eadgyth. "Have you seen what lies outside this tent?"

"Yes. Had your . . . husband . . . kept his oath, they might all be living still. Indeed, one can go back further. Had your husband's father not given six hundred Norman men to death at Gildenford, thirty years ago, King Edward would not have offered me the throne. You could say I have come to claim their weregild. That is the proper word, I think. I have succeeded in my claim."

Gytha, placing a hand quickly on Eadgyth's arm to quiet her before she burst out in frenzy, had said: "We can offer the weight of my son's body in gold, if you will surrender him to us."

"I am not a merchant, madame. I will not trade in flesh. What I refuse to give you, I will not sell."

But for Gytha's hand, Eadgyth would have sprung at him then. He saw it. "I am sorry," he said. "But I cannot have him buried where he will become a shrine and a gathering place for my enemies." The force of her frustrated sorrow turned her dizzy and she swayed. He called to a man sitting at the rear of the tent, in the shadow. "Malet! Bring that stool of yours here!"

William Malet brought it and somehow persuaded Eadgyth to

sit down. It was he who said: "When Harold was in Normandy, we were friends. As a friend, I have a suggestion. My lord?"

"If you can solve this difficult question, Malet, we're all willing to listen," William said. "What is your suggestion?"

"He fought well," said Malet respectfully, his brown eyes full of a genuine regret for Harold. "No one could have defended England more boldly. He died guarding what he thought, however wrongly, was his kingdom. Let him guard it still in death. He cannot lie in holy ground, but let him rest in a grave on the cliffs overlooking the sea, to watch the sea for invaders for ever. He was a great warrior. I mean it kindly."

William nodded his black cropped head. "I agree. Let it be done." He turned to the silent women. "I can offer nothing better. You had best leave now. I will provide an escort to see you off the battlefield. I do not ask for your forgiveness. I can't expect it. Will you believe me when I say I regret that? Malet, tell the guard to come in . . ."

"A fine, magnanimous conqueror England has," Eadgyth said now to Brand. "May he die in misery and be buried in shame himself! Brand, are you wounded?"

"Not beyond small things, no." He had a long, shallow cut on one forearm, he had discovered, a swollen and abraded knee, and a big patch of bruising on the right side of his chest, as if some blunt and heavy weapon had struck him there. He couldn't remember it happening. His mail had saved him, no doubt.

"We shall need every man who still lives and can fight," Eadgyth said with passion. "Harold is gone but he leaves sons. I have sent them away from here. They'll take the fight on where he left off, and they'll need every man they can get to help them. Such as you, Brand. You must come with us now. You can use the litter if you need to. We brought it for Harold but . . . Don't say again that you don't want to live. You must live. For Harold."

It might have been the Eadgyth of long ago speaking, he thought, the flamelike young Eadgyth who had lit the first love in the combustible young Brand. After twenty-two years and five children, the essential Eadgyth had not changed.

Not changed at all. She was still all Harold's. "You must live. For Harold." Because *she* had always lived for Harold and never for anyone else, and she expected it of him as well. And rightly. He had

no business to think of Eadgyth as anything but the widow of
Harold. No business to remember, even for an instant, what she had
once meant to himself. He managed to stand up and she managed to
smile at him and he was unexpectedly aware that she had followed
his mind. Quickly, to cover the awkwardness, he said: "I must get to
Fallowdene. I must see that Wulfhild is safe. What will you do?"

"Make for the West Country," said Gytha. "Exeter, perhaps. I
must get King Harold's sons well out of William's reach. London
will fight, I think, but we must not be in the city if it is taken. It will
take William a long time to reach the west and by the time he
does . . ." She spread her hands in a gesture which meant "we shall
see."

"Give Wulfhild our love," said Eadgyth. "Tell her . . . I wish
her a long life and happiness."

"I will. You . . . and Lady Aldith, of course . . . educated her
excellently," Brand said. He hesitated and then let the words form.
"Wulfhild is a debt I owe to you. I can never repay it."

"You can," said Eadgyth, and she had understood him fully; he
saw it in her eyes. She moved to remount her mule. "Help us to go
on fighting, Brand. Help us to drive off William. Will you promise?"

Oaths, in the past, had been his downfall and Harold's, but he
took this new one boldly, giving his heart to it.

"I promise."

They did not want to tell Aldith that her husband's body had been
unrecognisable after the battle, but she saw something wrong in
their faces and got it out of them. "Mutilated?" she asked. "Like
Gruffyd? Harold—and Gruffyd—*both*?" she said, stumbling back,
and they called her women.

"It was an easy birth, she was lucky after all," said the midwife
when Alveva, sent for urgently, arrived in haste at Chester.
"They're fine babies, if they were three weeks premature. Healthy
as you could wish."

"They?" said Alveva.

"Yes, yes!" The midwife's elderly face burst into a mass of
laughter wrinkles "Twins, madam, and both boys. Best with twins
if they do come early. Easier for their mother and . . ."

Alveva walked briskly into the birth chamber.

Aldith lay quietly after the catharsis of bringing forth, her head turned on the pillow to watch her offspring in their cradles by the bed. The bed had a black sealskin coverlet and on it lay the manuscript of Harold's book on falconry. Aldith's hand lay near it. She smiled as her mother entered. "I was too quick for you. It was over very soon."

"So . . . male twins." Alveva sat down by the bed. "A thousand pities their father isn't here to see them. But I congratulate you, my dear." She peered at the nearer cradle. There was a dusting of pale down on the baby's scalp. "I wonder, when they're grown, if they'll challenge our fine William? You'll have to guard them from him."

"I shall go abroad with them," said Aldith. "Norway, perhaps. But William need not worry. They won't return to challenge him, if I can help it."

"Your family should do well under King William, if your brothers are wise," said Alveva. "But still . . . these are King Harold's lawful heirs. You must rear them to know who they are."

"No," said Aldith.

Drowsiness had been overcoming her, but she pushed it back. She saw the bewildered indignation on her mother's face, and shook her head at it.

"My boys will be better off as private men, if I can only teach them that. They're *my* children, Mother. No one else's."

"They're King Harold's children," said Alveva sharply.

"Harold is dead. As Gruffyd is dead. That's what being a king, or fighting to be one, leads to. It does no one any good to fight over a throne."

She echoed, without knowing it, the words of another fugitive queen, in Sweden, nearly fifty years before. But Alveva had not had the experiences which bred that knowledge, and Aldith saw by Alveva's face that her mother did not understand.

Aldith regretted that. She tried again. "I am telling you that the course you recommend leads to death before one's time, hacked to pieces by swords." The startling authority in her voice kept Alveva silent. "Do you think I will ever forget what happened to the men who were the fathers of my children? I pray every day for the souls of Gruffyd and Harold. I never cease to grieve for them. I will not have my sons die as they did, if I can prevent it."

The blankness on Alveva's features only grew blanker. "You

pray every day," she said at length, "for Gruffyd and Harold. You pray every day . . . for *both* of them?"

"For both of them," said Aldith.

And Alveva, who had never spent a prayer on a man in her life, and her daughter, Aldith, who had mourned two husbands, regarded each other silently, across a chasm that they would never bridge.

After . . . ⁂ Winter 1066 A.D.

Rolf Ericson, fugitive of Hastings, came into Fallowdene on a cold December day, his feet crackling in the frosty fallen leaves as he trudged through the woods. He was too weak to move briskly. His awareness of his own sheer good luck in being there at all helped him along in lieu of muscle.

The hall looked as it always had, its hearth smoke lazily rising and the thatched roofs of the clustered buildings as comfortable as warm pelt rugs. Then he was in the courtyard and Wulfhild came out to meet him and the illusion of normality was gone. Fallowdene had not after all escaped disaster. She was thin and unkempt, her brown braids lank and her eyes dull as if with much weeping. "Thane Rolf," she said in a flat voice. "So you're alive." She in turn took in his condition, his shaky legs and tattered clothing. She added wryly: "Only just. You'd better come indoors."

They sat by the fire and Editha brought oat cakes and some ale in the glass beakers which Rolf himself had sold to Brand two years before. "Your father . . . ?" he said doubtfully to Wulfhild. He let his tone do the asking because he was not sure how to choose the words. There was such grief in her face that he thought he already knew the answer.

"Alive," Wulfhild said.

He waited. There was clearly more to come. Brand was wounded, perhaps . . . not dead but dying . . . or else crippled . . .

"Alive," said Wulfhild again. "And not hurt. Or not when I last

saw him." She stared into the fire. "He's been here," she said at
length. "He wanted to take me to Withysham Abbey but I wouldn't
go. I *couldn't* go! Someone must take care of Fallowdene and its folk.
Fallowdene is our home. We quarrelled."

She stopped with her head still turned away from him. She
must not cry, she said fiercely to herself. She had cried so much already. To have longed for years to find her father, and then to succeed, and to care for him as she had begun to care, and then to lose
him . . . like this. It was worse in one way than if he had died on
the field, for the dead do not leave you of their own accord.

"Stay here?" he had said on that searing day. "Wulfhild, don't
you understand? The war isn't over. One battle doesn't decide the
fate of the whole land. I am going to London. There will be a new
resistance; the city will fight when William attacks, as attack he will.
We shall stand siege . . ."

"And if London falls?"

"I shall go into hiding or into exile. Become an outlaw. I shan't
be alone. Other men, better men, will be in the same plight. We
shall gather a force and make ready to fight yet again. But . . ." He
was trying desperately to make her see. ". . . I shall be an *outlaw.*
There may be reprisals here. Fallowdene may be burnt, or given to
some Norman lord. And then you . . ."

"I understand." Wulfhild's voice shook. "Our home may be
ravaged, the people who live here, who look to us for protection,
may be killed or left to starve. You would let that happen and do
nothing?"

"What can I do? I made a promise to King Harold's wife and to
his mother, to go on fighting. In honour . . ."

"Honour! It's honourable, is it, to desert your manor folk?
They don't matter because their weregild is small. Is that it? I was
born a thrall, remember, and my weregild was small then. I can feel
for them, if you cannot."

"Stop it! You don't understand these things."

"I don't want to!"

"What can you do, even if you stay?"

"Lead them! Lead them to shelter in the forest . . . or treat
with William on their behalf." And even as she had said it, the desperate resolve that she'd made in these last few days was beginning
to take shape in her mind. "I would write to William if I had to, or

go to him, to save Fallowdene. He has seen me. He might remember."

"Treat with William?" said Brand. They stood staring at each other, hopelessly out of sympathy. To a warrior, making terms with such a foe was impossible, and one's own survival did not matter. To a woman, survival came first. But she had not expected what happened next: that Brand should spin on his heel without another word and walk straight out of the hall.

He had left Fallowdene within minutes. Not alone, she was glad of that. Odi Pathfinder had found his way to Fallowdene the day before his master. Odi went with him. It was all the comfort she had. She had cried all that day, afterwards, knowing what she had lost and how bitterly she had hurt him by attacking the foundations of his integrity and at the end deserting him for Fallowdene. Yet when she was among the manor folk, sharing their fear of the future and their sorrow for their dead—of all the village men who had gone to Hastings, only the miller had returned—she knew her choice was right. She was needed here.

"He went to London," she said to Rolf. "But where he is now, I don't know. In the West Country, with King Harold's family, perhaps. Or perhaps fled abroad. I don't know. Since London surrendered . . ."

Rolf sat up straight. "Has it?"

"Yes. It was given out in Chichester, a week ago. William will be crowned on Christmas Day. There was a siege but not much fighting; the leaders surrendered when William took to ravaging round about. Didn't you know? Where were you? Where did you come from this morning?"

"I've been lying ill in the hut of some forest dwellers. I came through the battle, with a knife blade in my shoulder broken off short." He raised a hand, reminiscently, to his right shoulder. He pressed it gently and grimaced. "Then I slept out for two nights, without food. I'd have died of the cold and of my wound if those folk hadn't taken me in. One of them got the steel out of the shoulder for me. I ran a fever for a long time. It was weeks before I was strong enough to leave them, and even now I'm not entirely well. But when I felt better I asked where I was and found I must be near Fallowdene. I came to get the news and ask after your father. The forest folk knew nothing of events."

Wulfhild threw more wood on to the fire. "What will you do now?"

"I don't know." He crouched near the warmth, his face drawn. There was little left, thought Wulfhild, of the plump, self-satisfied thane she had encountered when she first met him. His bones jutted and he had a queer yellow tinge to his skin. "I see no hope in these rebellions your father dreams of. A crowned king is a crowned king. William has always had luck with him. A remarkable amount of it. I believe in luck," Rolf said.

He had reason to believe in it. He had had experience of it. He'd been lucky to come through the battle, lucky to find help, and lucky to survive his illness. His hand went again to his sore shoulder. He had even, he reminded himself, had a special kind of good fortune during the battle. He, Rolf, never a mighty warrior, had found himself when the shield-wall broke grappling with a burly soldier who suddenly, in the midst of much swearing, addressed him by name. He was hand to hand with that dishonest slave merchant, Lyfing. Rolf had never been easy in his mind, knowing that somewhere in the world Lyfing lived, harbouring his knowledge of the most damaging episode in Rolf's life and probably believing that the younger man had ruined his chance of a double profit on Edward Edmundson's kidnapped person. The probability was confirmed all too forcefully as Lyfing, cursing his name, went for Rolf with crooked fingers and teeth and knife. Yet, astonishingly, Rolf had prevailed. It was he who rose living from that conflict, and Lyfing who stayed behind, blessedly dead. There had been times, since Edward's death, when Rolf felt he had merely exchanged one menace for another: the threat of Alfgar for the threat of Lyfing. But neither was a threat to him now. Lyfing was dead, at the cost to Rolf of only one knife thrust. He was free.

As if the thought of Edward Edmundson had sprung from his mind to hers, Wulfhild remarked: "You are right. William has been lucky ever since Edward, who was to have been the Atheling, died in London. Died of his own accord, apparently, and got out of William's way . . . and that after all the attempts to kill him had failed." Unexpectedly, she smiled. "Do you remember Ivon Taillefer, the minstrel knight who charged singing up the hill before the battle started, and was the first to die? Did you see him? My father spoke of him."

"Yes, I saw him. We all did." Rolf was puzzled by the non sequitur.

"I knew him in Normandy," said Wulfhild. The smile was one of kindly memory, but tears were in her eyes. She had cried for Ivon too, as much as for her father's going. "He was a minstrel with Edward Edmundson's following," she said. "He thought *you'd* murdered the Atheling."

Rolf's mouth opened. His eyes widened. He glanced quickly away from her to contemplate the heart of the fire again. "I don't understand. What are you talking about?"

"He said he saw you put your wine goblet down beside Edward's that day, and then pick the wrong one up. He only knew you as a merchant thane called Rolf, of course. I realised who Ivon meant when you told me you had been with Edward Edmundson's court too. It was lucky for you that Ivon was snatched away by his father that evening. Oh, I knew it was nonsense, that it could only have been an accident. After all, why should you try to hurt Edward Edmundson? You had nothing to do with Duke William, or Earl Alfgar, either."

"Earl Alfgar?" said Rolf tautly.

"Yes. He tried to injure the Atheling. His daughter Lady Aldith told me, when he died. King Harold believed that two different sets of people were out to kill Edward, you know. I heard all about that when I was with his suite in Normandy. I always supposed that the two were William and Alfgar. But it was generally agreed that whoever they were, neither succeeded—that it was the hand of God. As you say: William has phenomenal good luck."

"*Sweet Saints!*" said Rolf, and let his breath out on an audible sigh.

Wulfhild, hands round her knees, did not see the shock on his face. She was pursuing her own train of thought. "Even when William was about to invade," she said, "the wind held him back until Harald Hardraada could land first and draw our army north. Then it changed and brought him here just when our forces were least able to deal with him. It gives me the shivers to think of it. The hand of God, all the way. As if he were meant to be King of England . . ." She looked up. "That's one reason why I think my father is wrong, that his efforts will be useless. If God is against you, you'll never win."

"True, very true," said Rolf, and the gooseflesh rose on his skin.

He had thought himself fortunate. The sheer, staggering dimensions of that good fortune were only now becoming plain to him. He had walked unknowing on the verge of an abyss. All these years, fearing Lyfing's vengeance, when . . .

The day of Edward Edmundson's collapse sprang back into his memory, achingly clear. Himself, tired from a sleepless night spent tossing and fretting because, in spite of all Lyfing's promises, nothing seemed to be happening and if Edward were not disposed of soon he would be made officially Atheling and Rolf would be destroyed. All through that day he had moved slowly, miserably, exhaustedly, towards a desperate decision: to risk Lyfing's wrath rather than Alfgar's . . . to hope that because Edward was known to have a weakly stomach, poison might pass for disease

He had put the venom in his own wine and switched it with Edward's and Edward had duly died. And all the time, *someone had been watching.* He huddled by the hearth, seeking in its warmth a comfort for the cold terror pouring through his veins. If Ivon had not been whisked from the court that night but had stayed to point a finger . . . Come to that, if Wulfhild had learned of his dealings with Earl Alfgar, then . . . If, if, if! The array of *ifs* trooped through his horrified mind like an army of blackbeetles. His body, uncontrollably, began to tremble.

"I wonder," said Wulfhild, stirring the fire, unconscious of the sweat upon Rolf's temples, of the terror that pattered and gibbered through the mind of a man only four feet away from her, "if you intend, as I hear many thanes have done, to make your peace with King William? Do you?"

Rolf took hold of himself, pushing the past away and forcing himself to attend to the present. "I . . . yes. I think so. There's no alternative. Yes, I must." Think of the future, you fool, think of the future. And control yourself, don't let her see. Say what is expected of you. "What will *you* do? If the king is crowned, I suppose your father will be outlawed."

"Yes. Anything could happen to Fallowdene. It could be given to a Norman lord, or sacked. I know." Wulfhild spoke grimly. "I, too, have decided to make terms with William. I have a letter written already. I persuaded the priest to write it. Thane Rolf, if you intend to go to the king in person, will you take it for me?"

Rolf nodded. Not for a shipload of gold ingots would he cross Wulfhild today. She held knowledge too near to the truth. Oh God, would the past never cease to follow him?

Wulfhild pushed her seat away and went out of the hall. When she came back, she held a small parchment roll, which she offered to him. "This is the letter. You haven't asked what's in it."

"It's not my business," Rolf muttered, stretching out a hand to take it. "What is in it, then?"

"It asks William not to ravage Fallowdene. And it says that, if necessary, if he feels it must be given to a Norman lord, I am willing to marry that lord, so that I may stay at Fallowdene and perhaps mediate between the strangers and the village folk. At least I understand French. It asks him to send me a good and honest man."

"Nothing wrong with that. . . . Can you mount me? If so, I'll travel on tomorrow."

"Tomorrow? There's no need for such haste." Wulfhild sat down again and stirred the fire. "Rest here a day or two. You said, yourself, you're not fully healed."

Rolf said: "It would be better if I went at once."

He must go at once, or he would not get there at all. He put a palm once more against his shoulder and fought down the dread within him, the other dread, the one he had brought with him to Fallowdene. Moving, stretching out his hand to take the letter, he had felt the bite of metal still in his body. The forest folk had done their best. But a fragment of Lyfing's knife was still there and from it came this constant weakness, this sense of malaise. It had increased even since this morning. He could get that letter to London in three days, he thought. If he held out for three more days, he might save Fallowdene. It would be a kind of pilgrimage, whispered his frightened mind. Perhaps if he took that letter safe to William, it would buy him back to health. Perhaps if he did this for Wulfhild, God would let him live.

At a deeper level, he knew otherwise. The past would never cease to follow him and it had almost caught up with him now. But if he let that knowledge into the open, he would dissolve his being in terror. The knowledge must come and the terror must come, but he would hold them back while he could.

"Your course is wise," he said to Wulfhild. "But if you're set on it, you ought not to delay."

"My father wouldn't think it was wise," said Wulfhild. The tears that were never far from her eyes these days sprang to them again. "Wherever he is, I pray to God he's safe," she said. And she began to mend the fire again, clumsily, because all she could see of it was a blur of angry red. Like a burning city, or an enflamed and fevered wound.